Praise for *The*

"Brimming with drama, deceit and betrayal, *The Windsor Conspiracy* is a fascinating story of a young woman torn between loyalty to family and love of country and the immense courage it takes to accept the challenge of a lifetime. Compelling to the last page."

—Shelley Noble, *New York Times* bestselling author of *The Tiffany Girls*

"*The Windsor Conspiracy* offers a complex and compelling portrait of Wallis Simpson following the abdication, as told through the eyes of her trusted cousin and confidante. From Parisian chateaux to Bahamian estates, Blalock has weaved a chilling narrative about the lengths to which the embittered and myopic Duke and Duchess were willing to go to restore their grip on power."

—Bryn Turnbull, internationally bestselling author of *The Paris Deception*

"Georgie Blalock pens a vivid portrait of the lives of disgraced Edward VIII and Wallis Simpson through the downstairs viewpoint of Wallis's personal secretary in this glittering parade of European high society. *The Windsor Conspiracy* is the next best thing to being on the set of *The Crown*!"

—Stephanie Marie Thornton, *USA Today* bestselling author of *Her Lost Words*

"Georgie Blalock returns to the Windsors, this time taking sharp aim at the Duke and Duchess as they stand on the brink of World War II. Through the fresh eyes of Wallis Simpson's cousin and personal secretary, we get a unique and intimate portrait of this couple in all their entitlements as well as their alliance with Hitler and the Third Reich. Spellbinding tale, impeccably researched, *The Windsor Conspiracy* is a must-read for fans of the royals and historical fiction alike."

—Renée Rosen, *USA Today* bestselling author of *Fifth Avenue Glamour Girl*

"A fascinating deep dive into the turbulent waters of one of history's most controversial couples, the Duke and Duchess of Windsor, through the eyes of Wallis Simpson's cousin and companion, *The Windsor Conspiracy* is historical fiction at its best!"

—Christine Wells, internationally bestselling author of *The Royal Windsor Secret*

"A fascinating look behind the scandalous curtain of the life of Wallis Simpson in the early years of her marriage to the Duke of Windsor, who abdicated the throne of England to be with her, from the viewpoint of her cousin turned private secretary. Carefully researched and expertly woven into the sweeping pages of a novel, Georgie Blalock takes us back to mid–World War II, and a tense time for the royal family, where conspiracies and betrayal thrive. Intrigue abounds in this page-turner. Highly recommended for fans of the royal family and the drama of the century!"

—Eliza Knight, *USA Today* and internationally bestselling author of *The Queen's Faithful Companion*

THE WINDSOR CONSPIRACY

ALSO BY GEORGIE BLALOCK

The Other Windsor Girl

The Last Debutantes

An Indiscreet Princess

THE WINDSOR CONSPIRACY

A NOVEL OF THE CROWN, A CONSPIRACY, AND THE DUCHESS OF WINDSOR

GEORGIE BLALOCK

wm
WILLIAM MORROW
An Imprint of HarperCollins*Publishers*

This book is a work of fiction. References to real people, events, establishments, organizations, or locales are intended only to provide a sense of authenticity, and are used fictitiously. All other characters, and all incidents and dialogue, are drawn from the author's imagination and are not to be construed as real.

HarperCollins books may be purchased for educational, business, or sales promotional use. For information, please email the Special Markets Department at SPsales@harpercollins.com.

FIRST EDITION

Designed by Diahann Sturge-Campbell

Library of Congress Cataloging-in-Publication Data has been applied for.

ISBN 978-0-06-333984-2

24 25 26 27 28 LBC 5 4 3 2 1

To Grandmaster Floyd Burk and my Trad Am Karate family for the friendship, strength, and peace you've given me through training

Chapter One

Château de Candé, France, May 12, 1937

"Since the beginning of the service, Her Majesty, the Queen, has been sitting in the Chair of Estate. Now she moves forward for her anointing." The BBC radio announcer's voice crackled over the wireless and echoed off the oak-paneled walls and old books of the Château de Candé library. Heavy rain ran down the windows and obscured the view of the sprawling château grounds, adding to the room's heavy chill. "The Queen kneels at the altar. The Archbishop will pour the holy oil upon the crown of her head. He will put the Queen's ring on the fourth finger of her right hand."

Wallis Simpson tightened her fingers into a fist beneath her chin, and the nineteen-carat square-cut-emerald engagement ring from the Duke of Windsor glinted in the lamplight. Wallis stared stone-faced at the large Zenith radio but Amelia caught the slight deepening of the small creases at the corners of her mouth and the tightness in her already severe jaw. Amelia could practically hear her cousin thinking, *That should have been me.*

"Mrs. Simpson, Monsieur Mainbocher has arrived for your fitting," Mr. Hale, the Bedaux's English butler, announced in a baritone voice worthy of a radio announcer contract.

"Not now," the Duke of Windsor snapped, worrying his triple-band pinkie ring.

Fern Bedaux flinched, and Mr. Edward Metcalf and his wife exchanged a quick glance. Even Detto, Prisie, and Pookie, the Duke and Wallis's cairn terriers, kept to the hearthrug instead of his lap. The Duke's brother and sister-in-law were being crowned in Westminster Abbey instead of him and Wallis.

"The Archbishop brings the crown from the altar and sets it upon the Queen's head," the BBC announcer continued.

Aunt Bessie, one side of her aged face slack from a stroke a few years ago, caught Amelia's eyes and nodded at Mr. Hale.

Amelia jumped to her feet and hurried through the adjoining salon de musique. She nodded to the maids polishing the herringbone wood floor in preparation for the upcoming nuptials between the ex-king of England and the woman he'd given up his throne to marry.

Amelia stopped in the dark paneled dining room and drew in a deep breath. *This is my job now.*

She sighed then stepped into the château entryway. "Good morning, Monsieur Mainbocher. Mrs. Simpson is occupied at present but will be with you shortly. If you'll follow me, I'll escort you to her dressing room."

"And you are?" The American-born couturier stared down his aquiline nose at Amelia. His two chic assistants affected the same arrogant air. Even the one carrying the garment bag with Wallis's wedding dress eyed Amelia as if she were one of the contemptible throng of press crowding the château gates.

"Amelia Bradford," she whispered, then cleared her throat and spoke up. "Mrs. Simpson's new private secretary." She didn't mention she was also Wallis's third cousin. Her plain brown wool skirt and jacket already made her look like a poor relation. "If you'll follow me?"

"Of course." He motioned for her to lead the way.

"Whatever is she wearing?" the assistant in the tailored gray suit asked her companion in French as Amelia led them down the narrow Norman stone hallway with its wood-beam ceiling and up the spiral stone staircase to the second floor.

"Something she found in the bottom of an old trunk," the other woman sneered.

Amelia understood them perfectly. She'd excelled in French at Oldfields, baffling her mother, who'd wondered what she'd do with an education.

If Mother could see me now she'd be shocked, Amelia mused, assuming her mother could muster enough interest in her youngest child to care. Mother had barely noticed her before Father's death. Afterward, Amelia had been little more than an unwanted and embarrassing nuisance.

"*Taisez-vous,*" Monsieur Mainbocher commanded when they reached the second floor, and the assistants stopped their snide remarks. He smoothed his thick, pomaded hair away from his severe side part, offering Amelia a touch more respect as he encouraged her to continue. "Mademoiselle?"

"Madame, if you please, I am a widow," Amelia replied in perfectly accented French.

The assistants' cheeks went red. Monsieur Mainbocher didn't so much as raise an eyebrow.

"When I'm finished making a marvel out of Mrs. Simpson, I'll do wonders for you," he offered in French.

"That's very kind of you, monsieur," she replied in French, neither refusing nor accepting his offer. She didn't have the money for a new wardrobe, especially not one by the famous designer. "Here we are."

Amelia opened the door to the Bedaux's private suite. Mr. and Mrs. Bedaux, the owners of Château de Candé, were hosting the Duke and Wallis's wedding and Mrs. Bedaux had been kind enough to move to another room so Wallis could use hers. Amelia led the designer and his assistants through the small foyer and into the elaborate closet. It was larger than most of the servants' garret bedrooms, with pale green walls, built-in drawers with crystal knobs, and lighted cabinets with glass doors.

Down a short passage, just past the shoe closet, was Mr. Bedaux's dark paneled study, where Amelia and Aunt Bessie stayed, Aunt Bessie in the bed, Amelia on a trundle beside her. Mr. Bedaux was on a business trip to Germany and Amelia worked at his desk; at least, that's where she sat while she tried to figure out how to deal with Wallis's accounts, receipts, and the travel itineraries for the London florist, organist, milliner, and everyone else involved in the wedding.

The assistants, with their perfectly coiffed hair and manicured nails, carefully removed the pale blue dress from the garment bag and hung it on a gilded hook between the windows.

"It's beautiful." Amelia fingered the silk crepe skirt, wondering what her wedding dress might have looked like if things had been different. She'd married Jackson in her traveling suit at the First Presbyterian Church wedding chapel in Elkton, Maryland. She'd worried every second of the five-minute ceremony about her stepfather bursting in to stop them but it'd gone off without a hitch.

Amelia opened her fingers and let the fabric fall back into place. *I should've listened to Theodore.* It would've saved her a lot of heartache and trouble.

"I call the color Wallis blue," Monsieur Mainbocher announced in English. "I had the silk custom dyed to match the shade of her eyes. They're the most stunning I've ever seen."

"Then you can't have seen very many if you think so." Wallis's clipped tone with its odd mix of British and Southern accent carried over them as she swept in. Pookie, Prisie, and Detto followed obediently behind and settled on the rug near the heating grate. Wallis extended her hand to Monsieur Mainbocher, who raised it to his lips. His assistants curtseyed to Wallis as if she were the Queen while Aunt Bessie quietly joined Amelia. "I'm glad you're here. I couldn't endure another moment of that Fat Scottish Cook muttering her vows in that insipid voice of hers. It's like nails on a chalkboard."

Wallis stepped behind the screen in the corner and changed from her navy-blue-and-white wool suit into the wedding dress.

"It galls me to think she's gathering all the glory while I'm relegated to this French backwater."

"You'd outshine the woman even if you wore a potato sack." Monsieur Mainbocher took Wallis's hand when she emerged from behind the screen and helped her onto the stool in front of the window. "You don't need a crown to be a queen."

"But I need a king and I don't have one."

Everyone went stiff.

"Wallis, you have something better than a king. You have true love," Aunt Bessie proclaimed.

"Of course, and I'm deliriously happy." Wallis glared at the two assistants, who busied themselves marking the flared skirt and fitted waist with pins and tape measures.

When Monsieur Mainbocher was satisfied that everything was hemmed, nipped, and tucked to perfection, Wallis changed and rang for Mr. Hale to escort the couturier and his assistants out of the room.

"Wallis, you must be more discreet around outsiders," Aunt Bessie warned as she and Amelia followed Wallis into her bedroom. "Those pretentious shopgirls might repeat what you said to the press."

"If they do, they'll be blackballed from ever working in Paris again, and they know it. That should keep their thin lips sealed." Wallis strode to the pink marble fireplace mantel and straightened the gilded clock a maid had moved while dusting. The room was painted a rich butter color set off by white boiserie and a suite of Louis XVI furniture. The dogs hopped on the bed and settled into the fluffy, pale cream comforter. "Besides, I can't keep up this façade every moment of my life."

"If you don't, you'll be crucified for not making his sacrifice for you worth it."

"I never asked him to make the sacrifice, and now I'm stuck with it as much as he is, but he's getting what he wants, while I'm getting the short end of the stick." Wallis threw her arms out to the room, her usual stern composure slipping for the first time since Amelia's arrival last week. "He and all those simpering courtiers said I'd be Queen or the woman behind the throne, then they all jumped ship the moment it started to sink, leaving me to go down with the captain."

"A captain who's devoted to you," Aunt Bessie reminded.

"If he'd been devoted to keeping his crown we wouldn't be in this mess but in Westminster Abbey." Wallis sank into one of the silk-covered chairs and rested her head in her square hands, careful to keep her fingers arched out and not disturb her tightly parted, smoothed, and rolled dark brown hair. "He gave up with barely a fight. Instead of heads of state and hundreds of people watching and kneeling to us, I'm the cruel witch who stole Britain's beautiful king. I'm hounded by the press, run out of Britain, and Cookie is doing everything she can to turn everyone against me."

"You can't think about that," Aunt Bessie insisted. "You have to think of your future."

"That's all I think about." Wallis stood and paced, twisting the engagement ring around her finger. "What is there for us?

No home, no position, no real status. We have to make something of ourselves, and this marriage, and with the whole world watching and waiting for us to fail."

"You won't fail." Aunt Bessie rested her hands on Wallis's shoulders, settling her in a way no one else could. "You can't afford to."

Wallis clutched Aunt Bessie's wrinkled hands to her chest. "What'll I do when you go back to America? I can't endure this without you."

"You'll have Amelia here to help you."

They turned to Amelia, who wanted to bolt straight back to Maryland. Nothing in her Baltimore childhood, her married life in Wellesley, not even her year at the Katherine Gibbs School of Secretarial and Executive Training for Educated Women had prepared her to manage a duchess's personal affairs, but she couldn't run. There was nothing left for her in Baltimore or Wellesley. Like Wallis, she had no choice but to succeed. "Of course."

Wallis pursed her red lips. "We'll see."

The door swung open and the Duke marched in clutching a letter with the royal crest emblazoned across the top. He waved it over his blond head, shaking it as if he could flick off what was written there. "Sir Walter just arrived and what do you think he brought me? This! Buck House's idea of a wedding present."

The dogs started barking, agitated by the Duke's excitement. Sir Walter Monckton was the Duke's former attorney and the go-between for the feuding King George and his brother, as Amelia had discovered the first day of work when Wallis had fired off a telegram to him complaining about how bad the British press treated her.

"Silence!" Wallis commanded, and the dogs stopped barking and settled back into the comforter.

"The Palace is denying you the title of Her Royal Highness," the Duke fumed. "And they've cooked up some ridiculous legal reason why they can do it. A wife is entitled to her husband's honors. I'm a Royal Highness and you bloody will be too."

He flapped the paper in Wallis's face and she snatched it out of his fingers, pinning him with a reprimanding glare that made him bow his head. Wallis read the letter while the Duke waited with his hands clasped behind his back like a chastened schoolboy.

"This is the Fat Scottish Cook's doing. Your brother doesn't have the backbone to stand up to his wife or insist on something this underhanded." Wallis dropped the letter in the grate and it caught fire.

"I'll call my brother and instill some backbone in him," the Duke threatened in his high, nasally voice.

"You'll do nothing of the sort. They're trying to hurt us but they can't, not when we have each other." Wallis smoothed his lapels with quick circles of her broad hands. "We have our love, our life together. That's worth more than any extra-chic title."

"But . . . ?" The Duke cast a mournful look at the blackened letter.

"No, we'll deal with this after the wedding. If we make a fuss now, Sir Walter will hurry back to Buckingham Palace and tell Cookie her blow landed. We can't have that. See to our new guest as if you're deliriously happy and no shadow can touch you. We'll find a more appropriate time to argue our case."

"Of course. You're always so levelheaded. I don't know what I'd do without you." He pulled her close to kiss her but she turned and his lips landed on her cheek. He either didn't notice or didn't mind the dodge but let go and rubbed his hands together in delight. "I'll give Sir Walter nothing but reports of our joy to take back to Queen Elizabeth."

He practically skipped out of the room.

"That bitch," Wallis muttered. "I'll have my revenge on that old Scottish Cook and her entire country for the hell they've put me through."

"For the moment pretend to be in heaven," Aunt Bessie advised.

"That's all I ever do." Wallis flashed a million-dollar smile then left to join her fiancé, the dogs trotting behind her.

"Does she love him?" Amelia asked. Some American newspapers had called Wallis and the Duke's affair the love story of the century. The British ones on the Atlantic crossing had blamed Wallis for ruining their beloved king. They'd claimed she'd mesmerized him with strange sexual techniques she'd learned in China in the 1920s and divorced Ernest Simpson in her quest to become queen. They'd reveled in her failure to capture the crown.

"She cares for him, in her own way, but Wallis has never been content with her situation." Aunt Bessie's ample chest rose and fell with a resigned sigh. "She's always aimed high, too high this time. Now she must play the cards she's been dealt and it's put her under a terrible strain. It makes her say things she doesn't mean. I'm sure you understand her position better than anyone else." Aunt Bessie sat on the edge of the bed and motioned for Amelia to join her.

"I do." Amelia opened and closed her left hand. Her ring finger still felt light without the gold wedding band. She'd sold it to pay for her first semester of secretarial school. "You didn't tell her about my debts, did you?"

"I told her enough to secure your employment but we never discussed the nitty-gritty, just as you asked, but you'll have to tell her eventually."

"Not yet. I don't want her to worry I'll swipe the silverware to pay my attorney fees. She already thinks I can't do the job."

"She thinks nothing of the sort. Once things quiet down and you both settle in, you'll get on splendidly, the way you used to at Cousin Lelia's. You'll learn a lot from Wallis. She'll make you one of the most sought-after private secretaries in Europe. That's more than you'd have had in Baltimore. She'll also throw eligible gentlemen in your path. Perhaps one of them will sweep you off your feet and take you away from this life of drudgery. He might even have a title."

"No thanks. From what I've seen of aristocrats, they aren't worth the effort."

"I agree." They giggled together before Aunt Bessie sobered. "I'm so relieved you'll be here when I go home. Wallis needs all the support she can get, especially from family she can trust.

Promise me you'll do what you can to stop her from giving in to her worst inclinations. I've tried and failed enough times to know it isn't easy, but if you can't save her from herself then learn from her, especially her mistakes. Those lessons could serve you well."

"Haven't I learned enough over the last three years?"

"Everything except how to trust in yourself and your abilities." Aunt Bessie covered Amelia's fidgeting hands. "Promise me you'll try that too."

Amelia wasn't sure she could. She wasn't any better at following her instincts than Wallis, but she'd do what she could for Wallis and make Aunt Bessie proud. She was one of the only family members who hadn't judged her after she and Jackson had eloped, and especially after his death. Without her help, she might've sunk to who knew what indignities to survive. She turned her hands over in Aunt Bessie's and clasped them tight. "I'll do what I can."

"That's all any of us can do."

Chapter Two

Amelia approached Château de Candé's large stone-and-iron front gate. She'd walked to the village post office after breakfast, eager to see if the carnival of reporters had grown since last week. They blocked the road, waiting for anyone with the faintest connection to Wallis or the Duke in the hopes of getting details for articles. Some reporters sat at makeshift tables under the large trees, coats off, shirtsleeves rolled up, fingers flying over their portable typewriter keys. Amelia wondered why they bothered to sit here day after day, since they made up most of what they wrote, but she supposed they had to make a living too.

Amelia slipped past them unnoticed, until the gendarmes opened the gate for her.

"There's someone," a reporter shouted, and they leapt from their tables and typewriters and rushed the gate. Amelia stepped through and the gendarmes quickly closed it behind her.

"Any word on which royals will be at the wedding?" a reporter yelled.

"Is it true King George has forbidden the royal family from attending?" a young woman in a dark blue suit, her blond hair smartly done in tight curls, called out.

Amelia waved at them but said nothing as she turned to walk back to the château, hoping no one cared enough about her to print her picture in the newspaper. She might work for the most notorious woman in the world, but she didn't want to become one.

Especially not dressed like this. Even the reporters camped out on the street were better turned out than her. She kicked a small pebble with the scuffed toe of her black shoe. She'd never been a fashion plate, not with Mother pouring everything into her own style while leaving Amelia to figure it out on her own. At least back then, Amelia's clothes had been quality, not half-price basement knockoffs. However, the fine fabrics hadn't been enough to cover her awkwardness, and Amelia had blended into the woodwork during her debutante season, trying not to draw attention to herself, until Jackson had noticed her.

The noise of the crowd faded into the reverie of birdsong and the rustle of wind through the pine trees as Amelia walked up the long drive to the château. The rolling hills, large trees, and green grass reminded her of the woods behind her house in Wellesley. She used to cross through them on her way to meet Jackson's evening train. They'd walk home together, telling each other about their day or dreaming of a trip to Paris and a proper honeymoon. He'd promised her a fine hotel, cafés, and a chic new wardrobe. Three years later, she was finally in France, no thanks to him. Her entire life had collapsed through no fault of her own.

She tightened her grip on the package she carried, wrinkling the brown paper cover. This wasn't how things were supposed to be. She should be enjoying a quiet life in her home with a husband and children. Jackson's greed had stolen everything, including her future, and proved everyone right about their hasty marriage. All she'd wanted was love. It was all she'd ever wanted. All she'd gotten was heartache.

She wiped away tears with the back of her hand, careful not to let them fall on the special-delivery letters. Heaven forbid she mar the fine stationery from more guests sending their regrets. All the replies had been regrets yesterday, and it'd left Wallis in a foul mood. *You're typing too loud. You aren't sorting the thank-you list properly. Answer the phone before the second ring, the clanging bell will give me a headache.* Ugh!

The slate roof of the French castle with its crenellated towers, pointed blue slate turrets, and stunning views of the Loire Valley came into view through the trees. Amelia's stomach tightened at the prospect of another day of orders and reprimands. She'd grown up with servants. She never thought she'd be one.

"Everything well, Mrs. Bradford?" Mr. Dudley Forwood, the Duke's equerry, greeted when he emerged from the guesthouse. The Duke and his staff were staying there in an effort to convince everyone the Duke's relationship with Wallis was chaste. No one believed it, especially not Aunt Bessie or Amelia, but for propriety's sake they all played along. It was one of the many lies that made life with Wallis and the Duke possible, including the one about the grandeur of the wedding. Wallis was right: the château was no Westminster Abbey and this was no state event.

"Yes. I had a nice stroll to the village post office."

"How much did the reporters offer you for information?" Mr. Forwood asked as they crossed the sprawling lawn outside the front entrance. Mademoiselle Marguerite Moulichon, the Bedaux's lady's maid assigned to Wallis for her stay, walked Pookie, Prisie, and Detto. The dogs pulled at their leads, eager to go faster. A viper had killed Wallis's beloved Slipper a few weeks ago and the dogs were no longer allowed to run loose on the grounds.

"None, I'm afraid."

"They offered me one thousand francs for information the last time I strolled out, but of course I refused it." He raised his cleft chin in pride. "Faithfully serving His Royal Highness is more important than money."

Easy to say when you have the private income required of a royal equerry. She slid him a sideways glance. He was more distinguished than handsome, with a solid body and a very respectable lineage. He was a good catch but Amelia felt nothing for him other than the friendly camaraderie of someone in a similar position. If she were like Mother, she'd get her claws into him and marry herself out of this mess, but she refused to be like that awful woman. "I hope I can resist the temptation to tell all."

"I'm sure you will." He had more faith in her than she did. With Jackson's legal bills hanging over her, the right amount of francs in exchange for information might be too tempting to resist.

They passed beneath the entrance tower with the mosaic of

Saint Martin of Tours and the Beggar and into the château's wood-paneled entryway. The Duke strolled out of the reception room dressed in his plaid golf outfit with his plus fours above argyle socks, and a tam-o'-shanter cocked at an angle on his blond head. He was only one or two inches taller than Amelia, with a smooth face that was more boyish than manly, and appeared much younger than his forty-three years.

"Your Royal Highness." Amelia dipped an awkward curtsey. "Off to your morning game?"

"This very instant. Do you golf, Mrs. Bradford?"

"No, sir." Jackson had been the golfer. She'd been content to make friends with the country club wives, the same women who'd ostracized her after Jackson's illegal financial dealings had come to light.

"Wallis is in the reception room. Mr. Forwood, walk with me. We need to discuss Sir Walter's unexpected arrival." The Duke sauntered out the front door with Mr. Forwood in tow.

Wallis stood in the reception room inspecting the numerous wedding gifts laid out on the long medieval table in the center. People were hesitant to come but not to send presents.

"Another gift arrived for you." Amelia handed Wallis the package.

Wallis tore off the brown paper wrapper to reveal a slender yellow and black box with *Fendi* emblazoned on the top. Inside was a fine-tooled leather guest book. Her eyes lit up at the name on the attached card. "It's from Il Duce. Such a thoughtful man, unlike most of the people we invited. Any new responses?"

"Yes." Amelia opened one of the letters she'd picked up with the package. "Lord Brownlow sends his regrets."

"Of course he does." Wallis set the guest book and its box on the table between a candelabra and a silver tea service. "Cookie threatened to revoke the royal appointments of anyone who so much as looks at us from across the Channel. Two hundred eighty-four regrets out of three hundred invitations. At this rate, there'll be more press than guests at my wedding."

Wallis marched out of the reception room. Amelia hurried behind her, expected to follow.

Wallis flung open the door to her bedroom and Aunt Bessie looked up from where she sat on the sofa sorting through yesterday's fan mail. It arrived every afternoon from Britain, America, and various other parts of the world. Everyone everywhere had an opinion of Wallis and they all felt the need to share it with her.

"Why are you managing my mail? That's Amelia's job." Wallis sat behind the Louise XIV desk to paste Il Duce's card in her memory book. "You'll strain your eyes."

"I can't lounge around all day pretending to be the lady of the château." Aunt Bessie winked at Amelia while slyly tucking a few letters between the sofa cushions.

"What are you hiding?" Wallis rarely missed any detail.

"Whatever do you mean?" Aunt Bessie shifted on the cushion to try and conceal the evidence beneath her ample bottom.

"You're keeping letters from me when you know I want to read them."

"They'll only upset you."

"But they're so educational." Wallis held out her hand. "Every day I learn a new word for whore."

With a resigned sigh, Aunt Bessie handed Wallis the letters and Amelia's stomach tightened. Wallis was already irritated. The fan mail would make her a brute.

Wallis slid a dagger letter opener into the first envelope and slit the paper with a quick flick of her wrist. She tugged out the letter and pursed her lips at what must have been a particularly spicy note. "Amelia, what other good news do you have for me this morning?"

"A letter from Mr. Ernest Simpson." Wallis and Aunt Bessie exchanged a look. "Should I open it?"

"No, I'll take it and any others from him. His letters, like the safe in my closet, are off-limits to you."

"Yes, ma'am."

"He shouldn't be writing to you at all, and you shouldn't be writing to him," Aunt Bessie said.

"It's about our divorce. There are a few loose ends to tie up." Wallis slid the unopened letter in her suit pocket and returned to reading her fan mail.

"There's something from a Joachim von Ribbentrop." Amelia read the return address on the letter with the Berlin postage stamp.

"Another person whose letters are for my eyes only." Wallis took the letter and tucked it away with Mr. Simpson's.

"Another person you shouldn't be corresponding with," Aunt Bessie muttered. "But you will have your way, won't you?"

"Don't be such a worrywart."

"It's not as if you've ever given me anything to worry about."

Wallis frowned but had enough respect for Aunt Bessie to not bite her head off. Amelia was another matter. "Well, get on with it. I don't have all day to review the morning post."

"Here's your dry cleaning bill." Amelia held out the bill.

Wallis didn't even look at it, too engrossed in her fan mail to bother. "Mrs. Bedaux will see to it. When you speak to her, request another laundrywoman. My sheets must be ironed every night and my pillowcases changed every day. Dirty pillowcases are ghastly for the complexion."

Amelia tucked the bill in her jacket pocket, amazed at how Wallis and the Duke thought nothing of running up exorbitant bills and then casually handing them to the Bedaux to settle. That the Bedaux never failed to do so was even more astounding. Amelia wondered what they were getting from this arrangement.

"Don't put the bill in your pocket," Wallis snapped. "Put it in the notebook I gave you so you can enter it in the accounts the way I taught you."

"The notebook's in my office. I-I didn't have time to get it after I came back from the post office."

"What were you doing there?"

"I-I . . ."

"You attend to my affairs. The mailman sees to the mail. I need help, not hindrances. Keep the notebook with you at all times." Wallis set aside the second letter and began the third, the contents making her frown. If she wasn't careful, those sheets would spoil her complexion faster than a dirty pillowcase. "Has Lady Selby cabled about her arrival time?"

"Lady Selby?" Amelia tried to remember who that was.

"The wife of the British Attaché to the consul in Vienna." Wallis glared at her from over the top of the letter. "Didn't that school of yours teach you anything?"

Amelia bit back a curt reply. She'd spent a year at the Gibbs School learning to write thank-you letters to distinction, manage guest lists and correspondence, but no, she did not know who the wife of the British Attaché to the consul in Vienna was.

"Be kind, Wallis," Aunt Bessie gently scolded. "I doubt you knew who any diplomatic officials were when you were Amelia's age."

"No, but I quickly learned who was who and what was what when it was important." She fixed Amelia with a hard stare. "I suggest you do the same. Now, when Lady Selby arrives, assuming you can determine when that is without my help, she must have lilies for her room. Her husband isn't joining her so we needn't worry about him. Make sure the lilies are fresh and not drooping. I won't have people saying I'm as much a second-rate hostess as I am a"—she read from the letter—"'paltry companion to Britain's glorious king.'"

"I think that's enough of these little gems for today." Aunt Bessie slid the letter out of Wallis's hand; she was the only one brave enough to approach her when she had that murderous look on her face.

The clock on the mantel chimed the hour and Wallis rose

and straightened the pussy bow on her dark green blouse. "I must speak with the cook about the wedding luncheon. His menu is too extravagant. Food should always be perfect but simple. Too much of it makes people sluggish and boring. And no soup. It's the most uninteresting liquid and it gets you nowhere. Amelia, if it isn't asking too much of you to attend to your duties, finish the thank-you letter to Lady Williams-Taylor. I want it sent with the afternoon post, and make the writing sound more like my voice this time."

Wallis marched out of the room, her heels banging over the wood-plank floor.

"Which voice should I write in, the one Wallis uses with us or the sweet one she uses with her guests?" Amelia complained to Aunt Bessie. "How am I supposed to know who all these people are if she won't tell me?"

"You're smart. You'll find a way to figure it out. Now, off to work. You won't learn anything by standing around complaining."

Amelia trudged into Mr. Bedaux's study and the mahogany desk in the corner. She fell into the hard banker's chair and studied the stone fireplace in the corner and the large, turned-wood daybed where Aunt Bessie slept. The maids had pulled the bedspread tight and tucked in the corners. Amelia's trundle bed, like her portable typewriter and paperwork, had been put away. Wallis hated things to be out of place or cluttered.

Just like Father.

His office hadn't been as formal as Mr. Bedaux's but warm and inviting with blue walls and white chair-rail molding instead of this heavy paneling and red brocade. After he'd died, his associates had taken away the drawers full of files and Mother had changed it into a closet for her gowns, erasing all traces of him.

Amelia picked up the fountain pen and turned it over in her hands, the light from the window behind her reflecting in the black resin barrel. If Father hadn't died, everything would've been different. Mother wouldn't have launched herself into society in search of another husband, abandoning Amelia and her brother, Peter, to find their own way. Mother's indifference had been a mere annoyance for Peter. Father had planned his future so he could eventually take his place on the railway's board of directors. He hadn't done the same for Amelia. He hadn't even included Amelia in his will, leaving it to Mother to decide what money Amelia received, which had been nothing. Mother had said her future husband would take care of her. So much for that plan.

"This arrived for Mrs. Simpson, or should I say, Mrs. Warfield." Mr. Forwood walked in and handed her the official papers marking the change in Wallis's name from Simpson to her maiden Warfield. Wallis could change her name but there was no erasing her past. That would haunt her forever, just like Amelia's. "She filed the paperwork before you arrived."

"I see." At least she'd found out before she'd typed today's letters. She didn't want to be up all night redoing them.

"Mrs. Bedaux would like to see you."

"I'll go to her at once." Amelia gathered up her notebook, the bill, and the request for another laundress, feeling more like a beggar with her hat in her hands going to the chatelaine than she had the day she'd arrived on Aunt Bessie's doorstep. However, this was her job and fresh hell waited for her if she didn't do it Wallis's way.

Amelia passed the library, where Sir Walter and Mr. Metcalf, the Duke's longtime friend, onetime equerry, and best man, sat hunched over a half-finished puzzle, more involved in their whispered conversation than finding pieces.

"I'll pass on what I think is helpful but even I'm not privy to everything." Mr. Metcalf ran one hand through his wavy brown hair set over a long face. "Ever since the Duke became chummy with that Bedaux fellow, I've been all but shut out."

"I understand, but do what you can. We don't wish to be caught on the back foot," Sir Walter, the slender, bespectacled royal attorney with his dark hair parted in the middle and slicked down on either side, encouraged before noticing Amelia.

Both men stood. "Mrs. Bradford."

"Please, carry on." Whatever they were discussing, it wasn't for her ears.

She left them to their puzzle and climbed the curving stone staircase beneath a vaulted gothic ceiling. Large windows at the top let in the bright sun and offered stunning views of the poplars and willows surrounding the château.

I suppose this is as good a place to work as any. It was better than the dirty, dank insurance offices she'd interviewed at where even the rotund men in their cheap suits had heard of Jackson and his crimes. They'd locked their cash drawers then told her she wasn't suited for the position.

I'm barely suited for this one, she mused, but she had to make it work. There weren't any other options.

"Good morning, Mrs. Bedaux." Amelia stepped into a room of pale green walls and stately First Empire mahogany furniture.

"Bonjour, madame, thank you for coming to see me," Mrs. Bedaux greeted in an American accent tinged with a continental flair. She sat at a drop-front secretary, and wore an afternoon dress of cream lace over silk, her figure lithe and graceful like the black and gold Charles Lemanceau statue on the pink granite mantel.

"I was going to come see you. Mrs. Simpson asked me to give you this." Amelia handed Mrs. Bedaux the bill with more humility than Wallis had shown in asking her host to pay for it.

"I'll take care of it." Mrs. Bedaux set it on top of the bill from Cartier beside her correspondence.

"Mrs. Simpson also requests another laundress for her sheets, and lilies for Lady Selby's room before her arrival tomorrow afternoon."

"Of course. I'll speak to Mr. Hale about it. Nothing makes a guest feel more welcome and at ease than flowers."

Amelia thought of the flowers Mother used to fill their Baltimore home with after her marriage to Theodore Miller. There hadn't been anything personal or inviting about those gaudy and overdone arrangements. All they'd done was block everyone's view at the dinner table.

"When hosting guests, personal touches and attention to

detail should never be overlooked," Mrs. Bedaux explained. "What are your favorite flowers, Mrs. Bradford?"

"Pale pink roses, but only two or three of them with some greenery."

"You have simple but elegant tastes."

No one had ever called her tastes elegant. Common, Mother always used to say, amazed her daughter hadn't naturally adopted her opulent style. It'd never occurred to her to actually teach Amelia to appreciate her taste and fashion. She'd simply expected Amelia to magically develop them and she'd been disappointed when she hadn't.

Amelia waited in silence, expecting to be dismissed, but Mrs. Bedaux sat back in her chair and studied her. She was tall, with fine features beneath dark blond hair, her natural elegance enviably effortless. "How are you settling into your new position?"

"Wallis is very demanding." Amelia sighed before she caught her mistake. "I don't mean to sound ungrateful." This woman was Wallis's friend, not Amelia's confidante. She might tell Wallis what she'd said and then she'd be in for it.

"You're not ungrateful, merely young and out of your element." She flashed a warm smile and Amelia let out a relieved breath. Her time here would be short if she didn't lose the babe-in-the-woods smell clinging to her. "It wasn't easy for me either when I first came to France. I wasn't much older than your, what, twenty-four years?"

"Twenty-one." Although Jackson's arrest and death, and the need to make a living, made her feel ancient some days.

"Younger than me when I arrived in France. Grand Rapids high society did little to prepare me for European society. Let me offer you a little advice, a few rules to live by, as it were. First, watch Wallis and take note of her likes and dislikes, how she does things and prefers things done, then do everything that way. Learn to anticipate her needs and you'll make yourself indispensable. The second is to be nice to everyone no matter what their station. You never know when they'll be in a position to help you. Third is to read." She gathered up copies of *Le Temps* and *Le Figaro* and *Marie Claire* and *Vogue* from the round table between the tall windows. "You'll learn who's who and how they're acquainted or related. These will also inform you of artistic and literary trends, which will improve your conversation skills. I'll have my maid deliver my newspapers and magazines to your room in the evenings. If you read about something or someone you don't understand, don't hesitate to ask me about it."

"Why is Lady Selby coming to the wedding without Lord Selby?" Now was as good a time as any to ask.

"His Majesty's Government has commanded their officials not to attend the wedding. Lady Selby may come as a friend but her husband may not."

"Why? His Royal Highness is no longer King. What does it matter who he marries or what he does?" Royal things were always so complicated.

"Kings, like popes, don't abdicate, they die, and there are never two at once. Now there are, and it divides loyalties. That's dangerous to both men, but especially the one wearing the crown. His Majesty doesn't want any reminders that he could topple too. The royal family is trying to ignore a very inconvenient reality."

They aren't the only ones. Wallis was trying to maintain the façade of a grand royal wedding worthy of an ex-king, and every declined invitation chipped away at that illusion. No wonder she was cross.

"Another excellent way to discover who is who and what is what is to speak to those in the know. I'll convince Wallis to have you join us for dinner tomorrow night to fill out the numbers. Mr. Randolph Churchill will be there and I'll arrange for you to sit next to him. You'll learn a great deal from him, including what he intends to write about the wedding for the *Daily Mail.* Wallis is worried about that, and if you can ease her mind, she'll be grateful. Remember, Mrs. Bradford, your job is to always make her life easier. Do that and she'll adore you."

That no one was interested in making Amelia's life easier wasn't lost on her. She must have frowned at the thought because Mrs. Bedaux clasped her hands in front of her, calm and serene in the way Amelia wished Mother had been. "One more word of advice, rule number five, you could say. Never chafe or look irritated at being told what to do, no matter how difficult or silly you think the request is. I know it's hard at your age, but don't complain or be churlish, always smile and treat every encounter as an opportunity to practice poise, speech, manners, and all the skills that will further your career."

This might be the most difficult advice for Amelia to follow.

Chapter Three

I asked Lord Beaverbrook why he sided with His Majesty when everyone knows he's against the monarchy and do you know what he said?" Randolph Churchill asked Amelia from beside her at the table. The party of eight dined in the wood-paneled dining room with its beamed ceiling and tapestry wallpaper. They didn't use the Bedaux's fine china but the shell-pink Wedgwood set Wallis had inherited from her Warfield grandmother, a doyenne of Baltimore society who'd taught Wallis the social graces and how to sit without her spine ever touching the back of a chair.

"What did he say?" Amelia asked. Mr. Churchill liked to talk, especially about himself, but Mrs. Bedaux was right, he had a wealth of knowledge. She'd learned more about British politics and society in the last two hours with him than she had during the entire last week.

"He did it to bugger Prime Minister Baldwin for forcing the Duke to abdicate." Mr. Churchill chuckled into his champagne.

"Who's Lord Beaverbrook?"

"Newspaper owner, quite influential. My boss, one might say. He sent me here even though he knows I'm not going to write much. Father loves the old king and won't have me spilling the beans on his intimate affairs. Let the hacks outside the gates do it." He glanced around the table then leaned close to her, taking a quick glance at her décolletage hidden beneath the satin sash that crossed her chest and tied in a much too large bow at the back. The pale pink chiffon dress was a leftover from her debutante season and the only formal gown she owned. It paled in comparison to the other women's chic evening dresses, especially Wallis's fitted gold lamé gown with the high neck. "His Royal Highness is the only one who looks as if he's having a jolly good time. The rest appear as if they're here for a funeral. No one wants to read about that."

There's a relief. Amelia could tell Wallis she had nothing to worry about from Mr. Churchill. She might even be impressed Amelia was the one who'd discovered it.

"I understand you hail from Washington, D.C." Mr. Churchill tucked in to the last of his roast guinea hen, pomme soufflé, and asparagus in cream sauce. He resembled his father through the face and jowls but he didn't have his father's bulldog look of ambition and hard work she'd seen in the newsreels back home.

"Baltimore originally." Amelia waved away a footman offering more champagne. "But I spent a few years in Washington, D.C., after my mother remarried."

They'd been the second most miserable years of her life.

"Your father was a senator?"

"Stepfather. It was back in the late twenties. He's in the clothing manufacturing business now, the Daniel Miller Company. They don't do business in Europe." Thank heavens or Theodore would probably break his shunning silence to send her warning letters about embarrassing him overseas. However, she decided to play up her lineage. She might be a black sheep, but in the middle of all these lords and ladies, pride demanded they know she wasn't a complete nobody. "My father's family owns the Baltimore Southern Railway but Father died in a car crash in 1931." She'd been fifteen, and forced to watch Mother launch herself into society and land the very rich and well-connected Theodore. It'd allowed her to maintain her precious social standing, the one Amelia had threatened by eloping with Jackson. "My brother will take his place on the board of directors soon."

"Lady Metcalf, tell me all the gossip from London that isn't about me," Wallis said to the woman who sat across from her. She wasn't particularly loud but her crisp tenor always carried in even the most crowded room.

"Then I may not have much to tell you." Lady Metcalf laughed although she was half serious.

"But you must have heard something," Wallis insisted. "If you accept a dinner invitation, you have a moral obligation to be amusing. What about you, Fern? What does Charles write about Germany?"

"He says their factories are impressive and if Britain and France weren't so hostile to trade agreements, they'd all benefit from the new, industrialized Germany."

"Charles is right. We should embrace Germany instead of isolating it." His Royal Highness handed pieces of guinea hen to the dogs, who sat patiently beside his chair. "If I could visit

Germany and extend the hand of friendship, I'd do it and settle all this saber-rattling."

"Germany isn't interested in settling its aggressive talk," Sir Walter pointed out to much nodding from Mr. Metcalf and a frown from the Duke. "Herr Hitler has done nothing to conceal his ambitions or his blatant breaking of the Treaty of Versailles."

"Herr Hitler has no designs on Britain, Denmark, Holland, or the Netherlands; he's said as much in numerous speeches. He only wants to unite the German-speaking people and halt the communist spread," the Duke insisted. "I say leave him to it. The Bolsheviks are a greater threat to the world than Germany. Someone has to stop them. My brother isn't about to do it, and I don't want to end up on the wrong end of a bolshie bullet like my cousin the Tsar and his family did. All we need to do is stay out of Herr Hitler's way and he'll see to Russia and save us a damned lot of trouble."

"What about his treatment of the Jews?" Mr. Rogers, Wallis's old American friend who was here for the wedding, asked, exchanging a concerned glance with his wife across the table.

"Those stories are communist rubbish, exaggerations meant to smear a man who's accomplishing more for the working class than any other leader in Europe." His Royal Highness rapped his knuckles against the table.

"Sir, I advise you not to be so open in your admiration for Herr Hitler," Mr. Metcalf cautioned. "Such remarks could easily be taken out of context to smear you."

The Duke pinned Mr. Metcalf with an off-with-his-head look. "One may suggest things to me but they may not advise."

"My apologies, sir, I didn't mean to overstep. I'm merely trying to help."

"The Duke knows and appreciates how much you've done for us in the past, Edward," Wallis soothed. "Don't you, darling?"

"Quite right." The Duke picked up an asparagus spear with his fingers.

Wallis slapped the spear out of his hand. "Use your fork."

Shock rippled down the table. Amelia expected the Duke to rebuke Wallis for embarrassing him but he wiped his fingers with his napkin and picked up his fork.

The eating and conversation slowly resumed as if nothing had happened.

"Is Sir Walter right about Germany's ambition?" Amelia asked Mr. Churchill while they stood together by the fire in the library after dinner. Maurice Chevalier's "Ma Pomme" played on the gramophone and settled beneath the low conversation of Wallis and the other women on the sofa. The clink of chips punctuated the French singing as the Duke, Sir Walter, Mr. Rogers, and Mr. Metcalf played cards at the table near the large Skinner organ, a showpiece of the library and château.

"He is. I saw their armament factories when I was in Germany reporting for the *Daily Mail*. They're running at full speed, and every able-bodied man has joined an army the

Treaty of Versailles says shouldn't exist. I've told people there's more to worry about than Germany overrunning the Rhineland but they listen to me as much as the Greeks listened to Cassandra. His Royal Highness is quite mistaken if he thinks Germany and Russia will simply fight it out while the rest of Europe watches and waits for a winner."

"Unless the Duke knows something we don't. He must have seen all sorts of state secrets when he was King."

"None that he took seriously." Mr. Churchill chuckled into his drink. "Statecraft was not his forte."

"I tell you, Sir Walter, it isn't right." The Duke banged his fist on the gaming table, making the chips in front of him rattle in their stacks. "There's no legal basis for denying my wife the right to be styled Her Royal Highness."

"I'm merely His Majesty's messenger, sir, not the decider of titles," Sir Walter calmly replied.

Wallis watched the conversation, her hand tight on her highball glass, irritated at the Duke for bringing this up in front of Sir Walter and the other guests.

"Randolph, speak to Winston about it. He must have some pull," the Duke commanded.

"I'll see what I can do, sir," Mr. Churchill assured with the same deference everyone showed the ex-king.

"There's a good man." The Duke returned to his card game and Wallis eased her tight grip on the glass and resumed her conversation.

"I don't understand the Duke's concern with Wallis's title," Amelia said to Mr. Churchill. She barely understood all the titles and royal protocol and why everyone was so enamored with it, almost to the point of obsession. "She'll be a duchess when she marries him. What's so special about 'Her Royal Highness'?"

"It makes her a recognized member of the royal family, and the King and Queen don't want a jumped-up adventurer on the same footing as them or His Royal Highness's sisters-in-law, especially since they think the marriage won't last."

"She's gone through too much to chuck him over."

"Except he isn't the catch he was when she met him, is he?" Mr. Churchill sipped his Scotch. "If she'd respected the monarchy, understood the Crown and everything it means and stands for instead of spitting in its face, she wouldn't be in this predicament. Neither of them would be."

"It wasn't all her fault." She understood Wallis's position. Everyone had blamed Amelia for what Jackson had done, but until his arrest, she hadn't known that every dime she'd spent on her house, clothes, and car had been stolen from someone else. Her entire life had been a lie.

"She didn't help matters either. Who was she before she met him? Nobody. He made her someone but it wasn't enough. Now she wants everyone to curtsey to her with the same respect as the royal women who've supported the family they chose to marry into. Fat chance, that. She wanted all of it and she'll get none of it, except him. Good luck to them both."

"Wallis, your shoe buckle has come undone. I'll fix it for you." The Duke dropped his cards and rushed to kneel in front of Wallis and fastened her shoe.

How sweet, Amelia thought before she caught the horrified looks exchanged between Mr. Churchill and Lady Metcalf. Suddenly, she understood Mr. Churchill's irritation. The man who'd once represented everything they cherished about their country was kneeling at the feet of a commoner. Instead of demanding the Duke stand, Wallis let him buckle her shoe like a lowly footman. Mr. Churchill was right, she hadn't respected the Crown, she still didn't, and everyone knew it.

Chapter Four

June 1, 1937

Amelia stood in the salon de musique helping Wallis and Mrs. Bedaux with last-minute wedding preparations. The piano in the niche had been replaced with a large chest dragged in from the hallway to make a temporary altar. Its wooden sides were carved with naked Renaissance nymphs and the top supported a plain brass cross borrowed from a local Protestant church flanked by two tall candlesticks. Footmen dressed in the Bedaux's gold and blue livery carried in hired gilt chairs and arranged them in rows for the ceremony.

"Whatever is he playing?" Mrs. Bedaux peered through the open library door at Marcel Dupré, the premier organist in Europe, according to Mrs. Bedaux's newspapers, who sat at the Skinner organ practicing the ceremony selections. The music reverberated out of the large pipes concealed in the château's first- and second-story walls.

"'O Perfect Love,'" Wallis answered. "But it doesn't sound right."

"Because it isn't. I'll see to it." Mrs. Bedaux walked into the library and the music ceased.

In the quiet, the voices of Constance Spry, the London florist, and her assistants carried in from the dining room. Bunches of Madonna lilies and roses rested on week-old copies of the *London Times* on the parquet floor, waiting to be arranged.

"I don't know what I'd do without Charles and Fern," Wallis said as Lady Bedaux's pretty voice singing the proper version of "O Perfect Love" drifted in from the library. "They know how to treat royalty."

"Everything going well, darling?" The Duke entered with a bright smile, forcing the footmen to bow to him before leaving to get more chairs.

"You're as red as a beet and it'll never fade in time for the wedding," Wallis chided. "Wear a better hat when you golf or you'll look like a ripe tomato in the wedding portraits."

"Yes, darling." His bright voice broke like fragile glass. He bent over to peer at the newspaper on the floor, pushing aside a few white peonies with his foot to get a better look.

"What in heaven's name are you doing?"

"Trying to read the bloody *London Times*. I haven't seen it in ages and they're all damp."

"Go read a French newspaper. Constance doesn't need you interfering with her work."

"Yes, darling," he mumbled, and wandered off to find a dry newspaper.

Wallis examined the room, and Amelia waited for orders on what to change or arrange but all she heard was a deep sigh, and then: "Were you disappointed by your wedding ceremony?"

"Not at first," Amelia answered honestly. "I thought eloping was romantic."

"It was, and I was quite impressed with you when Aunt Bessie told me about it."

"You were?" People had expressed a lot of opinions about her wedding. *Impressed* wasn't one of them.

"Of course. I remember how spirited you were at Wakefield Manor, eating up everything I told you about China and London. I thought, *Here's a girl like me who doesn't want to sit under the thumb of chaperones and rules, but wants to live,* and you did. I was glad to see your father's loss and that awful mother of yours hadn't snuffed the life out of you." Wallis's proud smile faded as she surveyed the room. "My first wedding was in Christ Episcopal Church, if you can believe it. Mary Raffray was my maid of honor and there were six other debutantes as bridesmaids, a very proper Baltimore society wedding. It was the groom who wasn't right. Win was an awful drunk and mean as a dog but I was too young and naive to see the warning signs. After Win, I thought I'd never remarry. Of course, I never thought I'd divorce and wed a second time but here I am, soggy newspapers in a salon de musique. If you ever get married again, I suggest another elopement."

"If planning a proper wedding is this involved, I will," Amelia joked before her stomach dropped in horror at having forgotten her place. She braced for a browbeating but Wallis laughed instead. It eased the fatigue and strain of the past year, and for a moment, she was the Wallis who'd sat on the back porch at Wakefield Manor, the Virginia estate of Cousin Lelia, Father's sister, telling Amelia risqué stories about her time in China.

"Planning a wedding is only this bad when you're marrying the ex-king of England." Wallis laid a rare tender hand on Amelia's arm, her skin cold but her touch firm. "Be glad Jackson took the coward's way out. Life is easier for a widow than a divorcée. You'll have the freedom to follow your heart when the time comes. It's a rare gift."

Following her heart had already landed her in a fool's paradise. If she ever decided to marry again, she'd be far more practical about it, but she appreciated Wallis's concern. She'd endured enough fake condolences after Father's death, and even Jackson's, to know when people were throwing out expected words and when they really meant them.

"What are you two discussing?" Mrs. Bedaux strode in and Wallis let go of Amelia.

"I'm advising Mrs. Bradford to change her name to her maiden Montague."

Amelia tried not to look startled, not because they'd never discussed it before but because she'd never even considered it.

"What a wonderful idea," Mrs. Bedaux said. "It'll help give you a fresh start, and with your fluency, a French last name could help you catch the eye of a comte or chevalier."

"Imagine going home and having your mother and stepfather forced to bow to you," Wallis suggested in a conspiratorial tone. "It's a tempting idea, isn't it?"

"Is that what you'd imagined?" Amelia asked.

"The game isn't over yet, there's still time to win it."

June 3, 1937

The sunlight filling the salon de musique failed to brighten the guests' somber faces. They sat on either side of the makeshift aisle waiting for the ceremony to begin as the strains of Schumann played by Monsieur Dupré drifted through the château. Everyone appeared more relieved than excited that the big day was finally here. Only the Duke beamed like the two altar candles where he stood with Reverend Jardine and Mr. Metcalf. The groom and best man wore morning suits with matching Wallis-blue waistcoats. Two opulent arrangements of lilies and peonies stood behind the makeshift altar with the borrowed cross.

That darned altar. It'd cost Amelia no end of trouble this morning when Reverend Jardine had insisted they cover the nudes on the chest. Reverend Jardine wasn't even the true officiant, merely the only Church of England vicar Mr. Bedaux had found to perform an Anglican blessing, for a hefty fee. All the others had been scared off by the Archbishop of Canterbury. Dr. Mercier, the mayor of Monts, had performed the civil ceremony in the dining room a half hour ago. The religious one was simply for show, but Reverend Jardine had insisted on decency. While Cecil Beaton had taken Wallis and the Duke's wedding portraits, Amelia and the maids had torn through the already packed honeymoon trunks to find the silk cloth painted with stars that Wallis knew would perfectly cover the altar in the ex-king of England's makeshift wedding chapel.

Amelia glanced at the guests, all thirty-seven of them if one counted Mr. Philip Attfield, the Duke's Scotland Yard protection officer, the château staff, the few privileged correspondents invited in, the English guests, and Amelia and Aunt Bessie. Their meager ranks were swelled by the presence of Mr. Bedaux, who'd returned from Germany this morning and sat with Mrs. Bedaux in the front row.

Monsieur Dupré gracefully transitioned from Schumann to the Wedding March. Everyone rose to their feet and Amelia's shoes pinched her toes from all the running around in search of that hand-painted altar cloth. Mr. Hale pulled open the door and Wallis entered on Mr. Rogers's arm. No stunned gasps greeted the bride as they used to at Washington, D.C., and Baltimore weddings. They hadn't at Amelia's either. There'd been nothing but the echoing words of Theodore's crumpled telegram in her pocket threatening to disown her if she went through with the wedding. As usual, there'd been no word from Mother. Amelia hadn't expected any but sometimes she was an optimist.

Curse hope and its ugly promises. It still galled her that if she'd listened to Theodore then all the tragedies of the past three years wouldn't have happened. She'd be in Washington, perhaps engaged to a more suitable man with a pile of wedding presents instead of debts, and a promising future instead of this uncertain one.

Wallis came up the aisle at a regal pace but she didn't glow like a bride-to-be. Across the aisle, Lady Metcalf dabbed at tears that, given her expression, weren't ones of joy. The man who'd once been King of England, Emperor of India, who'd stood on the balcony of Buckingham Palace while a nation cheered and heads of state bowed, had only one unknown vicar and eight fellow countrymen at his wedding. Amelia hadn't expected cherubs to drop from the ceiling to give the ex-king and his new wife their blessing, but she'd hoped the joy of the day would transform it into something more splendid. It hadn't.

Mr. Rogers handed Wallis off to the Duke then took his seat beside his wife. Reverend Jardine performed the Anglican rite in the droning tone Anglican ministers seemed to learn in seminary. Twenty minutes later, after the Welsh gold rings and vows had been exchanged, the newlyweds faced their guests.

"Allow me to introduce the new, uh . . ." Reverend Jardine stammered. He'd bothered about a bunch of nymphs but hadn't thought to ask how to announce the new Duke and Duchess.

"His and Her Royal Highness, the Duke and Duchess of Windsor," the Duke hissed.

A ripple of indignation stiffened the backs of all the English guests. Even after the two ceremonies, they still didn't see Wallis as a Royal Highness.

"Of course." Reverend Jardine smiled in supplication. "Their Royal Highnesses, the Duke and Duchess of Windsor."

Polite applause muffled by gloves filled the room as the organist played the correct version of "O Perfect Love."

The guests lined up to offer the required congratulations but there were no glad smiles, no effusive wishes for a happy life and a fruitful union. The guests tipped their heads to Wallis but did not curtsey. They were too aware of Sir Walter, the King's representative, and his imminent return to Britain, where he'd give a full report of today's events to the royal family. Wallis's newlywed smile tightened as she realized even her most loyal friends and supporters were more influenced by the King and Queen of England than by her.

Aunt Bessie stepped up to Wallis and enveloped her in a large hug before moving aside to allow Amelia to come forward.

"Congratulations, Your Royal Highness." Amelia slid one leg behind the other and dropped into the deepest curtsey she could manage. People gasped from somewhere behind her but she ignored it as she rose to meet Wallis's astonished expression. Then a flicker of respect and appreciation passed through Wallis's eyes and Amelia resisted the urge to smile in triumph.

"About time someone got it right." The Duke scowled at the other guests, who averted their gazes in shame.

"You'd serve Her Grace better by helping her adjust to her new situation instead of living in a fairy tale." Sir Walter joined Amelia at the reception room window. Outside, Wallis and the Duke posed for the few reporters and newsreel cameras allowed onto the grounds. Mr. Metcalf read a prepared statement for the press, his words muffled by the château's stone walls.

"It's her wedding day. She deserves a few hours of happiness before reality sets in."

"I suppose." He wasn't as generous about what he thought Wallis deserved.

"Thank you for being here. It may not seem like it, but it's appreciated. There would've been more family but they couldn't travel." It was a lie. Wallis hadn't invited any of her American family except Aunt Bessie and Amelia. She had the sneaking suspicion Wallis didn't want people from home to see firsthand what a third-rate affair this had been.

"As someone who serves a challenging master, I understand your unique position. If there's anything I can ever do to help you, please don't hesitate to contact me." He spoke in the straightforward manner of an attorney giving professional advice. Her Boston lawyers had used the same tone with her many times after Jackson's death when the full realities of his life and her new one had taken shape.

"Thank you. I'm sure I'll need all the help I can get."

Wallis was wrong. The King's attorney general wasn't a lapdog but a servant ordered to deliver bad news who genuinely wished to help the Duke and his staff.

Wallis, the Duke, and Mr. Metcalf came inside as the footmen escorted the press back to the gates.

Mr. Hale approached Wallis with a large bouquet of roses. "From the Prime Minister of France, ma'am."

"How kind of him." Wallis was about to take the roses when Mr. Bedaux stepped between them and her.

"He isn't the only head of state to send his congratulations." Mr. Bedaux slid a gold box decorated with flowers out of his morning suit pocket and held it out to Wallis. "Herr Hitler asked me to personally deliver this to you. He wishes you both a lifetime of happiness."

"How very thoughtful of him." Wallis held up the box, turning it this way and that to admire the fine gold metalwork. "Isn't it beautiful, David?"

"As beautiful as you, darling."

"Herr Hitler also asked me to extend an invitation to you to be his guest for a state visit to Germany this fall so he can congratulate you in person."

"How wonderful. David, this could be your chance to extend the hand of friendship." Wallis moved a silver salt and pepper set from the King of the Belgians aside to place Herr Hitler's box front and center on the gift table.

"Perhaps." The Duke tugged at his white and blue pinstriped tie. "We'll certainly consider his offer, but not today. It's time for our reception."

The Duke took her by the elbow and escorted Wallis out to the back portico, where a buffet lunch of chicken à la king, lobster, and salads awaited them. The guests sat in the shade of wide umbrellas while footmen moved among them with silver trays of champagne from Mr. Bedaux's cellar.

"Wallis couldn't have asked for a more beautiful day." Aunt Bessie lounged in her chair sipping her third glass of champagne while Amelia enjoyed a rare break from her duties.

"Maybe this means things will be easier for them from here on out."

"I doubt that, but whatever is in store for them, she'll face it with her usual grit, poise, and charm."

Amelia watched Wallis chatting with her guests, wondering why these people had defied Their Majesties to be here today. Wallis didn't have Lady Metcalf's prestigious lineage or Mrs. Bedaux's lithe beauty. Even Monsieur Mainbocher's dress hadn't softened Wallis's hard lines and angles. No, there was something else there, the way she moved through the tables as if she were a queen, speaking with each person as if they were the only one here and flattering everyone with kind words and compliments, the way she used to do with Amelia at Cousin Lelia's. Amelia didn't know if Wallis meant a word of what she said but she spoke in a way that made people believe she did. Amelia admired her effortless manners and etiquette, and her resilience. Wallis had endured the abdication of the King of England, a very public divorce, and the scorn of the royal family and the British people, and it hadn't crushed her or dulled whatever sparkle that continued to draw people to her.

A footman refilled Amelia's champagne glass and she nodded her thanks to him the same way she'd seen Wallis do many times. Aunt Bessie was right; Amelia could learn a lot from Wallis, including how to face difficulties with grace and rise above her past.

Chapter Five

Paris, September 1937

Once the Duke and Duchess motored off to catch the *Orient Express* for their Austrian honeymoon, and Aunt Bessie had sailed for home, Amelia had traveled with Mr. Forwood and Mr. Schafranek, the Austrian chauffeur, to Paris to settle into their rooms at the Hotel Meurice. Mr. Hale and Mademoiselle Moulichon would join them next week when Wallis and the Duke returned from their honeymoon. Wallis had convinced the Bedaux's butler and lady's maid to come and work for her, a change in staff the Bedaux had surprisingly encouraged.

The Windsors had a large suite on the third floor with a sitting room, dining room, and private elevator. Amelia and Mr. Forwood shared an office off the Windsors' small foyer, allowing them to greet delivery boys and postmen without giving the curious a glimpse into the Duke and Duchess's private rooms. Wallis had chosen the Hotel Meurice because of its reputation for privacy, and the deep discount it had offered the Windsors for the honor of housing them. People clamored to stay at the same hotel as the infamous Duke and Duchess, hoping some of their glamour and notoriety might rub off on them. Amelia couldn't blame them. She hoped for the same thing.

"You're in early this morning," Amelia greeted Mr. Forwood when he entered the office. He usually didn't come in until 10 A.M., the Duke's habit of sleeping late dictating his hours. Amelia wished Wallis slept in. She'd miss the late start when Wallis returned.

"I had an errand to run at the British Embassy." He shrugged out of his light overcoat and hung it on the rack beside the door. The crisp fall air was begging to nip in and steal the warmth of summer. "This arrived for you, Mrs. Bradford."

"Mrs. Montague," Amelia politely corrected as he handed her a package. The final poll deed for her name change had come through last week. It had felt strange to fill out the paperwork, to try and erase the last three years through an act of government, but Wallis was right. Shedding some of the past did help her breathe a little easier.

Amelia opened the package to find copies of *Bottin Mondain* and *Tout Paris,* along with a note from Mrs. Bedaux.

> *The French social registers are a must for making invitations and seating charts for dinners. I advise you to visit the American Embassy Chancery and obtain*

a copy of the diplomatic corps list to help you with guest lists. Please let me know if I can be of any assistance. Yours truly, Mrs. Bedaux

Between this and the *Burke's Peerage* she'd sent, Amelia had quite the social reference library. She flipped through *Tout Paris,* admiring the advertisements for tailors and cafés and maps for each of Paris's twenty arrondissements. She set the books aside and resumed typing the letter regarding Wallis's donation to Lady Williams-Taylor's fundraiser for the Bahamian Humane Society. A loud knock at the door startled them.

"That'll be the postman." Amelia rose to see to him. "He still insists on personally bringing me the registered letters to sign."

"At least he's finally chosen a reasonable hour to do it."

"I'll say." The first week they'd been here, he'd knocked on her door at 7:30 every morning to get her signature.

"Bonjour, madame." The postman handed her the receipt book to sign. "The Duke and Duchess return soon?"

"On Friday." Amelia exchanged his receipt book for the letters, noting the one from Mr. Carter of Carter Ledyard & Milburn. Her stomach tightened. A letter from her Boston attorney was never good.

"Perhaps I'll meet them?" The postman was as excited as the gawkers in the lobby, eager to catch a glimpse of the hotel's rich and famous guests.

"Perhaps. *À demain.*" She closed the door and returned to her desk.

She read the letter from her attorney and her heart sank. She and ninety other entities had been named in a suit to recover the money Jackson and his two associates had looted from the investment trust at the height of their scheme. Hot tears blurred her eyes. What did the prosecutors think they were going to get out of her? Her meager eighty-dollar-a-year salary would barely put a dent in Jackson's outstanding attorney fees, much less pay back even a small percent of the money Jackson had helped steal. Whatever hopes for independence she might gain from this position evaporated. She'd be in debt for the rest of her life.

"Is everything all right, Mrs. Montague?" Mr. Forwood tugged the handkerchief from his jacket pocket and handed it to her.

"Some unpleasant news from home." She wiped her eyes and tucked the handkerchief in her pocket when Mr. Forwood waved away her attempt to return it.

Another knock at the door echoed through the room.

"I'll see to it." He closed the door behind him to give her a moment to compose herself, and she must. She had a full day of work ahead of her. She could fall to pieces in her bedroom tonight. She sat at her desk to write to her attorney about what to expect from this new development and how to proceed. It'd mean another hour of legal fees added to her already staggering bill but it was a pittance compared to what she'd owe if the court ruled against her.

"Mrs. Montague, a gentleman from the American Embassy is here to see you," Mr. Forwood said when he returned. "Should I send him away?"

"No, I'll speak with him." It might be about the lawsuit.

She checked her makeup in a pocket mirror then walked into the sitting room with the same confidence she'd seen Wallis employ at Château de Candé. Amelia nearly lost her poise at the sight of the gentleman waiting for her. She'd expected another of the many middle-aged men with thinning hair and thick round glasses who'd visited here over the past three months. This man was neither. He was tall and slender, with a fine pin-striped suit filled out by his wide shoulders and buttoned snugly over his trim waist. With his square face, defined jaw, and dark blond hair parted on one side and carefully combed back, he reminded her of Errol Flynn but without the mustache.

"I'm Robert Morton, Foreign Service Officer for Ambassador Bullitt, the American Ambassador to France." He held out his hand and she took it, impressed by his firm grip. "Mr. Bullitt is holding a reception in honor of Maître Suzanne Blum and he'd be honored if His Royal Highness and Her Grace could attend." He handed her an invitation with the Windsors' names in calligraphy on the front, but only the Duke was addressed as His Royal Highness.

"The Embassy isn't using 'Her Royal Highness' for the Duchess," she remarked.

"The British Embassy directed us not to employ the title with the Duchess."

"I see." Word had gone out from on high that the extra-chic title wasn't to be used by anyone official. "Do men in your position usually hand deliver invitations?" None of the others had been sent with this much personal attention.

"I make it a habit to get to know the staff of people of note. I would've called sooner but I was in America on business this summer." He produced a business card from his jacket pocket and held it out to her. "If there's anything I can ever do for you, don't hesitate to ask."

She took the card, careful not to let her fingers brush his. It was masculine in its simplicity, with none of the frilly edging or script on the ones from the Paris couturiers, jewelers, and milliners who'd visited over the past few weeks. "I don't suppose you have a copy of the diplomatic corps list?"

"I'll send one over this afternoon."

"I'll be near the Chancery tomorrow. I don't mind picking it up." There was a boldface lie if she'd ever told one, but Mrs. Bedaux had said to make as many influential connections as possible. She was simply following her advice.

AMELIA SAT ON a plush bench in the entrance hall of the U.S. Embassy Chancery in the Place de la Concorde, watching men in suits and military uniforms crisscross the white and black diamond marble floor. Some headed down the hallways while others climbed the white marble staircase with the brass railing.

"I don't know what's keeping Mr. Morton, but I'm sure he'll be with you any moment," Miss Harper, the receptionist behind the burled-wood desk, assured in a charming Southern accent. She was about Amelia's age, with perfectly manicured

red nails and a stylish mauve suit with a white collar as crisp as the stone arches carved in the walls. "Is there anything I can get for you? Water or tea?"

"No, I'm fine. Thank you." Amelia picked a loose thread off the hem of her brown dress, wishing she looked as fashionable as Miss Harper. At least Amelia's nails were done in a pretty pale pink. She'd purchased nail varnish and makeup her first week in Paris, doing what she could, despite her pitiful wardrobe and income, to look more stylish, but she wasn't half as chic as Miss Harper. However, if a humble Embassy receptionist could dress this well then there was hope for her. "Actually, there is one thing you can do for me. I simply adore your suit. Is it Chanel?"

"Oh no, I can't afford her pieces on my salary." The young woman blushed, flattered to have her dress mistaken for the famous designer's work. "I bought the material at Bucol, then took it to Madame de Wavrin in the Quartier du Sentier along with a picture of what I wanted and had it run up. All the girls here do it. It's how we afford to look our best." Miss Harper wrote down the information for Amelia and handed it to her. "Speak with Hillaire, tell her Miss Harper from the Embassy sent you."

Amelia tucked the card in her purse. "Being new to Paris, you have no idea how much I appreciate this."

"Oh, I do. Why, I felt like the biggest frump when I first arrived. It's hard not to with all these Parisian women looking as if they've stepped out of *Vogue*. It must be especially hard for you working for someone as fashionable as the Duchess of Windsor."

"You know who I am?" Amelia hadn't mentioned her title when she'd given her name.

"Oh honey, there's no anonymity in social and ambassadorial circles. When you're done with Hillaire, visit Antoinette's. I wrote her address down for you too. She's a wonder with hair. And if you ever need anything else, please don't hesitate to call and ask. If I can't help you, I'll find someone who can. I know how hard it is for a working girl to make her way in this city. You have to use every advantage you have."

"I suppose I do." Amelia had used her position to open doors at dressmakers, milliners, and even Madame Chanel's on behalf of Wallis. The idea that she should use it for her own benefit hadn't occurred to her until this moment.

"There's Mr. Morton."

He strolled across the lobby as if he were the ambassador and not simply a part of his staff. Amelia's heart fluttered in her chest at the sight of him but she beat it down. This was a business visit, nothing more. She couldn't afford for it to be anything else.

"Mrs. Montague, it's a pleasure to see you again. Here's the diplomatic corps list." He handed her an envelope, the manila paper still warm from where he'd held it. "I've included lists for the other embassies so you don't miss anyone important."

"You've saved me a great deal of running around Paris."

"I'm always eager to help a fellow American. I can share more information at lunch if you'd like? There's a wonderful little café not far from here with the best prix fixe menu."

"They don't mind you knocking off?"

"I have a bit of freedom in this position, especially when it comes to dealing with the Duchess of Windsor's assistant."

I bet he told Miss Harper who I am. She had a pile of work waiting for her at the hotel but getting to know him was worth falling behind for, and with Wallis returning on Friday, she had to take advantage of this little freedom while it lasted. "It sounds delightful."

"Miss Harper, I'll be back in an hour if anyone is searching for me."

"Yes, Mr. Morton."

Mr. Morton escorted Amelia out of the Chancery entrance, across the front drive, and past the marine sentries standing guard at the iron and stone gates.

"I'm glad you and Miss Harper had a chance to meet. She's a gem." They strolled down rue Royale, past old buildings with upper-floor apartments and ground-floor shops, restaurants, and small cafés where white-coated waiters served coffee to tourists. He didn't stop at one of these but led her toward the tree-lined Boulevard des Capucines. She didn't mind the extra walk, grateful to be outdoors on a fine day and with someone so friendly. He slowed his long strides to match her shorter ones and she caught the citrus notes of his crisp cologne over the scent of petrol and fresh bread from the boulangeries. "She's been here six months and already knows more people than I do."

"How long have you been in Paris?"

"Three years. I worked in Washington, D.C., before that. I'm from Boston originally. My family has been there for generations. I attended Groton then Harvard. My uncle worked for the State Department. I worked for the Cipher Bureau for a time and then became a Foreign Service Officer."

Ciphers, as in decoding secrets. Amelia waited for him to mention her past, sure he'd deciphered that bit of news from one source or another. It'd been quite the story in Boston when Jackson's swindle had come to light, and people loved to spread and remember juicy scandals.

"You must know all the best places to go when not working?" Amelia changed the subject fast, eager to keep him talking about anything except her.

"I do." He told her about which cafés to avoid and which were the best, of jazz clubs she had to visit, art galleries she must see, and bookshops where the tourists never ventured. She enjoyed his deep voice and the easy way he spoke to her as a fellow American in Paris, not the Duchess of Windsor's secretary, and she imagined visiting the places he described.

With whom? She didn't know anyone outside the Windsors' staff and they had families and friends in Paris, including Mr. Forwood, who was seeing a young secretary at the British Embassy. Amelia had no one, and once the Windsors returned, there'd be precious little free time to make friends.

"Here we are," Mr. Morton announced.

He held open the door to the plainly named Café Capucines at number 23 Capucines. The heady aroma of rich café Viennese struck her the moment they entered, as did the number of young men cluttering the tables and discussing European politics over small coffeepots and plates of rolls, meats, and cheeses. The American accents were as impressive as the marble and wood counter where a young woman with thick-rimmed glasses filled cups from the large copper coffee machine.

"This is a Chancery favorite. Close enough to walk to, but out of the way enough to privately discuss what we've seen and heard." Mr. Morton nodded to a couple of coworkers as he led her to a small corner table. He held out her chair then took the one across from her. The waiter exchanged pleasantries with him before taking their order for the prix fixe lunch then bustling off.

"What interesting things have you heard?" The cloak-and-dagger suggestion of what went on here between courses intrigued her as much as he did.

"That King Carol of Romania has invited the Windsors to dinner."

"How do you know? The invitation just arrived."

"It's my job to know what's going on in Paris, who's coming and going and why, especially people of note, and King Carol is certainly noteworthy. He's spent most of the summer here meeting with the French Foreign Minister and other gentlemen of interest."

"Well, I don't know much about him except he and his entourage are taking up the second floor of the Hotel Meurice while the Duke and Duchess are on the third. I'm housed with the servants on the fifth. I have a view of the Tuileries Garden and I can just see Notre Dame over the tops of the trees. I'm positively spoiled." She woke up every morning in expensive sheets with someone to change them and clean her room. It was simple compared to the Duke and Duchess's suite but far more elegant than anything she'd enjoyed in a long time. "I sit at the window at night and watch the city lights while I catch up on work. It's better than being in a stuffy old office."

She didn't dare say she stayed up working to distract herself from the loneliness.

"As someone working in a stuffy office, I'm jealous." He sat back to let the waiter set a coffeepot down in front of them along with a small creamer and sugar bowl. Mr. Morton plucked the lid off the sugar bowl and, using the tongs, picked up a sugar cube. He offered her one then dropped a cube in his cup before glancing up at her from beneath his brows, making her forget all about the steaming drink in front of her. "A word of advice to you and your employer about King Carol. His mistress, Madame Lupescu, is with him. The Queen is in Romania with the children. The less said about that arrangement the better."

Amelia reached for the creamer. *Business, he's talking business. I need to be businesslike.* "I'll tell Her Royal Highness. She'll understand the need for discretion. I certainly do."

"Everyone in Paris does because everyone here has a story and a few secrets." He pointed the sugar tongs at her. "Including you."

And there it is. She set down the creamer and sat back, the spell he'd woven with his sugar, advice, and good looks vanishing. "I'm not going to embezzle the Windsors' money if that's what you're worried about."

"Not at all." He pushed the sugar bowl aside. "It must have been hard being snared in someone else's machinations and then left to deal with the consequences."

Good Lord, this man was full of surprises. "It was."

"I'm very sorry for your loss."

And he was, it was there in his blue eyes, the way it'd been in Wallis's. "Thank you."

She didn't say the only thing she was sorry for was having married Jackson in the first place. The fines and other issues had died with Jackson but not the attorney fees, or the recovery lawsuit now hanging over her.

Stop it. Wallis wouldn't face something like this by looking back or playing the wounded widow. It was time for dignity, elegance, perhaps a bit of wit, not self-pity. She crossed her legs beside the table and leaned toward him as she'd seen Wallis do with people, giving him her undivided attention as she raised her coffee cup.

"Let's not dwell on the past. That's in America and I'm in Paris, making a new life for myself, and possibly some new secrets."

He raised one curious eyebrow, and humiliation flooded through her.

What the devil am I doing? She hadn't learned anything from Jackson if she was flirting with a man she barely knew simply because he was handsome and giving her attention. She almost set her coffee down and slid her legs back under the table but she didn't. She wasn't flirting but being confident, like Wallis. After all, she was an experienced widow, not a naive debutante, and she'd made a move; she couldn't look silly by chickening out.

She waited for him to laugh or make some snide remark, but he leaned forward on one elbow and clinked his coffee cup against hers. "To a new life, and new secrets."

"To secrets." Exhilaration swept away her humiliation. Whatever she'd done, it'd worked, and with a charming gentleman. She'd have to find out what a little more confidence might do for her.

Chapter Six

"I've taken the liberty of organizing your closet so Mademoiselle Moulichon can arrange everything according to color and style," Amelia explained to Wallis during the tour of their suite and Wallis's closet the morning after her return. "I had special tags printed with spaces to write when and where each outfit is worn so nothing is seen too many times at similar events." Amelia turned over the tag pinned to a ball gown to show the lines for each entry.

"How very clever of you." The Austrian mountain air and time away from reporters had done wonders for Wallis. She was relaxed and almost cheerful today, like the old Wallis from Wakefield Manor rather than Château de Candé. "I'll tell Mademoiselle Moulichon to arrange my shoes, hats, and gloves according to your system too. I want everything to be coordinated so I always look my best. I'm not the prettiest woman but I can be the best dressed, and David deserves the most fashionable wife."

Amelia didn't mention it was Mrs. Bedaux who'd suggested the closet organizing system. The generous lady had visited Amelia a number of times over the summer and taught her how to call for cars, inform hotel staff about Wallis's special preferences, to make seamless travel arrangements and reservations, and the many other skills expected of a private secretary. Amelia wasn't sure why Mrs. Bedaux had taken her under her wing but she was glad she had.

"I'd intended to spend this fall training you but I can see you have everything under control. Fern, who adores you, gave me a stern talking-to about how I treated you and made me see I'd thrown you in the deep end when I took you on. I'm sorry I was so harsh and short but I was under such an awful strain. I wasn't myself. I hope you can forgive me, and we can make a fresh start. I want you to enjoy this position and your time with me, not dread it."

"I do enjoy it, and all the opportunities you've given me." After the disastrous start at Château de Candé, Amelia had worried about how it'd be when Wallis returned. This conversation gave her hope that everything would work out swimmingly.

"Good, then let's get to it." Wallis led Amelia back to the sitting room and sat down at the narrow writing desk. Amelia stood in front of it, ignoring the chair beside her. Wallis frowned. "Why are you standing?"

"The staff were ordered to stand in your presence until invited to sit, in deference to your new status."

"Nonsense. We've known each other far too long for that. In public, or with anyone who isn't an intimate friend, you'll address me properly and behave as expected of a hired secretary. In private we can be much more informal, the way we used to be at Cousin Lelia's. Now, what business do you have for me?"

"I've prepared a calendar with all of your appointments."

Amelia sat down, took out her folio, and removed a few papers. "Mr. Guillaume Guglielmi is scheduled to arrive every day at four to set your hair, except on the nights when you go out, then he'll arrive at two. Miss Sage, the manicurist, will be here on Tuesdays and Thursdays at nine. I took the liberty of scheduling next Monday for Schiaparelli and next Wednesday for Mainbocher for you to review their winter collections."

Wallis examined the schedule, nodding in appreciation.

"This is a list of the invitations that arrived while you were away. I'm ready to RSVP or decline as you see fit." Amelia laid the typewritten events and dates in front of Wallis.

Wallis pursed her lips. "Your organization is top-notch. The number and quality of the invitations isn't."

She'd noticed that too. "I placed an announcement about your arrival in the newspapers. I'm sure more will arrive once people realize you're here."

"We'll see." Wallis opened her desk drawer and removed a few letters and handed them to Amelia. "Send these out with the morning post."

"Yes, ma'am." The top one was addressed to Joachim von Ribbentrop, the Nazi Minister of Foreign Affairs, not at his Berlin address but in care of the Paris Ritz. She wondered about this. Aunt Bessie had suggested Wallis not write to him and Amelia thought about reminding her then changed her mind. It was none of Amelia's business who Wallis wrote to. She was here to help manage the more mundane aspects of Wallis's life. She slid the hotel bill out of the folio. "Here's the hotel bill to settle. I reviewed it and I didn't see anything out of the ordinary."

"Good, then it shouldn't take me long to double-check it." Wallis took out a pencil and scrutinized each charge. "It's not that I don't trust you, but Grandma Warfield always said no one can take care of a woman's finances the way she can and she was right. If I hadn't scrupulously managed mine and Ernest's accounts after the stock market crash, we'd have been swindled poor by the grocer and foolishly spent the rent money. I can't tell you how many of our acquaintances did that and found themselves up the Thames without a paddle."

Amelia knew a little something about that. She'd left the household bills and accounts to Jackson, happily accepting her pin money and his assurances that he was taking care of things. She'd never be so foolish or naive about her financial security again, assuming she ever got back on her feet. Most of her salary went to pay down her legal bills, and if her calculations were right, she'd be in debt until she was fifty. She tried not to slouch under the weight of it. Perhaps someday, if she did a good enough job for Wallis, she might ask her for help with the outstanding bills.

Wallis went through the charges line by line until one made her stop. "Please remind Mr. Schafranek not to charge mineral water to our account. I won't have him racking up needless expenses."

"It's only a few francs for when he had to wait with the car in the Paris heat while I took care of business at Cartier."

"A few francs badly spent can add up to a great deal over time. David isn't as rich as Croesus, not with that petty brother of his threatening to hold back his stipend and us forced to pay expenses. We must watch every franc or we'll be bled dry."

"I'll remind him." Right after she paid the manicurist, the hairstylist, and Suzanne Belperron and Jeanne Toussaint for selling Wallis enough jewels to make Queen Mary blanch. If Wallis begrudged the chauffeur mineral water, she wasn't likely to help her with her financial troubles. Jackson might have gotten her into this mess but she'd have to get herself out of it.

Wallis set down her pencil and laced her fingers together on the desk. "I'm not being petty but prudent. When I was little, Mother used to beg stingy Uncle Sol, who was richer than his namesake, for money. I vowed never to be like her and there I was after my divorce from Win, poor as a church mouse, forced to rely on Uncle Sol and Aunt Bessie for everything. I wasn't clever like you."

"I'm not clever." If she were, she wouldn't have violated Mrs. Bedaux's rule and looked churlish about reprimanding the chauffeur.

"Of course you are, and quite the adventuress." Wallis picked up the pencil and touched the tip of it to her lips. "You wouldn't have eloped if you weren't."

"That was a mistake."

"So it didn't work out the first time, that's the risk we bold women take." Wallis shrugged as if the past three years of Amelia's life were an inappropriate ball gown she could simply change. "But you didn't give up. You wiped off the dust and gained real skills and a position for yourself. It was more than I did when I was a young divorcée. I never had the head for school or any talent more useful than how to meet well-connected people. Allow me to teach you another lesson, one

I had to learn the hard way." She pointed the pencil at Amelia. "It doesn't matter how secure you think you are, there's always something or someone ready to snatch it away from you, and you have to guard yourself against it. If I have to scrutinize every bill to protect my security, then I will. Tell Mr. Schafranek not to charge anything to the hotel account again."

"Yes, ma'am."

"And from here on out, when someone gives you a compliment, don't question or undermine it, simply say 'thank you.'" Wallis handed back the itemized bill. "You'll get further by acting as if the compliment is an accurate observation rather than a lapse in judgment."

"Yes, ma'am." This was as good a lesson for Amelia to learn as the one about money. It certainly wasn't anything Mother had ever taught her. The woman was as stingy with her praise as Wallis was with her finances but at least Wallis was willing to share her experience and knowledge with Amelia. Mother had been too busy with her own concerns to bother.

Mr. Hale rapped on the door then entered. "Mrs. Bedaux to see you, ma'am. I've shown her into the sitting room. Shall I order tea?"

"A detestable drink. I don't understand David's or anyone's fascination with it, but as I'm expected to serve it, I must." Wallis set the pencil on the bill and rose. "Order tea, Mr. Hale. Amelia, follow me, I want to ask Fern about the invitations and for you to note her responses."

Amelia followed Wallis into the sitting room, where Mrs. Bedaux stood studying the Duke's abdication desk and the red

Moroccan-leather dispatch box enjoying pride of place on top of it. The box had held his official papers when he'd been King and it and the desk were odd souvenirs he'd insisted on bringing to their temporary home.

"Welcome back, Your Royal Highness." Mrs. Bedaux curtseyed to Wallis before Wallis motioned for her to sit across from her at the claw-footed tea table. Mrs. Bedaux opened a box of Marquise de Sévigné's chocolates and offered them to Wallis. "Did you have a splendid trip?"

"I did." Wallis set her bonbon on the table. "Austria was so relaxing, especially with Amelia taking care of things here so I never had to worry. She's impressed me with the work she's done in my absence."

"I think she's living up to her full potential and will continue to amaze us." Mrs. Bedaux threw Amelia a conspiratorial smile as she offered Amelia a chocolate.

Mr. Hale entered with the silver tea service and set it in front of Wallis

"What amazes me is the few invitations I've received. It's as if I'm still gone." Wallis lifted the silver teapot and awkwardly poured Mrs. Bedaux a cup. Wallis was a natural with a cocktail shaker but looked awkward handling the heavy teapot and delicate china. Amelia made a note to arrange for discreet tea service lessons for Wallis from the Hotel Meurice staff.

"According to protocol, you must call on the important women first before they call on you." Mrs. Bedaux graciously accepted her cup from Wallis, polite enough not to mention Wallis had forgotten to offer sugar or milk.

Wallis set the teapot down with a clunk. "A duchess is expected to grovel before mere consular wives?"

"Yes, if you want the best invitations. It's the custom in diplomatic circles for the newcomer, no matter what their rank, to make the first call and announce their arrival. As you insist on your courtesies, they insist on theirs. Your card left with the butler will suffice and should secure a new round of invitations."

Wallis picked off a corner of her chocolate and slipped it in her mouth, the piece so small it was a wonder she could taste it. She chewed while silently debating between protocol and her vanity until reality finally won out. "Amelia, take the car and deliver my cards to the necessary ladies this afternoon. I don't want Cookie or anyone else thinking we're being snubbed when it's simply a mistake in custom. We've received an invitation to dine with King Carol. He's invited Amelia to come too."

"The perks of being Her Royal Highness's cousin, you get to dine with a charismatic head of state, but be careful, King Carol is quite the playboy," Mrs. Bedaux teased Amelia.

"Do you have anything appropriate to wear?" Wallis asked Amelia.

"I'm having a few dresses run up by a seamstress." She'd visited Miss Harper's seamstress and the woman had done wonders for her with the bolts of fabric Amelia had purchased from Bucol.

Mrs. Bedaux set aside her barely touched tea. "That's fine for every day, but not for something like this, wouldn't you agree, Wallis? How a lady presents herself is vital to her success. A well-turned-out one will go much further than a frumpy one. Remember that, Mrs. Montague, and live by it."

"I will."

"Wallis, you must see to it that Mrs. Montague has a proper wardrobe," Mrs. Bedaux instructed. "Your staff is an extension of you and how you run your household. Think of Mrs. Montague as a complement to you, such as a matched handbag or well-kitted-out footman. No offense, Mrs. Montague, but you understand my meaning?"

"I do." If Mrs. Bedaux could conjure the miracle of making Wallis part with a few francs for someone other than herself, Amelia would play along.

Wallis crossed her arms over her flat chest and touched her fingers to her jaw, studying Amelia as she considered Mrs. Bedaux's advice. Wallis might be a frugal duchess but she was also a social climber who'd clawed her way from obscurity to almost the pinnacle of high society. Wallis couldn't stop the vitriol flung at her for how she'd gained her position but she could mute it by always being impeccable, proper and perfect. Mrs. Bedaux had cleverly made Amelia an extension of Wallis's all-consuming need to impress her critics.

"David deserves to have his wife, family, and staff looking their best. Mr. Forwood's Savile Row suits are immaculate and David is designing marvelous uniforms for the footmen. I wouldn't want anyone to say my relative isn't properly attired. Amelia, inform Madame Schiaparelli you'll be accompanying me to her atelier and I expect her to take as good care of you as she does me. Tell her I'd also like a private dressing room with my usual special accoutrements."

"Yes, ma'am." Amelia wrote the instructions in her notebook, careful to conceal her smile. The onerous task of tactfully asking Madame Schiaparelli for a discount paled in comparison to the chance to be fitted and dressed by the designer on Wallis's dime. More than Wallis's manners and social knowledge was about to rub off on her.

AMELIA WALKED WITH Wallis through the Hotel Meurice's marble-floored lobby with its pillars, gilded ivy, and massive Versailles-style pier glasses. Guests and visitors mingling in the lounge area stopped their conversations to watch them. One young woman slyly raised her camera to snap a picture. The hotel wasn't particular about who sat in the lobby to star spot so long as they behaved. Mr. Attfield didn't interfere with the rubberneckers either, unless they approached Wallis, and no one did as Wallis stepped through the hotel's black and brass revolving door.

Outside, Mr. Schafranek stood by the dark blue Buick. The Duke had custom ordered it for Wallis in England and she'd brought it with her to France when she'd fled London in 1936 in a futile attempt to stop him from abdicating. The initials *W.W.S.*, Wallis Warfield Simpson, were outlined in gold on the driver's door. She'd changed a number of things in the past year but not this small detail.

The American car stood out among the French Citroëns,

Peugeots, and Simcas crowding the streets, causing people to stop and stare in the hope of catching sight of Wallis as Mr. Schafranek maneuvered the car through traffic.

"You don't know how nice it is to go shopping alone. David insists on following me and it's exhausting. Thank heaven he plays golf or I'd never have a moment's peace." Wallis crossed her gloved hands in her lap, her gray luncheon suit with the black patent belt and checked black blouse as impeccable as her hair and makeup. A sapphire-and-ruby broach from the Duke sparkled on the coat's lapel. Amelia had styled her hair in the simple rolls Antoinette had shown her, but her old brown suit and shoes threw off the effect. Wallis turned her black patent leather clutch over on her lap, the hard set of her jaw softening. "For the last year, it's as if there's a whole country working against me and it's been so hard. I can't even adjust to it in private."

"It was like that in Wellesley after Jackson's illegal dealings came out, and then in Baltimore when I went to Aunt Bessie's. I was a thief's wife and everyone thought I was in on it but I didn't know what he was doing. Jackson worked in the city, and I had no reason to riffle through his office, at least not until after he was arrested."

"How very prudent of you. I hope I don't have to worry about you digging through my things," she teased, keeping Amelia and the conversation from turning gloomy.

"Don't do anything illegal and you'll have nothing to worry about."

Wallis snorted out a laugh. "It'll be illegal how good we'll look when Madame Schiaparelli is done with us, and divine for you to finally pop into something more elegant. A woman can handle anything life throws at her when she looks chic."

Amelia couldn't agree more, and her excitement made sitting still difficult as Mr. Schafranek turned the car into the grand Place Vendôme. They passed the Chanel boutique with its blue door, Van Cleef & Arpels, and the Hotel Ritz's wrought-iron entrance. He brought the car to a stop at 21 Place Vendôme and the Hôtel de Fontpertuis, where the white sign with *Schiaparelli* emblazoned in black letters announced the fashion house. Mr. Schafranek came around and opened the door and Wallis and Amelia stepped out. Mr. Attfield escorted them past the gathering crowd of people on the sidewalk—tourists, judging by their practical clothes. The wealthy women walking in and out of the boutiques paid them no mind, and Amelia and Wallis offered them the same courtesy.

"Welcome, Your Royal Highness." Elsa Schiaparelli swept down the staircase and curtseyed to Wallis. She wore a fitted black dress with a slender belt and a square but very high neckline accented by a pearl choker. Her dark hair was pulled into a severe chignon that emphasized her wide brown eyes and full nose. "I have your usual fitting room prepared for you, and personalized just as you requested."

Madame Schiaparelli led them past tables with displays of blouses, hats, and perfumes, and glass counters with fine scarves and gloves laid out inside. Black-clad vendeuses with impeccable hair and makeup assisted women Amelia recognized from the society pages.

"Miss Viollet will assist Mrs. Montague this afternoon."

Madame Schiaparelli motioned to a brunette with tight curls arranged at the crown of her head and the woman joined their small party. "She's new to us and very talented."

"It's a pleasure to meet you." The vendeuse wasn't much older than Amelia but she dressed with the same chic all Parisian women appeared to possess. Thanks to Wallis, Amelia would soon look as good as this woman.

"May I offer my congratulations on your marriage, ma'am," Madame Schiaparelli said as they climbed the curving staircase to the first-floor fitting rooms.

"I wouldn't have looked as good on my honeymoon if it weren't for you."

"I'm always ready to do my best for my clients." She escorted them down the hallway past young mannequins wearing sample dresses for clients to inspect. Madame Schiaparelli didn't stop but continued up to the quiet second floor and into a gilded fitting room with a large chaise adorned with round satin pillows. Sheer curtains covered the windows, shielding them from the view of the fine establishments across the Place Vendôme. Beside the chaise stood a gilded three-paneled mirror with a white silk dress hung in the center.

"Mr. Dalí has outdone himself with this creation." Wallis held out the skirt to reveal the fanciful lobster hand painted on the front.

"His designs are among our most celebrated this season. He's honored to dress you."

"I'm honored to wear it. It'll give people more to talk about than my past for a few minutes." Wallis removed her tilt hat. "I can't wait to try it on."

"I have a fitting room ready for you, Mrs. Montague," Mademoiselle Viollet said. "If you'll follow me?"

"No yellows, oranges, or reds for Mrs. Montague," Wallis instructed. "They won't suit her coloring and a woman must always wear colors that blend with her skin's tint. She needs blues, greens, and pale pinks and yellows."

"Yes, Your Royal Highness."

Mademoiselle Viollet showed Amelia to her fitting room across the hall. It wasn't as large as Wallis's but it was a far cry from the bolt-filled seamstress's studio she'd visited for her other new dresses. Small gilded chairs lined one wall and the same sheer curtains as in Wallis's room covered the windows, illuminating the small dais flanked by tall mirrors. Another young woman in a plain black dress with a yellow tape measure draped around her neck waited for Amelia beside a rolling rack of sample outfits.

"If Madame will change, we may begin." Mademoiselle Viollet motioned to the screen in the corner and Amelia slipped behind it and out of her clothes. She sighed at the sad state of her old panties and bra, then covered them with a luxurious satin robe and stepped out from behind the screen.

"If you'll stand on the dais, madame," Mademoiselle Viollet instructed. The assistant removed the tape measure from around her neck, ready to take Amelia's measurements. "The robe please, madame."

Amelia slowly untied the sash, reluctant to take it off. She'd paraded in here beside Wallis for a private fitting, acting the wealthy client, but the minute she showed them her threadbare underwear they'd know she was a fraud.

"Madame?" Mademoiselle Viollet gently urged.

There was no avoiding revealing herself and she untied the sash and shrugged out of the robe. Amelia stood in front of the mirrors, bracing for the horrified looks. Neither of them flinched at the poor condition of her undergarments but treated her as they would any other client as they discussed the cut and fit of each potential outfit.

While Amelia stood with her arms out for the seamstress to take her measurements, the day she and Aunt Bessie had spent at Hutzler's department store in Baltimore the spring before her debutante season rushed back to her. Aunt Bessie had helped Amelia pick out her ball and tea gowns, the two of them constantly waving off expensive dresses in favor of cheaper, less stylish ones. While debutante mothers all over Baltimore had written out guest lists, menus, and invitations, Mother had left it to Amelia and Aunt Bessie to arrange everything.

"I'm paying for it. Isn't that enough?" Mother had snapped when Amelia had confronted her about it. Despite Mother's indifference, Amelia's coming-out ball had been a success, except for it being the night she'd met Jackson. Amelia winced at the memory.

"Did I stick Madame with a pin?" the seamstress asked from where she knelt adjusting the hem of the smart gray skirt with the matching jacket and a crisp white blouse beneath. It was the uniform of a secretary, not a debutante or a wealthy man's wife.

"No, everything's fine." It was all the work Amelia had done to arrange her coming-out ball that'd given Aunt Bessie the idea for Amelia to attend secretarial school.

An hour later, with her wardrobe picked out, pinned, and measured, it was time for Amelia to change back into her old clothes. By the time she was dressed, Mademoiselle Viollet had returned with a small shopping bag.

"For Madame, compliments of Madame Schiaparelli."

Amelia gasped when she opened it to reveal a new silk slip, chemise, panties, and girdle. "Oh, I can't." She couldn't afford them, and if Wallis scrutinized this bill the way she had the one for the hotel, Amelia would have to endure the humiliation of returning them.

"It's a gift. The clothes will fit better with the proper foundations, and what better advertisement for Madame Schiaparelli than Her Royal Highness's cousin well turned out."

She's right. No self-respecting woman could wear Schiaparelli skirts with old Woolworth girdles. She was in Paris to shape a new life and image for herself. This was part of that and a chance to take advantage of opportunities for improvement. She'd never thought of herself as a charity case and yet she was, like Wallis in her youth, constantly relying on the generosity of others for life's basics. Someday she'd find a way to be the one giving charity instead of the widow in need of it. "Thank you. I very much appreciate it."

"Allow me to suggest that Madame speak with Mademoiselle

Mele at Robert Piguet. She sells the mannequins' sample dresses at a discount to the right people. Tell her I sent you. Ask for something by Monsieur Dior. He's a fabulous new designer there."

"I will." A little thrill went through her at being considered one of the right people.

The vendeuse smiled as if she understood exactly what her generosity meant to Amelia, even if some small part of Amelia chafed at having to need it. "If you'd like to browse downstairs, Her Royal Highness isn't quite finished but she will be shortly."

Amelia stepped into the hallway, surprised to see a distinguished, middle-aged gentleman in a well-tailored suit standing outside Wallis's fitting room. Even if the small swastika lapel pin hadn't given him away, she recognized him from his pictures in the newspapers. They'd never been introduced but somehow, he recognized her.

"Mrs. Montague, it's a pleasure to finally meet Her Royal Highness's cousin." Herr von Ribbentrop held out his hand and she took it, noticing his fingers were as finely manicured as the Duke's. "She speaks very highly of you, as does Mrs. Bedaux. I understand you may be joining us in Germany."

"It's possible." The Windsors and Bedaux had been planning the trip since Mr. Bedaux had mentioned it at the wedding, and the secrecy surrounding it was as exhausting as the work of arranging it. They were so afraid Buckingham Palace would get wind of it, they'd clam up the moment anyone outside their immediate circle walked into a room. It'd made Mr. Metcalf's brief visit last week frustrating for him and the staff. It wouldn't be a secret for much longer if people like Herr von Ribbentrop brought it up this casually. Then the cables and calls between London and Paris would start flying. Amelia didn't understand the Duke and Wallis's admiration for Herr Hitler, what with his silly mustache and constant blustering about the fatherland, but an entire country and a good portion of society was mesmerized by him. "Are you enjoying your visit to Paris?"

"It's one of the most beautiful cities in the world but nothing compared to Berlin, as you'll see when you visit. Once Herr Hitler's vision for Berlin is complete, Paris will look like a sad shadow in comparison, but I prefer Paris to London. The weather and company are more enjoyable. Germany is lucky to have a friend in His Royal Highness. With his assistance, we might ease the tension between Germany and Britain. Good day, Mrs. Montague." He tapped his hat on his head and made his way downstairs.

He was mistaken if he thought the Duke had any influence over His Majesty's foreign policy but once the Duke was in Germany, Herr von Ribbentrop and the rest of his cohorts might see that. Assuming Herr von Ribbentrop joined them in Germany and didn't stay in Paris. She wondered what the German was doing here in the first place, especially on the second floor of Schiaparelli's.

Wallis's fitting room door opened and a number of suspicions rushed in, none of them good. "Did you enjoy your fitting?" Before the door swung closed, Amelia caught a glimpse of the satin pillows scattered across the chaise and floor.

"I did. There was one item in particular that suited me perfectly." Wallis led the way downstairs.

She meant the dress. She had to. After the mess Wallis had gotten into with the Duke she couldn't risk the scandal and gossip of a fling with a senior Nazi official. "I met Herr von Ribbentrop in the hallway. Did you see him?"

"I didn't know he was here. I'm sorry I missed him."

She studied Wallis. Nothing about her was odd or out of place, everything perfect as usual, even her smooth hair. *I'm jumping to conclusions.* Prudence wasn't Wallis's strong point but even she wasn't this foolish. Besides, Herr von Ribbentrop probably had a lover in one of the other fitting rooms and Wallis hadn't really known he was there. She could hardly condemn her cousin because of a few scattered pillows.

In the first-floor showroom, a slender young man with thick black hair combed back from his square forehead, and heavily bagged dark eyes that widened at the sight of Wallis, hurried up to them. "Here is the charming woman honoring us with her presence."

"Monsieur Dalí, the honor is all mine, your dress is a dream," Wallis gushed, genuinely starstruck. "Allow me to introduce my cousin, Mrs. Amelia Montague."

He turned his wild gaze on Amelia. "She has your natural beauty."

Wallis stepped between them, returning Monsieur Dalí's attention to her. "My family is filled with elegant ladies of respectable lineage, some going back to King George the Second."

"Your royal lineage is in every curve of your face and the

carriage of your body, Your Royal Highness." He said the title loud enough for everyone in the salon to hear, and made a bow worthy of a Hollywood soundstage.

Amelia thought he was laying it on a bit thick until she caught the horrified faces of the two women standing at the glove counter. She recognized them from the newspapers, the Countess of Pembroke and her friend Mrs. Martin Scanlon, the American wife of the United States Air Attache in Paris.

"You won't see me bend the knee to a commoner," Lady Pembroke sniffed to her friend as Monsieur Dalí escorted Wallis to the entrance, forcing them to walk past the disapproving women.

"I'm not about to curtsey to a fellow countrywoman, especially one of her reputation." Mrs. Scanlon eyed Amelia. "Other American ladies should have enough self-respect not to bow and scrape to that kind of woman either."

Amelia pretended not to hear them. She'd been publicly chastised before but never for who she did or did not curtsey to. That was a new experience, as was the rush of the crowd the moment she and Wallis left the ateliers. Gendarmes stood arm in arm holding back the curious as they shouted Wallis's name or hurled more savory words at her.

"Quickly, now." Mr. Attfield waved Wallis and Amelia into the car. Once he closed the door and was seated beside Mr. Schafranek, the dam of gendarmes broke and the people swarmed the Buick to get a closer look at Wallis.

"I detest gawkers." Wallis pressed back against the seat, and the Buick's sloping roof shielded her from the curious people as Mr. Schafranek drove off. "In Austria, people crowded the shop windows to stare at us as if we were marzipan confections and they were starving. It didn't bother David. He went about his business as if nothing was wrong but I could hardly shop with all those people watching us."

"His Royal Highness is used to it."

"I'm not. I want to go where I want, when I want, without being treated like a tiger in a zoo. I never thought I'd lose my privacy, or miss it so much when it was gone." Wallis opened a cocktail cabinet in the door panel, one of the car's many unique features, plucked out a bottle of vodka, and poured a finger into a highball glass. "Care for some?"

"No thank you, ma'am." Amelia had never been much of a drinker, much less at two-thirty in the afternoon and especially not on the light lunches Wallis and the Duke served. Not eating much was how they both stayed so slim. It'd done wonders for her own figure since their return.

"The people on the street I can forgive. They're curious. It's those catty society women I detest. They nearly lost their knickers when Monsieur Dalí bowed to me." Wallis finished the vodka and poured herself another. "Imagine what it'll be like at dinner parties with everyone wondering what to do or not do and always looking over their shoulder to make sure Cookie's spies aren't watching. It's all so ridiculous."

"If you and the Duke stand together in receiving lines or at cocktail parties, then people won't have to decide. One curtsey will do for both of you and if someone takes offense, people can always say they were honoring His Royal Highness and you just happened to be next to him."

"A brilliant idea. See, I said you were clever and I was right. You're also cunning. Good, the world needs more of that; I certainly do." Wallis poured more vodka but drank it slowly. "It's all jealousy, you know. The British are so particular about their titles and positions, they can't stand to see anyone outside their inbred circle move up in the ranks. Lady Pembroke is spitting nails now that I outrank her, and sallow Mrs. Scanlon is green with envy that I caught a duke and all she managed was some military man floating from embassy to embassy. I knew her when I lived in D.C. in the 1920s. She, Alice Gordon, and all those other awful political wives thought they could drive me from society with their petty gossip but I showed them. They think I've forgotten their slights and insults but I haven't. I'm nothing if not patient, especially when it comes to getting revenge, and I'll have it, especially in Germany."

"Or you'll be tarred with the same brush as Herr Hitler and make things worse," Amelia cautioned, deliberately breaking Mrs. Bedaux's rules in favor of Aunt Bessie's mandate to help Wallis not give in to her worst instincts. Amelia had as much influence over Wallis as His Royal Highness's family had over him, but she had to try.

"Herr Hitler is a powerful man. His recognizing me will force others to do the same." Wallis dropped the empty vodka glass in the door compartment and clicked it closed. "I want everyone who's ever looked down on me to have to look so far up at me their necks hurt. They deserve the pain for what they've put me through. You should think about doing the same."

"I don't want revenge." She wanted the happiness she'd enjoyed during the first year with Jackson, before it'd all fallen apart. The truth lingered under the new manners, tenuous confidence, and secretarial skills. She was still the debutante who wanted to be noticed, happy, and loved.

"Stop feeling sorry for yourself and moping over what you lost. Heaven knows I've done enough of it to recognize when someone else is doing it too. Let me tell you, it won't do anything but make you miserable. The best revenge is a life well lived. Isn't that why you're here? Hold up your head and prove to everyone you're better than they think you are; do it until you believe it too."

She was right. Amelia had spent so much time mourning her lost life or wishing things were different she'd barely noticed they already were. She was in France, and it'd taken a leap of faith to come here but she'd done it. Despite the early stumbles, she was succeeding. She was about to dine with the King of Romania and in a silk Schiaparelli gown. She'd write to Aunt Bessie and tell her to spread that little tidbit around. She'd send her brother a note about it too and he'd tell Mother. What she wouldn't give to see the look on her face then. Wallis was right. Amelia had mastered her new position; it was time to take pride in it and herself and concentrate on the future instead of the past.

Chapter Seven

"Your gown is beautiful," Mrs. Bedaux whispered to Amelia from beside her at King Carol's dinner table. Amelia wore her new organza evening gown imprinted with ferns. It had a modest neckline to flatter her not overly large chest and deny King Carol a good view of her décolletage, but it didn't stop him from trying many times during dinner in his suite.

"Thank you," Amelia whispered, and returned her attention to the Romanian monarch.

"What His Majesty's Government fails to understand is the importance of Germany's superior air and military power." King Carol sat at the head of the table in a uniform covered in epaulets, medals, and ribbons. His mistress, Madame Lupescu, sat beside him in a dark blue dress that set off her white skin and red hair to perfection. "Britain can't match it."

"I've seen the munitions plants in Germany, visited the flying schools and airplane factories. They're the best in Europe, far better than anything I've seen in Britain or America," Mr. Bedaux added.

"Is that true, Mrs. Montague?" King Carol sat back to allow a footman to remove his crème brûlée dish. "Are American airplane factories as lacking as British ones?"

"I can't say. I've never visited one." She mimicked Wallis's reserve and confidence to hide her nervousness at suddenly being the center of attention, determined to appear as if she did this every night. "Even if I had, I wouldn't know the difference between a good one and a bad one."

"I assure you, even the untrained eye can spot the difference." He flicked a glance at her chest then turned back to His Royal Highness. "It isn't only factories and munitions that convey superior strength but leadership. Germany has a powerful head not hindered by squabbling parties and coalition governments."

"Dictators do get things done." His Royal Highness tugged at his bow tie. He was seated at the other end of the table and dressed in a black tuxedo instead of a military uniform. "I wouldn't be surprised if England soon begs for one of their own."

"Or a real king with real power." King Carol pointed one ring-clad finger at His Royal Highness. "A king is ordained by God to rule and must wrest power from the plebeians and their ridiculous constitutions and limitations."

"Didn't your ministers mind you curtailing their power?" Wallis rested her elbows on the table and laced her gloved hands beneath her square chin, enraptured by King Carol. She sat across from Amelia and beside Mr. Bedaux, splendid in a black Mainbocher halter dress with a flared skirt and gold trim that crisscrossed the bust and encircled her tiny waist. It was unusually low-cut for Wallis and allowed her large sapphire-and-diamond necklace to shine in the candlelight.

"Ministers don't matter, only the people do, and I'm their greatest champion. I fed them when the ministers let them starve. I created work for them when the ministers left them hungry. The people saw what I did for them and supported my return to the throne. Soon, I'll dissolve the government and take complete control and the people will support me again."

"David, you always had a way with your subjects," Wallis flattered him, "especially the miners and such."

"I did, didn't I?" The Duke traced the base of his crystal wineglass with one finger. "Unlike my father, I wanted to improve the workers' plight. I still do. It's why we're going to Germany. Herr Hitler has created jobs and opportunities for his people. I want to study his methods and help other countries implement them. Sharing ideas will help encourage cooperation and peace between nations."

"You'll enjoy Herr Hitler," King Carol said. "He's a visionary, like you."

"Of course, it's easier to implement one's vision when one is still on the throne," Wallis said. If the Duke caught the dig, he didn't show it. King Carol noted it and smiled at Wallis like a snake.

"I was banished in 1925 for following my heart." He raised Madame Lupescu's hand to his lips and kissed it before he fixed his eyes on the Duke. "My government forced me to abdicate the way yours did, but I came back. An abdication is merely another obstacle to overcome."

"That's one way to look at it." Wallis slid the Duke a sideways glance, studying him as if she could see the path King

Carol had blazed, one the Duke might follow if given the opportunity.

Amelia sat perfectly still, hoping her surprise didn't show on her face. She hadn't known what to expect from this dinner but she hadn't expected revolution. This wasn't ordinary dinner conversation. It smacked of treason and something more dangerous. After everything Wallis and the Duke had been through with the abdication, they shouldn't even entertain these wild ideas.

"Of course, it's very different in England," His Royal Highness said at last, returning some common sense to the discussion. Amelia hadn't expected him to be the voice of reason.

"Of course, but war is coming. It changes things and creates opportunities. Who knows what it might offer you." King Carol threw Madame Lupescu a look that said he craved the opportunities of chaos.

"I do enjoy any chance for improvement." Wallis smiled, deepening her sharp cheekbones.

"Especially improvement in one's title and standing," Madame Lupescu said. "The one the wife of a monarch deserves. The one she was promised."

Wallis pinned the Duke with a hard look, his failure as heavy in the air as the lingering scent of dinner and cigarette smoke. His Royal Highness said nothing but continued to turn the delicate crystal glass by its stem, casting rainbows from the candlelight onto the white tablecloth.

"Of course, it's just a bit of fun, playing what if and what not." Madame Lupescu clapped her gloved hands together as if breaking a hypnotist's spell and everyone responded with nervous smiles. "Who's up for a game of bridge?"

"KING CAROL IS a remarkable ruler, with admirable ambition and will," Wallis remarked in the private elevator to their suite. "Look at what he's done for himself, his country, and Madame Lupescu."

The elevator doors opened and the Duke escorted Wallis into their suite. Wallis withdrew her hand from the crook of his arm but he caught her fingers and held them against his chest. "You know there's nothing I wouldn't do for you, darling. I'll get you the extra-chic title, I promise. Despite what some think, I still have supporters and pull in London."

She patted his hand, her emerald engagement ring clinking against his signet ring as she slid free of his grasp. "Good night, darling."

"Good night." Dismissed like a servant, His Royal Highness walked off to his bedroom.

Amelia slowly inched toward the door and the public elevator outside the suite that would carry her to the longed-for quiet of her room.

"Don't go," Wallis commanded. "Sit with me for a while. I'm not tired yet."

Despite aching for sleep, Amelia followed Mrs. Bedaux's fifth rule to not complain and walked with Wallis to her bedroom. Inside, Mademoiselle Moulichon bustled around arranging Wallis's night clothes and turning down her blankets. Pookie, Detto, and Prisie offered an obligatory wag but didn't get up from their baskets.

"What an evening." Wallis stepped behind the black lacquer screen, a souvenir from her time in China, and changed out of her evening gown, draping it over the top so Mademoiselle Moulichon could take it to be cleaned. "King Carol is quite a man. He didn't fold like a house of cards the minute his ministers objected to his relationship with Madame Lupescu." Wallis emerged in a full-length raw silk and lace peignoir that put Amelia's plain terry robe with the fraying sash to shame. What she wouldn't give to be in it now instead of discussing this questionable topic. Wallis shouldn't give King Carol or anything he'd said a second thought but here she was, still mulling it over.

Wallis sat down at her dressing table. "Help me off with my jewelry." She rubbed the back of her neck when Amelia unclasped the sapphire and diamond necklace. It weighed a ton. "What a relief."

Amelia laid the necklace in a velvet tray on the dressing table. "You shouldn't wear it if it gives you a neck ache."

"I have to. I must always look regal, for David." And she did. Wallis spent at least fifteen minutes of her already lengthy dressing time coordinating her jewelry with her outfits. Wallis removed her matching earrings then carried the jewelry tray to the small black-and-red-striped private safe in the closet. The carnation-shaped combination lock clicked as Wallis turned it back and forth before the clank of metal signaled the open door. "What King Carol said about wresting power from the political parties was very interesting."

"And dangerous. If things don't work out the way he plans, he and Madame Lupescu could end up in front of a firing squad." If the fear of death couldn't dissuade Wallis from whatever idea was germinating from the seed planted by King Carol, then nothing could.

The lock clicked again as Wallis spun it to lock it. Wallis returned to the dressing table and twisted open a jar of Elizabeth Arden cold cream. "That's what I adore about you, you're so sensible. I let my imagination run wild while your feet are firmly on the ground. You'd think after everything I've been through I'd have feet of lead, but I still catch myself believing in fairy tales. I don't mean David becoming King again—from what I've seen of monarchs I don't blame him for chucking it all—but living life on my terms again, with my reputation restored, but I suppose it's too late for that. People have memories like a vise grip when it comes to scandals." Wallis scooped out a dollop of cold cream and spread it over her face. "Look at Cookie. She won, she's Queen. Instead of being a gracious winner she insists on degrading me with her petty insults. My own mother-in-law won't even acknowledge me. She barely speaks to David."

"Perhaps you could write to her," Amelia suggested. "I broke the ice with Peter by writing to him and he wrote me back. We still talk sometimes. Who knows, maybe someday we'll have lunch together, not where anyone from the railroad might see us, but maybe at some out-of-the-way Woolworth's counter. Do you think Queen Mary would meet you at one of those?"

Wallis met her eyes in the mirror and a wide smile broke the severe lines of her face. "Does one wear a crown to Woolworth's?"

"Maybe just a small one."

The two of them burst out laughing.

"You always were a riot." Wallis gripped her side against a stitch from enjoying the image of Queen Mary ordering a milkshake a little too much.

Amelia didn't argue but graciously accepted the compliment. She was about to make another joke when Mademoiselle Moulichon's somber entrance sobered them.

"This arrived while you were out, ma'am. It's from Mr. Simpson." She held out the airmail letter to Wallis.

Wallis stared at it as if it were a summons from the Court of St. James then took it with a tenderness reserved for a rediscovered heirloom. There was a long silence as Mademoiselle Moulichon left and Amelia wondered if she should do the same. She was about to leave when Wallis spoke.

"After Jackson's arrest, did you ever think there was a chance you two could go back to the life you'd had before, even though you knew it was impossible?"

"Every day. Then he shot himself. I thought everything I'd been through before was awful. Losing hope was the worst."

"I haven't lost hope yet. If something happens to David, Ernest is still there, dependable, affable old Ernest." Wallis traced Mr. Simpson's solid script with one finger. They shouldn't be writing to each other. All it did was drag out their final separation but Amelia didn't have the heart to say so. Hope was as essential to Wallis as it'd been to Amelia. It's why Wallis had entertained King Carol's ridiculous suggestion about the Duke reclaiming the throne. It'd offered the slight chance she might regain some of what she'd lost during the past year, even if they both knew it was impossible.

Paris, October 1937

"His Majesty's Government views the German tour as a private one, and as such, there will be no reception at the British Embassy in Berlin," Sir Walter announced. The Duke had finally told Buckingham Palace about the German visit and His Majesty's Government had ordered Sir Walter to Paris to try and talk him out of it. With less than a week before their departure, and the schedules, accommodations, timetables, and official visits already finalized, it was a fool's errand.

"If it's so private then why did they send you to try and put us in our place?" Wallis sat on the edge of the sofa, her back straighter than usual, the dogs perched beside her like little lions.

"That isn't His Majesty's Government's intention, Your Grace."

"Your Royal Highness!" The Duke slapped the slick bar top, making the dogs jump to attention. "She's my wife and will be addressed as Your Royal Highness."

"David, you don't have to stand up for me," Wallis purred, savoring Sir Walter's reprimand as she settled Pookie in her lap.

"It's an honor to stand up for you, darling. If only some people had more honor." He glared at Sir Walter, who didn't flinch.

"I have no desire to cause insult, sir, simply to clarify the terms of the visit and ask you to reconsider the wisdom of making it. Everything His Majesty's siblings do and say reflects on the royal family, and Buckingham Palace doesn't appreciate the shadow cast by this visit."

"I don't care what they think, especially after the ghastly way they've treated us, denying my wife her rightful title and banishing us." The Duke carried a tray of his special Wallis cocktail to the Bedaux. Amelia wondered why they were here but since they were paying for the German trip, she supposed they had a right to listen in. "Our leaving England was never supposed to be permanent but that's what it's become, and now Bertie wants to manage every aspect of our lives too. He and you would be better off pressing the case for Wallis's HRH title rather than meddling in our travel plans."

Amelia admired Sir Walter's ability to not groan in exasperation. He must be as tired of hearing about the extra-chic title as Amelia was typing letters and cables about it.

"I don't understand why my family continues to close ranks against her, considering how admirably she behaved during all that business last winter, even in the face of the press's awful treatment, mobbing her car and forcing her to hide under blankets to avoid being photographed, living in exile like a criminal when she'd done nothing wrong." The Duke moved

Detto to make a space beside Wallis on the sofa. "She shouldn't be shunned but granted the correct and proper title."

"If Herr Hitler could confer the title on her, he would," Mrs. Bedaux said.

"His treating her like a queen when we're there is enough," the Duke said. "I want Wallis to experience a royal tour, to be shown some respect."

"And she will be," Mr. Bedaux assured.

Given the itinerary Amelia had seen this afternoon, the Windsors would be feted. Wallis wasn't excited about touring machine factories and mines but she was thrilled by Charles Edward, Duke of Saxe-Coburg and Gotha, the Duke's cousin, hosting a near-royal dinner in their honor. Amelia was also excited to attend what amounted to her first state dinner. She only wished it wasn't in Germany. She'd read enough newspaper articles about the Nazis' treatment of the Jews to know it wasn't the paradise the Duke believed, but it wasn't her decision where to hold the dinner. She was an employee, and like Sir Walter, her employer told her where to go and what to do. Someday that wouldn't be the case, but it was today.

"It's this treatment His Majesty's Government is concerned about. This tour could be mistaken for British approval of the Nazi government and undermine their official stance," Sir Walter explained in his steady but straightforward voice, no evidence of fatigue from his morning flight from London showing on his placid face.

"Bertie is more worried about my undermining his popularity than any official position. He thinks if he keeps me out of sight the British people will forget about me but they won't. No one in the royal family has ever cared for them the way I have."

That the Duke had loved Wallis more than his people seemed to echo through the room along with the city noises from outside but everyone was polite enough not to say so.

"The British people do not want their former king hailed by Herr Hitler, nor do they wish to see Herr Goebbels use your remarks in his propaganda," Sir Walter reasoned.

"David isn't a dupe if that's what you're suggesting." Wallis stroked Pookie hard, making the dog squirm and jump down. "He's too smart to fall for their tricks, and besides, it isn't Herr Hitler using David but David using him to highlight the needs of the working class and what can be done to help them, something His Majesty should worry more about than where we vacation."

"What if His Royal Highness refuses to make speeches or give newspaper interviews?" Mr. Bedaux suggested, trying to make peace. "If he says nothing then nothing can be taken out of context or used against him."

"Quite right." The Duke rose, forcing everyone to their feet. "You may return to His Majesty and inform him of our decision to continue as arranged."

The Duke took Wallis's arm and led her and their guests out onto the patio, Detto, Prisie, and Pookie trotting obediently behind them.

"A little kindness from Buckingham Palace would go a long way toward making them more cooperative," Amelia suggested once she and Sir Walter were alone.

"I've said as much to Their Majesties but they're as headstrong as the Windsors." Sir Walter snapped the handkerchief out of his breast pocket and rubbed his glasses clean. "His Royal Highness is placing himself in a very compromising and possibly dangerous position with this trip. He expects the treatment of a king and anyone who bows to that desire will exert a great deal of influence over him. The Germans know this as well as we do, as does Her Grace. She helped pull His Royal Highness down from his high place. She might be searching for an opportunity to push him back up into one."

"I think Her Grace has endured enough political maneuvering for one lifetime." With all the rot King Carol had shoveled at them, she couldn't blame Sir Walter for being concerned, but Wallis's desire for status and influence had already turned her into the world's most maligned woman. She wasn't likely to get herself in that kind of trouble again.

"I don't mean to disparage your cousin but I want you and her to go into this Germany trip with open eyes." He slid on his glasses and tucked the handkerchief in his pocket. "Be careful what you say or write when you're in Germany. Everyone there will be watching and listening to everything you do and say. The less you reveal, and this goes double for the Duke and Duchess, the better. Do your best to advise her to be cautious in her dealings with the Germans and not to let them or any of their new friends turn her head with their flattery. It won't lead anywhere good."

Chapter Eight

Berlin, October 12, 1937

"Heil Windsor, Heil Windsor!" the massive crowd shouted as Wallis and His Royal Highness stepped off the *Nord Express* at the massive steel and glass Friedrichstrasse Station. A band played "God Save the King" and Union Jacks hung beside Nazi banners from the steel girders. The Duke strode through the cheering masses and waved while Wallis walked beside him, smiling for the cinema and press cameras. Nazi officers in crisp brown uniforms, arms emblazoned with the red and black swastika band, formed a protective circle around them to keep back the people pressing in from all sides.

If the crowd inside was formidable, the one outside was overwhelming. The pop of multiple flashbulbs made Amelia blink as much as the bright sun, and the cheers were deafening. The police guided them through the crush to a line of shiny black Mercedes waiting to ferry them to the Hotel Kaiserhof, the first stop on the itinerary tucked inside Amelia's leather folio. She held it tight, afraid one of the many people reaching over and around the policemen to touch the Windsors would snatch it as a souvenir.

A thin woman in a beige coat broke through the police line and rushed up to Wallis. She handed her a bouquet of homegrown white roses and Wallis accepted the flowers with all the graciousness of Queen Elizabeth. The woman stared at Wallis in near reverence before a policeman tugged her back into the crowd. The Nazi officials ushered Wallis, the Duke, and Mr. Attfield into the first car while Amelia, Mr. Forwood, and Mademoiselle Moulichon climbed into the others. The cars lurched into motion, parting the sea of people surrounding them.

The caravan of cars drove through Berlin, passing beneath the imposing Brandenburg Gate and along the Unter den Linden. The Art Deco city was breathtaking except for the Nazi banners flying from everything higher than a fire plug. The red flags with their white circles and swastika hung from streetlights, draped the front of large buildings, and waved from the tops of department stores.

"What are all the flags for? Their Royal Highnesses or a festival?" Amelia asked the young Nazi officer with the Brylcreemed blond hair sitting beside her.

"They're for the majesty of the Third Reich," he answered in indignation. "They're always there, as the Third Reich will be."

She didn't know about that, but the second rule was to be nice to everyone so she didn't argue. She also didn't ask any more questions, not even when they passed a store with the word *Jude* scrawled on the window. Young men in brown uniforms paced in front of it, scowling and yelling at anyone who wandered too close. It was clear they weren't there to guard the business but to keep people away, to bankrupt and harass the Jewish owners. The sight of them pacing in front of the graffiti-scarred shop was as unsettling as the bright red flags against the gray baroque buildings. It was one thing to read about Germany in the newspapers, to listen to after-dinner conversation about a nation somewhere to the northeast. It was another to ride through the heart of it with the Nazi banners draped ominously over everything, making it clear the Nazi party wasn't simply a part of German life but the center of it.

Wallis and the Duke shouldn't have come. She shouldn't be here either, but this was her job. She couldn't pick and choose the best parts and leave the rest. It was a stark reminder of why she had to learn her position and create some future where she had a real say in her life instead of always being ruled by other people's whims.

AMELIA FOLLOWED WALLIS into her bedroom at the Hotel Kaiserhof and closed the door. The Duke remained in the sitting room with Dr. Ley, the stout German Labor Front leader and their guide for the week, and a few other officials, their rapid conversation in German carrying in through the closed door.

"David speaks German so well. Even with the translator, I can't keep up." Wallis pushed aside the window curtain to view the massive Reich Chancellery across the street, the stark façade brightened by the large red swastika banners draping the front of it. On the sidewalk below, the massive crowd that'd greeted them at the hotel sung in accented English for His Royal Highness to come to the balcony and wave to them.

"Listen to the people." Wallis opened the French doors to let in their cheers. "Britain never treated me like this."

"They're very welcoming." *And amazingly fluent English speakers. Suspiciously so*, but she didn't say it. She couldn't be churlish.

"I don't want to disappoint them." Wallis stepped onto the balcony and the crowd went wild. She threw out her arms to them, her gestures becoming more and more pronounced the louder they cheered, her thanks feeding their adoration in a vicious circle of praise.

"Wallis, remember the press," Amelia cautioned from inside. After two weeks of this, it'd be hard for Wallis to go back to her quiet life in Paris. No wonder Sir Walter had warned her about feeding Wallis's fairy tales. It made them too tempting to chase and reality too difficult to endure.

"I don't care about them. Listen to the people."

"What'll Cookie say if she sees pictures of you waving like an opera singer? She'll say you're acting common or the crowd was paid to be here and you fell for the ruse."

Wallis whipped around. "They aren't paid."

Amelia wasn't so sure about that. "I know, but Cookie will say they are if pictures of you waving like that make the papers. Remember, you're as dignified a consort as she is, and much more fashionable."

Wallis looked back and forth between Amelia and her admirers, wanting to revel in their praise but afraid to look the fool. "You're right. I can't embarrass David, this trip is too important to him and our future, and I'm not about to give that Fat Scottish Cook another reason to sneer at me."

With one last dignified wave, Wallis backed into the room and pulled the balcony doors closed, pausing to listen to the muffled cheers before facing Amelia. "What's on the agenda for this afternoon?"

"A tour of the R. Stock & Company machine works and then a special concert by the factory workers' orchestra."

"Heaven forbid." Wallis picked up the bouquet of white roses the woman at the station had given her and admired the delicate blooms. She plucked the bouquet from Dr. Ley out of the vase on the sideboard and dropped it in the trash and arranged the white buds in the crystal. "And tonight?"

"Nothing, but tea with Herr Goebbels and Herr Goerlitzer."

His Royal Highness stepped into the room, as jovial as he'd been on his wedding day. "It's time to leave for the Gruenewald factory. Are you coming, darling?"

"No, I'm too tired after the train ride. I'll stay here and rest."

"Good. I'll see you this evening." He pecked her on the cheek and, with Mr. Attfield at his side, left with the Germans.

The Duke was barely gone five minutes before Herr Rudolph, the butler assigned to assist the Windsors during their stay, announced, "Herr von Ribbentrop to see you, Your Royal Highness."

Wallis's exhaustion from the long morning instantly vanished. "Show him in."

Herr von Ribbentrop entered dressed in full Nazi uniform with gleaming black boots and a black jacket. He swept off his cap and made a deep bow to Wallis. "Your Royal Highness."

He straightened and handed her a bouquet of red carnations.

"How kind of you to think of me." Wallis admired them with more delight than the diamond brooch the Duke had given her last night.

"You're always in my thoughts. I'd be honored if you'd accompany me to the Palace of Sanssouci. I know how much you adore eighteenth-century decor."

"I'd be delighted. I need inspiration for when I finally have a home of my own to decorate."

Amelia bit back the urge to remind Wallis that with the eyes of the world on her, she should be more discreet about who she spent time with. However, with His Royal Highness escorted around by Nazi officials, Wallis going out in public with Herr von Ribbentrop shouldn't raise too many more eyebrows than were already lifted because of this trip. It was not something Amelia would do, but little of what Wallis did was anything Amelia would ever do.

Wallis must have felt her subtle judgment because she handed Amelia the carnations. "Put these in a vase then return to your duties."

"Yes, ma'am." Amelia took the flowers to Wallis's bedroom, irked at being dismissed like a servant, but after all, that's what she was, and not as deferential a one as Mrs. Bedaux had advised. She was trying, but Wallis made it difficult sometimes.

WITH THE DUKE and Wallis gone, and the frenzy of sorting luggage and settling their entourage over, Amelia decided to step out and see Berlin. She had some free time before the tea and this might be her only chance to poke around the city. She settled her peaked hat over her hair, tucked her purse under her arm, and made for the door.

"Where are you going, Frau Montague?" Herr Rudolph asked in a respectful but firm tone.

"To do some sightseeing."

"I don't advise traveling without an official guide."

"I'll stick to the main areas, I'm sure I'll be perfectly fine." She moved for the door and he stepped between it and her.

"Allow me to ask Frau Koch if she can accompany you." He barked something in German and Frau Koch, the maid, stepped out of the adjoining room. The two of them began a lively discussion in German, the gist of which was neither of them wanted Amelia to leave. She should just go and let them try and stop her, but she wouldn't put it past them to try. She wasn't about to get into a tussle with the German staff.

Frau Koch picked up the telephone and made a call in German. A moment later, Mr. Forwood entered the room.

"Is there a problem?" He glanced back and forth between Amelia and Herr Rudolph.

"I want to walk around Berlin, but they say I can't."

"It's not advisable." Herr Rudolph pled his case in German

to Mr. Forwood, who spoke the language as fluently as he did French and English.

When they were finished, Mr. Forwood pulled Amelia aside, out of their hearing. "I think you should stay here."

"Why? What are they afraid I'm going to do? See something I'm not allowed to see?"

He flashed a look that said that was exactly what they were afraid she might do. The truth dawned on Amelia. They weren't here to see the real Germany, but a pretty picture postcard with none of the ugly things she'd glimpsed during the car ride here. Amelia glanced over his shoulder at the butler and maid watching and trying to listen. They spoke fluent English. She hoped they didn't speak French. "They're spying on us, aren't they?"

He nodded, then answered in French, "They probably think you're a spy too. This isn't Paris. Things are different here and I can't vouch for your safety if you veer from our itinerary."

He was right. She'd read newspaper stories about American gentlemen being mistaken for Germans and punched when they didn't give a proper Nazi salute. She didn't want to be pig-headed and get herself in real trouble.

"I'll stay. I have things to do anyway," she replied in English loud enough for the maid and butler to hear. They exchanged relieved looks then returned to their work.

"Thank you. I'll try and arrange an outing for you."

Amelia removed her hat and set her purse on the table, then thought better of leaving it where anyone, including Herr Rudolph, could riffle through it. She set up her portable typewriter on the desk near the window. The view from the hotel was all of Berlin she was going to see.

"IT'S EXACTLY LIKE it was when I was here in 1918." The Duke slapped his knee in excitement at the picturesque views of farms, fields, and rolling, tree-covered hills on either side of the Autobahn. "Of course, we didn't have this magnificent road then, but everything else is the same. I had so much fun with Uncle Willie and Aunt Augusta. This brings it all back."

"This road is one of the finest in the world. Feel how smooth it is." Dr. Ley positioned his squat body between the two rows of seats. He raised his hands to show how steady he was then wobbled and quickly grasped the backs of the seats.

"He'd be a great deal steadier if he weren't constantly drunk," Wallis whispered to Amelia, who choked down a laugh. Dr. Ley often took discreet sips from the bottle of schnapps he kept in his uniform pocket whenever he thought no one was looking.

"His Royal Highness should be careful where he lights his cigarette. It might ignite the fumes surrounding our host," Amelia whispered back, and Wallis's face lit up in amusement.

The two of them sat together near the back of the large and luxurious Mercedes bus ferrying them to a military school on the Pomeranian border. The Duke sat at the front and reveled in the view of the German countryside. Amelia didn't care what she saw so long as it wasn't the same four walls of the Hotel Kaiserhof. She'd barely been outside since their arrival, buried under a constant stream of press inquiries, callers, deliveries, and cables.

Despite Mr. Forwood's assurance, no sightseeing had been arranged for her but more work had piled up. She suspected someone was making sure she had extra tasks to keep her busy and off the streets of Berlin. She'd diligently done what was asked of her until Herr Hermann Goering had insisted she change the Windsors' Leipzig hotel reservation because the hotel owners were Jewish. Amelia had politely declined, turning the onerous task over to Mr. Forwood.

"We have all the modern conveniences on board." Herr Goering, a barrel-chested man with dark, slicked-back hair, pointed to the telephone on a small shelf beside him. "Wireless telephone, we can call anyone from anywhere."

"Marvelous." The Duke was thrilled by the custom Mercedes bus with its large windows, small kitchen, and the two waiters in white coats and black trousers who served canapés and drinks. A radio played a selection of music from Wagner's operas.

The flatness of the Autobahn soon gave way to the rolling hills of the Crossensee as the bus climbed up a winding mountain road.

"There it is, Ordensburg." Dr. Ley pointed out the window at the stoic fortress of angles and hard stone perched on the side of the hill. It was an austere and chilling place with long, low buildings broken by a single, ominous tower.

"You've received quite an honor today," Herr Goering said as the bus pulled to a stop at the front of a column of black-uniformed soldiers standing in front of a contingent of students in identical khaki shirts and green shorts. "This is where the SS Totenkopf train. They're the elite of the elite and here to welcome you."

"What does *Totenkopf* mean?" Amelia whispered to Mr. Forwood as they followed the others off the bus.

"Death's head."

That couldn't be good no matter how much Herr Goering or anyone else talked it up.

The soldiers in their high, shiny boots and black uniforms broken by red swastika armbands threw up their hands and shouted, "Heil, Windsor!"

His Royal Highness raised his right arm in return as the Death's Head band played "God Save the King." The British anthem drifting over the brutal fortress and surrounding countryside was more chilling than the cold fall day.

I should have stayed in Berlin. She'd wanted to see Germany. Now that she'd had a good look at it, she didn't like it at all.

Nothing about the salutes or the rigid line of soldiers bothered His Royal Highness. He inspected them as if they were his old Welsh Guards regiment, stopping every few feet to speak with the soldiers in German and accepting and returning their salutes. The train station had practically been a melee. This was a well-coordinated show of strength and power.

They passed from the parade ground into the school's main building, where more students and officers greeted them. The interior was as austere as the outside with heavy, exposed-beam ceilings and stark white plaster walls broken by a large map of Europe with Austria and Germany painted as one country.

"In the Great War, I used to inspect the troops like this. They loved me and I couldn't get enough of them," His Royal Highness said to Wallis before he stepped up to the line of officers and officials inside who showed him the military respect he'd been denied since leaving Britain.

After the formal greeting, Herr Goering and Dr. Ley escorted His Royal Highness on a tour of the school. Frau Goering took charge of Amelia and Wallis.

"Ladies, if you'll follow me, I've arranged for a nice tea." Frau Goering led them to a small sitting room, clearly a man's office given the dark wood walls and the lack of decorative pillows or patterned furniture. Large windows showcased the stunning view of the tree-covered hills and the young men doing calisthenics on the field below.

"Quite the stoic institution." Wallis sat in one of the wood and leather chairs surrounding a low table. A silver tea service engraved with the Nazi eagle sat in all its Art Deco formality in the center beside a similarly decorated china platter with tea sandwiches. The gold eagle was also stamped on the china cups, saucers, and teaspoons.

"It's an honor to attend Ordensburg. Only the best are selected for admission. Students receive a very comprehensive education in strengthening the body," Frau Goering explained in her heavily accented English as she poured the tea. She was a stately Swedish woman with wavy blond hair parted in the center and pulled loosely back from her oval face. According to Wallis, she'd been a famous actress in Germany before she'd married Major General Hermann

Goering. “The rest of the time they attend classes on racial biology and German history.”

Amelia didn’t ask what a class in racial biology was, not sure she wished to know.

“They also study politics, especially Bolshevism.” Frau Goering handed Wallis her teacup. “One must know their enemies to face them.”

If the Germans placed so much emphasis on studying the Russians then perhaps His Royal Highness was right about the two countries fighting it out and leaving the rest of the world alone.

“I noticed the map in the entrance hall doesn’t have the border between Germany and Austria,” Amelia remarked, earning a scrutinizing gaze from Wallis, who barely touched her food.

“Germans in Austria dream of being reunited with the fatherland. In time they’ll decide to make that dream a reality.” Frau Goering turned to Wallis. “I must offer my deepest condolences on His Royal Highness being forced to abdicate. Herr Hitler feels it is a great loss to Britain and Europe. You would have made a glorious queen.”

“How kind of you to say so.” Wallis practically glowed under Frau Goering’s flattery. “His Royal Highness was driven from England because they were afraid of his desire to make peace instead of war. Rest assured, His Majesty’s Government will regret what they’ve done, perhaps not today, but in time.”

“I have no doubt they will.” Frau Goering sipped her tea as if they were discussing finding a good maid, not the tenuous future of Germany and Europe. "Mrs. Montague, will you join Their Royal Highnesses at Berchtesgaden to meet the Führer? It's an honor any German girl would die for."

"If Amelia wishes to come, she's more than welcome to join us," Wallis said, waiting for her response with the same eagerness as Frau Goering.

Amelia set her teacup and saucer on the table so they wouldn't clatter in her hands. She should agree and prop up Wallis's standing with the highest-ranking woman in Germany, as expected of any good employee, but she couldn't. Everything giving her the willies here would be ten times worse at Berchtesgaden, and she wasn't a talented enough actress to hide it. Amelia lowered her gaze to her lap and assumed the most subservient attitude she could muster. "The honor of meeting a head of state is for royalty, not for private secretaries."

It shouldn't be for Wallis either but with Frau Goering puffing her up and rattling on about what a grand honor it was to meet Herr Hitler, there'd be no talking Wallis out of it. How she could ignore the death's head insignia, the anti-Jewish signs they'd seen on the way out of Berlin, and the constant flattery, she didn't know, but if there was one thing Wallis was good at, it was seeing only what she wanted to see. Right now, all her cousin could focus on was the honors being heaped on her by the German heads of state, even if those heads stunk to high heaven.

Chapter Nine

Nuremberg, October 20, 1937

"I can't tell you how pleased this will make His Royal Highness." Mr. Forwood beamed as bright as the Duke. He and Amelia stood on the fringes of Wallis and the Duke's conversation in the Grand Hotel receiving room waiting for a call to duty, the two of them more like furniture than guests. "Duke Charles Edward is the first European royalty to acknowledge Her Royal Highness. It'll encourage others to follow, perhaps even His Majesty and his brothers."

Amelia doubted the acknowledgment of the Duke of Saxe-Coburg and Gotha, Queen Victoria's grandson and His Royal Highness's cousin, carried much weight with the royal family. His coziness with the German hierarchy gave royals all over Europe palpitations but it didn't appear to trouble the Duke. He chatted with his cousin, who was much taller than him with thinning white hair, a high forehead, and a full mustache.

Duke Charles Edward wore a military uniform adorned with more medals and ribbons than anyone else in the room. His Royal Highness stood out in his somber black tuxedo beside Wallis in her cream silk dress with a fitted bodice, slightly flared skirt, and a black sequined jacket that covered her wide shoulders. Her diamond and emerald set outshone the tiaras of the titled women who rushed to curtsey to her.

"Mr. Forwood, it's a pleasure to see you again." An older woman in a long navy-blue dress, her blond and gray hair twisted into a fancy chignon, greeted the equerry. "Will we see you in London this spring?"

"Not this year, I'm afraid. Lady Williams-Taylor, may I introduce Mrs. Montague, the Duchess of Windsor's private secretary."

"A pleasure. You must meet Miss Heastie, my private secretary. She couldn't accompany me to Berlin but you'll see her at my parties in Paris. The two of you will get on splendidly," she assured in her posh English accent. The seventy-year-old socialite was the queen of Bahamian society and the wife of the manager of the Bank of Montreal and spent her time among her homes in Nassau, England, and Paris. She was also one of the few socially prominent people who hadn't shunned Wallis. Seeing her in Germany, Amelia finally understood why. "Ah, there's Frau Goering. I must say hello. Enjoy your evening, darlings."

The Duke motioned to Mr. Forwood to assist him, leaving Amelia to stand by herself. She smiled at passing guests, thankful for the pale pink and silver-trimmed Schiaparelli dress Wallis had bought for her. She didn't shine as grandly as the wives of the dignitaries around her but she held her own.

"You must be Mrs. Montague." A woman with an American accent approached Amelia and shook her hand. "I'm Alice Gordon."

Amelia recognized the name. "You knew Her Royal Highness in Washington in the twenties?"

"Back when she was plain Wallis Warfield. What an interesting place to see her again." Mrs. Gordon accepted a glass of champagne from a passing server. "My husband is the American minister to The Hague. It's how we received the honor of being here tonight. Ask if Her Grace will speak to me."

Amelia wondered why Mrs. Gordon didn't simply approach Wallis herself, or why she hadn't gone through the receiving line, but it wasn't her place to ask questions. She was here to carry out orders and requests. She approached Wallis and while the Duke spoke to Herr Goering, she whispered in her ear, "Mrs. Alice Gordon, an old acquaintance of yours, would like a word with you."

Wallis locked eyes with Mrs. Gordon, and the sparkle that'd ignited them the instant they'd stepped into the Grand Hotel vanished. "I have no desire to talk to her."

Amelia returned to Mrs. Gordon, remembering Mrs. Bedaux's advice to be kind to everyone. Wallis might not want to see her old friend but it didn't mean Amelia should be rude. "I'm sorry, Her Royal Highness is unable to meet with you this evening."

The sting of the slight hung in the air like the woman's Chanel No. 5. "She's mistaken if she thinks she can erase her past by ignoring it. She was a penniless nobody when I launched her into Washington society and introduced her to Felipe Aja Espil. I'm sure she's mentioned him."

Amelia shook her head. Wallis enjoyed name-dropping but she'd never said his.

"He was first secretary at the Argentine Embassy back then, with a promising ambassadorial career ahead of him and quite the looker. Everyone was stunned when he took up with her, but her talent for collecting influential men is impressive. However, an ambassador needs money, and she had none. The woman he married did."

Amelia listened, amazed again at how free people in social and diplomatic circles were with gossip. They might not say anything above a whisper but they certainly whispered. Of course, if Mrs. Gordon had been the making of Wallis in D.C., back when helping her had gained her nothing, then no wonder she was mad at the snub. Wallis should have at least greeted her. A simple acknowledgment would have smoothed some old wounds instead of reopening them.

"I've always admired Wallis's ability to social climb, but, as George Mallory learned the hard way, not all climbers are successful. Sometimes they topple down before they reach the summit." Mrs. Gordon sipped her champagne then nodded at the very tall, silver-haired man bowing to the Windsors. "There's a mountaineer Wallis should stay away from. Mr. Axel Wenner-Gren, owner of Electrolux, among other businesses, and a close friend of the Nazis. He and Frau Goering knew each other in Sweden before Frau Goering shot to prominence in Germany."

"The Bahamas is a delight this time of year," Mr. Wenner-Gren said to Wallis in his thick Swedish accent. "The heat is finally gone and construction on my estate's deepwater harbor can resume."

"What do you need a deep harbor for?" Wallis asked.

"My yacht, of course. One's yacht can never be too large or too well-appointed."

"Just as one can never be too rich or too thin."

Mr. Wenner-Gren's deep chuckle joined Wallis's gratingly high laugh.

"Let me give you a piece of advice to pass on to Her Grace," Mrs. Gordon said. "Photos of Their Royal Highnesses giving Herr Hitler the Nazi salute are circulating in newspapers everywhere and people aren't happy about it. Lie down with the dogs and rise up with the fleas. Also, be wary of Her Grace's friendship. She isn't as good at keeping friends as she is at cultivating them."

She walked off, leaving Amelia to chew on that bit of wisdom. She didn't have long to mull it over as the banquet hall doors opened and everyone spilled in to find their places.

The Grand Hotel's belle epoque banquet hall was breathtaking. Large gilded mirrors reflected the gleam of the white tablecloths, china, and gold silverware laid out on the long tables beneath the heavy crystal chandeliers. Magnificent paintings of Wagner's operas adorned the walls below the arched white ceiling and gilded columns.

"This is amazing," Amelia said to Mr. Forwood as the two of them took their places well below the salt.

"This is nothing compared to the state dinners we use to have at Buckingham Palace."

"I'm glad I didn't have to make those seating arrangements." *It'd be a nightmare getting everyone and their titles and positions straight.*

Wallis and the Duke sat at the head table with the Duke of Saxe-Coburg and Gotha, who stood and settled the room into silence. "I can't tell you what it means for relations between our two countries for me to have my cousin in Germany. All of us who desire friendly relations between Germany and England know that his presence here represents a new and fruitful element for cooperation between the two nations." Duke Charles Edward raised his champagne glass. "To the friendship between Germany and Britain, and the continued ties between the House of Windsor and the House of Saxe-Coburg and Gotha. To His Royal Highness and the very beautiful Her Royal Highness."

"To Her Royal Highness!" The cry went up along with a hundred champagne glasses.

Amelia and Mr. Forwood stood with the rest and raised their glasses.

Down the table, Mrs. Gordon stood but didn't toast the guests of honor. Her warning about the pictures of Wallis in the newspapers rang with the guests' cheers. The Windsors giving the Nazi salute sat badly with Amelia. She could imagine how it must look to people outside Germany. Wallis was oblivious to the brewing trouble as she beamed in triumph at the head table, no longer Wallis Warfield Simpson, the twice-divorced American who'd toppled a king, but the most important woman in the room, the wife of royalty and royal in her own right. A woman too important to greet an old friend, assuming that's what Mrs. Gordon really was. Very little about Wallis and her life and past were straightforward. There was no telling how much of what Mrs. Gordon had said was the truth and how much was spite.

"WHAT HAPPENED BETWEEN you and Mrs. Gordon?" Amelia asked.

Wallis sat at her dressing table doing her morning facial exercises. In the adjoining room, Mademoiselle Moulichon supervised the German maids in the packing of Wallis's things. Despite the late night, Amelia had been up early to make sure the Windsors' massive amount of luggage was delivered to the train station. There'd be no fanfare for their departure and Amelia was glad. She'd seen enough German flattery to last a lifetime.

"You mean the witch who drove me from Washington." Wallis rubbed Elizabeth Arden cream into the delicate skin beneath her eyes. The hectic pace of the trip had taken its toll and she appeared more tired and drawn than usual. "Oh, she played at being my friend, but when Felipe left me for that ugly woman with more money than brains, Alice made sure to tell everyone I'd thrown myself at a man who wasn't interested in me. She humiliated me in front of D.C. society. I had no choice but to leave and salvage what was left of my reputation. But I don't suppose she told you that."

"No, she didn't." No wonder Wallis hadn't wanted to speak to her. It's why Amelia had hesitated about returning to Baltimore after Jackson's death. After they'd eloped, there wasn't a lie so awful that her old friends and even Mother wouldn't repeat it.

"Hypocritical cowards, all of them, judging me as if they don't have a hundred skeletons in their closets. I know what Alice got up to in the twenties and heaven knows what she's mired in now. She's probably a government spy. Here's a lesson for you. It's not the diplomats but their wives you have to worry about. No one suspects a woman but the women are connected to everyone and everything. Why, the government paid me to carry secrets to China when I went out to join Win, and I assure you I wasn't the only one. Don't think Alice is any different. Mark my words, she's already told everyone what she saw and heard last night. It'll be all over the diplomatic community by the time we reach Paris, and for once, I'm glad. Everyone can hear how I brought European royalty to their feet." She rubbed cream onto her neck with quick upward motions, willing her skin to defy gravity.

Amelia couldn't blame Wallis for wanting cheers and adoration, especially after the way she'd been maligned by the world and the royal family, but it was a mistake to search for it here.

"Let me share another lesson I learned in Washington." Wallis leaned into the mirror to apply her makeup. "A woman is nothing without money and standing. It's why I wasn't about to slink off to some dark corner to die in shame and anonymity when all this abdication nonsense started. No, I married David and became a duchess and I'll have the extra-chic title if I have to nag Sir Walter about it forever. I suggest you follow my lead and catch a titled man or millionaire of your own. It'd make your life a great deal easier and give all the naysayers back home something to chew on."

Amelia doubted that. She'd seen something of the aristocrats and millionaires floating around Europe. They exchanged partners like gloves, suffering through one public divorce or scandal after another. No title, standing, or revenge was worth that trouble and heartache.

"Look at the press coverage. It's marvelous." The Duke slapped the German newspaper with the picture of Wallis at the Nuremberg dinner. "Our trip was a success."

"'A divine woman in a divine dress,'" Mr. Axel Wenner-Gren's heavily accented voice carried above the hum of the train wheels as he read over the Duke's shoulder. Herr Hitler had offered the Windsors his private plane to take them home but Wallis's fear of flying more than prudence had forced them to politely decline the offer. Mr. Wenner-Gren had stepped in with his private Pullman car, which they'd gladly accepted. The Duke and Wallis were experts at getting other people to pay for things. For once Amelia didn't mind, simply glad they were leaving, and she breathed a little easier with every mile the train placed between them and Germany.

"She's number five on the International Best Dressed List," the Duke boasted.

"She deserves the honor," Mr. Bedaux complimented. "And the opportunity to shine again. You should do an American tour."

Amelia paused in organizing correspondence at the back of the Pullman. She was looking forward to the peace and quiet of her mundane Paris schedule and wasn't wild about the extra work of another trip. She also wasn't ready to venture back across the Atlantic and see how well her new confidence stood up under the old scrutiny and criticism.

"I've spoken to a number of entities in America who are eager to host you," Mr. Bedaux added, sweetening the pot.

Wallis set down her detective novel. "Who?"

"I've received a cable from the Women's National Press Club inviting you to their annual luncheon, and the Secretary of the Interior sent a list of housing and reclamation projects you could both tour. You might even meet the president."

"I've never cared much for Washington or its people." Wallis tucked a bookmark in the novel. "They can never let go of anyone's past."

"All the more reason to tour America and show them you aren't the old Wallis." Mrs. Bedaux leaned forward and rested one elbow on her silk-stocking-clad knee. "Imagine the faces of everyone who's ever snubbed you when you return home a duchess feted by the president. They'll be green with envy."

"They will, won't they?" Wallis trilled her fingers on the novel cover.

"You can meet the president without setting foot in Washington," Mr. Bedaux assured. "My family's New York home is next door to Mr. Roosevelt's and we know them well. I can arrange a meeting with him there, all very informal and chummy."

"Think what you can accomplish by speaking to President Roosevelt, sir," Mr. Wenner-Gren proposed to the Duke, who'd been forgotten in this discussion of Wallis's potential American triumph. "You could be a voice of reason in this insane world, a figurehead for Americans eager to stay out of a war. A prince of peace."

"A prince of peace." The Duke rolled the phrase across his tongue, getting a real taste for it before reality quashed the fantasy. "An American tour would be expensive. I can't afford anything so extravagant."

"I can arrange it as I did this one but we must act fast, ride this wave of momentum, keep Your Royal Highness and workers everywhere foremost in everyone's mind."

"I think it's a marvelous idea," Wallis said. "If your brother won't give you a position worthy of your skills and talents then you must create one. You, surrounded by hundreds of adoring Americans, will show the world you're still popular and a force for change. If America is eager to welcome and listen to you on workers' welfare and the need for peace, it'll encourage more countries to do the same. Everyone who was afraid to come to our wedding will flock to you and we'll show Buck House we're too important to be ignored."

"Quite right," the Duke said, breaking his fruit tart lunch into pieces and eating one.

This isn't right at all, Amelia thought, pretending not to listen but hearing every word. Buckingham Palace had fretted over their German trip. They'd be livid at the Duke acting as an unofficial British ambassador to President Roosevelt. Sir Walter's warning about Wallis being flattered by people with questionable motives, and her desire to lift up a man she'd helped pull down, echoed in Wallis's words. Of course, it was all talk. Wallis could barely get French or British notables to call on her. The idea she could suddenly summon them to raise the Duke to some grand height was ridiculous, or was it? Her ego more than the concerns of the working class were driving this new idea, and where Wallis was concerned, that was rarely good.

Chapter Ten

Paris, November 1937

"Seventy of the one hundred thirty-five trunks were sent to Calais yesterday. The rest will go by truck with us when we leave to board the SS *Bremen*," Amelia reported to Wallis, who sat in bed with a breakfast tray and a stack of morning papers. She didn't lean against the large pillows behind her but sat ramrod straight. Simply looking at her hurt Amelia's back. Detto, Prisie, and Pookie lay at her feet, their square bodies covering the embroidered *WE* topped with a coronet on the satin blanket. Wallis had stamped the crown and their entwined initials on everything from the silverware to bathroom soap cakes. "Speaking of which, Sir Walter cabled to say His Majesty's Government doesn't approve of you sailing on a German liner. They think it sets a bad example."

"They think our simply breathing sets a bad example, but they have no one to blame but themselves. If they hadn't insisted we not darken their shores we could've sailed on another liner but the *Bremen* is the only one that doesn't stop in Britain on the way to New York." Wallis ignored the grapefruit on the tray as she thumbed through the newspapers. "Another splendid article on our German trip. Paste it in the scrapbook with the others."

She folded the newspaper and handed it to Amelia, who motioned to the ones on the floor. "And these?"

"Their stories aren't nearly as delightful."

Mrs. Gordon was right; not everyone was impressed with Wallis and the Duke visiting Herr Hitler and they said so in print. However, there were enough flattering stories to keep too much censure from tarnishing what Wallis believed was the first of many glorious triumphs.

"Aunt Bessie wrote you." Amelia handed her the letter then sat at Wallis's writing desk to open and sort the rest of the morning mail.

"Let's see what the old gal has to say." Wallis opened the letter and began to read before gasping in horror. "Listen to this, someone purchased the East Biddle Street house Mother and I used to rent and turned it into a museum to me. People pay twenty-five cents to sit in the bathtub in Mother's old room and have their picture taken. Can you imagine?"

"It's outrageous. They should charge at least a dollar for the honor."

Wallis covered a laugh with one hand. "That's what I love about you, your pep and sense of humor. You can see it in even the most ghastly situations."

"Oh, it's simply good clean fun, that's all."

"Stop it or I'll never finish this letter and I can't lounge in bed all day." Wallis turned to the second page and her already pale skin went a shade whiter.

"Is something wrong?" Amelia asked, afraid Aunt Bessie might have had another stroke.

"Aunt Bessie's fine." Wallis snatched up the bell from her bedside table and gave it a sharp shake and the maid hurried in. "Take the breakfast tray away."

The maid clutched both sides of the tray and started to move it when Wallis flipped back the covers, catching the side and nearly upending it. "I said remove it! Can't you do anything right?"

"Je suis désolé, madame," the maid stuttered.

"Your Royal Highness," Wallis screeched. "Your Royal Highness!"

The maid scurried away with the tray, the china rattling with her shaking hands. The dogs jumped off the bed and trotted to their baskets, smart enough to lie low in the middle of Wallis's fury.

"Dismiss her." Wallis stormed to the window and stared out at the Paris skyline.

"Yes, ma'am." The girl didn't deserve to be sacked but there was no reasoning with Wallis in this state. Amelia wanted to slip out of the room but she never left until she was dismissed, and Wallis had not dismissed her. Time stretched out while she waited for Wallis to either send her away or say something.

Finally, Wallis picked up Pookie and settled in a chair,

stroking the dog from head to tail. "Ernest married Mary in New York last week."

The same death of hope Amelia had experienced when the policemen had told her about Jackson washed over Wallis's face and Amelia's heart dropped. She'd met the vivacious and dark-haired Mary Raffray in Baltimore a few years ago during one of Wallis's visits. Mary had introduced Wallis to Ernest, and during her last visit to England, she'd been kind enough to give Wallis the evidence she'd needed to sue him for divorce for adultery by posing as Buttercup Kennedy, the woman the maid had found Ernest in bed with at the Hotel de Paris in Berkshire. Apparently, the two of them hadn't been pretending.

"She was my oldest and dearest friend. We went to Oldfields together. I thought we'd be friends forever. How did I get it so wrong?"

"Do you think something was going on before the divorce?"

"I suspected it, especially when Ernest started making so many business trips to New York. The business of screwing my friend." Wallis looked at the letter again. There were no tears, but a longing for something lost that resonated in Amelia. She'd thumbed through the photo album of her and Jackson's first year so many times, wishing she could go back to that halcyon time instead of existing in the middle of her wrecked life. "I loved him, in my own way, and we were happy together. I thought we always would be. Now he's gone for good."

She didn't know how Wallis could be surprised that Ernest would find someone else while she'd enjoyed the dubious position of *maîtresse-en-titre* but Wallis rarely saw how her actions led to her troubles. Amelia couldn't be too hard on her. She'd done the same thing during the first few months after Jackson's death, refusing to see how her unwillingness to question him about his late nights at the Boston office, his ridiculous reasons for why bills were paid late or not at all, and her blind faith in him had helped create her current troubles. She'd given up everything to be with him and she'd wanted her sacrifice to be worth it and it hadn't been. "I'm so sorry things didn't turn out as you'd hoped."

"Do they ever? I'm sure your mother, my mother, and Aunt Bessie didn't expect to become widows so young."

"I don't suppose they did. I didn't."

Amelia waited for one of Wallis's proclamations about standing up in the face of difficulty with grace and poise and carrying on with determination, all the things Amelia admired about her, but the words didn't come. Instead, Wallis stared out the window, dejected in a way Amelia had never seen before.

Finally, she let out a deep, tired sigh. "Call Antoine in New York and arrange to have him meet the *Bremen* at the dock. Have an Elizabeth Arden makeup artist there too. I must look perfect when I step off the liner. I want Mary to open her newspaper over her eggs and see me, a duchess, a woman of note, splashed across the pages."

There was more spite than determination in the command. Amelia didn't try and coax her out of her blue mood but left to make the appointments. This was Wallis's grief, and she needed to sit with it.

Amelia returned to her office to find a letter from Peter waiting for her on the blotter. At least someone in her family besides Aunt Bessie still wrote to her. It wasn't often but it was something. Hopefully, his news wasn't as alarming as Wallis's, and it wasn't, but it took until the bottom of the first page for Peter to finally get to his reason for writing.

I'm working in the New York office and I'd love to see you when you're here with the Windsors. Cable me when you're available. I miss you, Melly.

Tears misted her eyes. It'd been years since anyone had called her Melly, and just as long since she'd seen Peter. He'd been one of the few bright spots in the years after Father's death, even if, with college and then the railroad, he'd spent more time away from home than in it. The chance to see him again was the only thing about the American trip she looked forward to, especially when she read the rest of his letter.

> *Mother saw the pictures of Wallis with Hitler. She was relieved you weren't in any of them and told everyone you'd stayed in Paris. Typical Mother, more concerned about her reputation and her social standing than anything else. I'm trying to convince her to come up to New York to see you when you're here, to bury the hatchet as they say, but she won't hear of it. I'll try and change her mind. I miss being a family and want that again. I hope you want that too. War might come and then who knows what will happen to any of us.*
>
> *Your loving brother, Peter*

Amelia folded the letter and leaned back in the chair, grateful he'd extended the invitation and terrified at the same time. At least she'd land stateside better turned out than when she'd left, but a Schiaparelli wardrobe and a smart hairdo wouldn't silence the old critics. People had long memories and once they got wind of you not being up to their standards, it didn't matter what you did afterward, past sins always defined you. At least as the secretary she wouldn't be front and center like Wallis. She could hide behind her cousin and hope no one noticed her, exactly as she'd done during her debutante years.

Until Jackson noticed me. If Mother hadn't ignored her, she might never have eloped. She wouldn't have wanted to escape, to be seen and loved.

She'd make sure to stand out this time.

She called Antoinette's and they were more than happy to squeeze her in for a haircut and manicure before she left. Let the old Baltimore biddies whisper about her. It no longer mattered.

THE DUKE STROLLED into the dining room with his arms loaded with shopping bags from Schiaparelli and Mainbocher. "I picked up everything you asked me to collect, darling, but the items from Cartier weren't ready. I'll fetch them tomorrow. I want you to look your best in America."

"Thank you, David," Wallis said from over her light lunch, and the Duke beamed under her praise like a new footman during his first week of work.

"A letter for you, Your Royal Highness." Mr. Hale held out a silver salver with an envelope on it.

The Duke exchanged the shopping for the letter. His enthusiasm immediately dropped when he read it. "Charles is canceling the American tour."

Well, that was a waste of money, Amelia thought as she admired her freshly painted nails.

"But we leave in three days," Wallis cried. "The tickets are purchased. Our trunks are at the dock. He can't cancel now. Think what people will say."

"Well, he has." The Duke dropped the letter beside Wallis's plate then slumped in his chair, waving away the footman trying to serve him his usual fruit tart.

Amelia wanted to groan in frustration. All her hard work arranging travel and schedules had been for nothing. It'd be a hassle to get the luggage back from Calais and a massive embarrassment for Wallis. The press reveled in reporting on the number of trunks the Windsors traveled with, and it was considerable. They'd go into raptures over the luggage returning to Paris because the trip was canceled.

"Charles says the labor unions used that picture of us at Berchtesgaden to rile up their members against the trip. They threatened to boycott his companies if he carried through with it. It sent his stock spiraling. Their uproar made the manufacturers jittery, especially the New York Clothing Manufacturers' Exchange, and for once they threw in with the workers."

Wallis looked at Amelia. "Your stepfather was the exchange's president once, wasn't he?"

"I don't know. He never discussed business with me," Amelia lied to avoid catching any of Wallis's simmering anger. As far as she knew, Theodore Miller was still a prominent member of the exchange, and he might have had a hand in torpedoing this trip, or maybe not. She didn't know.

"It's more than the labor unions." The Duke picked a flake of tobacco off his dark burgundy lounge suit. "A number of politicians raised concerns about the trip because of our German one. Of course, we are free to go at our own expense . . ."

Wallis flung down the letter. "Then we should and not allow anyone to bully us from staying out of yet another country."

"Let's not be hasty, darling. A tour of that magnitude is expensive and we're far from wealthy. I'd hate to compromise our ability to afford our future home."

"I don't care about the future, I care about the present and how people will gloat when we cancel," Wallis seethed. "I'll be humbled yet again before everyone who's ever insulted or sneered at me, all those old Baltimore biddies, Alice Gordon, Mary Raffray, everyone."

"I'm sorry, darling, I'm sorry." The Duke hung his head in shame.

"No, you're not. So long as you don't have to spend a farthing you don't care what happens to me or what I have to endure." Wallis rose and bent over him. "If you stood up to your brother and forced him to pay the promised allowance, demand he give you a position worthy of your talents and rank, we could afford the trip. I could hold my head up high, recognized by your family and with a proper title."

"I've never wanted to fail you. I've always wanted the best for you." Fat tears rolled down the Duke's face and dropped on the tablecloth, leaving wet rings on the silk.

His crying drove Wallis's fury and her voice rose two octaves. The footmen quietly left while Amelia remained perfectly still, attempting to blend into the woodwork.

"You're weak and pathetic. You let them push you off your throne and you'll let them shove you aside like some forgotten plant and force me to wilt in the dark with you. I won't have it, I tell you. I won't."

Amelia silently willed the Duke to stand up for himself but he didn't. He simply sat there and took the berating, sobbing like a chastened child.

"You make me sick." Wallis stormed out of the dining room.

Amelia quietly followed, eager to leave the Duke with some dignity. She returned to her desk and made arrangements for the luggage to be shipped back from the Norddeutscher Lloyd dock. A half hour later, Wallis sent her a note instructing her to cancel all of her afternoon appointments, even the hairdresser. This wasn't like Wallis. The world could be coming to an end and her hair would be perfectly coiffed.

Amelia knocked on Wallis's bedroom door and poked her head in. "It's Amelia. I wanted to make sure you're all right."

"How kind of you to think of me. So few people do." Wallis sat bolt upright on the sofa, eyes red, a tissue clutched in one hand, the other stroking Pookie. It was a strange picture of sadness and proper posture. She patted the cushion beside her and Amelia sat down. "I shouldn't have spoken to David like that but he doesn't understand how hard it's been for me, always having to be perfect, never able to admit to anything except utter bliss and happiness and hated by everyone." She wiped her damp cheeks with the tissue. "He grew up an adored prince, never wanting for anything. I've spent my whole life fighting for respect and every time I think I have it, someone steals it from me: Win, Alice Gordon, Mary Raffray, Felipe Aja Espil, Emerald Cunard."

"Who?"

"The woman who supported me in England until David abdicated, and then she had the gall to say she didn't know me. They were my friends when they thought it'd benefit them. They dropped me like a hot potato when it didn't." Wallis crumpled the tissue and set it with the others on the coffee table then tugged a fresh one from the box. "Do you know what it's like to have everyone abandon you when you need them the most? It's one of the loneliest feelings in the world."

"I know. I thought after the elopement, people would simply accept it and everything would go back to the way it'd been before. It wasn't great then either, but at least people spoke to me. The first time I went back to Baltimore, reality hit me smack in the face like a dead fish. I was naive to not see that coming."

"Experience doesn't make any difference. Look at me. I thought I could have all the fun and none of the pain but the piper must be paid and I pay him every day. Do you know what I loved most about Germany? For the first time in a long time I wasn't David's sole source of amusement and companionship;

he had something useful to do, real purpose. You don't know how stressful it is to constantly entertain him."

"Maybe he needs a new hobby, such as house hunting? I could put together a list of available properties and he could inspect them."

"I wouldn't trust him to find a suitable house. David and I have very different tastes."

"You don't have to live where he chooses, but it'd get him out of the house for a while. You could suggest properties outside Paris. The extra driving will keep him away longer."

Wallis studied Amelia with impressed admiration. "Your cleverness strikes again, and you're right, house hunting will do us both a world of good. We can't go on living in hotels. We need a place to put down roots, to build a proper future, then the past won't matter so much. Contact the finest estate agents in Paris, tell them we're on the hunt for a home worthy of a king."

After taking notes on what Wallis wanted in a house, Amelia contacted realtors to help create a list of possible prospects. While she read the listings, she thought of house hunting in Wellesley and the joy of finally finding the right one. Jackson had purchased it immediately and she'd never asked him where the money had come from, there'd been no reason to back then. She'd assumed he'd made enough as an attorney or had been left enough by his deceased parents to support her and pay for the maid and the car. His parents had left him nothing but debts when they'd died. He'd stolen money to keep up the façade of a rich and successful lawyer and heir. Someone else's money had paid for the furniture and the house, and all of it had been sold to pay his debts. Someday she'd have a home of her own again, but this time on her terms and her dime so no one could take it away from her.

Beneath the rental listings were the employment ones.

Lady seeks shorthand-typist or preferably secretarial position.

Lady desires secretarial position, experienced secretary, fine business capabilities, shorthand-typing (130/60), highly recommended.

Young Lady shorthand typist required with general knowledge of office routine. Commencing salary 30s to 35s according to ability.

Amelia had read a hundred of these in Baltimore, and placed a few before Aunt Bessie had struck on the Wallis idea.

Wallis.

She set down the newspaper, an idea coming to her. There must be hundreds of girls like her, graduates of secretarial schools eager to work somewhere more prestigious than a bank. With her new connections and experience, she could open her own secretarial agency someday. She'd have a business and income of her own and could help other women the way Wallis and Mrs. Bedaux had helped her. It was only a germ of an idea, and she had no idea how to make it a reality, but she'd figure it out and find a way to finally stand on her own two feet.

Chapter Eleven

Thanksgiving 1937

"I simply don't understand why, with all the grand homes around Paris, we can't find something suitable," Wallis whispered to Mrs. Bedaux. They sat together in the pew of the American Church during the Thanksgiving service. Amelia sat behind them, listening to Ambassador Bullitt's clear voice as he read a copy of President Roosevelt's Thanksgiving address.

"'I, Franklin D. Roosevelt, President of the United States of America, hereby designate Thursday, the twenty-fifth day of November 1937, as a day of national thanksgiving. The custom of observing a day of public thanksgiving began in Colonial times and has been given the sanction of national observance through many years. It is in keeping with all of our traditions that we, even as our fathers in olden days, give humble and hearty thanks for the bounty and the goodness of Divine Providence.'"

Amelia's eyes misted with tears. The proclamation wasn't as moving as the memory of the last Thanksgiving before Father had died. He had sat at one end of the long oak table in their Baltimore house carving the turkey while Mother had sat at the other chatting with the friends and relatives seated between them. Amelia couldn't remember everyone who'd been there, but she remembered who'd attended Father's funeral. The church for his service had looked like this one, with its massive wood and pipe organ behind the altar, the gothic marble arches, and the tall stained glass windows.

Amelia hadn't enjoyed another happy Thanksgiving until her first with Jackson. Her turkey had been a dry disaster but he'd eaten it, pretending to enjoy it. They'd cuddled in front of the fireplace afterward, discussing how to decorate the house for Christmas and hoping there'd be a baby by next year. Nothing had come of their nights together. Aunt Bessie had said it was for the best. Amelia couldn't care for a child and rebuild her life, but to have had one wonderful thing come out of that mess would've made her sacrifice to be with Jackson worth it. In the end, it had all been illusions and dreams.

Amelia touched her gloved finger to her eye to catch the tear before it fell. A white handkerchief appeared over her shoulder and she turned to see Mr. Morton leaning forward from the pew behind her. She smiled gratefully as she took his handkerchief. He settled back in his seat and she faced the altar, thankful someone had seen her pain.

"'The harvests of our fields have been abundant and many men and women have been given the blessing of stable employment,'" Ambassador Bullitt continued. "'A period unhappily marked in many parts of the world by strife and threat of war finds our people enjoying the blessing of peace. We have no selfish designs against other nations.'"

"I don't intend for us to remain in exile or live like snails for the rest of our lives," Wallis whispered to Mrs. Bedaux. "David wants to return to Fort Belvedere but we've been ordered not to darken dear Britain's shores unless invited by the King. He and the Fat Scottish Cook are terrified David will come back and upset that milquetoast king's so-called popularity. If he's so popular, why is he worried about us?"

"A friend of ours in the South of France has a lovely château he's looking to lease. It'd be perfect for you and His Royal Highness," Mrs. Bedaux said. "You could be in by Christmas."

"A winter house in the South of France sounds divine."

After the service, they mingled with other American expatriates on the sidewalk outside the church, the crush of guests giving Wallis and David some protection from the photographers and newsreel cameras across the street.

"Mrs. Montague, it's wonderful to see you again," Miss Harper said, pretty in her powder-blue dress with matching hat. "Is everything all right? You looked so sad in the church."

"All the talk of Thanksgiving made me a little homesick."

"I know the perfect cure for that. I'm having an old-fashioned Thanksgiving dinner at my place tonight and I'd love for you to come. There'll be nothing but Americans and it'll feel just like home, except for the cramped garret and the bad heating. Mr. Morton will be there."

"I will." Mr. Morton stepped up beside Miss Harper. It'd been months since Amelia had last seen him but the same thrill raced through her today as the morning he'd introduced himself at the Hotel Meurice. He wore a navy suit cut well across his wide shoulders, his dark blond hair a touch shorter than the last time she'd seen him.

"Thank you again for your handkerchief." She handed it back to him and his fingers brushed hers as he took it but she didn't pull away. She shouldn't be this electrified by him or think of him as anything more than another resource for her job, but she couldn't help it. He was still the most charming man she'd met in Europe.

"My pleasure." He tucked the silk in his breast pocket, politely ignoring the smudge of eye shadow on the corner.

"Tell me you'll come," Miss Harper insisted, forcing the two of them to look at someone besides each other. "Mr. Morton, tell her she must come."

"No one can refuse Miss Harper's Southern hospitality," Mr. Morton said with more than polite persuasion, "and I'd like to chat again. You've had quite the exciting time since we last had lunch."

"I have." He'd been keeping tabs on her. Surely his interest in her was purely political.

"Then say you'll be there," Miss Harper pleaded. She glanced at Mr. Morton with a little too much enthusiasm and Amelia wasn't sure if it was for the possibility of her joining them tonight or Mr. Morton. Amelia's stomach dropped. She shouldn't have let her imagination run wild, not when the two of them might be an item. Apparently, she'd learned nothing from the past three years. She was as bad as Wallis. "Pretty please?"

The old Amelia wanted to decline but this Amelia in her deep green velvet Nina Ricci dress with the matching picture hat couldn't stand the thought of spending Thanksgiving alone in her room. So what if Mr. Morton and Miss Harper were a couple? There were other men in Paris and some of them might be there tonight. This could be her chance to cultivate a few friends, a gentleman or two to escort her to the theater or the art galleries and cafés Mr. Morton had told her about the last time they'd met. With Wallis and the Duke going to dinner with their American friends, she'd be a little daring, meet new people, and put a little of what she'd learned from Wallis into action. "I'd love to join you."

MISS HARPER'S APARTMENT was in the rue du Conseiller Collingon in a quiet block of Haussmann buildings with their many windows, cream limestone walls, mansard slate roofs, and balconies protected by wrought-iron railings. A round-cheeked Frenchwoman let Amelia into number 21 and with bright talk and greetings directed Amelia to the curving staircase leading to the fourth floor. The old building had been divided into flats, the grandeur of better days concealed by dim lighting, chipped paint, and faded gilding. Amelia climbed the stairs, clutching the bottle of wine she'd brought as a gift but her steps slowed when she neared the top. All afternoon she'd debated backing out. If Mr. Morton knew about her past then everyone else here probably did too. She didn't relish an evening of whispers and sideways glances.

I'll be social and ignore anything bad anyone says. It's what Wallis would do and she'd darn well do it too.

All of Amelia's reservations vanished the second Miss Harper opened the front door. The scent of turkey, sage, and pumpkin pie hit her as strongly as the American music and the energy of the guests perched on the chairs and sofas. It'd been ages since she'd been around people her own age. She hadn't realized how much she'd missed it or how insulated her life with Wallis had become. She'd never been a grand socialite, but she'd had friends in Wellesley, at least until they'd learned about Jackson.

"Mrs. Montague, I'm so glad you could come." Miss Harper enveloped her in a hug that smelled of cinnamon and champagne.

"Call me Amelia. This is for you." She handed her the wine.

"I'm Susan. How kind of you to think of me." Susan passed the bottle to a young man in an evening jacket with a slender pipe balanced precariously between his lips. "Daniel, you're a wine man, see to this."

He read the label. "Château Haut-Brion. Impressive."

"Come on, I'll introduce you to everyone." Susan linked her arm in Amelia's and pulled her into a long, rectangular gallery with faded and scuffed parquet floors, elaborate white molding, and a graceful marble fireplace with a fire burning inside. The heat and cheer of the fire were matched by the chatting guests sprawled on mismatched French furniture with a few modern pieces sprinkled in. "Everyone, this is Amelia. Amelia, this is everyone."

The tuxedo-clad men, and the women in chic knockoff evening dresses, stopped talking and raised their glasses in a collective "Hello!"

"What department do you work in?" Daniel returned with a wineglass and the open wine bottle and poured Amelia a healthy serving.

"She doesn't work at the Embassy, she's the Duchess of Windsor's private secretary," Susan corrected, loud enough for everyone to hear.

He stopped pouring and there was a noticeable lull in the conversation. The old desire to run and hide hit Amelia but she held her ground, facing the silence with poise and grace.

"You raid the ex-king's wine cellar for this?" Daniel clinked his glass against hers and broke the spell.

"Something like that." Wallis had sent the wine with her because she didn't like the British aristocrat who'd given it to her. "I'll do it again if I'm ever invited back."

"Bring wine like this and you will be."

Susan batted a hand at him. "Ignore him. Daniel works in the press office, that's why he has no manners. You have to meet Lisa. She's in the visa department and can do wonders if you ever need travel documents."

"What's it like working for the Windsors?" Lisa asked as soon as Susan maneuvered Amelia to the empty place on the sofa beside her. "Is she a dear or a monster like the newspapers say?"

"Don't bother her about that," Susan chided. "You don't want to talk about your work. I'm sure she doesn't want to talk about hers."

"She's probably the only one who can talk about her job; the rest of us are sworn to secrecy." A tall man named Christopher dropped down on Amelia's other side.

"Are you kidding, her privacy clause is probably stiffer than ours." Lisa's tortoiseshell glasses slid down her nose and she pushed them back up.

"Is it?" Christopher asked.

"What do you think?"

"See." Lisa laughed. "I told you she has to keep more secrets than we do."

"Then stop trying to pry them out of her." Mr. Morton's voice carried over the crowd as he crossed the room in a few long, strong strides. He stopped in front of Amelia and Christopher, towering over them, his dark tuxedo making him appear even more impressive. He tilted into a bow and motioned for her hand. "Mrs. Montague?"

"Amelia." She slid her hand in his, enjoying his smooth skin and firm grasp.

"Robert." He squeezed her fingers before letting go, his gaze never leaving hers, and the entire room fell away. She could've sat like that all night but he flicked a glance at Christopher, who looked back and forth between them before jumping to his feet.

"I'll get another glass of wine. Can I get you one, Robert?"

"Thank you." Robert sat on the faded brocade beside Amelia, and she inhaled the light cedar scent of his aftershave. It smelled young and fresh, unlike the deeper sandalwood scents of the Duke and his friends.

"That's quite a party trick. Forcing a man from his seat with little more than a look."

"I didn't force him to do anything. He got up of his own free will." He flashed a devilish smile that made Amelia's toes curl in her patent leather pumps and she wondered if it was the look or the wine making her head fuzzy. "How was Germany?"

"Eye-opening, even if I didn't see much. The Germans don't like visitors poking around unaccompanied."

"I don't suppose they do."

"You must see loads of famous people at the Hotel Meurice. Isn't Marlene Dietrich there?" Lisa gushed, her sheath dress with the halter top similar to one Amelia had purchased from Susan's seamstress.

"She is, and she's as beautiful in person as she is on-screen." Amelia indulged in this little indiscretion, remembering Wallis's dictate that dinner guests have a moral obligation to be entertaining.

She and Lisa continued to exchange stories about the Hollywood stars they'd seen in Paris before talking about Lisa's prior posting in Mexico. While they chatted, Amelia waited for Robert to politely excuse himself and work his way around the room to Susan but he remained beside her. If he and Susan were a couple, he wasn't eager to be with her. Perhaps they were being discreet in front of their colleagues or maybe there was nothing to whisper about. It shouldn't matter to Amelia one way or the other but the longer he sat with his leg pressed against hers, his breath whispering delicately across her exposed neck beneath her upswept hair, the more it did.

"Dinner is served," Susan announced, and everyone rose and made for the dining room with the faded and scratched Louis XIV table surrounded by mismatched chairs. Fine china, stemware, and a matched silver service were expertly laid on a linen tablecloth that would impress even Wallis. "Amelia, you're over here."

Susan led her to a cane chair and she was about to sit down when Robert stepped up and held it out for her. "Allow me."

"Thank you." Amelia draped the fine linen napkin over her lap. "This is quite a table setting."

"Don't let her fool you, none of this is hers." Lisa laughed. "She's friends with the staff of everyone who's anyone and they let her borrow their china and crystal."

"Guilty," Susan said without shame as she passed a bowl of mashed potatoes. "The ambassador's cook is such a dear. He offered to whip up a little extra for me while he was preparing the Ambassador's dinner. All I had to do was pick it up."

"She has a knack for making connections," Robert said, serving Amelia from the platter of turkey.

"I'll keep that in mind." It was a talent Amelia herself was developing as she got to know the staff of Wallis's friends. She'd add more people to her list of acquaintances tonight.

The turkey, stuffing, and green beans, cooked to perfection, didn't stop the steady flow of conversation about prior overseas postings and the quirkier aspects of their jobs. During the taxi ride here, Amelia had worried about being different from Susan's friends, but the more they talked, the more she realized she wasn't so different from them, at least not where her work was concerned.

When the pumpkin pie was sent around, the discussion finally wandered to politics.

"I predict Herr Hitler will roll over Austria in the next few months," Daniel said.

"It would set off an international crisis," Lisa said.

"He's ridiculous but not foolish enough to start a war, not with the French and British ready to lick the Germans the way they did in the Great War," Christopher insisted, and a number of people nodded in agreement.

"Amelia, you were in Germany. What do you think?" Susan asked, drawing everyone's attention to her.

The old urge to mumble something innocuous and fade into the woodwork caught the words in her throat before she sat up straight. They'd asked for her opinion. Given her position and experience, she was as qualified as they were to share it. "Germany will annex Austria. I can't say when, but I'm sure it'll happen. Frau Goering mentioned it and there was a map at Ordensburg with Germany and Austria combined. I don't know if they're planning more but all those factories and soldier schools the Duke toured aren't for nothing."

"That certainly puts a grave spin on things." Daniel exchanged concerned glances with Christopher. Amelia's firsthand observations of Germany's ambitions, and what they might mean for everyone at the table and Europe's future, hung as heavy in the air as the cinnamon.

"Let's go back to the gallery. I still have oodles of champagne you have to drink up," Susan encouraged, reviving the holiday cheer.

"I hope I didn't bring everyone down," Amelia said to Robert as he pulled out her chair.

"You didn't. They already suspect it from the daily reports. It's just rare to hear it blatantly confirmed. Would you like to step out on the balcony?"

He offered her his elbow and Amelia slid her hand in the crook of his arm. Something primal rose up inside of her at the feel of his muscles beneath her fingertips as he escorted her through the glass doors and onto the narrow balcony.

She let go of him and stepped up to the wrought-iron railing, needing the fall air to cool her skin and a little space from Robert so she could breathe and think straight. The city was beautiful under the stars. The lighted windows in the buildings glowed in the semidarkness, and the tip of the Eiffel Tower was just visible over the slate roof of the apartments across the way.

Robert joined her at the railing and she resisted the urge to lean into him. "Where are the Windsors tonight?"

"La Restaurant de la Tour Eiffel. Lady Mendl is hosting the party and Wallis heard a rumor that Rose Kennedy might be there. She's desperate to have Mrs. Kennedy to dinner but she's declined every invitation."

“I’ll tell you why if you can keep a secret.” He brought his face down close to hers so she could see the flecks of gold in his blue eyes in the soft light spilling out from inside.

Amelia cocked her head at him, doing her best to remain levelheaded. “I work for the Windsors.”

Robert chuckled at her frank answer. “Ambassador Kennedy told Ambassador Bullitt he won’t let Mrs. Kennedy dine with the Duchess because”—he changed his voice to mimic Ambassador Kennedy’s Massachusetts accent—“‘my position doesn’t obligate my wife to dine with a tart.’”

Amelia burst out laughing. “That’s awful but it’s a riot. Who told you that?”

“I never reveal my sources.”

“Then I can trust you with my secrets?” She adjusted the wide strap of her deep burgundy velvet evening gown with the gold trim along the scooped neck, noting the flick of his glance to her chest before he met her eyes again.

“You shouldn’t trust anyone in Europe.” He slid her a sly smile and she trilled her fingers on the railing, enjoying this flirting even if she shouldn’t. There was danger in the rich tones of his voice and their easy conversation, and how wonderful it was to speak to someone without all the curtseys and *sirs* and everything else.

“Do you trust Susan?” She surprised herself as much as him with that question, but she had to know before she got too carried away.

“We’re simply friends. She has a fiancé in medical school in Georgia, so while he’s there, she’s here getting a Parisian polish.

She's having too much fun to leave but she'll have to go home if war breaks out. Most of us will. It won't be safe to stay."

"Hopefully, it won't come." The brisk fall air whipped up the wide avenue of similarly styled buildings and made her shiver. She wanted more time to make friends, to enjoy nights like this where she felt she belonged and no one judged her. It was something she hadn't experienced in a long time. "Europe suffered so much from the last war. It's awful to think it could happen again."

"Then let's hope for the best." He laid his arm over her shoulders and drew her into the warm curve of his body. He was a foot taller than her and she fit perfectly against him. She shouldn't be this close to him but it felt so comfortable she couldn't pull away. "I understand the Windsors are going to the South of France for Christmas."

"How did you . . . Oh, that's right, it's your job to know what's going on."

"It is." He didn't apologize for it. There was a lesson. She should never apologize for what she did or who she worked for either.

"We'll be there well into the new year."

"That's too bad." He drew her against his wide chest and as he pressed his lips to hers she forgot everything except the strength of his embrace. As a widow, she knew what she was missing, a warm body against hers, the nighttime pleasures of caresses and kisses. She might live a sheltered life right now but it didn't mean she wanted to become a nun. She was tempted to lead him into a dark and quiet corner and forget about tomorrow or next week and follow this passion wherever it led, but she knew better than to toss consequences to the wind. There were only so many second chances a woman could expect. She couldn't ruin this one by losing her head again over a man she barely knew.

"I'm sorry, I shouldn't." She stepped out of his arms, missing the heat of him the moment the chill bit her exposed shoulders. "I, well, it's been quite a year, quite the last few years."

"Don't apologize for being cautious. I know what it's like to be burned." He rested his elbows on the railing and peered at the bright city. "My last year of college, I was engaged to a girl I'd known for years. I thought I had it all figured out, graduation, marriage, a position with a congressman in Washington, D.C. It was perfect, until six weeks before the wedding when she told me she didn't love me, she never had. I was simply an old friend. She married a fellow classmate a month later. It's how I ended up in Europe. I wanted to get as far away from her and everything that might have been as possible."

"I know the feeling." Through a window across the street, Amelia watched a family sit down to dinner. The happy scene tugged at her heart. "I'm sorry you had to go through that."

"In the end, it was for the best. If she hadn't broken it off, we might have been miserable and I wouldn't have come to Paris or met the Duchess of Windsor's secretary."

"A dubious honor, I'm sure." She studied him, wondering if someday she'd thank Jackson for having ripped the scales from her eyes, and be glad for what he'd done because of where it had led her. She hoped so.

"Don't sell yourself short. You have a great deal to offer anyone who's smart enough to see it, but you have to appreciate it first."

She nearly said that wasn't true then closed her mouth, taking Wallis's advice not to argue with a compliment. "Thank you for your confidence in me."

"Don't thank me. I'm buttering you up so you'll meet me for breakfast at Café Capucines. I can't manage a week of work without at least one café Viennese and croissant."

"I'd love to join you. Perhaps we can make it a regular event?"

"I think that can be arranged."

Chapter Twelve

Paris, March 1938

Germany Invades Austria! the *Daily News* headline proclaimed from the corner newsstand rack. The London paper hadn't arrived with the morning post and Amelia had walked here to buy it and take a break from the flurry of activity at Boulevard Suchet. The crowd of workmen and movers there was nothing compared to the people nervously reading the reports here.

A nearby church bell rang and Amelia tucked the newspaper under her arm and hurried down the street, oblivious to anything but the awful news, when a familiar voice stopped her.

"Amelia?"

She turned to face the man, hoping she was wrong about who it was but she wasn't. "Theodore?"

"I thought it was you." Theodore Miller examined her from head to toe, taking note of her gray suit and silk shirt. It was one of the suits she'd had run up from a bolt of fine Bucol wool. After a lifetime in the garment and clothing manufacturing industry, her stepfather could spot quality fabric from a mile away.

"What are you doing in Paris?" It was the last place she'd expected to see him. He hadn't dealt with European markets or manufacturers when she'd known him.

"The threat of war is making the smart businesses stock up, and they're looking for suppliers from everywhere. I don't need to ask why you're here." He sneered at her as he had the one time they'd met after her marriage. "I'm not surprised you've thrown your lot in with Wallis. You were always a terrible judge of character."

"Just like my mother."

That wiped the sneer off his flat face. "She had the good sense to protect her reputation and honor while you've done everything you can to throw yours away."

"How dare you thumb your nose at me when you pay your workers a pittance to slave away in your horrible sweatshops. I read about the strikes at your factories."

"Yes, the Windsors are quite the crusaders for laborers, aren't they? I bet they haven't given the working man a second thought since they left Herr Hitler."

She couldn't argue with that. The Duke had forgotten about the working poor the moment the American tour had been canceled. He'd returned to Paris and fallen into his old habits of golfing and following Wallis around while she shopped.

However, she wasn't going to crumble under that bit of truth. "You helped cancel the American trip, didn't you?"

"It wasn't just me." Theodore straightened his tie. "The New York Clothing Manufacturers' Exchange didn't want the Windsors ginning up workers with their champagne socialism. Besides, the idea of that awful woman meeting the president is as sickening as you having no shame in working for her."

"She stood by me when you and everyone else wouldn't give me the time of day."

"A woman with that much scandal hasn't got anyone else to stand beside except a fellow guttersnipe. Tell me, was Jackson worth throwing it all away for?"

Theodore wanted her to admit he'd been right but she wouldn't give him the satisfaction. "If by *it all* you mean my oh so caring and attentive mother and your sad respect, then yes, it was worth it."

"You poor fool. If you think Wallis is going to stick by you then you have another thing coming. She's betrayed or driven away everyone who's ever tried to help her, including your mother and most of her old Washington, D.C., friends. Someday, when it suits her, she'll discard you too, like a wilted bunch of roses. Mark my words, she doesn't care about anyone but herself, her social standing, and money, and you have none of that."

"I don't have to listen to this." She whirled to leave but he dashed around her, blocking the way, just as he'd done in his office the morning she'd said she'd marry Jackson with or without his permission.

"Degrade yourself as much as you want but be discreet about it for once. I won't have you dragging my family name in the mud along with your own."

"You abandoned me when I needed my family the most. Don't think for a moment I'll worry about how anything I do reflects on you." She stepped around him and hurried away.

"You'll regret this. Wallis will ruin you the way she ruined the King," he yelled.

She didn't look back but kept walking until she reached Boulevard Suchet. She leaned against one of the large trees dotting the sidewalk, struggling to see through the tears stinging her eyes.

He's wrong about Wallis. He didn't know her like she did. Wallis had been there for her when others hadn't, and she'd taught her more in the past few months, given her more confidence and hope in the future and herself, in a year than Mother had in a decade. Theodore simply hated her for the same reason he hated Amelia: because she hadn't followed his or society's rules. Instead, Wallis had done what she'd needed to do to survive, they both had, and made something of herself despite all of his dire warnings. She'd looked at his and society's scorn and thrown it right back in their faces and he despised her for it.

A matronly woman with gray-streaked brown hair stopped and looked at the newspaper clutched in Amelia's hands and the tears staining her cheeks.

"It's awful, isn't it? I lost my brother in the last war. I might lose my son if Germany starts another one." The woman pressed a handkerchief to her face and hurried off.

Amelia dried her eyes, selfish for crying over someone who no longer mattered while Europe stood on the brink of war. It would change everything, including the life she was working so hard to build for herself.

She tucked the handkerchief in her purse and walked to 24 Boulevard Suchet. On the narrow lawn between the high iron fence and the square house stood a mess of packing crates, furniture wrapped in blankets, and small boxes. Workmen in coveralls unloaded crates from the three trucks parked outside the fence, arranging them on the grass under the watchful eye of Monsieur Hardeley, the house's caretaker, and Mr. Carter, the clerk tasked with bringing them safely to France from where they'd been stored in England.

Detto, Pookie, and Prisie ran around sniffing the crates, and Detto lifted his leg on the side of one.

"Don't you dare, you little gangster," the Duke scolded Detto while he dug through the hay and newspapers to get at what was inside.

"David, stop making a mess," Wallis commanded from the front doorway.

"It's my Garter Banner. Isn't it marvelous?" He shook out a rolled flag of gold, blue, and royal lions and held it up.

"It'd be more marvelous hanging in St. George's Chapel, where it belongs. I don't know why you shipped all this over from England. Where do you think it's going to go? The house is furnished."

The Duke kicked at a bit of hay at his feet. "I'm sorry, darling, only it's been so long since I've seen everything."

"You could've lived with it every day if you hadn't abdicated." Wallis stalked back into the house, leaving David to pout among his boxes of treasure.

Amelia exchanged a strained glance with Monsieur Hardeley, who quickly shuffled off to see to his other duties.

"Your Royal Highness, have you heard the news about Austria?" Amelia showed the Duke the newspaper.

He read the headline while tugging at the knot in his tie. "Dreadful, but it isn't all bad. Herr Hitler will whip the Austrian economy into shape the way he did Germany's. You there, careful with that painting, it's from the reign of Charles the First." He leapt toward two men carrying a portrait of a baby into the house.

Amelia went inside to find Wallis. She walked through the marbled foyer and paused at the center table to flip through the Fendi guest book laid out on top. The Duke liked to display it everywhere they lived, and had everyone who visited write their names in it, making sure they saw the other famous and important people who'd signed it before. It made him feel important, as though he was still someone of note, especially since he had no real business or official duties to fill his days. She closed the book and made for the stairs, passing the caryatid candelabras flanking the doorway and the Louis XVI sunburst clock before climbing the curving staircase leading to the second floor and Wallis's study.

"The Germans invaded Austria," Amelia announced when she stepped inside.

"I know." Wallis slid some papers into the top drawer of the antique cashier's desk with the high, curved sides and locked it with a small key she dropped in her Chanel jacket pocket. "It's why I wish David hadn't dragged all his knick-knacks here. It's bad enough he hauls the abdication desk around with us like some old skin. He should break it up for firewood. Everything else would be safer in England, and one less thing for me to worry about if it all goes south, but he never thinks about anything so practical, it's always left to me to manage."

"Hopefully, we won't have to move in a hurry."

Wallis looked at her as if she didn't believe it any more than Amelia did. "Your optimism is one of the things I adore about you. I was an optimist once. Life put me off it. Is there any uplifting news in the morning post?"

"Mr. Maugham sent you something." She handed Wallis the package.

"Another book of his. I could barely make it through the last one." She tore off the brown paper to reveal a copy of *Theatre*, then handed it to Amelia. "You read it for me, choose a notable quote, then type it out for me to memorize. It's an old trick I learned years ago when dealing with authors. Commit to memory a line or two then repeat it back to them with glowing praise. It flatters them every time, and saves me a great deal of boredom."

"Yes, ma'am." Amelia didn't mention she'd read all of Mr. Maugham's works after meeting the famous author at his New Year's Eve party in the South of France. They'd sat on the balcony of his villa and enjoyed a rousing conversation about *Of Human Bondage*. Since returning to Paris, she'd purchased the rest of his novels from the booksellers' carts along the Seine. She looked forward to talking with him again when they ventured to Château de la Croë this summer. There was no point discussing books with Wallis. Except for detective novels, neither she nor the Duke bothered with reading. He had few interests beyond golf and making Wallis happy.

Mr. Hale knocked and entered. "Your Royal Highness, Herr von Ribbentrop is here to see you."

"Show him in." She rose and stood in the middle of the room to greet him.

The German foreign minister didn't throw the Nazi salute but clicked his boots together and bowed to Wallis then handed her a bottle of champagne. "A housewarming gift, one of the finest my company has to offer."

"How thoughtful of you." Wallis admired the bottle then handed it to Amelia. "That's all, Mrs. Montague."

"Yes, ma'am." Amelia curtseyed then left, noting Wallis hadn't asked her or Mr. Hale to fetch the Duke to help her welcome their guest.

Amelia went downstairs to the small room near the back of the house. From her desk, she had a fine view of the garden. The perfectly manicured boxwood trees and the red roses didn't distract her today. Theodore's accusations did. She tried to focus on the back wages owed to yet another fired maid but she couldn't concentrate on anything except the slim chance Theodore might be right. He'd recognized Jackson for the snake he'd been while she'd been too infatuated and naive to notice. That he might see some fatal flaw in Wallis that Amelia missed made her chest constrict as much as the new letter from her Boston attorney.

Chapter Thirteen

April 1938

The prosecution is asking me to voluntarily return to the United States to answer questions for the suit about Jackson's involvement in looting that trust. I told them everything I knew at Jackson's trial, and it wasn't much back then. Jackson never discussed business with me. I can't afford passage home or the time away from work and I don't want to ask Wallis for the money."

"Does she know about this?" Robert read the letter from across the Café Capucines table, the remains of a croissant littering his plate.

He'd made time to meet her this morning after she'd called him yesterday in desperate need of his levelheaded advice. Ever since she'd returned from the South of France, they'd enjoyed croissants and coffee together every couple of weeks, careful not to cross the line between friendship and affection. She wasn't ready to risk her heart or her position in France, and thankfully, he hadn't pressed for more. Even if she'd wanted to start something, her schedule and his didn't allow for much free time, so they met when they could to share stories of their pasts or their experiences in Europe and what little they could reveal about their jobs.

"She knows what Jackson did and my lack of money, it's part of why she hired me, but she doesn't know about the outstanding legal fees or this new suit. What'll she think when she finds out I'm in debt up to my eyeballs and involved in a major lawsuit?"

"Do you think she'll fire you?"

"She knows what it's like to have legal troubles, especially after her divorce, but between the three maids she's sacked and her foul mood lately, I don't want to chance it." She shouldn't doubt Wallis, but after the run-in with Theodore, she'd be lying if she said she wasn't concerned. Wallis did have a tendency to burn as many bridges as she built but it wasn't always her fault. Mrs. Gordon had spread vile lies about her and forced her to abandon the life she'd tried to build in D.C. Amelia didn't know what had happened between Wallis and Mother but knowing Mother, she was sure Wallis had been right to walk away from her. Amelia should trust in Wallis and tell her about the suit and her debts but she couldn't. Even confiding in Robert felt like a terrible risk but she had no choice. She couldn't afford to lose her job and leave Europe. "Is there anyone you know who can help?"

"Mr. Carlton in the Embassy legal department might be able to do something. Can I show this to him?"

"Please, but it has to be soon. Word came down from Buck House for the Windsors to make themselves scarce during the King and Queen's Paris visit, so off to the South of France we go."

"I'll do what I can, but I think you should come clean with your cousin in case there's nothing Mr. Carlton can do. Better she finds out from you instead of someone else or when it's a crisis and you have to spring it on her." He flashed the charming smile she'd come to enjoy over the past few weeks. "Don't worry. I'm sure it will all turn out better than you expect."

"When you say it like that, I can almost believe it."

BREAKFAST DIDN'T SIT well with Amelia while she and Wallis inspected the baroque tables the antiques dealer had sent over for her selection.

"This one's too large for the foyer. This one's too small." Wallis touched the tops of the tables and Amelia made a note to add them to the list of the ones going back. Wallis stopped in front of a gilded table with a marble top. "This is perfect. How much are they asking?"

Amelia checked the list. "Five thousand francs."

"Offer them three thousand."

Wallis and the Duke bought so many things for Boulevard Suchet and Château de la Croë, the antiques dealers weren't likely to refuse and risk losing one of their most lucrative and notable clients.

"Let's look at the side tables. I hope this lot is better than the last. I'm decorating the house like Versailles, not a New Orleans bordello."

"Before we do, there's something I need to discuss with you." Amelia opened and closed her fingers on her notepad. As much as Amelia didn't want to bring it up, this might be as good a time as any before the stress of moving to Château de la Croë began. "It's about my business in America. I know Aunt Bessie told you some of it."

"She said you were in need of a paying position, and was kind enough to remind me I was once young and without a husband or income. It's awful, and naturally I wanted to help. Is there something more?"

"There is." Amelia took a deep breath and told her about the outstanding legal fees, the new court case, and the letter requesting her appearance for a deposition. With every word, she waited for Wallis to erupt in rage and banish her from the house. She'd almost prefer that to the composed woman listening to her as if she were explaining the carpenters' fees.

"Aunt Bessie didn't tell me things were quite so dire."

"I'm paying down the bill with my earnings, but if I have to return to America, it means I'll be away." She didn't have the courage to mention she might need to borrow money for the fare. She was too busy trying to read Wallis's reaction, to determine if this was the end of her employment or if things would simply carry on as usual.

"Why didn't you tell me this before?"

"Between the press, the title, the wedding, and Germany, I didn't want to bother you with my troubles too." She didn't dare say she'd been afraid of being shipped off on the first boat to America if Wallis thought Amelia and her debts weren't worth the risk. She should have had more faith in her cousin but after all the people who'd already abandoned or betrayed her, it was hard to trust even her.

"I hate to pry into your affairs, but how much do you owe?"

"Four thousand dollars."

"Good heavens." Wallis laid a hand on her chest, her engagement ring clinking against the jeweled flamingo brooch on the lapel of her blue suit with the yellow belt. "You'll never pay it off on your salary."

"I know." It hung over her like a sword every time she wired half her pay to America while her savings stagnated and her future dwindled under the debt. "I've paid off some of it but this new suit threatens to raise it again."

"You should have come to me sooner."

"I've been fighting everything alone for so long, it's hard to ask for help. I always think I can figure it out on my own."

"Not anymore. I want to help you, the way you've helped me. You deserve it for putting up with me. I'll discuss it with David. There has to be something we can do to ease the burden that bastard husband left you with."

"Please don't. It's my problem to deal with. You don't need to get involved."

"Nonsense, and if you're ever in trouble again, I want you to tell me at once."

"I will." *Theodore was wrong. I can count on Wallis and I should have trusted her.* Wallis had understood and was going to help her. She had no idea what Wallis or the Duke could do, but if they could get discounts on antiques and hotels, perhaps the power of their names and titles might work some miracle on her behalf.

"Good. A woman must make her own life, and I'd hate for you to be like me, past forty and finally finding it after too many difficulties and disappointments. Despite everything I've been through, I've never gone under, even when people tried to push me, and you won't either. We'll put our heads together and come up with some respectable method for you to make your way in this world."

"I did have one idea. I've thought of opening my own secretarial agency and placing young women in good positions with society ladies."

"What a wonderful idea, especially with all the old biddies in Europe. Finding employers will be like shooting fish in a barrel and give good women somewhere more illustrious to work than an insurance agent's office." A determined fire lit Wallis's eyes and it caught hold inside Amelia.

"I hope so."

"Hope will get you nowhere. Doing something will. I'll speak with my friends and put the word out. We'll build a list of potential employers and have you set up in no time. Not too soon, of course, because I'd be lost without you. Now, let's get back to these tables before the Duke and I have to leave for the races. I need time to decide which broach and bracelet I'm going to wear with my new cream suit."

Amelia followed her around the rest of the antiques, almost too giddy to concentrate on what was going or staying. If Wallis helped Amelia with the same determination she employed when tracking down the perfect foyer table, Amelia would soon be one step closer to building a life and future of her own.

July 1938, Château de la Croë, South of France

Amelia dug through the morning post, stopping at a letter from Robert. She usually left personal correspondence to the end of the day but she couldn't resist opening his. They'd been writing to each other ever since she'd left Paris, their conversations in the post similar to the ones they'd enjoyed over coffee. He told her about the goings-on at the Embassy and she told him about dining with Maurice Chevalier and Marlene Dietrich and antique hunting with Wallis in Nice. This time, his letter wasn't full of gossip but the news that Mr. Carlton, the Embassy attorney, had arranged for Amelia to respond in writing to the prosecutor's questions instead of appearing in America. The Embassy attorney had also argued against her being included in the suit but the prosecutor hadn't made a decision yet. It left Amelia with some hope that at least one of her problems might soon be resolved. She had no idea how to thank him but she knew where to start.

She picked up the telephone and dialed the Chancery. "Susan, it's Amelia. I'm sending something special to Robert and Mr. Carlton. Can you make sure they're delivered to their offices the minute they arrive?"

"Sure thing. Are they expensive?"

"Yes, but the salesman always gives me a discount because of how much Windsor business I send his way."

"I told you that'd win him over. Can you get me a box of those exquisite chocolates you sent to Lisa from that little chocolatier, and at a discount?"

"I'll ring them as soon as we're off."

"Thanks, you're a gem."

Amelia called the chocolatier, and once that was done, gathered up the recent invitations and her notepad and left the small gatehouse where she and Mr. Forwood worked. There wasn't enough room inside the château for her and him to have an office. Amelia enjoyed the short walk with the stunning view of the ocean between the tall pines. The Duke's yellow and black Duchy of Cornwall flag fluttered in the breeze on the flagpole at the top of the château. Amelia waved to him where he stood on his study balcony watching the yachts sail past Cap d'Antibes. He'd decorated the study to resemble a boat and christened it the *Belvedere* after his beloved home in England, the one he hadn't seen in two years and wasn't likely to visit anytime soon. Decorating it had amused him for a good part of the summer, giving Wallis a much-needed break from his cloying attention.

Amelia walked into the château and nodded to the footmen in their light gray summer uniforms. The Duke had designed the footmen's attire, with light wool for summer and red wool with gold collars, cuffs, and buttons for the winter. More than one person had remarked on their similarity to the Buckingham Palace footmen's uniforms, including the tailor Amelia had hired to sew them. Amelia stopped at the dining room door and looked at the painting of the Duke as a young man riding a horse. Beneath it stood the mahogany abdication desk with the red morocco-leather dispatch box on top.

The Duke's past had as much hold over him as Wallis's and Amelia's did over them.

Amelia continued through the house and out onto the back terrace. Wallis lounged in one of the wicker chairs, reading a Paris newspaper and shielded from the sun by curtains and a tall, rounded colonnade. It was hot but not miserably so and without the humidity that used to make Baltimore summers unbearable.

"The French are embarrassing themselves by fawning all over the Fat Scottish Cook. The way they're carrying on, you'd think no one had ever worn white before." Wallis handed Amelia the newspaper and motioned to a nearby wicker chair. Amelia looked at the pictures of the King and Queen at the Élysée Palace with President Lebrun. The Queen, dressed in white for mourning for her recently deceased mother, appeared chic in her long dress and coat. The article was in raptures over her and her fashionable new wardrobe.

"Imagine her getting all the attention while I'm banished here." Wallis stroked Pookie, who lay draped over her lap.

"It isn't too shabby a place for a banishment." The bright blue Mediterranean sparkled in the distance and Amelia could hear the waves crashing against the cliffs and the small bathing area at the end of the long walk. Wallis wore her Nile-green swimsuit with a white and red polka-dotted wrap skirt and a matching hair scarf.

"It isn't Buckingham Palace either. Oh, I can dress it up to the nines and everyone who stomps through here curtseys and calls me Your Royal Highness, but I'm not a queen."

"Do you want to be one?"

"Of course not, but after the support I've given the French fashion industry, you'd think they'd fete me with a state visit. Oh, they put me on the best-dressed lists and flatter me when they want my business, but I'll never be more than an ex-king's wife." Wallis lowered her white-rimmed sunglasses over her eyes and continued to pet Pookie. A quiet moment passed with the seagulls calling to one another from the beach before Wallis spoke again. "Sometimes, I wish Herr Hitler would start a war and bomb Britain into oblivion. I'd love to see the fat queen and her imbecile husband knocked off their gilded thrones the way they pushed David off of his, the two of them forced to wander in ignominious exile. If I thought there was some way I could make it happen, I'd do it."

"You don't really mean that. War would be awful."

"I know, I'm simply tired of people like Sir Walter telling us where we can and cannot go and kicking around Europe like the rest of the useless aristocrats. You can't throw a stone without hitting one." Wallis settled back against the chaise and stared at the ocean. "I really thought I was someone when David first noticed me. I knew what I was doing was wrong, especially to Ernest, and Aunt Bessie told me enough times, but after years of being nobody, I had respect, influential friends, everything it meant to be the woman behind the King. Then it all went to hell in a handbasket." A seagull glided over the long lawn leading down to the ocean before flying out to sea. "Enough bellyaching. What's on the agenda for today?"

Amelia went over the daily business, most of which involved the soon-to-be-arriving furniture from Wallis's last excursion to the Nice antique shops. "I also have news about my American legal case. The attorneys have agreed for me to give evidence via letter instead of traveling to America."

"That is good news. Better news would be you not being involved at all."

Amelia stiffened at the snarky tone Wallis usually reserved for the Duke when she chipped at him about the abdication. It ruffled Amelia's feathers but she'd mastered rule number five, to never look churlish, and held her bright smile. "Mr. Carlton is hopeful they'll drop me from the suit once they see there's nothing to get from me."

"Good." She set Pookie on the ground and he trotted into the house. "Speaking of money, how'd you like to do some work for Syrie Maugham while David and I are on our cruise? Her regular secretary is off nursing a sick mother and since you won't have much else to do while we're gone, you can assist her and make a little something on the side. Katherine Rogers needs you too."

"I'd be glad to help them." Both the Maughams and the Rogerses lived nearby so she wouldn't have to travel far. She could use the extra money, experience, and connections and it meant Wallis was keeping good on her promise to help her.

Wallis swung her feet down onto the marble. "Then I'll phone them this afternoon."

AMELIA SPENT THE rest of the summer dividing her time among Wallis, Syrie Maugham, and Katherine Rogers. Amelia assisted Syrie with her husband's fan mail and book schedules and helped Katherine organize the aid station she and her husband ran for poor farmers. The women had very different styles, with Syrie and Katherine far more relaxed than Wallis, but they both appreciated the order Amelia brought to their endeavors and were generous with payments and tips at the end of Amelia's service. Being at the Maughams' villa also gave Amelia the chance to use the many passages from Mr. Maugham's works that she'd memorized for Wallis.

The summer wasn't all work and flattering writers' egos. There were walks along the Saint-Tropez seaside, visits to the Monte Carlo casinos, and free afternoons swimming in the pool or the sea. During a shopping trip in Nice, Amelia found an antique silver tie tack with *bonne chance* engraved on it. She sent it to Robert to wish him luck during his travel with Ambassador Bullitt to Italy to join Prime Minister Chamberlain in trying to woo Il Duce away from Herr Hitler. She missed his regular letters but hoped the statesmen were successful in weakening Germany's growing influence. Ending the threat of war would mean ending the threat to her time in Europe with Wallis and Robert and her new life.

Toward the end of summer, when most of the trunks had been sent ahead to Boulevard Suchet and their tickets on the Blue Train to Paris were booked, they spent an afternoon aboard the Rogerses' yacht *Gulzar.* Amelia sat in the back soaking in the late afternoon sun, deepening the tan that'd browned her Paris pallor. The subtle vibration from the schooner's motor radiated through her and the sea spray sprinkled her exposed arms and legs and dotted her sunglasses. At midship, the Rogerses lounged with their guests beneath a large canopy. The Duke stood behind the bar mixing the Wallis cocktail, going through generous amounts of Cointreau, peppermint, gin, soda, and lemon juice while jaunty French tunes drifted out of the wireless. Across the water, the white walls of Château de la Croë were just visible above the cliff.

Wallis stepped out of the shade of the awning and the wind caught the hem of her blue and green agate-patterned dress. She staggered with the gentle roll of the yacht and grasped the back railing to steady herself as she came to sit in the deck chair beside Amelia. "Glorious day, isn't it?"

"I hate to leave it." Amelia's tan would fade in Paris, and the days were already getting shorter, but she was eager to see Robert again.

"Me too, but I have something to make your Paris return a little sweeter." She slid a letter out of her dress pocket and handed it to Amelia.

Amelia held the letter tight to keep it from blowing away. It was from her American lawyer but addressed to Wallis. She had no idea why he was writing to her or how she'd failed to see it in the post. She opened and read it, unable to believe it. "You paid my legal debts!"

"We negotiated down the bill in return for payment in full. In the future, if anything else arises, you'll speak with Lord Jowitt, the Duke's solicitor. He's already on retainer and won't cost you a penny."

"This is too much. I can't accept it. I'll pay you back, I will."

"Don't even think about it. It's a gift. I want to help you." Wallis clasped Amelia's hand, forgetting their pact to be formal in front of others. "You've been like a daughter to me, someone to share my strange and hard-won knowledge with, and you've used it well. I'm so pleased with how confident and capable you've become." Wallis beamed at her with the same pride she'd shown at Amelia's Oldfields graduation when she'd welcomed her as a fellow alumnus. It meant more to Amelia than the paid debts. "I can't protect you from heartache or loneliness but I can help give you financial security and perhaps keep you from making a mess of your life the way I did."

"It all turned out in the end."

"It could have been better, but I was so chummy with uncertainty, I almost preferred it to security, the thrill of it, at least, and I practically ran after it. I don't want you to develop the same bad habit. You're too good for that and the likes of me, and I adore you more than you realize."

Amelia threw her arms around Wallis, saying with her embrace what she couldn't put into words. Wallis didn't jerk away, but wrapped her thin arms around Amelia and rubbed her back the way Aunt Bessie used to do. Amelia held on tight to her cousin, inhaling the fruity notes of her Teo Cabanel perfume, touched to know how much she really meant to Wallis. "I don't know how I'll ever repay you for everything you've done for me."

Wallis sat back and held Amelia at arm's length, her blue eyes sparkling with the same unshed tears stinging Amelia's. "You can start by finding someone to replace Mr. Schafranek. Hiring a new chauffeur will give you practice for when you have employees of your own one day."

"I'll hire the best one I can find."

"I know you will."

"Darling, you have to hear what Herr Goering said about Queen Elizabeth. You'll die of laughter," the Duke called to Wallis.

"I'm coming." Wallis patted Amelia's arms then let go, the intimacy gone but not the joy softening her face. She staggered back to the shade, leaving Amelia to dream about a future she couldn't have imagined a year and a half ago. The long shadow of Jackson's crimes receded into the background, finally a part of her past instead of a weight on her present and future. It was more than she could've ever asked for, and none of it would've been possible without Wallis.

Chapter Fourteen

Paris, November 1938

"The German diplomat that Polish man shot died this morning," Robert said from across the Café Capucines table.

Amelia pushed her half-finished croissant away, her appetite gone. "I met Herr vom Rath at a party for Herr von Ribbentrop last year. He was nice and not much older than us."

"Everyone at the Chancery is on edge because of it. We wonder if one of us might be next."

"Don't say that." She reached across the table and took his hand. He caressed her palm with his thumb, sending little shivers racing through her. She wanted to slide up beside him and lay her head on his chest and have him tell her everything would be all right. Instead, she let go of him, aware of the diplomatic staff sitting around them and pretending not to watch.

She didn't want to start any more rumors than their regular breakfasts might have already aroused, unwilling to face them or her deepening feelings for Robert.

"It's worse. The Germans unleashed their thugs on the Jews last night in retaliation." Robert added sugar to his coffee. "The reports coming in from Berlin are terrible. They destroyed businesses, set fire to synagogues, and killed a number of people."

Amelia thought of the twisted rage on the faces of the soldiers who'd stood guard in front of the Jewish shops in Berlin. She could imagine them attacking their fellow countrymen. "Is anything being done about it?"

"International condemnation and outrage. President Roosevelt ordered the German ambassador home and there are rumors he won't appoint a new one. The Germans are surprised by how quickly this has turned countries against them."

"Let's hope international pressure is enough to keep Herr Hitler in check."

He shook his head to say he didn't believe it any more than she did. So much for the *bonne chance* she'd wished him while he'd been in Italy. He might wear the tie tack but it hadn't helped him or anyone slow down the wave of war threatening to crash over Europe. Despite Mr. Chamberlain signing the Munich Agreement with Herr Hitler at the end of September, the tension in Europe was increasing instead of simmering down.

WHAT TO DO about Germany was the talk of the evening at Lady Williams-Taylor's cocktail party in her impressive Paris townhouse. Amelia stood on the periphery of the guests in one of her pale pink Schiaparelli dresses shot with gold stripes along the wide skirt. She usually entertained a host of conversation partners at these events. Her status as Wallis's cousin drew people to her but no one was interested in chatting her up tonight. They were too busy talking politics.

"Mr. Chamberlain was right to negotiate for peace," the Duke insisted to Lady Williams-Taylor, Mr. Wenner-Gren, and a coterie of people in designer dresses and tuxedos. They held highball glasses and cigarette holders while debating the possibility of war as if speculating on a horse race and not something capable of ruining millions of lives. "He has the right idea. Give Herr Hitler the land he needs for his people and keep us out of war. Let the Germans have Czechoslovakia, it isn't a real country anyway, simply something President Wilson created out of whole cloth with that damned Treaty of Versailles."

"There's no need to swear, darling," Wallis reprimanded, smiling apologetically at the others.

"If there's any time to swear it's now. Those bloody fools in London will get us into a mess over this little bit of nothing. If I could've negotiated with Germany about Czechoslovakia ages ago and saved Mr. Chamberlain the bother, I would have. Herr Hitler is not a madman but a head of state to be reasoned with."

"Mrs. Montague?" A voice pulled Amelia's attention away from the conversation. "I'm Miss Heastie. Lady Williams-Taylor said I had to meet you." A colored woman in a fine emerald-green satin sheath dress, her British accent tinged by a slight Caribbean flavor, shook Amelia's hand.

"I'm glad to finally meet you. Lady Williams-Taylor has told me about you." She understood why Miss Heastie hadn't accompanied her employer to Berlin. Herr Hitler had no more love of colored people than he did of Jews. His fury over Jesse Owens winning the gold medal at the 1936 Berlin Olympics was legendary.

"How are you enjoying the party?" Miss Heastie asked.

"I've heard a number of very interesting things since I've been here."

"They do love their gossip. Speaking of which, have you heard Mr. Dalí has taken up with Mademoiselle Chanel?"

"Madame Schiaparelli will be jealous."

"Won't she just. Tell Her Royal Highness as soon as possible. Employers love it when you give them juicy news, especially when they're among the first to know."

"I'll keep that in mind." It was good advice she'd never heard from Mrs. Bedaux but she supposed employers liked to believe their staff didn't gossip about them. Another of the many illusions everyone maintained to keep society running smoothly.

"Want to get away for a few minutes? I know where we can take a breather."

"I don't know if I can. Her Royal Highness might need me."

"They're pretty well occupied and won't miss us. One of the footmen will find us if they do."

With Wallis deep in conversation with Lady Williams-Taylor and Mr. Wenner-Gren, now was as good a chance as any. "All right."

Amelia followed Miss Heastie through the house, pausing

at the study door to look at the large portrait of Herr Hitler staring menacingly out at her from over the fireplace. "Lady Williams-Taylor has interesting taste in art."

Miss Heastie rolled her eyes. "That, she does."

"How do you manage it?"

"The same way you and every other secretary does. We take the good with the bad, and there's more good to Lady Williams-Taylor than bad. She was the only one willing to hire and train me after I graduated from high school. Most of society wasn't as open-minded as she was."

Odd, considering her political leanings. "I understand. Her Royal Highness isn't perfect but she's done more for me than almost anyone else."

"I knew we'd get on splendidly." Miss Heastie led Amelia into the kitchen, where the staff greeted Miss Heastie with happy waves and smiles. "Señor Garcia, let me know if anyone is looking for me. You know where to find me."

"Sí, señorita," the chef answered with a wink.

"He's from Cuba, and the best chef this side of London, but don't tell your Duchess that. These aristocrats are so particular about their chefs' reputations. To hear them tell it they all have the best one but I've eaten at enough houses to know that's not true." Miss Heastie took two cola bottles from the icebox, popped off the caps on the wall opener, then led Amelia outside onto the narrow balcony off the kitchen. Miss Heastie handed Amelia a cold bottle, the moisture of it dampening the palm of her satin glove. "I don't want to get you in too much trouble."

"I haven't had cola in ages." Amelia enjoyed the sweet taste and fizz. It reminded her of long-ago summers with Father and Peter when they used to sit on the back porch of their lake house during the hot and humid evenings. She missed them and those simple days.

"Lady Williams-Taylor keeps it in stock for the maids and footmen. A little taste of home when we're here."

"Where's home?"

"All over." Miss Heastie set down the cola bottle and wrapped her gloved hands over her bare arms for warmth. The chilly fall air was preferable to the smoke-filled sitting room. "Lord Williams-Taylor is the Bank of Montreal manager so we spend time there or at their apartment in New York or here, but mostly at Star Acres, their estate in The Bahamas."

"How long have you been with her?"

"Five years. I grew up in Nassau. My father owns a number of businesses there, but he really made his money running rum to Miami during Prohibition. I learned to read on his boat while we waited offshore for American clients."

And Amelia thought she had a scandalous past. "Does Lady Williams-Taylor know?"

"It's why she hired me. She used to buy from Pops." Miss Heastie took a drink of her cola. "She looks like a proper English lady but when she speaks you'd better not be easily offended or a gentleman in tight trousers or you'll hear about it."

"No!"

"Yes. With her money and influence, she can get away with almost anything."

"Now I'm jealous." Suddenly a man with money and a title

who could afford to give her a devil-may-care attitude looked appealing.

"Enough about my employer. What's your story?"

"I'm a widow from Baltimore." Despite everything, it was as simple as that.

"I'm sorry for your loss."

"Don't be. He went to jail for stealing money from an investment trust."

"We're quite the pair, then, aren't we, Mrs. Montague." She clinked the neck of her cola bottle against Amelia's.

"Call me Amelia."

"I'm Eugenie. Are you staying in Paris for the winter?"

"We'll go to the South of France for Christmas but until then, we're here. How about you?" She liked Eugenie and wanted to get to know her better.

Eugenie shook her head, her long black curls bouncing against her round face and high cheekbones, which emphasized her deep brown eyes. "We go to Nassau for the winter. So you know the lay of the land when you head south, Marlene Dietrich has taken up with Erich Remarque."

"The author?" She had a feeling *All Quiet on the Western Front* was about to be her next assigned reading. Mrs. Dietrich had been a regular visitor to Château de la Croë last summer. They were sure to see her and her author lover at Christmas parties this year and Wallis would want to impress him.

"The very one. Greta Garbo's maid, Alma, told me about it when they were here last week. Her mother is Bahamian so we had a lot to discuss. The affair is quite the secret, but with me and Alma going on it won't be for much longer. She said the affair probably won't last. Mr. Remarque is planning to go to America. He doesn't want to risk staying in Europe and ending up on the wrong side of a potential war, not after the Germans revoked his citizenship and accused him of writing unpatriotic books. He's seen the situation in Germany with his own eyes and it isn't good."

Amelia thought of the Austria and Germany map and how prescient it'd been. "No, it isn't."

Wallis's cutting laugh carried through an open window, interrupting the tranquility of the balcony before it faded back into the quiet murmur of conversation and light music.

"I wonder if they ever think about all this coming to an end," Eugenie mused.

"Her Royal Highness does. She's worried she'll have to protect His Royal Highness's heirlooms if it all goes south. Of course, she hasn't done anything to move them to safety, but I imagine if things get dicey, Herr von Ribbentrop will give her some warning and then I'll be busy."

"She swore up and down in that *New York Times* interview last year that she hardly knew him."

"That's a lie. They've been friends for years, ever since London. They see each other whenever he's in Paris," Amelia said before she caught herself. "I shouldn't have told you that. You won't tell Lady Williams-Taylor, will you?"

"Of course I will, but I won't say I heard it from you. We private secretaries have to protect one another. Besides, she probably already knows and is thrilled they have such an influential friend in common."

Senor Garcia poked his head out the door. "Lady Williams-Taylor is looking for you."

"Well, back to work." Eugenie finished the last swig of her cola. "Write to me in Nassau. I want to hear all the French gossip while I'm gone."

Paris, Boulevard Suchet, March 1939

Amelia closed her letter to Eugenie with news of H.G. Wells taking up with the reporter Martha Gellhorn, who was thirty-two to his seventy-four. She'd heard it from Constance Coolidge's secretary, who'd told her Mrs. Coolidge was in a rage because she was having an affair with him too. It was about to become the talk of France and Amelia didn't want Eugenie to miss out. They'd been writing to each other since they'd met, exchanging gossip or commiserating about work, and Amelia enjoyed having a friend who understood the unique challenges of her position. She was about to start on the rest of the mail when Mademoiselle Moulichon poked her head in the office.

"You have to hear this."

Amelia followed her into the sitting room, where Wallis, the Duke, and most of the staff stood listening in tense silence to the wireless.

"With the German invasion of Czechoslovakia in direct violation of the Munich Agreement, Prime Minister Chamberlain is expected to announce Britain's support of Poland, which Herr

Hitler may have his eye on next. Britain and France will declare war if Germany invades Poland," the BBC reporter announced.

"Someone must take a stance against this ridiculousness," the Duke exclaimed. "We can't have another generation of young men dying in French mud."

"Darling, this could be your chance to help pull Europe back from the brink of war. You could be a voice of reason, make a radio address and appeal directly to the people to pressure their leaders to negotiate instead of fight. You could be a prince of peace." Wallis used the same title Mr. Wenner-Gren had dangled in front of the Duke on the train from Germany. "Remember that lovely NBC chap who used to come to my London parties? I bet he'd jump at the opportunity to get you on air, not just in Europe but America."

"A radio address to America." The Duke tapped his empty pipe against his palm. "That's the ticket. They're the only ones with enough sense to stop Britain and France from rushing into another war."

Amelia and Mr. Forwood exchanged uneasy glances. She might as well book a hotel room for Sir Walter. The moment Buckingham Palace got wind of this he'd turn up in Paris.

Verdun, France, May 8, 1939

I am speaking tonight from Verdun, where I have been spending a few days visiting one of the greatest battlefields of the last war. Upon this and other battlefields throughout the world, millions of men suffered and died, and as I talk to you from this historic place, I am deeply conscious of the presence of the great company of the dead; and I am convinced that could they make their voices heard they would be with me in what I am about to say." The Duke began his speech from the bedroom in the Hotel du Coq Hardi where Mr. Bates and his NBC crew had set up the microphone. His words were broadcast around the world via shortwave radio, except in Britain, where the BBC had blocked the broadcast, much to the Duke's chagrin.

The Duke's plans for a radio address had set off a firestorm of correspondence between His Majesty's Government and Boulevard Suchet. Mr. Forwood had been privy to most of it, but Amelia had taken a few letters from Wallis to Sir Walter. More than once she'd had to stop Wallis's tirade and suggest a more delicate turn of phrase. Surprisingly, Wallis had listened. However, nothing anyone said or wrote had changed anyone's minds and so here they were.

"I cannot claim for myself the expert knowledge of a statesman, but I have at least had the good fortune to travel the world and therefore to study human nature. This valuable experience has left me with the profound conviction that there is no land whose people want war. This I believe to be as true of the German nation as of the British nation to which I belong, as it is to you in America and of the French nation, on whose friendly soil I now reside."

The Duke might be in France but the King and Queen of England were on their way to America to shore up support for

Britain in the event of war. Wallis had known that when she'd suggested this date, and Sir Walter had been kind enough to point out how the Duke's speech, no matter what his intentions, undermined the King's efforts in America. The Duke had almost relented until Wallis, his staunchest supporter, had stiffened his resolve. She stood beside him now in a black coat dress with a white scarf tucked into the collar, her usual ostentatious jewelry shunned in favor of a simple Cartier diamond bracelet with jeweled cross charms.

"I feel that my words tonight will find a sincere echo in the hearts of all who hear them. It is not for me to put forward concrete proposals. That must be left to those who have the power to guide their nations towards closer understanding. God grant that they may accomplish that great task before it is too late!"

The red light on the table turned off. The Duke hadn't said anything incendiary but Amelia could almost hear the pearl-clutching from London. The Duke had promised in his abdication speech not to meddle in politics, and here he was, at Wallis's goading, stepping into international affairs. If they thought Buckingham Palace was difficult before, it'd be even worse after this.

"Well done, Your Royal Highness," Mr. Bates congratulated as the operator took off his headphones. "Truer and more inspiring words were never said."

A cheer went up outside the closed window and Amelia peeked out to see a large crowd gathered in the street below.

"*Vive le Roi! Vive le Roi!*" they shouted.

"They're calling for you, David, they're calling for us. We have to greet them." Wallis linked her arm in his and drew him onto the balcony. The people erupted in applause, and the pressmen across the street snapped pictures of Wallis and the Duke waving as if they were the King and Queen of England on the Buckingham Palace balcony on Armistice Day.

It reminded Amelia too much of Berlin and she wanted to pull them back inside. There was nothing more to this than waving but it didn't sit right with her, as if they weren't here for peace but for themselves. Guilt nagged at her for doubting Wallis, especially after everything Wallis had done for her, but she couldn't shake the feeling. Whatever they were doing with this "prince of peace" business, she hoped they didn't live to regret it as much as they had the abdication.

Paris, June 1939

The United States ambassador's residence at 2 Avenue d'Iéna was filled with gilded woodwork and Louise XVI furniture overseen by a full-length portrait of George Washington. The doors to the magnificent garden were open and guests milled about in the cool evening air, accompanied by the soft notes of a grand piano. Wallis dazzled in her white dress, the pale color setting off the deep red of her ruby necklace. The distinguished guests danced and mingled to celebrate Wallis and the Duke's June birthdays. With Wallis and the Duke safely occupied inside with Ambassador Bullitt, Amelia and Robert were free to explore the crushed-gravel path near the back of the walled garden. Amelia paused at a small pond to watch the goldfish flitter beneath the lily pads.

"We toured the military cemetery in Verdun the morning of the Duke's NBC broadcast. The endless rows of white crosses were heartbreaking. If only the Duke's speech had made a difference." The Duke's attempt at being a prince of peace had fizzled as fast as his crusade for workers. "All it did was cause more trouble for them with His Majesty's Government."

"And Britain. Herr Hitler views the Duke's pleas for peace as British weakness." Robert stood beside her, the two of them reflected in the water's glassy surface. "The more uncertain things become, the more guarded he should be with what he says and does. He should also be careful with who he is and isn't friends with." Robert dug a coin out of his pocket and tossed it in the pond, sending ripples spreading across the still surface. "For instance, their staff. How many of them came from Bedaux's château? They're probably all spies."

"If they are, they must be bored hearing about jewelry, clothes, and antiques. Buckingham Palace doesn't send the Duke birthday cards much less dispatch boxes full of state secrets."

"It doesn't mean I'm wrong."

Amelia fiddled with the skirt of her silver lamé dress, a piece more form-fitting than usual, run up by her Paris seamstress and modeled after one of Robert Piguet's designs. All the servants in Germany had been spies. It wasn't a stretch to believe the ones here might be too. "I've worked with Mademoiselle Moulichon and Mr. Hale since the wedding. I've never seen anything out of the ordinary with them."

"I'm glad to hear it."

They wandered deeper into the garden where the boxwood hedges were cut low to show off the many statues on pedestals adorning the walks. They stopped behind a statue of Diana the Huntress.

Amelia leaned against the smooth, cold stone, the goddess's wide, flowing toga shielding them from the house and party. "What'll happen to you if war comes?"

"I'll stay in France until ordered to leave. What about you? Have you thought of returning to America before any trouble starts?"

"Everything I have is here, my work, my friends. It might take bombs to make me give it up." She hadn't saved enough to start her own business and she wasn't likely to get a job in Washington, D.C., or Baltimore. She could use her connections to find a position in New York but the thought of starting over with an employer who viewed her as nothing more than an expendable employee, not a cousin, confidante, and cherished member of her staff, wasn't appealing.

"Promise me, no matter what the Windsors do or where they go, you'll follow your instincts and keep yourself safe."

"My instincts haven't always been reliable."

"They're better than you realize." He rested one hand on the statue and brushed her cheek with the other, his touch light, comforting, and searching. "Promise me you'll stay safe."

They shouldn't be intimate where anyone could see them but with the world hurtling toward an uncertain future, she couldn't push him away. "I promise."

"Good. It'll give me one less thing to worry about if things go sideways." He leaned down and pressed his lips to hers. She shifted closer and slid her fingers beneath the satin lapels of his tuxedo, delighting in the firmness of his chest beneath her fingertips. With war looming on the horizon, this could be their last time together and she didn't want to waste it. She'd lived with enough regrets about Jackson and her family, she didn't need any about Robert. He'd been a friend and confidant for the past year, never judging her, always believing in her. She couldn't lose this. War might interrupt it but she wouldn't willingly toss it aside.

Chapter Fifteen

Château de la Croë, September 1939

Sir Walter called. Britain has declared war on Germany." The Duke walked to the end of the diving board and with a graceful hop, sprung off it and into the pool. He swam to the shallow end, where Wallis, Amelia, and Mr. Metcalf stared at him in horrified silence.

War. It'd been rising all summer like the heat in the air in the mornings. Invitations to parties had been few and far between, and Wallis had canceled most of her picnics and dinners, unable to bear more regrets. The shuttered villas and empty hotels had made it seem as if no one but the Windsors, the Rogerses, and the Maughams were left in this corner of the world. Even the staff had been forced to reckon with it as one by one the footmen and even the chef had been called up for military duty. Only the men too old to serve, such as Mr. George Ladbroke, the new chauffeur, remained. Even Mr.

Forwood had been forced to abandon his sovereign and rejoin his Scots Guards regiment. Mr. Hale should have gone back to England but Wallis had fought with Sir Walter to have him exempted from service so he could remain with her.

"We should make arrangements to return to England before it's too late." Mr. Metcalf rose from his chair, leaving his drink on the table to melt in the sun. He'd replaced Mr. Forwood as the Duke's equerry while his wife remained safely in England. "With Germany on the move, the Italians might decide to invade and we're too close to the border to be safe."

"I'll make train reservations to Paris. We can travel to the coast from there." Amelia was eager to do more than sunbathe while the Germans plotted their next move.

"We aren't going anywhere," the Duke said while floating on his back. "We're perfectly safe here; besides, with everyone else gone, there'll be plenty of space on the trains for us and our things if we choose to leave."

Amelia looked to Wallis, expecting her to insist they go. She sat in her lounge chair in her Nile-green bathing costume, oddly silent, her opinion and thoughts as hidden as her eyes behind her white sunglasses.

AMELIA PICKED UP the telephone receiver and turned the dial with a pencil, her fingers shaking too much to do it. She reached the operator, who tried to put her through to Robert at the Chancery but the line was blocked.

"I'll ring you back when I make the connection." The operator sounded as frazzled as Amelia. Thousands of people were clogging the phone lines with frantic calls home to decide what to do and where to go. It was a good hour later when the phone rang and the operator came on the line. "I have the connection."

"Are you on the way back to Paris?" Robert asked.

Amelia breathed a sigh of relief at the sound of his voice. The German blitzkrieg was mowing over Poland like a tractor while governments scrambled to respond and here she was with Mr. Metcalf trying to convince Wallis and David to get to safety. They might as well bang their heads against a wall for all the good it was doing. "No, the Duke won't leave. He doesn't think we're in danger. Are we?"

"The Germans aren't likely to move from Poland just yet, giving everyone some breathing room, but if they decide to push through Belgium into France it could get bad. The King of England's brother is a prized catch. The Windsors should get to England immediately."

"Mr. Metcalf and I are trying to convince them but they won't budge. I don't know why they're being so stubborn. Wallis is an expert at looking out for herself but she's awfully cavalier about this."

"Then you should go."

"I can't leave them to fend for themselves. Wallis would never abandon me like that, and they need people around who can talk some sense into them and help them when they finally decide to go. I don't think they can even make train reservations by themselves. I also can't leave the staff and merchants. I have to settle those accounts so they have money for food and whatever else they need for whatever is coming."

"You never fail to think of others. I admire your sense of duty."

"I just hope I don't regret it. Besides, as much as the royal family doesn't want them, they don't want the Germans getting them either. If I stay with them, I should be safe."

"True. One moment." Muffled voices pulled him from the conversation before he returned to the line. "I have to go. Things are crazy here. Stay safe."

"You too." The line clicked silent and Amelia dropped the receiver on the base, missing the anchor of his voice. She was scared and wanted to be anywhere but here but she couldn't leave. If she didn't have work to keep her busy, she might dissolve into a puddle of tears the way Mademoiselle Moulichon did every night. She'd quietly made arrangements for the Windsors and their things to return to Paris, ready to flip the switch the minute the Duke and Wallis changed their minds.

If only they'd change their minds. She still couldn't understand why they were being so stubborn.

She picked up the receiver and rang for the operator to put her through to the one person who might be able to convince Wallis and the Duke to leave.

"THE PLANE IS waiting to take you and your remaining staff to England. Space is limited so you can only bring one suitcase each," Sir Walter explained. The poor man had barely had time to change since braving the Channel, a quick plane ride south, and the long drive to the château. The dark circles under his eyes and his wrinkled suit betrayed the strain of his travels, but at least he'd agreed to come when Amelia had explained the situation. She and Mr. Metcalf needed all the help they could get.

"Nonsense," the Duke scoffed. "I'm a prince not a traveling salesman. I won't spend this ridiculous war with nothing more than what I can stuff in a valise."

"I won't fly. I absolutely refuse." Wallis was more hysterical about boarding a plane than possibly getting caught in a war zone. "I saw too many planes go down when I lived on the air base with Win. I won't hurtle to the ground in a ball of flames."

"You won't have to." The Duke patted her hand, the calming and reassuring one for once. "Because we aren't leaving until my brother grants her the Royal Highness title, and the Queen and my mother agree to meet and acknowledge her. No more pretending she doesn't exist or she isn't the center of my life. They'll place an announcement of the meetings in the Court Circular in order to assure her social acceptance."

Amelia held back a groan. Now wasn't the time to discuss this.

"I'll convey your wishes to His Majesty but at present, there are more pressing matters than etiquette and society."

"He must also have a position when he returns," Wallis demanded, having recovered her composure now that she wasn't forced to fly. "David won't sit around knitting in some castle while everyone else is doing something for the war effort."

"I've been authorized by His Majesty to offer Your Royal Highness one of two positions. Deputy Regional Commissioner in Wales, where you'll oversee civil defense efforts, or Liaison Officer with the British Military Mission in Paris, where you'll inspect the strength and security of the Maginot Line on behalf of His Majesty's Government."

"He'll take the Welsh position," Wallis answered before the Duke could even open his mouth. "At least in Wales he won't risk getting his head shot off in this foolish war, and we'll finally be able to return to England."

"I'll tour the British regiments and commands, visit the troops, and buck up the men's spirits as I did in the Great War. Her Royal Highness will accompany me." The Duke paused, waiting for Sir Walter to react to his use of the HRH title, but Sir Walter had the most impressive poker face Amelia had ever seen. "She'll live at Fort Belvedere."

"Fort Belvedere hasn't been maintained since you left," Sir Walter said. "I suggest you make arrangements for other lodgings when you return."

"If my family wants us home then they can make proper lodgings for us," the Duke thundered.

"I'll convey your wishes to His Majesty via phone this evening. I'm staying at the Hotel du Cap. I'll return in the morning to discuss various arrangements." Sir Walter bowed then left.

Amelia was surprised he didn't sprint back to the car and the hotel. He'd taken a beating from the Duke and there'd be another in the morning or when he called His Majesty. The poor man was being batted between the Windsors and Buckingham Palace like a badminton birdie.

"Sir, might I advise accepting Sir Walter's plane and seeing to the details of titles, housing, and positions when you're safely in England?" Mr. Metcalf entreated.

"And lose our bargaining power?" Wallis answered for him, rising and forcing the Duke to his feet. She eyed Mr. Metcalf as she would a maid who'd dared to question her. "David failed to secure his income and my title before he surrendered his crown. He won't make the same mistake twice. So long as we're here they must pay attention to our demands. Come, David, we have things to discuss."

"Yes, darling."

She walked out the door, the Duke, Detto, Prisie, and Pookie trotting after her.

"They're bickering over titles when we could be bombed by the Italians at any moment." Mr. Metcalf ran his hand through his hair in frustration. "One would think the abdication would've taught them the cost of being stubborn but they haven't learned a thing. At least he wants the Welsh position. It'll get him away from the likes of that Bedaux fellow."

"The Bedaux aren't that bad. At least Mrs. Bedaux isn't." She didn't see Mr. Bedaux enough to know much about him but Mrs. Bedaux had been nothing but kind to her. She wouldn't have gotten as far as she had with Wallis if it hadn't been for her.

"Mrs. Bedaux is a gem but that husband of hers is too close to the Germans. I've been with His Royal Highness since 1922 and I've never seen him shy away from being influenced by the worst sort, neither does Her Grace. I wonder sometimes if I've been a fool for being so loyal."

"Someone has to help them or they'll get into even more trouble." Amelia loved Wallis but she wasn't blind to her lack of judgment sometimes, and the Duke wasn't much better.

"Very true, Mrs. Montague, very true."

Chapter Sixteen

Fort des Ayvelles, Belgium–French Border, February 1940

"Buckingham Palace shouldn't have worried about us returning to England. We'll die of boredom before we die from bombs," Wallis complained as she brushed the mud from her khaki French Red Cross uniform skirt. Amelia nodded her agreement. Nothing had happened since war had been declared. The *Drôle de Guerre,* the French called it; the Phony War, the British and Americans named it, as everyone went about their usual lives while waiting for something they prayed would never come. "But we must do our part, mustn't we?"

"We must." Mrs. Bedaux closed the Buick's now empty trunk, the chocolates, cigarettes, and knitted socks they delivered twice a week to the French troops stationed along the Maginot Line near Fort des Ayvelles gone. The three of them were part of the Section Sanitaire and when they weren't handing out care packages, they spent the better part of the week with French society women in the Ritz ballroom assembling treats for the bored soldiers guarding the border between Belgium and France at the far end of the Ardennes Forest. "It'd be unpatriotic for us not to help."

"And to think I tried to join the British Red Cross but those snooty tarts wouldn't have me." Wallis slid into the front seat beside Amelia, took a compact out of the glove box, and touched up her lipstick.

"They don't deserve your help, not with the ghastly way they've treated you." Mrs. Bedaux sat in the back seat and straightened her garrison cap over her finely curled hair. They might be in the mud-strewn wilds of France but they still insisted on looking their best.

Amelia didn't have time to freshen up as she started the car and maneuvered it over the wet and narrow streets and past the low-slung buildings of the medieval lanes toward the Duke's barracks outside of town. Whenever they finished delivering packages, they always met him for tea and coffee in his quarters before returning to Paris, the three of them splitting the driving on the long trip back.

"Where is Charles these days?" Wallis asked Mrs. Bedaux as the car bounced over the muddy and undulating ground beneath the tall and thin bare trees.

"Still in The Hague overseeing his businesses."

"It must be nice to have a husband with a real job, not just busywork." Sir Walter had returned to la Croë the morning after his September visit and told the Duke the Welsh offer had been rescinded and only the French posting was available. It'd thwarted their plans to have the upper hand in negotiating for Wallis's title, and after wrangling about ranks, uniforms, and other meaningless things, the Duke had finally traveled to Vincennes to take up his duties while Wallis and Amelia had gone back to Boulevard Suchet. "Here we are, darlings. Smile, we have to make the little man feel important."

"ISN'T SHE WONDERFUL?" the Duke asked Mr. Metcalf at the end of lunch when Wallis had finished telling him about their work in Paris, making it sound much more interesting than it really was. "What happened to the newspaper stories on Wallis's war work? I want people to see her in uniform, to know she's doing her part."

"I contacted Lord Beaverbrook about running a story but it hasn't happened," Mr. Metcalf explained as he checked the coffeepot. At the Duke's request, Mr. Metcalf had been made the Duke's Aide-de-Camp. "I'll write to him again."

"We'll try the American newspapers too, darling," the Duke assured Wallis. "We'll show everyone you're a model volunteer."

Mr. Metcalf returned the lid to the coffeepot with a frown. "We're out of coffee. I'll walk to the canteen and fetch more."

"I'll go with you," Mrs. Bedaux offered. "I want to stretch my legs before the drive back."

They stepped out into the dreary gray day, leaving Amelia to finish her lukewarm coffee with Wallis and His Royal Highness. She took another fresh-baked donut from the china tray in front of her, enjoying the warm food while she could. There was little civilization between here and Paris, with most villagers and farmers wary of strangers, especially at night.

A large boom echoed through the barracks, making the old stone walls with their small framed windows rattle.

"What was that?" Wallis jumped to her feet, ready to run to the car and back to Paris.

"Artillery fire, nothing to worry about, they practice every day." The Duke settled Wallis in her chair then sat down in his. He removed a pipe from his shirt pocket along with a pouch of tobacco and packed the bowl. "A waste of artillery if you ask me. I've seen the fortifications and defenses. They aren't worth a damn."

"But the Maginot Line is supposed to be impregnable," Wallis said, still uneasy about the cannon fire.

"The Maginot Line is like Swiss cheese through the Ardennes. Bloody French fools think tanks can't get through the trees but they're wrong. If Herr Hitler wants to invade, he should do it through there. He wouldn't meet any resistance, not with the French refusing to keep reserves. When the Maginot Line breaks, there won't be any troops to plug it back up."

Amelia paused in sipping her coffee, wondering what the devil she'd just overheard. The Duke was discussing confidential military matters as if they were cricket results.

"The British aren't much brighter." The Duke lit his pipe and shook out his match. "I was at Dunkirk last week. Our flying boys are run ragged and in no shape to fight or defend anything. I'm constantly pointing out flaws in the French defenses but no one listens. You'd think someone in Britain would at least acknowledge my reports but they haven't. All they do is deny my request to tour the British lines. I want to see our defenses and compare them to the French ones."

"It's your brother's doing. He hates you, he always has, he was simply better at hiding it when you were on the throne. If he weren't so shortsighted, he'd read what you've written and know the line and army is in trouble. They dismiss it as they do your talents, except this time they'll regret it," Wallis grumbled, as if the Germans invading France would be nothing more than a minor social cut and not a disaster for Europe and Britain.

The door swung open, and Mrs. Bedaux hurried in with a gust of cold air before Mr. Metcalf closed the door behind them, the empty coffeepot dangling from one hand. "My apologies, everyone, the canteen had nothing prepared, as usual."

"The French Army is the most disorganized I've ever seen," the Duke complained. "If they had a brain they'd be dangerous, but there isn't one to be found among any of them. For all the bragging about being strong enough to fight, they'll be hopeless if the Germans invade."

Wallis straightened her garrison cap over her hair in the small mirror tacked up above the Duke's wash table. "We must be going if we hope to get back to Paris at something resembling a reasonable hour."

"I'll drive down to see you next week, darling." The Duke picked up Wallis's heavy wool coat and helped her into it.

"Sir, you were in Paris last week," Mr. Metcalf tersely

reminded him. "It might be more prudent to remain here and attend to your duties."

"What duties? I haven't a thing to do. They'll probably be glad to be rid of me for a day or two."

"I'll be expecting you," Wallis said as she pulled on her gloves.

AMELIA RESTED IN the back seat while Wallis took her turn driving. It was near sunset, the sky red above the brown fields. In the distance, a light here and there from a farmhouse or château twinkled in the cold air. The long length of muddy roads crisscrossed by rivulets of water from patches of melting snow was broken by small groups of refugees in tattered and dirty clothes struggling to push carts and bicycles weighed down with their belongings. They'd come from conquered Poland, walking hundreds of miles to escape the brutal Germans and their ironfisted rule. She had no idea what they'd do once they reached Paris. The city's charitable organizations were already bursting with refugees.

"We should stop and give them something to eat. They must be hungry and cold," Amelia suggested.

"We can't." Wallis swerved around a peasant man leading a sad-looking and tired donkey. A young woman in a thin coat and mud-covered shoes followed him. "We don't have any care packages left."

"We could give them our blankets and donuts."

"We might need those. The roads are so bad, we could have a flat and be stranded all night and freeze to death." Wallis jerked the wheel right to avoid a large ditch and Amelia steadied herself against the back seat. "Besides, if you hand out food, they'll swarm us like pigeons. We might be robbed, or worse. I swear, Amelia, sometimes you are so naive."

"I'm not naive, I simply hate to see people suffer," Amelia snapped, irritated by Wallis's callousness.

Wallis threw her a hard look in the rearview mirror. Amelia instantly regretted making Wallis look like a heartless witch but she couldn't help it. She was tired from the long day of driving, the long months of waiting for the other shoe to drop, and horrified by the misery surrounding them.

"We'll bring some extra care packages to hand out next time," Mrs. Bedaux suggested, the polite compromise easing the tension between the cousins. "It's the least we can do to help these poor people."

"That's a splendid idea," Wallis agreed with little enthusiasm.

Amelia rested her head against the back of the seat and closed her eyes. The hum of the engine lulled her into a light sleep.

"You remember what King Carol said about war and opportunities. Charles's business is booming. There could be opportunities for you and His Royal Highness too." Mrs. Bedaux's low, melodious voice melded into the soothing engine noise.

"I hadn't thought so until David told me about the Ardennes." Wallis's carrying voice, even in a whisper, jolted Amelia into full consciousness but she pretended to be asleep, curious to hear where this was going. She listened in shock as Wallis told Mrs. Bedaux what the Duke had said about the weakness in the Maginot Line, the lack of reserve troops, and how the Germans could come through the forest.

Having heard enough, Amelia sat up and pretended to yawn, stopping Wallis from saying more. "Are we there yet?"

"Not far. Another half hour or so." Wallis opened and closed her gloved fingers on the steering wheel and focused on the road. Mrs. Bedaux said nothing but stared out the windshield at the tall and leafless trees lining the road.

Amelia didn't fall asleep again, afraid of what Wallis might say if she did. Amelia appreciated everything Mrs. Bedaux had done for her but there was no ignoring her husband's Nazi friends. If she were as indiscreet with her husband as the Duke was with Wallis, there was no telling what damage it might do.

Amelia walked into the Chancery and was stunned by the change. She expected the sandbags out front, the taped-up windows, and the double guards; those were everywhere in Paris these days. It was the spacious foyer crammed with desks and chairs filled by Embassy officers helping desperate families get out of France that shocked her. Nothing was normal anymore and it deepened the unease already draping her.

She made her way past the line of people, her Red Cross uniform giving her some status. She wasn't trying to cut the line but to reach Susan and find Robert.

"Amelia, I don't suppose you're here to lend a hand?" Susan half-jokingly asked, somehow managing to not look disheveled in the midst of the controlled chaos. She directed a young couple to the chairs along the wall where numerous other tired and anxious men and women waited.

"I wish I could." Amelia spied Lisa and many other Embassy friends delivering or fetching papers from the desks. "Is Robert here?"

"It's the only place he's been for the last week." She made a quick phone call and within moments he appeared from the hallway.

Deep circles beneath his eyes marred his face but he lit up at the sight of her. If the foyer hadn't been filled with such misery and desperation she might have rushed across it to throw her arms around him. He would've run to meet her too, she could feel it in his quick steps.

"I need to speak to you, in private. Do you have time?"

"A few minutes. Susan, I'm out for a brief walk. I'll be back soon." He led her out of the Chancery. "Let's go down to the Seine. I need some fresh air. It's a madhouse here."

"It's a madhouse everywhere."

"It'll only get worse if the Germans press on toward France."

"That's what I want to talk to you about. I'm worried about Wallis." They crossed through the Place de la Concorde, passing posters plastered on buildings proclaiming France and her allies were strong enough to defeat Germany. The faith in the French Army and the Maginot Line rivaled anything found in Notre Dame. After everything she'd heard from the Duke, she prayed that faith wasn't misplaced. "I don't know if I'm turning a molehill into a mountain or if I should even tell you about this but I didn't know who else to talk to and it's been bothering me for days."

They reached the walk along the Seine where the booksellers with their green carts crowded with books and prints for sale sat waiting for buyers. There weren't many people browsing today and most of the stalls were locked up tight.

"What happened?"

"Maybe I'm overreacting and she isn't saying anything people don't already know but she's gotten herself into so much trouble before. That'll be nothing compared to sharing information during war."

He jerked to a stop. "Tell me what she said and I'll tell you if you're overreacting."

She studied him, his strong face serious as he waited, but she hesitated. She shouldn't betray Wallis but she couldn't risk Wallis doing something that might come to haunt her more than losing the extra-chic title. "Promise you won't tell anyone at the Embassy about this."

He laid his hands on her shoulders. "I won't."

She rested her hands over his and took a deep, soothing breath. She had to believe she hadn't misread him or his feelings for her and that she could trust him. "I think Wallis and the Duke are being too free with sensitive information and with the wrong people."

She told him about the Maginot Line and what the Duke had said about the weakness through the Ardennes, the lack of reserve troops, and Wallis telling Mrs. Bedaux. He listened, his expression tightening with every sentence. She'd been right to be worried. “She didn’t do it on purpose, I’m sure of it. Wallis can be shortsighted but she isn’t a traitor.”

“Not everyone would agree with that. Europe is becoming a very dangerous place and even innocent discussion could be taken the wrong way.”

“Could they be tried for treason?”

“Anything’s possible but I doubt it. The backlash would be terrible and the Duke still has supporters in England.”

“Wallis doesn’t.” She’d seen the correspondence between the Duke and Mr. Churchill and the loyalty of men like Mr. Forwood and Mr. Metcalf. Wallis didn’t have those kinds of allies. “They could hang her.”

“I doubt it’ll come to that.” He pulled her close and she settled against him. “His Majesty’s Government knows the Duke is careless with sensitive information. When he was King, he used to leave government papers lying around Fort Belvedere where anyone could see them, including Herr von Ribbentrop, who was a regular guest. Cabinet members knew it and began holding things back. They wouldn’t have sent him to the Ardennes if they thought he could get into real trouble there.”

He was trying to comfort her but there’d been no mistaking his alarm when she’d told him what she’d overheard. The situation was more serious than he was letting on. She had to warn Wallis to be careful.

AMELIA KNOCKED AND entered Wallis’s bedroom. “Can we chat?”

“You should be in bed. We have another long day of packing

boxes tomorrow." Wallis licked her finger and turned the page of her book, sitting ramrod straight in bed as always.

"I know." Amelia twisted her satin robe sash. "But I wanted to talk to you about what His Royal Highness told us about the Maginot Line and the Ardennes. Why did you tell Mrs. Bedaux about it? If she mentions it to her husband, he might pass it on to the wrong sort of people."

Wallis didn't look up from her book. "One would think you'd have some faith in her after the faith she's shown in you."

"I'm grateful, but . . ."

"You're accusing her and me of what amounts to treason."

"I'm trying to protect you from accusations. If the newspapers or Buckingham Palace get wind of this, you could be in for a world of trouble."

"Who's going to tell them? You?"

"Of course not." That was a whopper of a lie and it made her stomach hurt. "But war makes everyone and everything much more suspect. Even innocent things can look bad."

"Or, as King Carol said, there could be opportunity, perhaps a changing of the guard."

"You mean for His Royal Highness to be King again?"

They locked eyes, neither of them flinching from the other's gaze.

"Of course not." Wallis waved a dismissive hand at Amelia, breaking the standoff and allowing Amelia to finally exhale. "He was glad to be rid of the job, but war could mean a more prestigious position for him than inspecting the French, who, if he's right, are going to lose anyway."

"War is precarious, and no one can be certain of any outcome, no matter how secure they think they are."

"Something both of us should keep in mind." Wallis slid her finger in the book and closed it. "I need to know I can count on you, that you're on my side."

"I've always been on your side. That's why I wanted to talk to you about this."

"I'm glad to hear it, and that you mentioned it to me. I should be more careful about what I say and to whom. I don't want people to take my words out of context and think poorly of me; it'll reflect on you too, especially given your past. I'd hate to ruin your reputation and standing. Thank you again for being so sensible. I don't know what I would do without you. Now, off to bed. We have another long day tomorrow."

Wallis resumed reading, dismissing Amelia.

Amelia padded down the cold hall to her room. With heating oil rationed, the house wasn't warm like last winter and a perpetual chill hung over everything. She crawled into bed and pulled the thick covers up under her chin, shivering more from fear than cold. Wallis's ability to inadvertently get herself into trouble was more terrifying than the German Army, except this time, if Wallis made a grand mistake it might cost Amelia too.

Chapter Seventeen

Paris, May 10, 1940

The wail of air raid sirens broke the morning stillness. Amelia and Wallis looked up from their breakfast and cocked their ears to listen.

"Is it a drill?" Wallis went pale beneath her makeup.

"I don't know." There'd been fighting in Norway for days, the Phony War quickly turning into a real one. Every day, the newspapers reported on the battles inching closer to France while assuring readers the French Army would stop any German attempt to cross the border. Everyone prayed it was true, but the very real possibility that it was a lie was growing by the moment.

They waited, listening, until they heard the sound that settled it. The antiaircraft guns boomed, rattling the windows and the chandelier hanging over the dining table. The drone of airplane motors flying low above the city echoed beneath the sirens.

"They're going to kill us," Wallis cried.

"To the wine cellar." Amelia hurried around the table and pulled a near frozen Wallis to her feet. This snapped her out of her shock and she broke from Amelia's grip and without a look back bolted for the wine cellar, leaving Amelia to gather the maids; Mr. Phillips, the Duke's new equerry; Mr. Ladbroke; Mr. Hale; and Mademoiselle Moulichon and guide them to safety.

They waited between the racks of dusty wine bottles for over an hour for the sirens and the barrage of antiaircraft fire to end. They expected bombs to explode at any minute but they never came, and an hour later the all clear sounded.

"Go up and see if it's really over." Wallis pushed Amelia toward the stairs.

Amelia wondered why it was up to her to check but she supposed someone had to do it. None of the others were capable of moving. Mademoiselle Moulichon had spent the last hour crying into the maid's arms while the cook and Mr. Ladbroke had sweated profusely. Wallis had twisted her handkerchief between her hands, nearly catatonic with fear. Amelia had given up trying to talk to or calm any of them.

Amelia climbed the stone steps, pushed open the cellar door, and listened. Everything was still, like in the middle of the night, but the sun was up and catching the bits of dust hanging in the air. Outside, the street was unusually still, the steady stream of cars missing. Whatever the situation, she couldn't gauge it from here. There'd be a better view from the roof, where she could see something of the city but she'd be exposed. As she crept up the stairs, she hoped a fighter plane didn't shoot her or blow the house to smithereens.

She stepped onto the roof and saw the small puffs of dark smoke from the antiaircraft artillery drifting off with the breeze. They lost their shape and faded into the sooty morning air fed by coal fires in homes all over Paris. She approached the edge to get a view of the street and some of the taller buildings around Boulevard Suchet. They were all standing, with no fires raging. A man hurried by on the sidewalk below.

"What happened?" Amelia called down to him.

He stopped and looked at her, one foot turned to go. "German fighter planes crossed Paris then headed west. They're all over Western Europe. The Germans invaded the Low Countries and are pushing south through Belgium." He rushed off without saying more.

"It's all clear," Amelia called down the cellar stairs, and one by one the others came up. Amelia turned on the radio in the sitting room and everyone listened to the BBC report of German bombers over the Thames and coastal France. They hadn't attacked, and the newscaster suggested they'd been a distraction from the German movements through the Low Countries.

"Will they invade Paris?" Mademoiselle Moulichon asked in French thick with panic and worry.

Wallis sat closest to the radio, playing with her emerald engagement ring.

"I'm sure we're perfectly safe here. The French Army won't let Paris fall to the Germans," Amelia reassured the frightened staff but she wasn't sure if they believed it. "Isn't that right, Your Royal Highness?"

"What?" Wallis finally noticed the servants waiting for her to take the lead. She suddenly remembered herself and her place as chatelaine. "Of course, but if any of you wish to go home, you may do so."

Mademoiselle Moulichon, Mr. Hale, Mr. Phillips, and Mr. Ladbroke chose to stay. The chef and most of the maids and footmen decided to join their families on the outskirts of Paris.

Amelia spent the rest of the morning settling their wages and typing up letters of reference. She was glad for the work. It kept her mind off the radio blaring news of German movements, especially when Monsieur Giraudoux, the French Minister of Information, came on to declare, "The real war has begun."

They lived as normally as possible for the next four days while listening to radio reports of the Germans pushing deeper into Belgium and Luxembourg toward the Maginot Line. They went to the Ritz to pack boxes for the refugees arriving with each new train from the north. Half the volunteers went to the station to help tend to the people's wounds, offer food, and reunite separated children with their desperate parents. The volunteers returned with horrific stories of German airplanes strafing civilians at the Belgian stations. The American hospital was filled with the wounded.

On the fourth day, Amelia leaned against the cream stone of the Ritz, her neck and shoulders stiff from work and worry. She closed her eyes and allowed the May sunshine to caress her face, but kept her ears alert for air raid sirens, artillery, or the roar of planes. The Paris skies had been clear since that first morning, and she heard nothing except the usual hum of traffic on the boulevards.

"Mrs. Montague, thank heavens I found you."

Amelia opened her eyes to see Mr. Metcalf hurrying toward her.

"What are you doing here? You're supposed to be in Vincennes with His Royal Highness."

"We were until things turned dicey."

"He deserted?"

"He said he'd done enough and there wasn't any reason to stay. I have no idea what he'll do next but he'll do something; it won't be the right thing but it'll be something."

His lack of faith in the Duke was as unnerving as his being here.

"We have to get back to Boulevard Suchet." Mr. Metcalf frowned. "His Royal Highness wants the Duchess moved to Biarritz. With the Germans on the move, the roads are full of people, and if we don't start soon, who knows where we'll get stuck."

IT TOOK HOURS to pack up the three cars and the truck Amelia was forced to hire because the Duke and Wallis were determined to take everything but the kitchen sink. Trying to talk them out of it was like trying to convince a child to let go of a lollipop. Amelia understood the Duke wanting to move his priceless antiques, they were practically historic artifacts, but Wallis clung to her things like a lifeboat. She stood in the dining room with Grandmother Warfield's china set in piles on the glossy table, arguing with the Duke and Amelia about packing them.

"I won't leave it behind." Wallis clutched one of the pink dinner plates to her chest. "This and Grandma's brooch are the only things of hers I have, the only mementos Uncle Sol would give me. I can't lose them."

"They'll be safer here than bouncing along a road where they might be stolen or broken." Amelia was ready to smash the entire set and be done with it. Every moment they wasted arguing over these silly things was one the Germans spent creeping closer to France.

"Or looted once ruffians realize we're gone," Wallis screeched, her voice higher and coarser than usual.

"Monsieur Hardeley will be here to watch over the house as he's done every time we've traveled, and the gendarmes will protect the neighborhood," Amelia assured her.

"I don't trust the French police as far as I could throw them."

The Duke, with uncharacteristic sternness, slid the plate out of Wallis's fingers and laid it on the stack with the others. "Mrs. Montague is right, it's safer here. After I get you settled in the south and am on my way back to the regiment, I'll speak to Ambassador Bullitt about placing the house under American protection. I'm sure the French Army will stop them and we'll be back in no time."

Amelia waited for Wallis to tell him he was a fool to think their precious things would be protected simply because an ambassador marked their house with a red notice stating it was under American jurisdiction. However, with their luggage already overwhelming the truck and the three cars taking them, the dogs, Mr. Hale, Mr. Phillips, Mr. Ladbroke, and Mademoiselle Moulichon to Biarritz, Wallis listened to him.

"All right, I'll leave it. But I'm not leaving my linens."

"That's fine, darling."

He might be all right with it but Amelia and Mr. Metcalf wanted to scream in frustration at the additional delay caused by packing and loading them into the already overstuffed cars.

It was well past noon by the time they drove away from Boulevard Suchet. The busy avenue was eerily quiet and the large houses lining it closed up and deserted. It was slow going getting out of Paris and the road to Biarritz was choked with everything from horse-drawn carts and bicycles to wheelbarrows. People walked with suitcases, others pushed prams full of household goods while older children carried their infant siblings. Those lucky enough to have a car sat bumper to bumper in traffic, the whole teeming mass forced to pull off to the side of the road every few miles to allow army vehicles to pass on their way north. Broken-down cars were abandoned or their owners sat dejected on the running boards, unable to move their haphazardly packed things.

At sunset, the line of traffic stopped and people climbed out of their cars to prepare to bed down on the side of the road for the night.

"There must be somewhere more suitable than this." Wallis slammed the car door closed. "I won't sleep on the ground."

The Duke stepped out on the other side, followed by Mademoiselle Moulichon, who took the leashed dogs into the field to do their business.

"We'll find you something, darling. Mr. Ladbroke, see what's near here. There must be a château or a respectable house willing to put us up for the night."

Mr. Ladbroke, the lines of his face much deeper since he'd driven them away from Paris, trudged off toward a group of small buildings in the distance.

"He's sending him on a fool's errand," Mr. Metcalf grumbled, but Amelia didn't have the energy to agree with him as she sat against the car to eat a can of tinned sardines and crackers. Two hours later, Mr. Ladbroke returned to say there were no respectable lodgings to be borrowed or purchased and they'd have to sleep on the ground or in the cars. Wallis didn't argue this time, but allowed the Duke, Mr. Metcalf, and Mr. Phillips to remove some of the suitcases from the back seat and make a bed for her with her precious linens.

The Duke was shaking out one of the fine sheets when a radio announcement echoed through the line of cars and made him stop.

"King Leopold of the Belgians has formally surrendered to the Germans. Belgium is now German-occupied territory."

Quiet settled over the road of refugees. Belgium was the last defense between the German Army and France.

"If I were still King I could do something to help them; instead look at me, at us." The Duke opened his arms to the small group of tired servants sitting on old blankets in the beaten-down grass. "I hate being this useless."

He slumped beside the car, buried his head in his hands, and sobbed. Wallis marched up to him and yanked his hands away from his face.

"Stop it, stop it this instant, do you hear me? Stop it! You aren't useless. You'll have your chance to do something. I'm sure of it."

"Yes, darling." He tugged a wrinkled handkerchief out of his coat pocket and wiped the dust and tears off his face. "You're right, as always."

The Duke couldn't fall to pieces at a time like this, but Wallis's conviction made Amelia wonder. If she weren't so tired and overwhelmed by the misery in every face around her, she might think more about it. Instead, she lay on her jacket, tucked a sweater under her head, and fell into a fitful sleep.

THEIR CARAVAN ROLLED into Biarritz the next afternoon and any relief at having reached safety vanished. The seaside resort was packed to the gills with fancy cars overloaded with things and people, many of whom Amelia recognized. Some planned to remain in Biarritz to see which way the winds of war blew. The rest were trying to secure whatever passage they could find out of Europe. Amelia had no idea where the rest of the refugees had fled but the rich were apparently coming here.

The Duke paid more money than he was comfortable with

to rent four rooms at the Hotel du Palais, one for the male staff, one for the female staff, another for Wallis and himself, and the fourth for their luggage. Mr. Metcalf and Amelia were ready to chuck the luggage in the Mediterranean when they were forced to find footmen willing to carry it into the hotel because Wallis was afraid it would be stolen from the cars.

"For once I have an ocean view." Mademoiselle Moulichon pushed aside the lace curtains in her and Amelia's room. "How long do you think we'll be here?"

"I don't know." Amelia fell on the clean bed, eager to sleep after the hard ground last night. There'd been no talk of anything except getting south. Now they were here and she hadn't heard any plans about what they intended to do next. "I suppose we'll wait until we can get to England." Assuming the Windsors decided to go to England. After last year, Amelia wouldn't put it past them to refuse to return, but with real bombs and bullets flying she couldn't imagine them being foolhardy enough to stay.

"It's too crowded," Wallis complained three days later while she and Amelia walked back to the hotel after refugee beggars had driven them away from a pleasant stroll along the boardwalk. The poor people moved among the rich, who sat in beach chairs while waiting for news of passage on the next ship out of Europe. It was the strangest gathering of the wealthy on the Riviera she'd ever seen, all of them overdressed and over-jeweled in a desperate attempt to leave France with as many of their valuables as possible. "There're too many of the wrong sort here."

"Are there really a right and wrong sort at a time like this?" Amelia was too tired and worried to follow Mrs. Bedaux's fifth rule. Whatever Wallis and the Duke's next move, they hadn't shared it with her or Mr. Metcalf and neither of them appeared to be in a hurry to get to England.

"There are a right and wrong sort in every situation." Wallis sidestepped a woman with a baby sitting in a shop doorway begging for money or food. "One of the many things I learned on my way to Peking, when the American diplomats were in a tizzy because there was fighting around there, is that war doesn't make anyone give up their prejudices. You should have heard the things those diplomats said about me because I wouldn't cower in fear but insisted on traveling."

"You were very brave." Amelia slipped the beggar woman a coin, raising her finger to her lips to silence the woman's gratitude so Wallis wouldn't hear.

"A woman has to take a few chances if she wants to get anywhere in life."

They strolled into the hotel lobby, where every chair and bench was filled with people. A radio on the porter's counter blared reports of the war. They could hardly go anywhere without hearing news from one wireless or another. They weren't two steps into the lobby when the BBC broadcast was interrupted by a German voice reading the latest Nazi propaganda.

"No one is beyond the reach of the Third Reich. We know the Duke and Duchess of Windsor are staying in suite 305 of the Hotel du Palais. Herr Hitler hopes they enjoy their holiday and will soon see them in Paris."

Everyone turned to glare at Wallis and Amelia. Amelia hadn't endured this much hate since the day she'd walked into Hutzler's department store with Aunt Bessie and run into her old debutante friends. The disgust on their faces had been nothing compared to this. With that single announcement, Wallis had gone from the crème de la crème to one of the wrong sort.

"We'll be bombed to bits because of them," a woman whispered to her friend.

"There must be spies here. How else did they know she was here?"

"She's a Nazi lover. You saw those pictures of her and Hitler."

Wallis pretended not to hear the nasty remarks but raised her chin and straightened her shoulders as she walked to the elevators, collecting more suspicious looks and sneers from the well-heeled guests. Amelia mimicked her as best she could as the whispers about Wallis and the danger she posed to the other refugees flew through the hotel.

"How did they know you were here?" Amelia asked in a low voice as they stepped into the elevator and the operator slid the grate closed.

"I have no idea, but we can't stay."

"We won't go to England," the Duke insisted. "We'll go to la Croë."

"I would strongly advise against it, sir." Mr. Metcalf tried to reason with him and Wallis as they sat in their room surrounded by Louis Vuitton trunks. They'd gone round and round about it for the past half hour and gotten nowhere. "We have to find passage to England before the situation in France turns dire."

"Nonsense. Sir Walter paraded in here last year carrying on about risks and nothing came of it. It's the same this time. I refuse to run like a scared rabbit back to England only to be treated with the same disdain as before. I'm a prince, I have my pride."

"Your pride," Mr. Metcalf scoffed. "France is falling, women and children are being shot on the roads, and all you care about is yourself and your pride. Stop being so selfish and start seeing what's around you. Europe is at war."

"AMELIA, WHERE ARE you?" Robert's sturdy voice sounded over the crackling phone line. She'd risked the long-distance charges to call him, willing to pay for them out of her own salary to hear his voice. She wanted his opinion so she could tell Wallis the situation, gain more ammo, as it were, to convince them to leave France before it was too late. What she wouldn't give to be in his arms and indulging in the strength of him instead of here, but she couldn't fall to pieces.

"La Croë." Through the open gatehouse windows, she could see the sloping lawn leading down to the cobalt-blue ocean. With the crashing waves and seagulls calling to each other, she could almost pretend the world hadn't gone mad, but it had.

"What are you doing there? You should be in England or on the next ship to America."

"Good luck convincing them of that. The Duke went back to his regiment but only because Mr. Metcalf guilted him into doing it. I doubt he'll stay there. No one can stop him from doing what he wants and he wants to be with Wallis. What about you?"

"Washington wants Ambassador Bullitt home but he won't leave. America is a neutral country and we're working like hell to get out anyone at risk, especially Jews. We're bending a lot of rules to do it but once we go, there won't be anyone left to help them."

She admired his bravery and his reasons for staying and feared what might happen to her and many others when he was finally forced to leave. "How bad is it?"

"The Germans are pushing through the Ardennes and it'll only be a matter of days before they're in Paris."

A chill raced through Amelia. The Ardennes was the weak point the Duke had told Wallis about and she'd told Mrs. Bedaux. Who had Mrs. Bedaux told? No, there were thousands stationed there. If the Duke saw the weakness, a hundred others must have seen it too and some of them were sure to be spies. "What about the French Army?"

"There isn't one, and the British forces were evacuated at Dunkirk. Paris has been declared an open city and the French government is gone. Ambassador Bullitt is the highest-ranking official left and he's doing everything he can to make sure the Germans don't bomb the city when they enter it. Try and get the Windsors to leave while they still can, before there isn't anyone left to help you."

"They won't do anything to the Duke."

"You don't know that. Prince Ernst of Hohenberg and his

American wife were arrested after the fall of Vienna and no one has heard from them since. Her parents are frantically trying to find her but she's disappeared. The same could happen to you. Once you're in the Germans' hands, God help you. Staying is part of my job, but I know damn well it's not what you signed up for."

"Yes, it is. If I don't help Wallis have better sense than to stick around and be captured by the Germans, who will?"

He paused before he finally answered. "I understand." Urgent voices sounded in the background. "I have to go. I love you, Amelia."

She closed her eyes, the phone warm against her ear, his voice rough with emotion that echoed inside her. "I love you too."

This wasn't how she'd wanted to tell him, or admit it to herself, but with the Germans bearing down on France, it was possible she might never see or speak to him again. The world had gone insane.

Chapter Eighteen

La Croë, June 1940

"Thank heavens you're safe." Wallis embraced the Duke the moment he stepped out of his car. "I told you not to go back to Paris. You could've been hurt or killed if you hadn't left before the Germans marched into France."

"Where's Mr. Metcalf?" Amelia didn't see him among the trunks and items from Boulevard Suchet being carried into the house by the local men under Mr. Phillips's direction.

"How the devil should I know?" the Duke tossed at her with an indifferent shrug.

"You left him in Paris?"

He eyed her with a reprimanding stare. "He's resourceful, he'll find his way back to England. Besides, that's not important now. This madness has to be stopped before the politicians get millions killed. Mr. Phillips, come, we have work to do." They marched inside.

Wallis narrowed her eyes at Amelia. "Watch your tone when you speak to David. He isn't one of the servants."

"He left Mr. Metcalf in Paris to fend for himself."

"He doesn't matter. What matters is how you treat David in front of the servants. They won't help us if they don't respect us, and we might need them to get our things to a port if we have to leave." She spun on her heel and marched into the house to be with the Duke.

Amelia stared after her, unable to believe what she'd just heard. Mr. Metcalf had served the Duke for years, been the best man at their wedding, and after all that, they'd simply discarded him like a dirty tissue when it'd suited them. If they could cast off an old friend this easily, who else might they abandon when it was convenient?

Wallis wouldn't treat me like that. I'm like a daughter to her, and she needs me.

Amelia watched the footmen carrying the Duke's things inside. They eyed Amelia with unease and she felt the vulnerability of the Windsors' position and hers.

TENSIONS REMAINED HIGH in the house after that. The Duke and Mr. Phillips locked themselves in the Belvedere to compose telegrams to everyone from Mr. Churchill to the Italian king, whom the Duke encouraged to plead with Il Duce for peace. Amelia and Mr. Phillips had a devil of a time getting the cables sent without being censored, with Amelia forced to explain to the telegram operator that these were personal wires from the Duke of Windsor. It hadn't moved him. When Mr. Phillips came to her, red-faced, asking for help in sending a telegram to Herr Hitler, she'd flatly refused. She wanted no part of that.

She spent the rest of her time arranging for many of Wallis and the Duke's valuable and difficult-to-pack items to be sent to a monastery deep in the hills. Mr. Maugham had recommended it before he and Syrie had sailed away on their yacht, their generous offer to take the Duke and Duchess with them refused, much to Amelia and everyone's irritation. Hiding the Windsors' things had cost the Duke a whopping twelve thousand francs, and it was the first time Amelia had ever seen him willingly pay so much for anything. Heaven knew if they were really safe but she'd fought with the bank about the wire transfer, passing on their concerns that if the Germans invaded, the Windsors' French funds might be frozen. Wallis and the Duke hadn't done anything with that information but Amelia had wired her savings to an account Aunt Bessie had opened for her in America to keep her money safe from the Germans.

Wallis spent her days locked in her room talking to people on her private telephone line. Amelia didn't know who Wallis was calling but figured she was probably fretting over some piece of frippery at Boulevard Suchet. Amelia almost wished a bomber would hit the house and burn it to pieces so the stubborn people would stop worrying about their things and leave.

In between securing rationed petrol reserves for the cars, acquiring food for the house, and soothing crying and nervous maids and belligerent footmen, Amelia had cabled Lady Metcalf, eager for any news about her husband, but she had no idea where he was. No one had seen or heard from him in days and

Wallis and the Duke hadn't given him another thought. When the postman finally handed Amelia a telegram from Mr. Metcalf, she tore it open with relief.

He left me without a word or a car or any way to get back to France. When I saw him the night before, he wished me goodnight as he did every night and I returned to my lodging, only to learn the next morning that he'd absconded with both cars and the rationed petrol and left Paris at 6am without one word to me. After all my years of loyal service, to be treated worse than one of his dogs is beyond comparison. By sheer luck I made it to Cherbourg, hitchhiking and walking for miles, and secured passage on one of the few remaining ships leaving for England.

After twenty years I am through. I utterly despise him. He deserted his job in 1936; well he's deserted his country now, at a time when everyone is trying to do what he can. It is the end. I have had not one word from him and I can only surmise that he intends to stay where he is now. I am out of his service and I feel sure it is the only thing to do. I am through with the Windsors. Stay safe and be cautious Mrs. Montague, and look out for yourself. In these trying times you cannot count on anyone else.

Amelia folded the telegram. Mr. Metcalf had every right to curse the Duke. She hoped she never had a reason to do the same.

"You dance divinely," Maurice Chevalier complimented the Duchess in his heavily accented English as he swung her about the terrace in time to the radio. The Duke watched his wife and the famous French singer from where he lounged on one of the chaises, a martini in one hand, his pipe in the other.

"*Enchanté,* madame. *Livin' in the sunlight,*" Monsieur Chevalier sang along to the orchestral version of his song, his rich voice as soothing as the warm sunshine and bright sky.

Wallis had invited Mr. Chevalier to lunch, hoping to lighten the cloud of doom hanging over the house. The Duke tapped his fingers against the chair's arm in time with the music, thoroughly enjoying himself.

Mr. Chevalier twirled Wallis off and with a laugh she planted herself in the chair beside the Duke. "No more for me."

"Madame?" Mr. Chevalier leaned over in his white linen suit, a wicked smile curling his lips beneath his pencil mustache as he held out his hand to Amelia.

She didn't want to dance and pretend everything was wonderful but she couldn't ruin the mood and risk another dressing down from Wallis. She didn't want to wake up in the morning to find everyone gone and her left to fend for herself.

Mr. Chevalier took her in his arms, his hand very low on her back while he guided her in a waltz beneath the shade of the columned roof. At any other time, in any other place she would've written Aunt Bessie about it. It was too absurd to write about now.

A breaking bulletin interrupted the song. "In a speech from Venice Square in Rome, addressing the Italian people, Dictator Mussolini has declared war on the United Kingdom and France."

Mr. Chevalier let go of her, picked up his hat from the side table, and set it over his black hair. "*Excusez-moi, Son Altesse Royale*. I have enjoyed my time here and thank you, but my wife is Jewish and we must hurry to consider our next move. I wish you both well. Until we meet again, hopefully under happier circumstances. *Au revoir.*"

He bolted inside, imploring Mr. Hale to call for his car.

"I'll make arrangements to close up the house," Amelia said, still standing in the center of the terrace.

"No need to run around like chickens with our heads cut off." The Duke sipped his martini. "There's nothing to worry about."

"Except the Italian border is only forty miles from here, and the French Army hasn't done a thing to stop the Germans up north."

Wallis threw her a warning glance but she ignored it, as short-tempered with their stubbornness as Mr. Metcalf. The Duke and Wallis weren't taking this seriously and she couldn't understand why.

Inside, the phone rang and Mr. Hale answered it, then came out and announced, "Mr. Rogers is on the line. He says it's urgent."

"I'll speak to him." The Duke rose from the chair with a huff, annoyed anyone should be worried when he clearly wasn't. The Duke was no sooner done assuring Mr. Rogers that he and Wallis were safe when the phone rang again. Amelia could tell by his reaction it was someone else calling with the same advice. After the fourth phone call, the Duke stopped picking up.

"WHY ARE THEY still there?" Sir Walter asked when Amelia finally got through to him in London.

"The Duke says he won't have Wallis sleeping in cars again, and he'll only leave if His Majesty sends a destroyer for them and all their things."

"There isn't one to send. Doesn't he understand? Britain is fighting for her very existence. The intractable fool."

Things must be bad for Sir Walter to lose his cool. It took every ounce of Amelia's strength not to run for the next ship to America, assuming she could find passage.

"Is there something else going on?" Sir Walter asked.

"I don't know. They spend most of their time in their rooms making calls but I don't know who they're talking to; it certainly isn't me or anyone who could help get us out of here. I think Wallis spoke to Mrs. Bedaux but only because she promised to look after Boulevard Suchet." Their obsession with their things was maddening.

"She's better off not talking to her or anyone so closely aligned with the Nazis."

"I know. I'd tell them I'm on the line with you but they'd only start arguing for the extra-chic title again. A lot of good that'll do them if the Italian Army marches through here."

"I'll make a few calls and see if there's someone who can talk some sense into them."

Amelia was overseeing a delivery of wine on the front steps, the locals eager to make a few francs off the Windsors before war put an end to everything. She was inspecting bottles when the low rumble of an engine caught her attention. A small plane painted in green and black camouflage emerged from behind the wispy early summer clouds and dipped down so low over the trees, Amelia could see the red, green, and white circle on the tail.

An Italian fighter plane.

It flew off over the trees, the putting rhythm of the engine almost mesmerizing before the crack of machine-gun fire and a loud explosion broke the spell. A tall column of black smoke rose up from the nearby village, marring the fine blue sky.

"We're under attack!" the deliveryman yelled.

Everyone dropped the crates of wine and scattered, taking cover behind columns and bushes. Amelia crouched behind the van then peered over the hood as the plane reemerged above the trees. She covered her head with her arms, waiting for another rattle of machine-gun fire or an explosion to finish her off but it never came. The whir of the plane's engine faded into the distance and everyone slowly stood, scanning the skies for more danger. Amelia brushed the dirt off her skirt, wincing at the scratch on her leg from a sharp pebble.

"What happened?" Wallis rushed out the front door, the Duke close behind her. "What's going on out here?"

"An Italian fighter plane bombed the village."

Wallis and the Duke watched the large black plume rise into the sky above the trees.

"That's how Herr Hitler will bring Britain to her knees," the Duke whooped. "Charles thought I was silly when I said so but he'll see I'm right."

"Shut up, David," Wallis commanded. "Don't be such a blabbermouth."

"We have to leave at once," Amelia insisted, tired of being timid. "We aren't safe here."

"Nonsense, there're always rogue pilots trying to make names for themselves." The Duke picked up a broken bottle. "Who did this? Clean up this mess at once."

"That wasn't a one-off. The pilot deliberately targeted the village. I saw it. He could've done the same to us if he'd wanted. If we stay, there might be more planes next time and more than shattered wine bottles to worry about."

"Come with me at once." Wallis grabbed Amelia by the arm and pulled her up the front stairs and into the sitting room. The cool ocean breeze, heavy with salt and moisture, made the tall yellow curtains flanking the open windows move. "Why are you scaring everyone?"

"Because if you listen carefully you can hear the French shelling Genoa." Amelia shook out of her grasp. "Why are we still here? Why haven't we left?"

"Because there's no reason to go traipsing around France like vagabonds, leaving our precious things to be looted."

"They're just things. They can be replaced."

"They aren't just things but a part of our wealth, and if we can't get our money out of French banks, we'll need them to live on. I won't be poor again. You of all people should understand that."

"You won't need money if you're dead."

"No one is going to die." Wallis took a steadying breath. "I have assurances that no matter what happens, we'll be safe."

"From whom?" Her cousin had gone mad over flatware.

"Herr von Ribbentrop. I've spoken to him numerous times and he's promised that we and our things will be perfectly safe."

"Is that who you've been holed up in your room talking to?"

"That's none of your business."

"It is when my life is at stake too. What if you're wrong or he's lying and the Italians march in here and hand you over to the Germans, then what? Queen Elizabeth won't lift a finger to help you; she'll probably be glad to be rid of you or say you threw in with the Nazis and everyone will believe her because of those pictures of you and the Duke saluting Herr Hitler in Germany. Whatever deal you think you've got, whatever you're planning, if we leave, you'll have a stronger position to bargain from than if you fall into their hands."

Wallis turned her emerald engagement ring around on her finger. "I hadn't thought of that."

"It's always better to have choices, especially since you have no diplomatic papers or safeguards, and if the Duke is captured, they might treat him as a combatant because of his military rank." It was every argument Sir Walter had given her to try and reason with them.

"His position was only an honorary one."

"They don't know that, and you don't know what nefarious game Herr von Ribbentrop is using you for. Stop playing into their hands. We've got to go while we still can."

Wallis began to pace, contemplating everything Amelia had said. Amelia hoped she'd come to her senses. If she didn't, Amelia would call Prime Minister Churchill herself and tell him to make them leave at gunpoint.

"I think you're right. We can better bargain with them if we aren't in their hands," Wallis said at last.

"Bargain about what?"

She didn't answer but faced her as she had every morning when she'd given Amelia her daily tasks. "I'll speak with David. Prepare the household for our departure."

"YOU WANTED TO see me?" Amelia joined Wallis in the sitting room. "The cars are filled to the brim. We can't squeeze much else in." The packing list had grown like a fungus over the past twenty-four hours. Major Hugh Dodds, the British consul at Nice, had told the Duke the only way out of France was by car through neutral Spain and then on to Lisbon. Amelia hadn't been able to find a truck driver willing to drive that far.

"It isn't about the luggage. I left my safe in Paris when we fled. I can't leave it behind. I'd like you to go to Paris and arrange to have it shipped to us in Lisbon."

Amelia stared at her, unable to believe what she'd heard. "You can buy new jewels. I did the insurance paperwork myself. I won't risk my life for things you can replace."

"It's not about my jewelry but some personal papers and correspondence."

She didn't like the sound of that. "What kind of correspondence?"

"The sort that in the wrong hands could be read in the worst light." Wallis rearranged the flowers in the vase on the abdication desk, the last bit of furniture left to pack. "I'm friends with very influential German men. I've known them since London, it's all perfectly innocent, but you know how quick people are to disparage me and they would over this. Then I and everyone associated with me will be dragged through the mud, the way they dragged you over Jackson. I know you don't want to go through that again. I can't bear it, and in these uncertain times, anything taken in the wrong light could mean the difference between being safe and being at risk."

She didn't want to be dragged again but she didn't want to end up with the Germans either. "Why didn't you bring the safe with us when we left?"

"You saw everything abandoned on the road. I couldn't risk it being dropped in some field for anyone to find, and I didn't believe, I never imagined, we couldn't go home or that France would fall. I can't risk desperate people breaking into Boulevard Suchet and stealing it."

"Then have your German friends send it to Lisbon."

"They're much too busy to bother with something like this, and I don't want them digging through my things either. I have to send someone I trust."

"It's too dangerous."

"You'll be perfectly safe. The Germans are being generous with Americans, they don't want to drag us into the war by mistreating those still in France. You'll have not only the protection of the U.S. Embassy but the highest German officials." She opened the top drawer of the abdication desk and removed a few papers and handed them to Amelia. There was a ticket on the Blue Train to Paris and German travel documents signed by Herr von Ribbentrop granting Amelia free movement through France and Paris. "Here's a list of some other things I'd like you to get from the house. You can use them to hide the safe when you ship it. Once you finish in Paris, you'll meet us in Lisbon and travel with us to England. It's all been arranged."

"You did this without asking me?"

"I trust you, and you know all the right people, the correct routes, how to arrange things so no one will ask questions. I'd do it myself but David is helpless without me, and if we have any hope of getting back to England, I must stay with him."

She was right. Without Wallis, the Duke might linger somewhere inappropriate and place everyone from Mademoiselle Moulichon to Mr. Phillips in danger. Amelia had to think of their welfare too. If they stayed with the Windsors they'd get out of Europe with them, assuming Wallis didn't waste precious time demanding the Duke use this opportunity to gain more titles and honors for her.

There's opportunity in chaos.

A chill filled her. There was more to this than chasing after old letters, she could feel it. "Is there something you're not telling me?"

"Not at all." Wallis's cool blue eyes and bland expression betrayed nothing. She'd spent her life pretending to the press, society, and the Duke that she was above worry or care or human emotion. It'd become as easy to her as breathing. "I'm simply looking out for you and everyone's best interests."

"By sending me into the lion's den?"

"I'd never ask you to do this if I thought it was dangerous."

"You wouldn't ask me to do it if you cared about me."

"I've told you before, you're like a daughter to me, but this is no time to be overly sentimental. You're a brave, adventurous girl. It's nothing you can't manage."

"I won't go."

The ice of controlled anger hardened Wallis's blue eyes and made Amelia take a step back. "You owe me this, especially after all I've done for you. I educated and dressed you, introduced you to influential people, and made something of you. Aren't you grateful?"

Amelia's stomach dropped. "Of course, but—"

"Then it's time for you to help me, and a great deal to lose if you don't. I paid off your debts. I'd hate to have to undo that arrangement."

Amelia stared at Wallis, her cousin unrecognizable and familiar all at once. "It would ruin me."

"Then let's not allow it to come to that."

It was like a punch in the gut, hitting her so hard it was a wonder she could stand up straight. For the first time, she saw what Theodore, Mrs. Gordon, and others had seen, the demanding woman who placed her own self-interest above everyone and everything else. She didn't doubt for a moment Wallis would call in the debt if she refused to go and she struggled to think of some excuse to stay, a reason why this was an awful idea, but deep down she knew there was no argument she could make. Wallis wanted that safe and nothing else, not even Amelia and everything they'd been to one another, mattered.

Amelia fiddled with the button on her blouse, one Wallis had bought and paid for at Schiaparelli. Everything Amelia had, from her social connections to her career and the very clothes on her back, had come from Wallis, and suddenly her present life wasn't a new start but a silver web spun by Wallis to entrap her. No matter which way she turned she was caught.

How did I end up in this position again? She'd trusted Wallis, believed in her, stood beside her, and in the end, Wallis was willing to hold it over her head to make Amelia do what she wanted. She had no idea what Wallis was even doing or what she was really asking Amelia to do. She could be accused of passing information to the enemy or whatever else Wallis was embroiled in, and it was clear Wallis would drag her down with her if it all went bad. But Wallis could ruin her if she refused.

"Well?" Wallis demanded, and Amelia flinched. There was no way out of this.

"I'll go." She couldn't afford not to.

Chapter Nineteen

Paris, June 20, 1940

Amelia disembarked from the Nice train at Gare de Lyon station, shocked to hear more German than French and see the mass of gray uniforms on the platform. The Blue Train had taken two days to reach Paris instead of the usual five hours, delayed by the confusion of transporting people and troops. Amelia had been forced to sleep in her seat, and with no energy for the long walk to 24 Boulevard Suchet, she stepped aboard the Paris Metro, one of the few civilians brave or foolish enough to travel with so many German soldiers. The metro trains were still running, the Germans keeping Paris moving for their convenience, not the Parisians'. The soldiers on board were courteous and polite, enjoying their odd holiday, but she sensed that could change in an instant. She kept her head down and made herself as small and unnoticeable as possible. Thankfully, the Germans ignored her and she emerged from La Muette metro station with no incidents and made the short walk to Boulevard Suchet.

The street was eerily still and her knock at the front door sounded like cannon fire. Mr. Hardeley, his face as somber as the few others' she'd seen on the walk here, let her in. Amelia stood in the foyer as her eyes adjusted to the darkness. The closed shutters let in only slivers of light that illuminated the dust covers over the furniture. She'd spent hours with Wallis planning every detail of the decor and now it was protected by nothing more than a few locks, an old caretaker, and the red letter pasted on the door stating the house was under the protection of the American government. The lack of life inside reminded her of standing in the Wellesley house before she'd left it to the creditors and her past forever.

How did I end up in this situation again? She'd asked that question over and over on the train to Paris. Another person she'd loved and trusted had played her for a dupe, and she'd allowed it to happen. She'd been too enamored of Wallis, too eager to be like her, to be loved and admired by her and others, to see who Wallis really was. Jackson had ruined her life. Wallis might be the end of it if she wasn't careful.

"We need to get to work," Monsieur Hardeley urged. "You don't want to draw too much attention to yourself or the house."

Together, they hid Wallis's safe in a trunk beneath the furs, shoes, and other odds and ends from Wallis's list. Monsieur Hardeley and his son loaded the trunk into his truck. She'd negotiated with him to drive it south, the caretaker eager to get paid to leave Paris and spend the war in the country with his family. Amelia gave them a little extra for their troubles before they drove off. She wasn't certain she or Wallis would ever see those things again, but she'd upheld her part of the bargain. It was time for her to go.

But where?

She locked up the house then stood on the stoop, debating what to do. She didn't want to go back to Wallis, but Wallis and the Duke could get her to England. London was full of titled and rich women in need of private secretaries. She could start a new life there, free from anyone's influence, or she could walk away from Wallis now and find a way to succeed on her own.

Wallis can go to hell.

She hurried toward the train station but her determination slowed with her steps.

She couldn't afford to leave Wallis. She had nothing but her traveling suit and one change of clothes in her leather satchel. Her savings was in America, and if she distanced herself from Wallis, Wallis might force her to repay the debt or whisper nasty things about Amelia to her wealthy friends and ruin any chance she had of starting over. Everything she owned was with Wallis but she wasn't, and neither were her friends or Robert. They were at the Chancery, and they were the one thing she had that Wallis didn't own. They'd help her decide what to do and where to go next.

She skipped the metro, afraid to risk another ride with the soldiers, and decided to walk instead. She hurried down the quiet Avenue du Président Wilson, stepping over and around piles of things discarded by fleeing people, their lives left on the asphalt to be picked over by scavengers and dogs. Overhead, the evening sky was clear of fighter planes, and the sunset was less orange and red without the usual haze of chimney smoke and car exhaust to filter the light. Even the bird songs were louder without the roar of traffic to drown them out. Beneath their twittering, the hum of a single car engine caught her attention. She glanced over her shoulder and saw a black Mercedes idling on the curb down the block. She pulled her light coat closer around her and walked faster. The sooner she reached the safety of the Chancery, the better.

She turned the corner to another street, this one as quiet as the last except for the subtle hum of the Mercedes as it turned the corner too.

He's following me.

She took a deep breath, determined not to panic while trying to decide what to do. She walked toward a bar just up the block, a small place not listed in Baedeker, eager to get off the street. Inside, despondent Parisians drowned their sorrows in cognac and Grand Marnier, the Germans uninterested in their misery.

"What are you doing in here?" the bartender barked when she approached him, eyeing her as if she were a member of the Totenkopf and drawing everyone's attention to her.

"Can I use your telephone?" She dug a crisp franc note from her purse and slid it across the bar.

He slapped his hand over the money and tucked it in his apron pocket then jerked his thumb toward the phone in the corner.

"*Merci.*" She hurried to it, not wanting to spend more time in here than necessary but afraid to go back outside in case the Mercedes was still there. She dialed the number she knew by heart and breathed a sigh of relief when Susan answered the phone. "Susan, it's Amelia. Is Robert there?"

"No, he's with Ambassador Bullitt. Where are you?"

"In Paris."

"What are you doing here?"

"I can't explain over the phone but I need somewhere safe to stay."

"Get here as soon as you can and you can bed down with us. Everyone's living here now."

"I'll be there in a few minutes."

"I'll meet you at the gates. Be careful, honey."

"I will."

Amelia hung up and, under the bartender's disapproving stare, walked back out into the dimming evening light. She paused in the doorway to survey the quiet street. The Mercedes was gone. She started off, walking quickly but not fast enough to call attention to herself as she passed quiet or empty buildings. She barely noticed them until she turned the corner into a square and saw the pocked and mutilated brick and the large crimson stain on the ground in front of it beside a discarded cap. People had been lined up here and shot.

What the hell am I doing in Paris? She wanted to sit down on a nearby bench and weep but she couldn't. She had to stay strong, to keep her wits about her. She'd find a way out of this the way she'd found her way out of her troubles before.

You never found a way out. You simply changed one rotten situation for another.

She kept going despite the doubts and fears, crossing the square as the evening darkness deepened around her. The streetlights didn't come on, the electricity, like petrol, confiscated and controlled by the Germans. Theodore's and Alice Gordon's warnings about Wallis echoed with each footstep on the pavement but she couldn't let them stop her or slow her down. She had to get to the Chancery. She could berate herself when she was safe.

She finally reached the Champs-Élysées. It was only a short walk to the Chancery from here but it felt as if she'd stepped into a whole other world. The bloodred Nazi banners that'd dominated Berlin swathed Paris, including the large Nazi flag hanging from the Arc de Triomphe. The sidewalk cafés rang with the laughter of German troops enjoying cappuccinos and ordering the French waiters around. The chic Parisian ladies had been replaced by young soldiers buying presents for sweethearts or taking pictures in front of the Arc de Triomphe. The streets were empty of cars except for German military vehicles. The few Parisians who dared to be out walked with their heads down, careful to avoid eye contact with their conquerors. Their faces were forlorn and mournful, beaten down by this start to a long and difficult road. The only consolation was the lack of fighting. The German soldiers were too busy sightseeing to shoot, and judging by what she saw, Ambassador Bullitt had succeeded in sparing the city from the destruction the Germans had wrought in Rotterdam.

She picked up her pace, about to cut through the Jardin des Champs-Élysées when the black Mercedes pulled to a stop in front of her.

Three German officers in dark uniforms with the death's head insignia on their caps stepped out and surrounded her.

"Please come with us," the tallest one said in perfect British English.

"I'm an American citizen." She dug through her pocket for her papers.

"We know who you are, Frau Montague."

She drew on every ounce of poise and secretarial training to hide her fear. "Then you know I have the proper papers, issued by your government and arranged by the Duchess of Windsor with Herr von Ribbentrop, to travel freely in Paris." She handed him the papers.

He barely glanced at them before sliding them into his breast pocket. "Come with us, please."

The other two men waited patiently for her to comply or resist. They didn't seize her or shackle her but there was no mistaking they'd get her in that car one way or another. She'd be at their mercy once she was inside it, but she couldn't resist. She'd seen the bullet holes and blood on the street. She knew what they were capable of and allowed them to lead her into the Mercedes.

"WHAT'S IN THE safe, Frau Montague?" SS-Standartenführer Helmut Knochen asked from across the gilded and marble-topped tea table. He wore a black uniform with an Iron Cross hanging from one pocket. He spoke English with a mild German accent, and with his neatly combed and parted hair and pleasing manners, he looked like the many gentlemen she'd met in Berlin or at various parties before the war. Except this was no cocktail party.

She'd sat alone in the large salon of the Hôtel Lyon-Broussac for three hours, according to the gilded cherub clock on the sideboard. She'd been here once before when she and Wallis had joined Lady Williams-Taylor and Eugenie for a farewell tea last October. Lady Williams-Taylor admired Herr Hitler but not enough to stick around and risk his jackboots treading over her. The socialite had smartly decamped for Nassau. If Wallis had possessed half as much sense, she and Amelia might be in England or America and then Wallis wouldn't be on the road somewhere in the south and Amelia wouldn't be here trying not to shiver in fear.

If I'd possessed any sense, I never would've allowed Wallis to lead me into this mess in the first place. There was no time to think about that. She had to stay sharp if she wanted to survive. "I don't know. Her Royal Highness didn't give me the combination to the safe, but I imagine it's only her jewelry inside."

"I find it hard to believe she sent you all the way to Paris for jewels."

"She's very particular about her things. Ask Herr von Ribbentrop, he'll tell you. He's a close friend of hers and gave his personal assurance that I'd be safe. I'm sure Herr von Ribbentrop won't appreciate his orders being ignored."

"There's nowhere in Paris safer for you than here, and we've treated you well."

"I haven't had a thing to eat or drink since I arrived."

"An oversight and my apologies." He snapped his fingers and the young officer standing guard at the door left. "We've only just taken up residence and things are, as the English like to say, in sixes and sevens."

"Establishing a new household is exhausting." She spoke to him as if they were talking about the difficulties of running a large château, not the occupation of Paris, eager to keep him in a good mood. She didn't want to see the angry side of him. When Amelia didn't arrive at the Chancery, Susan would tell Robert and he'd find a way to get her out of this, assuming he could do it in time. Princess Hohenberg had disappeared. The same thing might happen to her.

"The Windsors left for Spain the same day you left for Paris. The last anyone heard from them was in Perpignan, near the Spanish border. According to Italian radio reports, Prime Minister Churchill has ordered their arrest if they enter England, so they can't be there. Do you know where they are?"

"All I know is I'm supposed to meet them in Lisbon. I left before they told me how they were getting there." It didn't seem possible for them to get lost. They had a habit of making themselves conspicuous everywhere they went. She also didn't know what the Germans expected to get out of her. Other than being Wallis's cousin, she knew nothing of value.

"Our contacts in Lisbon say they haven't arrived."

"Then I can't tell you where they are."

The soldier returned with a bowl of meat stew and a crystal goblet of water. He set it in front of her with the flourish of a waiter, hinting at his former occupation.

"Thank you." Amelia smiled at him and he hesitated, thrown off by her cordiality, before returning to his post by the door.

Amelia ate with dainty bites, refusing to fall on the food like a ravenous dog, determined to maintain her manners and composure in the face of her fears and this awful situation. The clock chimed the half hour. "This is very good."

"We enjoy only the best Paris has to offer."

Easy to do when you march in and take it. Amelia held her pleasant smile. "If you're looking for the best of everything, there's a young woman at the American Chancery, Susan Harper. She knows all the best places for wine, chocolate, something for your wife, everything. Speak to her if you get a chance, tell her I sent you. She's the most connected woman in Paris. It's how I used to get everything for Their Royal Highnesses, and at a deal. They like fine things too."

"I'll be sure to speak to her."

With any luck, he'd drop Amelia's name and give Susan and Robert some clue as to what had happened to her.

Another officer entered the room and whispered something to Herr Knochen. He nodded then smiled at Amelia. "I'm afraid I must end our little chat. You'll be shown to a room upstairs where you'll stay during your time with us."

"How long do you think that will be?" Amelia asked, as if waiting for a florist to finish a boutonniere for an evening dance. "I'm sure Her Royal Highness is eager to have me back."

She never wanted to see Wallis again but that didn't mean she wouldn't use her name to try and win favors or her freedom.

"I can't say, but once we're in contact with the Duke and Duchess, we'll send word of your delay."

"That's very kind of you. Might I write to Herr von Ribbentrop to let him know you're taking excellent care of me while I'm your guest?"

"We'll see, Frau Montague."

The new man and the young soldier escorted her through the lobby and up the stairs to a guest room on the first floor. Her satchel waited for her on the bench in front of the double bed, the zipper only half closed. Clearly they'd riffled through it because everything inside was a mess. She left it and lay down, too tired and on edge to undress. Thankfully, she was in a room and not some dank cellar. For a prison this was the best she could expect but it was still a prison and her situation could change at any minute.

Outside, the nightingale songs were accompanied by the voices of German soldiers walking along the elegant Avenue Foch. Whatever waited for her tomorrow would be easier to face if she got some sleep, but fear, disappointment, and disbelief tumbled through her, tensing her already frazzled nerves.

All I wanted was love and a little success. All I've been is hurt and betrayed. She rolled on her side and squeezed her eyes closed tight against the pain. She thought she'd been alone before. This was worse.

Exhaustion eventually overcame her and she drifted into a light and fitful sleep broken by a piercing scream. Amelia sat bolt upright as the horrific yell sounded again and again. She hurried to the window, looking to see if someone outside was hurt, but she couldn't see anyone in the faint moonlight.

It's coming from downstairs.

Harsh German voices barked out commands in the brief spaces between the howls and Amelia crawled into bed and pulled the covers tight around her. She covered her ears with her hands until a single shot split the night and the screams stopped. The silence afterward was far more terrifying.

Chapter Twenty

Paris, July 5, 1940

"Did you tell Her Royal Highness I've been delayed in joining her in Lisbon?" It'd been two weeks since Amelia's arrest and the monotonous days had melded one into another as she'd waited in dread for something to happen.

"We sent word through the German Ambassador to Spain while they were in Madrid," Herr Knochen said as he brought her the British newspapers. After the third day of nothing to do, she'd asked for something to read and he'd granted her request. It helped pass the time, especially on the nights when the screaming kept her up. It didn't happen every night but it had happened three more times since her arrival. She hadn't had the courage to ask about it, pretending every morning when she saw her captors that she was fine and nothing was wrong. It was an exhausting and demanding performance. "We've received no reply."

"She probably hasn't had a chance to cable or write back, what with all the confusion of moving from Madrid to Lisbon." That lie was as much to raise her flagging spirits as to convince him she wasn't worried. Once the Windsors had reemerged in a small village in France, the newspapers had followed their every move, allowing Amelia to track their progress from France to Madrid to Lisbon. The reports of their Italian capture and Prime Minister Churchill threatening to arrest them had been false but it wouldn't be long before they moved on to England. The possibility that Wallis and the Duke might abandon her to rot in German custody the way they'd left Mr. Metcalf to find his way home kept her up on the nights the tortured men didn't.

"Would you be so kind as to send word to her in Lisbon?"

"I'll cable Baron von Hoyningen-Huene today." He clasped his hands in front of him, more amused this morning than the previous ones. "I now understand your employer's fascination with her things. She had the Americans fetch a certain green swimsuit she left behind in the South of France. Apparently, she cannot live without it. It's no surprise she sent you to collect her jewels. I must thank you for your recommendation of Miss Harper. I paid her a visit at the American Chancery and she was most helpful with recommendations for wine merchants."

"I'm glad I could help." Her spirits soared even while she kept her expression serene. At least Susan had some idea of where she was and could tell Robert. Whether he could do anything to get her out of here remained to be seen but it was the first hope she'd enjoyed in days.

"May I write to some friends? Mrs. Bedaux, perhaps?" She never hesitated to drop names of the influential people she knew. She hoped one might do the trick and impress him enough to release her. So far, it hadn't. "It'll help pass the time."

"I'll send up some paper."

He did and she wrote to Mrs. Bedaux, telling her in the mildest terms possible that she was at the Hotel Lyon-Broussac as Herr Knochen's guest and it would be wonderful if she'd visit. Amelia didn't complain about her imprisonment or suggest Mrs. Bedaux use her influence to have her released. The Germans were sure to read what she wrote before sending it.

Mrs. Bedaux arrived at the Hotel Lyon-Broussac three days later with a box of chocolates and some magazines.

"You're looking well, Mrs. Montague." French occupation hadn't dampened Mrs. Bedaux's sense of style but it had taken a toll on Amelia, who had no makeup and dark circles under her eyes, and still wore her wrinkled traveling suit.

"Herr Knochen has been very kind to me." She didn't dare say what she really thought about him. The guard at the salon door spoke French and was sure to report their conversation to his superiors. She hoped he didn't speak English and switched to that language but she was still careful with her choice of words. "He's contacting Her Royal Highness in Lisbon on my behalf but I'd hoped you could write to her about my situation."

"She already knows of it and that you're perfectly fine."

"I'm not perfectly fine." She was about to jump out of her seat.

"But you are. No one has hurt you and no one will. All you need to do is sit tight and wait."

"For what?" What the devil was she caught up in?

"His Majesty's Government is being particularly difficult about Their Royal Highnesses leaving Europe when they'd prefer to stay a little while longer."

"Why do they want to stay?" It made no sense. Nothing did anymore.

"I can't say much except all will soon be revealed. If you thought your position was grand before, it will be nothing compared to what she'll offer you when this is over. All you need to do is your part, which is to be patient and wait. Your being here gives Her Royal Highness a legitimate reason to remain in Lisbon. Now I must go. I'm expected at Mademoiselle Chanel's Ritz suite at noon."

Mrs. Bedaux stood and Amelia grabbed her arm. "Her sending me here was never about the safe, was it?" She'd sent her to Paris knowing what would happen, using her for whatever end she was trying to achieve. Jackson had been bad but he'd never dragged her into his schemes. Amelia had practically walked right into Wallis's plans. *You fool.*

Fear flashed through Mrs. Bedaux's eyes and Amelia let go of her, afraid she'd call for the guard.

"Remember your place, dear." Mrs. Bedaux straightened the wrinkled Chanel knit sleeve. "And no matter what's asked of you, don't balk or look churlish. Enjoy the magazines."

She rose and left without a backward glance.

Amelia barely noticed the walk back to her room, too stunned to think straight. It wasn't until the door locked behind her that she snapped out of it. She tore through the magazines, hoping to find a hidden note or message from Mrs. Bedaux about her situation but there was nothing. She sank down onto the floor in the middle of her room, surrounded by the ripped and creased pages. *What the hell is happening?*

She'd trusted Mrs. Bedaux, as much as she'd trusted Wallis, and when she'd needed her, she'd left Amelia to her Nazi friends. They'd both betrayed her and she still had no idea why.

A WEEK AFTER Mrs. Bedaux's arrival, Amelia read the British newspaper article about the Duke of Windsor's appointment as the Governor-General of The Bahamas and his plans to set sail for Nassau. Mrs. Bedaux had said the whole point of Amelia being here was to keep the Windsors in Europe. If they set sail for Nassau, the Germans and the Windsors wouldn't need her anymore.

I have to get out of here.

She stood and paced the room before stopping at the window to try and gauge the distance between it and the ground. She could jump but she might break her leg and then they'd shoot her in the garden instead of dragging her off to wherever they tortured those men at night. She'd rather be shot than tortured to death.

The sudden entry of the guard made her nearly jump out of her skin.

"You have five minutes to gather your things," he barked.

"Where am I going?"

"Five minutes." He slammed the door closed behind him.

With shaking hands, Amelia packed up her satchel, trying not to let her mind run away with her. She'd just zipped it closed when the door opened again.

"Come with me."

She followed the guard out of the room and down the stairs. Ahead of her, the hotel's front door slowly closed behind the soldiers who'd just entered. If she made a run for it she might escape or gain a bullet in the back for her troubles. It might be preferable to whatever was waiting for her at the end of this walk.

The guard led her down the hall to the salon, the only other room she'd seen since arriving. Inside, a man in a gray suit spoke to Herr Knochen in firm but fluent German. After much talking and gesturing and some polite arguing, Herr Knochen waved his arm at Amelia.

"You may take her. It was a pleasure, Frau Montague." Herr Knochen bowed to her and she smiled, her final performance with the German before the other gentleman approached. She didn't know if her ordeal was over or about to begin until he spoke to her in perfect English.

"Mrs. Montague, I'm George Kennan, the American Ambassador to Berlin. I happened to be in Paris and Mr. Morton asked me to offer you some assistance. It's a pleasure to meet you."

AMELIA CLUNG TO Robert as she sobbed in his arms, the weeks of worry and terror leaving her in a flood of tears. She was free, he'd found her. She was safe.

"We called every contact we had to see if there was some rumor about where you were but there was nothing," Robert explained when her tears finally stopped. He settled her on the sofa in his Chancery office and handed her a cup of coffee. "It was as if you'd disappeared off the face of the earth. I even sent Daniel to the morgue to check for you. You don't know how surprised we were when that Knochen fellow came in here asking to speak to Susan and mentioned your name."

"I didn't know if he would."

"German bigwigs march in here once a day trying to flex some muscle but they don't have any authority here, so far. Once we had a lead, we knew where to look. Knochen is head of the secret police and itching to get control in Paris but there's some infighting between the Gestapo and the German Army so he's biding his time. It's why Ambassador Kennan was able to intervene on your behalf. If Knochen had full control, there's no telling what might've happened to you."

Amelia shivered despite the hot mug clutched in her hands. "Wallis left me there to rot."

"I know."

"How? Why? Why did she do that to me?" Fresh tears stung her eyes and she wiped them away with the back of her hand.

Robert slid a file off his desk and sat beside her. "What I'm about to show you is top secret. I trust you not to say anything to anyone, but I warn you, you won't like what's in here."

"I don't like a lot of things right now." Including about herself and how she'd landed in trouble.

"With good reason." He rested the file on his lap and opened it. "The Windsors refused to leave la Croë because they were in talks with Herr von Ribbentrop."

"I know. Wallis spoke to him before she sent me to Paris. She said he'd guarantee my safety." She set the coffee cup on the table. It stung to admit she'd been a gullible dupe.

"They were discussing more than that. Herr Hitler expects England will crumble as fast as France, and when it does, he plans to put the Duke on the throne as a puppet king with Wallis by his side."

Amelia stared at him, unable to believe what he'd said. Wallis was bad but she wasn't that awful—or was she? If five years ago someone had told Amelia that Wallis would divorce Ernest and help pull a king from his throne, she'd have laughed in their face, and yet it had happened. This must be true. "Oh my God. Mrs. Bedaux said she was entangled in something. I never thought it was this."

"I don't think she meant to involve you this deeply."

"Until she saw the chance to use me for her own ends." She couldn't say she wasn't warned, but once again she'd ignored it, insisting on seeing what she wanted instead of what was right in front of her.

"Apparently, she's been planning it for some time." He opened the file and handed her copies of private letters from Wallis to Herr von Ribbentrop and other German officials. Some were as recent as June, others stretched back to 1935 and 1936 when Wallis had been the King's mistress. Buried between comments about difficult staff or new antiques were bits of information that when taken alone seemed harmless, but when read together painted an ugly portrait of state secrets stolen from the King's dispatch boxes and passed to the Germans. Amelia wanted to tell Robert these were forgeries, an attempt by someone, probably the Queen of England, to besmirch Wallis but she couldn't. She recognized Wallis's elegant handwriting and the tone and flair of her phrases. There were also official government documents that made it all but certain, especially the memo to J. Edgar Hoover, Director of the Federal Bureau of Investigation.

MEMORANDUM FOR THE DIRECTOR

For some time the British Government has known that the Duchess of Windsor was exceedingly pro-German in her sympathies and connections and there is strong reason to believe that this is the reason why she was considered so obnoxious to the British Government that they refused to permit Edward to marry her and maintain the throne.

Shortly prior to the designation of the Duke to be Governor of The Bahamas, field agents established conclusively that the Duchess of Windsor had recently been in direct contact with von Ribbentrop and was maintaining constant contact and communication with him. Because of their high official position the Duchess was obtaining a variety of information concerning the British and French government official activities which she was passing on to the Germans. Accordingly, the British government moved them to Biarritz.

"That's why the Germans announced which room the Windsors were staying in, in Biarritz," Robert explained. "The Duchess told them where they were and they used the threat as a credible reason to go to la Croë. It's also why they refused to leave there. They were waiting for word or instructions from the Germans. They still are." He handed her another document. "We intercepted and decoded this communiqué from Baron von Hoyningen-Huene in Lisbon to Herr von Ribbentrop."

I have heard through my sources that the Duke of Windsor believes continued heavy bombing will make England ready for Peace. He will postpone his journey to The Bahamas for as long as possible to see if the winds of war change in his favor. Her Royal Highness, given her need to interfere in politics, and her limitless ambition, has not abandoned hope of becoming Queen of England.

He laid another paper on top of it. "There are also rumors the Duchess and Herr von Ribbentrop are lovers." He placed a typewritten memo in front of her. Much of it was redacted but what wasn't confirmed her suspicions about Wallis and Herr von Ribbentrop long ago at Madame Schiaparelli's.

MEMORANDUM TO THE DIRECTOR

[Redacted]

She also told me again that there was no doubt whatever but that the Duchess of Windsor had had an affair with Ribbentrop, and that of course she had an intense hate for the English since they had kicked them out of England.

Amelia thought she might be sick. Wallis's deceit had been in front of her the whole time but she hadn't seen it because she'd convinced herself Wallis had learned from her mistakes. She'd been as wrong about that as Wallis's concern for her.

Robert set down another one. "This one was intercepted three days ago. It's from Herr von Ribbentrop to the Duchess."

Germany is now determined to force England to make peace by every means of power. It would be a good thing if the Duke were to keep himself prepared for further developments. In such case, Germany would be willing to cooperate most closely with the Duke and to clear the way for any desire expressed by you. The direction in which these wishes tend is quite obvious and meets with our complete understanding.

"The Nazis were eager to keep the Windsors in Europe to see how things developed with England but Sir Walter was kind enough to travel to Lisbon and explain to the Duke that Prime Minister Churchill was ready to court-martial him if he didn't leave for Nassau immediately. The Germans intended to use you as a valid reason for the Windsors to stay, until I stepped in and had you released."

"Mrs. Bedaux is in on it too. Everything she did for me was to help make me Wallis's pawn." Amelia wished a bomb would fall on the building and blow them and the papers to hell so she didn't have to face this. It was like the morning the lawyers had laid Jackson's crimes out to her in their office, destroying all of Jackson's excuses and lies and her hope that the prosecutors had been wrong. The veil had been pulled from her eyes and she'd seen everything with horrifying clarity, as she did today, and nothing afterward had been the same. "I thought Wallis had learned her lesson, that she hated Britain because of what'd happened, the way I used to complain to Aunt Bessie about everyone who'd been mean to me. I didn't think she'd do something like this. If I'd known, I would've done something to stop it. But I did know. I heard what she told Mrs. Bedaux about the Ardennes. How many people are suffering because of it?"

He clasped her hands in his. "There's nothing you could've done to prevent the invasion. The Duke and Duchess weren't the only ones feeding information about the defenses to the Germans, but you telling me allowed me to tip off people to keep a better eye on them."

Another awful truth began to dawn on her and she slid her hands out of his. "You were spying on me the whole time, weren't you, using me to get information on the Windsors?"

"I didn't need you to gather information. The Duke wasn't exactly subtle in his admiration of Herr Hitler."

"But you still used me to do it. That's why you helped with the deposition. Did you have Mr. Carlton tell the prosecutors not to order me home so you could keep me in Europe?"

He sat back against the sofa. "I didn't but my superiors did."

Amelia jumped to her feet and paced the room. "I thought you were helping me because you cared but you were using me like all the others."

"That's not true. In the beginning I followed orders to make contact with you, but the more I got to know you the more I began to like and admire you." He stood before her, forcing her to stop and look at him and the sincerity in his blue eyes. "I love you, Amelia, I do, and I was in a panic when you didn't turn up here. I've spent the last two weeks trying to find you. When Susan told me the Germans had you, I used every contact I had, pulled all the strings I could to get you out."

"You lied to me."

"Not about wanting to be with you, but this is bigger than us, and no matter what my feelings or yours, I have a duty to my country to do everything I can to protect it and Americans in France. You'd do the same if you were in my shoes."

"I don't know what I'd do anymore. Theodore was right, I can't judge anyone and look what it's cost me. I have nothing real, and no one because I'm a naive fool."

"You're a caring person who tries to see the best in the people she loves. There's nothing wrong with that."

"Isn't there? My job is gone, along with most of my things. The people I relied on for experience and connections betrayed me. I can't believe this is happening again." Like Wallis, she'd learned nothing from her life experiences.

"You can't expect things to be cut-and-dried in this crazy world. You can only take what chances you're given to find happiness and joy. It's all any of us can do."

He was right. In a time when every maxim had been crushed by German tanks and plots, the old rules didn't apply. He'd done his job as she'd done hers, and both of them had been caught in a situation out of their control. If she could think straight, if the world weren't so dark, she might understand and sympathize with this but she couldn't. All she could feel was another letdown, another failure by someone she'd loved and believed in, and she'd fallen for it because she'd wanted to be loved and useful, valued and important. Despite the couture clothes, the European polish and experience, she was still the overlooked debutante suckered in by anyone who'd give her a second look.

"I want to go home to America." At least there weren't bombs and plots in Baltimore.

"Susan and most of the unessential staff are being evacuated to London tomorrow. You can go with them and the office there will help you find passage home. Or you could join the Windsors in Nassau, and report to us about what they're doing and stop them from undermining Britain, the last bastion of freedom in Europe."

"You mean spy on them the way you spied on me?"

He ignored the dig, assuming the posture of an ambassadorial official, the one who'd first greeted her at the Hotel Meurice ages ago. "The Bahamas aren't far enough away to keep the Windsors out of trouble, not with Axel Wenner-Gren there. He's up to no good and he'll draw them into whatever plot he's hatching. He's already arranged for payment to the Windsors from the Germans through a Swiss account. America plans to build air bases in The Bahamas and, along with the British, are worried about the Windsors feeding Mr. Wenner-Gren information about American naval movements. You couldn't stop your cousin from causing trouble before but you can help stop her from doing whatever she's planning now."

"You mean have my revenge." She'd seen what it had done to Wallis and she no longer wanted to be anything like her.

"It isn't revenge, but a way to keep bad people from doing more awful things. Charles Bedaux is already overseeing the takeover of Jewish factories, and word is, he's leaving for Africa to help the Vichy government build oil lines. You can't stop him, but you can help stop others."

"By living another lie. I won't do it again. Wallis can go to the devil for all I care, and you can go with her."

Chapter Twenty-One

London, September 7, 1940

Four-forty. Over an hour to go before Amelia was off work for the day.

"You have a hot date tonight?" Susan teased from across the desk as her fingers flew over the typewriter keys. They both worked as typists at the American Embassy at 1 Grosvenor Square, glad to have paying positions while they waited for a berth home. The number of Americans trying to leave was growing by the day but every transport in or out of Britain was dedicated to the war effort and the movement of men and machines. Everyone else got space when it became available. "Robert, perhaps?"

Amelia stopped typing the travel request. "I told you not to mention his name."

"He came back to London last week with the rest of the Embassy staff. He'd love to see you."

That thrilled her more than it should have. "He told you that?"

"Of course he did."

Amelia resumed typing the travel request for a mother with two young children, determined not to think about Robert. He was nothing but trouble, but when she and Susan walked home at night through the blackout, she often couldn't help but wonder where he was and if he was thinking about her. Apparently, he was. It didn't matter. She'd work in London until her travel ticket came up and then she'd put Europe, him, and Wallis behind her for good.

"Any word from you know who?" Susan was determined to bring up all kinds of ghosts today.

"Not so much as a postcard." Amelia pulled the finished transportation request out of her typewriter and rolled in a new one. The last she'd heard, Wallis and the Duke had set sail from Lisbon for Nassau at the beginning of August without a second thought for her. She shouldn't be surprised, but a small part of her still hoped a little of Wallis's care for her had been real. Letters and cables came through the Embassy every day from people trying to contact friends and family but none of them were from Wallis to Amelia. Wallis hadn't even sent a thank-you note for the safe or a short wire to say she was thrilled Amelia had been released. She must have heard about it by now from one of her Nazi friends. All there'd been was silence. The bitch. "The Caribbean can have them. I'm through with them."

"Do you think we'll ever get back home?"

"I'm not sure I want to go back. There isn't a lot there for me." She'd cabled Peter and Aunt Bessie when she'd arrived in London to let them know she was safe. They'd cabled back, relieved to hear from her. There'd been nothing from Mother, who probably hoped a bomb would spare her the humiliation of running into her daughter in Baltimore. Luckily for Amelia, the only bombing raids had been along the docks and the coast, with the German planes only venturing inland to attack RAF bases and communication facilities.

"You don't have to go home. There's a position open in Mexico City. The State Department would send you out on the next ship if they hired you."

"I don't speak Spanish, and if the weather there is anything like today, I don't think I could stand it." Amelia dabbed the perspiration from her forehead. The fans and the breeze coming in the open windows did little to ease the heat of this unusually hot day. Outside, people were strolling in the shade or lounging in the parks in an effort to cool off.

"With your knowledge of French, I bet you could learn Spanish real quick."

"If it means not going back to Baltimore, I might take lessons."

The air raid sirens began to wail.

"Down to the shelter, girls," Mrs. Griffith, the head typist, ordered, and the women filed toward the door with the calm quickness they'd practiced numerous times over the past few weeks.

"That's a strange noise," Susan said.

Amelia noticed it too, a droning louder than anything they'd heard before. They went to the windows and saw an ominous black shadow marring the blue sky, like a massive murder of crows as hundreds of bombers flew in formation toward the city. "I've never seen so many planes."

Their belly doors opened and strings of bombs began to fall. The lights and desks rattled as explosion after explosion ripped through London. Somewhere nearby, a powerful blast shook the Embassy walls and threw the women off-balance.

"They're targeting the city!" Susan cried as Amelia helped her to her feet. They were tossed against the walls two more times before they reached the shelter and descended with the others. The old wine cellar had been fitted with air filters and reinforced walls after Ambassador Kennedy had shipped the wine home before he'd fled Britain, certain the country was lost even before the first Luftwaffe raids had begun.

Explosions rocked the city to its Roman foundations. Amelia and Susan clasped hands in silent support as sprinkles of dust drifted down to cover the staff huddled together waiting for it to end. Each moment of quiet between the blasts teased them with the possibility that it might be over but it went on for two agonizing hours. Amelia feared they'd go crazy from the constant thudding and pounding until the echoes of the last explosion finally faded into real silence.

The all clear signal sounded and everyone filed upstairs. Dark plumes of smoke and greedy flames engulfed London and the red orange of the fires cast strange and menacing shadows on the Embassy walls. The women gasped in horror while others burst into frightened tears as they stared at the devastation outside.

Tears slid down Amelia's cheeks. The Duke had said this was how Herr Hitler would bring Britain to its knees. Curse Wallis and the Duke, the selfish bastards.

"You'll stay here tonight, girls. There's no way you'll get home through that, and the Bosch might be back before dark," Mrs. Griffith said.

The Embassy staff spent the next two hours gathering food, blankets, pillows, and anything else they could use to make tonight a little less uncomfortable. There wasn't time to collect it all as the sirens started to wail again, accompanied by the awful droning of bombers.

For the next nine hours, everyone huddled together in the bomb shelter, unable to sleep, wondering if a bomb would fall directly on top of them and make this their last breath. Amelia sat with her knees tucked under her chin and her arms wrapped around her legs, afraid and guilty.

Wallis is to blame for this, and so am I. If she hadn't been blinded by the clothes, manners, and Wallis's empty concern and promises of help and a future, she might have seen what she was up to and put a stop to it.

THE NEXT MORNING, the staff emerged from the shelter into devastation they'd only seen in newsreel footage of the Luftwaffe destruction of Rotterdam. Huge swaths of London were on fire. Buildings reduced to rubble were strewn across roads in a twisting skeleton of charred timbers and scattered bricks.

Injured people staggered among the wreckage, stunned, hurt, and lost, not knowing where to go or what to do or think.

"We have to help," Amelia said.

She, Susan, and many others offered blankets, food, and whatever care they could to the suffering Londoners. Amelia's anger with Wallis and her stupid plot to become Queen grew stronger with each wound she bandaged, every shell-shocked person she passed, and every new sheet-covered body laid in the streets.

Hours later, with the wreckage of the city still smoldering, Amelia staggered back through crumbled brick to where Susan sat giving water to a little girl with a bloody bandage around her head. The girl clutched a ragged teddy bear, her eyes wide with shock. Susan looked hopefully at Amelia, who shook her head. She'd helped search for the girl's mother but the rescuers had found her buried beneath the wreckage of her house.

"Her father's coming."

Susan nodded and held the girl until her father, his soot-covered face streaked with tears, gathered her in his arms, his fingernails black with grime and dirt from helping dig his wife out of the rubble.

"I want to talk to Robert," Amelia said to Susan as they watched the man carry the child away. "He asked me to do something, and I've decided to do it."

AMELIA EMERGED FROM the St. James's Park underground station and walked with the rest of dazed London past the wreckage to the address on Caxton Street that Susan had given her. She passed weary people digging out what little they could salvage from their destroyed houses while everyone around them led as normal a life as possible with hell raining down on them for the past three nights. The German bombers had returned in their quest to bomb Britain into submission, but the British stood strong.

Amelia stopped, surprised to find herself at St. Ermin's Hotel. "This can't be right."

Nothing in London was right so she walked past the sandbags and went inside. Men and women hurried through the Victorian lobby with its balconies and hugging staircase, their drab military uniforms a sharp contrast to the elaborate Victorian decor. Amelia wondered what she was doing here but supposed she'd soon find out.

"I have an appointment with Mr. Morton," Amelia said to the female soldier behind the reception desk.

"One moment, please." The woman picked up the telephone and made a call.

Prime Minister Churchill's voice coming from the many radios around the lobby caught her attention and everyone stopped to listen. "What he has done is to kindle a fire in British hearts, here and all over the world, which will glow long after all traces of the conflagration he has caused in London have been removed. He has lighted a fire which will burn with a steady and consuming flame until the last vestiges of Nazi tyranny have been burnt out of Europe and until the Old

World—and the New—can join hands to rebuild the temples of man's freedom and man's honor, upon foundations which will not soon or easily be overthrown.

"This is a time for everyone to stand together, and hold firm, as they are doing. I express my admiration for the exemplary manner in which all the Air Raid Precautions services of London are being discharged, especially the Fire Brigade, whose work has been so heavy and also dangerous. All the world that is still free marvels at the composure and fortitude with which the citizens of London are facing and surmounting the great ordeal to which they are subjected, the end of which or the severity of which cannot yet be foreseen."

"Mr. Morton will see you now." The receptionist led Amelia up the hugging staircase with its lush hotel carpet and past the ballroom to a small salon away from the bustle of the main hallway. She opened the door to reveal Robert standing inside.

The sight of him nearly took Amelia's breath away. He wore a dark blue United States Navy uniform with gold buttons, his white cap tucked under one arm. He was far more dashing than was good for him or her heart.

"You enlisted," Amelia blurted as the receptionist politely left.

"I've been in the Navy all along. My real title in France was Lieutenant Robert Morton, Naval Attaché in the Office of Naval Intelligence."

There went her excitement at seeing him. "Was anything you told me about yourself real? Your fiancée, your uncle?" All the things he'd said to gain her trust in the beginning, until her heart had run away with her.

"All of it, except my job title. My fiancée did chuck me over for a classmate, and my uncle does work for the State Department. He arranged for my position, but I had to enlist to accept it. I wasn't lying when I said I loved you or that I admire your ability to care for people."

"Even if they don't deserve it." She crossed her arms over her chest, guarding herself against his flattery and how it made her heart skip a beat. She shouldn't be so weak around him but she couldn't help it, not when he looked at her with such earnestness.

"You did your best with Wallis."

"I didn't see her for who she really is, and look what's happened because of it."

"You aren't responsible for what she did. If she'd cared for anyone besides herself the way you cared for her, you wouldn't be in this position, but I'm glad you're here. I knew you couldn't watch everything that's happening and not do something about it."

"I should've done more."

"You will, and I'm proud of you for it. Be proud of yourself."

After everything that'd happened, he still had faith in her. Maybe she should give herself a little grace too. She could have fled to America, but she was here helping with the war effort. It was more than Wallis or even the old Amelia would have done.

The door opened and a brunette of about thirty dressed in a sensible green suit entered. "Mrs. Montague, I'm Miss Bright with the Military Intelligence Research Division of His Majesty's Government." She motioned for Amelia to sit at the table.

Robert held out a chair for her. She tried to ignore the nearness of him as he pushed in her chair, but she felt the faint caress of his fingers against her back before he moved to take the seat across from her. She didn't pull away from it but allowed it to touch her heart as much as his faith in her had. "I can't tell you how happy we are that you've decided to help us. Before we begin, please sign this."

Miss Bright laid a copy of the Official Secrets Act in front of Amelia. If she signed it and then told anyone what they were about to discuss, she could be tried and hanged for treason.

"You have a great deal of trust in me."

"You come with the highest recommendations." She glanced at Robert, who watched her with the impassive air of a man deeply involved in secrets and spying.

I've misjudged him. She wanted to hate him for lying to her but she couldn't. He had a sense of duty that Wallis and Jackson had never possessed, and more than once he'd helped her when she'd needed him. He hadn't asked for anything in return, not even secrets. She'd given those to him of her own free will. What he asked of her now was to help others in an effort to end this war and keep more people from suffering. She couldn't stay mad at him, not when there was so much more than the two of them and their troubles at stake.

She signed the paper and Miss Bright slid it into her leather case then removed a folder stamped *classified* and set it in front of Amelia.

"As you're aware, Axel Wenner-Gren is a prominent member of Bahamian society. Our contacts in Nassau believe he's up to something. He was caught during the harbor construction on his estate taking aerial photography of the outer islands under consideration for American air bases. With President Roosevelt pledging to give Britain fifty destroyers in exchange for the right to lease land for bases in The Bahamas, we need to know what Mr. Wenner-Gren is up to and if or how the Windsors are involved. We need someone inside the Windsors' household, someone they'd never suspect who can gather information for us. You won't be there to stop them but to observe and report so something can be done to keep leaks like the Ardennes from happening again."

"I want to help, but I'm not an actress or a spy. I can't pretend to be close to Wallis again, not after everything she's done. She used me as an excuse to not leave and then abandoned me, the way the Duke did Mr. Metcalf."

"That's not entirely true." Miss Bright removed a few cables from her valise and handed them to Amelia. The telegrams were from Wallis to the American Embassy in Britain asking if Amelia was safe. "Once the Germans told her you were free and in London, we intercepted her communications to you. We didn't want her to know you were moving freely in Britain but to think you were having difficulties here. It'll give you a reason to pretend to dislike the British and help you regain her trust. We need her to trust you, as she did before, and to have an excuse for further delays in joining them so we have the chance to train you."

Amelia read the telegrams, not sure what to think. Wallis had searched for her. She had been concerned with her safety.

Not enough to have me released until I was no longer of any use to her. For all the good Wallis had done for Amelia there was no dismissing the wrong she'd done for many years, some of it right under Amelia's nose, and all the people who were suffering because of it.

"We won't send you to Nassau unprepared," Miss Bright assured. "We'll train you in intelligence, radios, codes, psychology, everything you need to gather information while blending in. You won't interfere, simply observe and report so others can step in and stop anything nefarious. You'll make contact with our agent in Nassau, who'll pass on your reports to the FBI in Miami. It isn't without risk but trust us, we'll do everything we can to keep you safe."

Trust. It's what had gotten her into this predicament in the first place. She needed to do it again, while betraying Wallis's trust, not that she didn't deserve it. "You want me to judge people and their motives. That isn't my strong point."

"Your instincts are better than you believe, and there's no one else who can do what we're asking," Robert assured, his faith in her strengthening hers in him.

"Will they be tried for treason if I find something?" Wallis had thought her divorce hearing had been a madhouse. A treason trial would knock a war off the front page.

"No. Their positions and high connections guarantee them a protection none of us enjoy," Miss Bright answered. "But whatever you find will undermine their plans or plotting and keep real damage from being done."

Watch and observe Wallis. Mrs. Bedaux's first rule for being a private secretary. Amelia had become a master at it and they were asking her to turn it against Wallis in order to help others and she would. There'd been no one to check Wallis's ambitions when she'd toppled the King but Amelia would sure as hell be there to stop her from trying to topple an entire country and push the Duke back on the throne.

Portsmouth, Late October, 1940

A cold wind lashed the dock where the men, women, and children who'd finally been granted passage across the Atlantic waited to board. They crowded together with friends and family for tearful goodbyes, not sure if or when they'd see each other again.

There were no luxury accommodations on board. The ship was too full of supplies and armaments to care about passengers' comfort. Amelia was one of the few people granted a room and the privacy needed to study the code book she'd been given to memorize.

Robert stood beside her and Susan on the crowded dock. Susan's departure had been quickly arranged so she could help Amelia prepare for her mission during the two-week crossing to New York. Amelia would travel on to Nassau and whatever waited for her from there. She'd spent the past six weeks in Bournemouth with a number of Miss Bright's other recruits learning the ins and outs of shortwave radios, how to write and decipher codes and observe human nature, and about acting. She hoped when the time came the training would pay off and she could give the performance of her life.

"Our agent in Nassau will make contact with you as soon as it's safe. She'll be wearing a pale pink rose," Robert said, his heavy blue wool peacoat speckled with drops of drizzle.

After six weeks of training with women bound for occupied France and Belgium she wasn't surprised her contact was a woman. However, it was the most she'd been told about the only other person in Nassau who'd know what she was up to, at least the only one she was aware of. She'd learned in Bournemouth that if she didn't know who the other operatives were she couldn't betray them if she was found out.

She pulled her wool coat tighter around her, more chilled by this than the misty day or the dread of crossing with U-boats prowling the Atlantic.

"If you're ever in doubt about what to do, rely on your training. It could save your life."

"I will."

"I got you a present." He handed her a small velvet box and she opened it to reveal a fine gold necklace with a disk charm, *bonne chance* engraved upon it in a flourished script. "A little something to remember me by."

"To remember you by or to let my contact know who I am?" She peered up at him through her lashes, wanting to stay and banter with him forever but she couldn't. Too many people were counting on her. She couldn't fail.

"Both." He flashed a charming but guilty smile, then took

her hands in his and clasped them to his chest. They were warm and solid, confident, the hands of a man sure of himself and his position, one who understood the importance of duty and honor and real love. "I chose this charm so you'll know I'm always thinking of you."

He took her in his arms and pressed his lips to hers. She savored the taste of his lips, not caring who was around them or what they saw; no one did, not with these last precious moments slipping away before they had to let go of each other for what might be forever.

The ship's horn sounded and the teeming mass of people began to move toward the gangway.

"It's time," Susan said, her reluctance to intrude as strong as Amelia's to let go of Robert.

She stepped out of his embrace and slowly backed away from him, her gaze never leaving his until she had no choice but to turn and walk away.

Chapter Twenty-Two

The Bahamas, November 1940

Corporal Sawyer, the Duke's new chauffeur, drove Amelia along Bay Street after he collected her, and Wallis's many packages, from Oakes Field airport. Her months in London had accustomed her to driving on the left side of the road and it stopped her from flinching every time he turned in a way that seemed so unusual to her in France and America.

"Is it ever cool here, Corporal Sawyer?" she asked. The few thick clouds in the brilliant blue sky did little to cut the intensity of the sun. The air was thicker here and the heat higher despite it being fall.

"No, it's merely not as hot or humid," he answered with a chuckle, "but the breezes help keep things tolerable. It's nothing like England."

"No, it's not." There was color here with the brightly painted shops and hotels, and peace. The buildings might be weathered and old but they hadn't been bombed out. If she were on the island under different circumstances, she'd see it as the paradise it was, but she wasn't. Amelia rolled down the window and drew in deep breaths of the tangy sea air. She was about to give the performance of her life, pretending to be thrilled to see Wallis and with no hard feelings about what had happened in Paris. She had to pretend she knew nothing about what they or their associates were up to while always being on the lookout for evidence of their scheming. She hoped she was up to the challenge. She had to be. Robert and Miss Bright were counting on her.

Their progress up Bay Street was slow, and Corporal Sawyer was forced to stop numerous times to let the horse-drawn fringe carriages ferrying tourists in their linen traveling clothes pass. Policemen in white jackets and black trousers stood under umbrellas in the middle of the street directing the steady stream of traffic. One policeman held up his hand to stop two local women balancing baskets of vegetables on their heads from stepping out from between the cars parked along the busy sidewalk. American tourists visited the saloons, restaurants, and hotels lining the street while locals loaded and unloaded trucks or sold postcards and shell trinkets. The color, warmth, and activity were so different from the somber gray and destruction of London, one could almost forget there was a war. Almost. War was why she was here.

She said a little prayer for the women she'd trained with. They were going behind enemy lines in France and Belgium to undermine the Nazis. If they were discovered, they'd be shot or worse. Amelia had been sent to a tropical paradise and would be shipped home if she was found out, or so she'd told herself in the middle of the night when worry had kept her up. If Wallis was willing to collude with the Nazis in the destruction of a country to capture a crown, there was no telling what she or her friends might do if they discovered a traitor in their midst.

Corporal Sawyer turned off Bay Street onto George Street and drove up the hill past brightly colored pink, green, and turquoise balcony houses and wide, spreading trees. Flashes of red bougainvillea and other bright flowers she didn't recognize bloomed in window boxes and along fences. A marble Christopher Columbus stood guard over the massive staircase leading up the hill to the Governor-General's residence with its grand view of Nassau.

Corporal Sawyer guided the Duke's Crosley station wagon through the brick and iron gates of Government House, where the Royal Bahamas Police Force guards in their crisp white uniforms stood at attention. The Union Jack rolled with the sea breeze over the top of the pink-walled and white-trimmed classical building dotted with green hurricane shutters. They crossed the courtyard and pulled to a stop in the shade of the front portico.

"You're finally here." Wallis flew out of the massive oak front door with the Duke's Order of the Garter insignia etched in gold on the glass. She clasped Amelia in a large hug, her gardenia perfume encircling the two of them. "I was so worried when you didn't turn up in Lisbon. Thank heaven you're safe."

"I was worried about you too." Amelia slowly wrapped her arms around Wallis, surprised and torn by the effusive greeting. This wasn't the prim and proper Duke's wife but the cousin she remembered from Wakefield Manor. For all her sins, Wallis had genuinely missed her. It made Amelia's head spin from more than the heat. Her cousin was welcoming her back as an innocent, and she was here to stab her in the back. Wallis deserved it. She was a traitor who'd been willing to leave Amelia imprisoned by the Nazis when it had served her plans.

Amelia stepped out of her grasp, determined not to fall for Wallis's silver-tongued lies and false concern again. "The French newspapers said you and the Duke went missing in Spain and were captured by the Italians. What happened?"

Wallis escorted her into the house, the hem of her stylish blue and red polka-dotted dress fluttering against her slim legs as they walked. She wore her more subdued sapphire set, the one that had been in the Paris safe. At least it had reached her and Amelia's escapades hadn't been entirely for nothing. "It was dreadful traipsing across France, sleeping out in the open or in flea-infested hotels. I thought we'd be fine when we reached Spain but it was nothing but problems there too. They shooed us out of Madrid because the French government in exile thought we'd get them bombed to pieces so we had to drag on to Lisbon. It was worse than fleeing Paris, worse than this awful place. It's been a mess without you, there isn't anyone who can organize my life the way you can."

They crossed the wide foyer as the four Bahamian footmen carried Amelia's things and Wallis's packages from Saks Fifth

Avenue and Bergdorf Goodman up the Grand Staircase under Mr. Hale's watchful eye.

"The house is stunning." A portrait of Wallis hung over the fireplace in the formal stateroom, overlooking furniture that was far more restrained than in Paris. Everything was simple lines and bright, printed fabrics that melded with the tropical surroundings. A few well-placed antiques, including the abdication desk, added to the regal feel, with the massive gold-framed mirror in the entrance hall the single nod to Wallis's usually extravagant tastes.

"It was an absolute mess when we arrived. We had to fight tooth and nail to make it habitable. His Majesty's Government didn't believe it needed work until a piece of the ceiling almost killed me, assuming it was an accident. One can never tell these days. I'm sure Sir Walter would like to see the end of me. He complained every time we asked for money, telling us the funds would be better spent on Spitfires. What rot. They might as well set the money on fire for all the chance Britain has of winning anything. At least spending it here means they get something for it. Maybe when Cookie ends up living here, she'll thank me for sprucing it up." Wallis locked eyes with a footman who had the bad luck to pause at the top of the stairs. "You can tell that to Buckingham Palace."

He didn't stop to ask what she meant but hurried to place a small crate in a room down the high-ceilinged central hall.

"Careful what you say." Wallis lowered her voice as other footmen strode past to collect more packages. "There are spies everywhere. I don't know who they are but I know they're here."

Amelia swallowed past the knot in her throat. If Wallis suspected the staff of harboring spies, she'd have to work extra hard to cover her tracks. It was already difficult pretending to be happy to be here while knowing about Wallis and how she'd betrayed her. She was going to put everything she'd learned in Bournemouth about concealing her true feelings to use. "I'll keep that in mind."

Wallis led her into a bedroom on the second floor. "This is where you'll sleep."

Tall windows stood open to allow in the breeze and stunning views of Nassau. The turquoise-blue waters of the harbor between Nassau and nearby Hog Island sparkled in the sunlight. The roofs of the balcony houses lining the streets poked up between the tops of palm trees and rubber trees except for the square spire of Christ Church Cathedral and the wide British Colonial Hotel towering over the bayside streets. The room's veranda overlooked the massive back garden with its straight main path. The outbuildings along the periphery were nearly hidden by coconut palms and other plants and trees she didn't recognize. The sound of shovels and rakes carried up from where the Bahamian staff trimmed the potted plants and trees on the terrace below. "It's beautiful."

"Don't let the palm trees and beaches fool you. This is nothing but the 1940s version of Elba," Wallis complained.

"You mean St. Helena."

"Does it matter? It's still an exile."

"There are worse places to be exiled."

"You won't say that when you're sweating through your

summer dresses. The war needs to hurry up and end so we can leave before the heat returns. I don't intend to be here for long."

Amelia wondered how long she'd be here. They'd never discussed the length of her mission, simply that she'd see it through.

"DID YOU FINISH that letter to the press?" The Duke leaned on Amelia's desk in her downstairs office, the smell of whiskey on his breath too heavy for this early in the morning.

"Yes, Your Royal Highness. I'll send it out at once." Amelia rolled the mimeograph paper out of the typewriter and looked over the memo directing the American press to address Wallis as Your Royal Highness instead of Your Grace. With the trade embargoes, poverty issues, and arguments with the Bay Street Boys, the elite island businessmen who refused to give up one iota of their power over Nassau, one would think the Governor-General would have more to worry about than his wife's title, but he didn't. Some things never changed.

"Good girl." He winked at her, and wobbled a bit as he straightened up. "Mr. Phillips, come along, we have the airfield lease and the oil imports to discuss. Tedious business." The Duke staggered out of the office.

"Doesn't he have The Bahamas Economic Commission meeting?" Amelia asked Mr. Phillips.

"Good luck reminding him of that. Too boring to bother, he says," Mr. Phillips complained as he gathered up his files. He occupied the desk across from hers in the small downstairs office they shared near the back of the house. Even from here, the views of the garden out the windows were stunning. "I'll be surprised if he discusses the airfield or oil with me. He'll probably talk my ear off about golf and then what'll I tell the officials? I can't say he's too drunk to bother, can I?"

"Has it been that bad?"

"Yes." The new equerry was far more candid in his opinion of the Duke than Mr. Forwood had been.

"I'll mention it to the Duchess." Wallis was the only one with any influence over the Duke and everyone knew it.

Ever since her arrival, Amelia, Wallis, and the Duke had fallen into their old routines as if no time had passed. The humid air and beautiful vistas lulled everyone into believing everything was right in the world, as did the mundane tasks of Wallis's new position, but it wasn't. Amelia had yet to meet her contact, going about her days as she had in Paris but always on the lookout for something dubious. Other than the Duke and Duchess's regular sailings with Mr. Wenner-Gren, she'd seen and heard nothing suspicious. There were no hidden notes or telegrams, only the usual letters to friends that Amelia steamed open before sending. They were all about how bored and lonely Wallis was here, how there was no real society and begging her friends to visit. There was no hint of the stolen intelligence or treason that Robert had shown her in Paris. If Wallis was sending someone information it wasn't through the post. Whatever Wallis was up to, she hid it well.

Mr. Hale entered the room, the Duke having pulled enough strings to keep him from being conscripted. "Mrs. Montague, a Miss Alice Jones would like to speak to you on behalf of the Infant Welfare Clinic."

"Send her in."

Mr. Hale paused. "Mrs. Montague, might I remind you that colored people are discouraged from calling at Government House?"

"I said, send her in," Amelia firmly insisted, refusing to follow that awful rule.

With a curt nod he escorted Miss Jones in then left to probably grumble to Wallis about this breach in their so-called etiquette.

A colored woman in a crisp white nurse's uniform approached with polite determination.

Amelia came around the desk to shake her hand. "It's a pleasure to meet you. What can I do for you today?"

"I'm the sister in charge of the Infant Welfare Clinic. Our nurses attend to the poorest mothers and infants and we can't make rounds to the outlying area without proper transportation. I've come to personally petition Her Royal Highness to help us. We're in desperate need of a car."

"I'll speak to her on your behalf and arrange a meeting for you to discuss it."

"Will you or are you putting me off the way she has the last three times I've come here?"

Oh dear. Wallis was making her usual friends and enemies everywhere she went. Amelia was tempted to let Wallis stew in her failure, but she couldn't turn away someone working to improve Bahamians' lives. Nassau benefited from the tourists, but the poverty in the areas south of Government House in Over the Hill and Grant's Town was heartbreaking. It was even worse in the Out Islands. She'd visited those with the Duke and Wallis and seen firsthand the poor Bahamians scraping out a hard living harvesting sponges and growing what they could in the loamy soil. Wallis could fall on her face somewhere else. "I'm sure Her Royal Highness didn't mean to overlook you. She's been without a private secretary for some time. Now that I'm here, I'll see she meets with you, and put in a good word for you and your cause."

"You seem like a woman who can get things done."

"So do you. Please don't hesitate to let me know if there's anything else I can do for you." Amelia took Miss Jones's information then called for Mr. Hale to see her out.

She climbed the stairs to Wallis's room for their regular morning meeting. It was across the hall from the Duke's with a large bedroom, study, and screened veranda with stunning views of Nassau and the ocean.

"Has my dry cleaning arrived from New York?" Wallis asked the moment Amelia entered. She sat at a rectangular bentwood writing desk, her cashier's desk still in France, her expression as stern as the judge who'd passed sentence on Jackson.

"It'll arrive tomorrow. The plane was delayed by a storm." The Bahamian sun and the tropical breezes scented by plumerias made it easy to forget the cold weather creeping into New York, London, and Paris. Amelia felt sorry for the people of

London and Paris who'd have to endure the coming winter in bombed-out houses or with the Nazis stealing their food and heating oil.

"It'd better get here soon or I won't have a thing to wear to Lady Williams-Taylor's party." Wallis capped her fountain pen and slid whatever she was writing into the desk's top drawer and locked it.

"Wouldn't it be easier to send your clothes to someone on the island instead of all the way to New York? It'd save time, hassle, and money and would help the local economy, build some goodwill for you and the Duke." Miss Jones wasn't the only visitor who'd grumbled about the Duke and Wallis not attending to their duties. Mrs. Solomon, the white chairman of the Bahamian Red Cross, had called yesterday to complain about Wallis not taking up her position as their head, one reserved for the Governor-General's wife, and how it was delaying their war aid efforts.

"I'll build goodwill with something other than my wardrobe. There isn't anyone here who can clean it properly, and with the Fat Scottish Cook making sure we can't leave Elba without royal permission, I have to make my clothes last. I want to look like a proper Governor-General's wife."

"Speaking of which, Miss Alice Jones, the nurse from the Infant Welfare Clinic, visited to request a meeting with you."

Wallis frowned. "Yes, Mr. Hale told me she was here."

Amelia ignored this. "The clinic is in need of a car. Mrs. Solomon from the Red Cross called again too. They need your assistance arranging care package transportation."

"All the local horrors do is pester me for help with this or that." Wallis was surly today, her delayed dry cleaning elevated to a national crisis.

"That's because everyone knows you're the one who gets things done."

"A dubious honor."

"An advantageous one. The press ignored your Red Cross work in France but they can't ignore you here. The Governor-General is the King's representative, making you something of a Queen. Imagine how regal you'd look coming to the aid of mothers and infants. It'd change the way people see you. Cookie would hate that."

"She would, wouldn't she?" Wallis trilled her fingers on her desk while she mulled over the idea. If logic couldn't work with Wallis, then flattery usually did. "All right, arrange the meeting and figure out what she needs and how I can give it to her. Contact the Red Cross woman and do the same and make sure the press knows about it. You're right, I'm all but a queen here. I suppose I have to take some interest in my people."

"A queen usually does," Amelia mumbled as she wrote a note about arranging the meetings.

The deafening quiet made Amelia stop writing and look up.

Wallis's stare sent a chill racing up Amelia's spine. "Is everything all right?"

Amelia caught her mistake, and felt her cheeks burn with a flush. "Y-ye-yes. Why?"

"You're different since you've returned, almost the way you

were those first weeks in France, except far better organized and capable of doing your job, and a touch more surly."

"I'm sorry." Amelia closed the notepad and slid the pencil in the holder. "Paris was hard, not knowing what was going to happen to me, unable to contact you or get help from the British, who were utterly useless there and in London, which was an awful city," she lied, using her training to maintain Wallis's confidence by sympathizing with her dislike of Britain. "The Americans were the only ones who helped me. They gave me a job and somewhere safe to stay during the Blitz but it was terrifying to go to bed not knowing if I'd survive the night, then wake up every morning to fire, hurt and killed people, and London destroyed."

"They deserve it for what they did to me. A whole country against one lone woman."

"That's too harsh."

"No, it's not. You saw what happened to me." Wallis narrowed her eyes at Amelia as if she were a back-talking maid.

"You're right, it wasn't fair what they did to you." Amelia struggled to look humbled, Wallis's callousness grating. Wallis didn't care a whit about what Amelia had been through or the millions of suffering people. All she cared about was her ambition and revenge.

"That's a very interesting necklace. I don't remember you having it before." Wallis approached and slid her fingers under the *bonne chance* charm and raised it to examine it. Her nails brushing Amelia's skin made it crawl but she forced herself not to flinch or pull back. "Where did you get it?"

"Susan Harper, a friend of mine from the American Embassy in Paris, gave it to me. She said it's for luck." Amelia drew on memories of when she'd believed in Wallis to hide her disgust. Everything had to appear as it had been before, with nothing wrong, no secrets, no betrayals, nothing.

"An Embassy friend?"

"We were stuck in London together, but because of you I got passage out before she did."

Wallis settled the pendant back against the boatneck top of Amelia's striped pencil dress. "David and I are sailing with Axel this afternoon. See to it the car is ready for us at four. Also, schedule the nurse meeting at the clinic. As you are aware, colored people are discouraged from making social and business calls at Government House. It's the way of things here, Miss Jones should have known better. Please remind her."

She'd do no such thing. "His Royal Highness is here to represent everyone and they need his help and leadership, not restrictions."

"David sees no reason to risk a future, better government position by causing trouble in this one. Bahamians can work here but not make social or business calls, otherwise we'll have no end of people traipsing in and out of here with every problem and petition they have and we'll never have a moment's peace. That goes for the white people too or I'll have to invite all the assemblymen's wives to every tea, dinner party, and official reception. What a bore. What passes for society here is slim pickings already. I won't make it worse." Wallis strode off to her closet to change.

Amelia had to hold her notebook tight to keep from lobbing it at the back of Wallis's perfectly rolled and pinned coiffure. The nerve of that woman, looking down on anyone after everything she'd done and was still doing.

I shouldn't have been surly. She had to behave as if everything was the way it had been before. Judging by Wallis's cold scrutiny, Amelia hadn't been pretending as well as she thought. *Or maybe Wallis is as jumpy as I am.* Given what Wallis was embroiled in, Amelia wasn't surprised, but it was Amelia's fault Wallis had noticed something was off. Wallis already believed half the staff were spying on her; Amelia couldn't give her any reason to question her or she'd never discover anything about what she was up to.

Speaking of which. Amelia glanced at the desk to see if there was anything interesting lying on top but it was clean as a whistle. If she had to guess, anything worth seeing was locked in the top drawer. Wallis had been writing to someone when Amelia had interrupted her, she usually was, but the number of personal letters Amelia mailed wasn't equal to the number Wallis wrote. It could be because the censors refused to grant Wallis an exception for her correspondence but Amelia doubted it. Wallis was so desperate for word from her friends, she'd risk a civil servant in some stuffy postal office seeing her letters in order to write to them. However, something more important was getting by somehow, Amelia was sure of it.

Mr. Hale's steady footsteps muffled by the hallway runner sounded outside the door and Amelia beat an orderly and refined retreat. She couldn't risk him catching her lingering or snooping around Wallis's room. She'd done everything she could over the past few weeks to appear as innocent and trustworthy as possible, despite regularly searching Wallis's room for evidence. It wasn't easy, especially with Mr. Hale and Mademoiselle Moulichon always hovering around. Amelia had no idea what they were up to but she wouldn't put it past them to be searching through her things as much as she was searching Wallis's. Amelia didn't trust anyone in Government House, especially not the Bedaux's former employees.

Chapter Twenty-Three

Nassau, December 1940

"David, I was telling Axel about the wonderful dinner we had with King Carol at the Ritz. What did you think of His Majesty?" Wallis asked when the Duke swayed up to Wallis and Mr. Wenner-Gren. They mingled on the terrace of Star Acres, Lady Williams-Taylor's Hog Island estate. Strings of white lights decorated the palm trees beside the riser where Blind Blake Alphonso Higgs and his band from the Royal Victoria Hotel played goombay songs and jazzy versions of Christmas carols. Lights from the house and torches set up along the back terrace illuminated the white foam waves breaking on the beach; the contrast between the winter season and the tropical weather was jarring but Amelia loved it. She wished Robert were here to enjoy it with her, but like her, he was somewhere working to help end this awful war. "Wasn't he a charming man?"

He was a snake. Amelia kept her opinion of the former Romanian king to herself as she stood on the periphery of their conversation, careful to remain bland-faced.

"He was quite the visionary." The Duke drained his martini. "He could have done much more for the Romanian people if his ungrateful government hadn't run him out again." The Duke motioned to a footman for another drink. In September, King Carol had been forced off the throne and had fled to Mexico City with Madame Lupescu and, if the rumors were true, a good chunk of Romania's treasury.

"With his ambition, I'm sure he'll land on his feet." Wallis trilled her fingers on her champagne glass.

"He already has. He and General Maximino Camacho, the brother of Mexico's president, are involved in Mexican oil drilling," Mr. Wenner-Gren said, almost confirming the rumors about the King and the treasury. "If the Lend-Lease Act passes, importing Mexican oil to fuel military ships and planes crossing the Atlantic will bring in much needed revenue to The Bahamas."

"You mean your Bank of The Bahamas. You have more of Herr Goering's money in there than yours." The Duke chuckled into his martini.

"Darling, you know those rumors are nonsense," Wallis insisted through a tight smile. "Axel runs the bank on behalf of The Bahamas. If it thrives then the country thrives. Think of what he's already done for the workers who built his deepwater harbor."

"The harbor is awfully large for the *Southern Cross*," the

Duke said. "And you have enough fuel there for a whole fleet. What do you do with it all?"

"One has to be prepared in the event of a hurricane," Axel answered, and Amelia looked at her satin shoes, pretending not to listen. "I don't want to be caught unawares and not be able to move *Southern Cross* if a storm whips up."

The bank and the unusual size of the deepwater harbor and the Mexican oil supplies could be nothing or they could be something important. Mr. Wenner-Gren was familiar with Nazis but he didn't goose-step around the island with a swastika on his armband. Amelia suspected that he, like Wallis, was more interested in exploiting the opportunities the Germans offered than he was a true believer. Either way, he was up to no good.

"Darling, listen, he's playing our song." The Duke tapped his foot as Blind Blake and his band launched into "Love, Love Alone," his song about His Royal Highness's abdication. "Shall we dance?"

"Oh, I just love this little ditty," Wallis said through gritted teeth, not nearly as flattered by the tune as the Duke, but she took his hand and allowed him to lead her onto the dance floor.

Amelia fell back to the periphery of the party as she always did at these events. She wore her silk Schiaparelli, the light dress the most appropriate for the warm Bahamian fall. She'd been reunited with her things when she'd arrived but the designer clothes didn't delight her like they used to. She didn't feel successful in them but owned lock, stock, and barrel by Wallis. She'd sent the heavy winter ones, along with the more impractical and expensive accessories, to Aunt Bessie for safekeeping. That lark in Paris had almost robbed her of everything she'd need for her future. She wouldn't make that mistake again.

Eugenie slid up to her. "I hear you're finally getting someone up at the red light district to take their duties seriously."

"The red light district?"

"That's what the locals call Government House because of Her Grace's history with men."

Amelia hid her laugh behind her hand. Meeting up with Eugenie had been one of the highlights of returning to Wallis's service. The two of them usually stood together at parties or met at the British Colonial Hotel to exchange gossip over tea. Eugenie knew more about The Bahamas and the people, both the socialites and the business owners, than anyone else. She always knew which Assemblymen spent more time on Booze Avenue, as the locals called Bay Street, than in the House of Assembly, and who of note was coming in on the next Pan American flight from Miami. Amelia used most of the gossip to keep Wallis informed and to stay in her good graces, just like in Paris. "What else do they say?"

"That Her Grace is the real governor of The Bahamas because His Royal Highness consults her on everything."

"Well, he made his bed, they both did."

"I'll say. Want to take a break? There's a little room where we can kick off our heels for a while, and someone there I'd like you to meet."

With the Windsors dancing, she was free for a bit. “Lead the way.”

Eugenie led Amelia into the house, through the crush of people mingling beneath large potted palms and whirling fans. They wove their way down the curving hall to a room so far from the terrace they could barely hear the band or guests. Eugenie ushered her into a book-filled office and Amelia stopped dead.

Lady Williams-Taylor stood in front of a Honduran mahogany bookshelf in a gorgeous Mainbocher black silk gown with a lovely pale pink rose pinned beneath her diamond brooch.

“You’re my contact?” It didn’t seem possible.

“I am.” She held out her hands and bowed like an actress at the end of a play. “I can’t tell you what a pleasure it is to have you here to help me, and we need help fast.”

“But the portrait of Hitler?”

“All part of the show. It has to be convincing, doesn’t it, Eugenie?”

“It does, ma’am.”

“You knew?”

“Of course. I wouldn’t have put up with all that Hitler nonsense otherwise.”

“She keeps me grounded,” Lady Williams-Taylor said. “We don’t have much time so let’s get down to brass tacks. What have you heard?”

“Not much except Mr. Wenner-Gren is working with King Carol on a scheme to import Mexican oil to fuel ships and airplanes crossing the Atlantic.”

"Probably German ones, given the reports of U-boats in the area. Keep an eye on that," Lady Williams-Taylor instructed. "What else?"

"There are shady dealings with Mr. Wenner-Gren and the Bank of The Bahamas."

"I know. Word is, his Swedish factories are manufacturing arms for Germany and he's funneling those profits, and Nazi funds, through it to finance activities in Mexico. One of his many questionable endeavors. Anything else?"

"The deepwater harbor is finished and there's enough oil stored there to fuel a fleet."

Lady Williams-Taylor and Eugenie exchanged a concerned look.

"That's bad," Eugenie said.

"I thought it was bad back in Prohibition when the island was crawling with bootleggers, but it's nothing compared to now." Lady Williams-Taylor removed a few books from the shelf behind the desk to reveal a small safe. "They were open and honest about what they did, good people trying to make a living off a unique opportunity. These new ones dress up and pretend at civility but they'll shoot you in the back over nothing faster than a bootlegger ever would've. Bootleggers were at least gentlemen, weren't they, Eugenie?"

"They were, ma'am."

Lady Williams-Taylor rolled the combination lock back and forth until it opened then removed a small paper from inside. She unfolded it on the high polished mahogany desk and invited Amelia to have a look. "This is a map of Hog Island and

Axel's estate, Shangri-La." She laid a gloved finger on a spot on the far side of Hog Island that was difficult to see even from the high ground of Government House. "I tried to keep the Windsors away from him when they arrived but they're stubborn when it comes to falling in with the worst sort."

"They practically run at them." Amelia tugged the *bonne chance* charm back and forth on its chain.

"Axel is one of the most despicable. He didn't appreciate my meddling in his friendship with the Duke and Duchess and it's caused a bit of a rift between us. He'll come to my parties because, of course, everyone who's anyone here does, but he stopped inviting me and my friends to his. It's made it hard to get evidence of what's going on at Shangri-La and especially in that harbor. Most of his staff are Swedish military men, all of them pro-German and loyal beyond being bribed, but there's one Bahamian maid who works in the house and she's on our side."

"Barin Rolle," Eugenie added. "I'll introduce you to her."

"She's there every day but restricted on where she can go. The other Bahamians he employs are gardeners and they're never allowed in the house or on the grounds at night, but they've told Eugenie of a shortwave antenna that could broadcast Count Basie halfway to Russia."

"What's he using it for?" Amelia asked.

"Nothing at the moment, but when he finally does fire it up, I doubt it'll be able to keep up on the price of whores in Stockholm."

Amelia snorted in laughter.

"The deepwater harbor is here." Lady Williams-Taylor pointed to a small bay around an outcropping of land just down the beach from Shangri-La. "The Bahamian groundsmen aren't allowed there but according to them and Barin, the Swedish employees are regularly there during the day. None of them have seen anything suspicious but they aren't there at night when everything of interest probably takes place. We can't sail a ship past there or fly a plane overhead without arousing suspicion, but one person taking a peek at it from the bushes shouldn't raise any alarms. See if you can find a way to get a look at it when you're there for cocktails or dinner with the Windsors."

"Should I look around the house too?"

"No, it isn't safe, especially with you so close to your mark." Lady Williams-Taylor folded up the map and returned it to the safe. "Nassau can be a very dangerous place, with desperate people willing to do anything for money. I can afford security. You're much too young to end up in an alley with a slit throat."

Amelia touched the gold necklace. "Wallis can be awful but she isn't that bad."

"She isn't, but I don't trust Axel as far as I could throw him. Be careful, dear. People may call this the Isles of Perpetual June but it's full of vipers."

Chapter Twenty-Four

Nassau, February 1941

Amelia lounged with Eugenie in the Windsors' private cabana at the Emerald Beach Club. With little to no society in Nassau, there weren't the endless invitations, dinner parties, and balls to attend to, fewer thank-you notes to write, and much less correspondence in general. It gave Amelia more free time than she'd ever enjoyed in Europe.

"Hard to believe there's a war on when the ocean is so peaceful," Amelia said to Eugenie as they watched the waves roll up onto the sand. Wallis was kind enough to let them use the cabana when she wasn't using it, which was often. Wallis detested the heat but Amelia loved the thick air tempered by the sea breeze, the clear skies and the constant ocean tang. She wished Robert were here to enjoy it with her. She hadn't heard from him since arriving, and what little news she'd had of him came from Susan's letter. He was in Washington, D.C., and Susan saw him sometimes when she and her fiancé, who'd finally graduated from medical school, drove up for dinners with her old Embassy friends.

"It does make one almost forget all the world's problems." Eugenie wiggled her fingers at the club maître d', who'd given Amelia no end of grief the first time she'd brought Eugenie here, insisting coloreds weren't allowed in Emerald Beach Club. Amelia had thrown her official position in his face to ensure Eugenie never had trouble coming with her again. It hadn't stopped him from tossing the occasional sour look in their direction.

"Almost." Above the roar of the waves, the whir of a fighter plane engine made Amelia tense. Memories of London were hard to escape, especially with the American fighter planes from Florida regularly stopping at Oakes Field to refuel. It was a reminder of why she was here and what she and the world were fighting against.

"Any luck getting into the Duchess's drawers?" Eugenie asked with a smirk.

"No. There's hardly ever a chance. Between Mademoiselle Moulichon hovering over Wallis's dry cleaning or Mr. Hale bringing in packages from Miami, and the maids, laundresses, and footmen, it's like Grand Central Station in there." She knew where Wallis kept the key to the desk drawer; she'd found it between hatboxes one afternoon while Mademoiselle Moulichon was off and the Duke and Wallis were sailing with Axel. She'd pinched it and had a copy made in Bay Street. She'd tried to get a look inside the drawer but Mademoiselle Moulichon had come back early and almost found her. It had scared her off any more searching, for the time being.

"See if you can get in there. Mr. Wenner-Gren finally fired up his antenna and he's got a new code they haven't cracked yet. See if you can get any idea of what he's sending and to whom. Lady Williams-Taylor's contact thinks it might be something about supply ship positions. If those get out, it'll make them sitting ducks for U-boats and who knows how many sailors will die."

"I'll do my best."

Christ Church Cathedral's bells sounded the time and Amelia checked her watch. "I have to get back."

"Me too. No rest for the wicked, eh?"

"I'll say."

Amelia strolled up quiet George Street to Government House. After a mild Caribbean winter, she didn't know how she'd ever endure a frigid Baltimore or Paris once again. Perhaps when the war was over, and all this was behind her, she might settle in Miami. There were plenty of wealthy women in need of private secretaries there and she could easily set up a placement agency to serve them. She no longer needed Wallis's help to do it, not with Lady Williams-Taylor on her side.

Amelia greeted the guards as she walked into Government House. She was about to go up to her room when the Fendi guest book on the table in the State Drawing Room caught her attention. Mr. Hale only brought it out when people visited, and no one was on the calendar for the Duke and Duchess today. Wallis was busy with her hairdresser and the Duke was at the weekly meeting of the Governor's Executive Council. Wallis had finally persuaded him to take his duties as Chairman seriously, eager for him to look like a king as much as she wanted to appear like a queen. Besides encouraging him to govern, she'd forced him to cut down on his drinking and the entire household had thanked her for it.

She glanced at the book to see Axel Wenner-Gren's bombastic signature above General Maximino Camacho's. Mr. Wenner-Gren rarely visited Government House, especially not unannounced and not with a Mexican general involved in the oil trade in tow. Miss Bright had taught Amelia to be on the lookout for anything unusual no matter how insignificant, and this was unusual.

Footsteps sounded behind her and she straightened. Mr. Hale bustled in and flipped the book closed then slid it off the table and tucked it under his arm. "May I help you, Mrs. Montague?"

If she hadn't suspected him of being a spy before, she was sure of it now. He didn't want her to look at the book. "Where's Her Royal Highness?"

"Upstairs with Mrs. Bethel, who's seeing to her hair for tonight's dinner."

Amelia entered Wallis's suite to find Wallis dressed in a robe and seated in a white wicker chair in the shade of the veranda while Mrs. Bethel did her hair. In a nod to boosting the local economy, Wallis had agreed to fly Antoine in from New York only once a month and he'd trained the Bahamian Mrs. Bethel to do Wallis's hair every other day.

"How is business, Mrs. Bethel?" Amelia asked.

"Busy as ever. I had to hire another girl to help out. Every American tourist wants to have their hair done where the Duchess of Windsor has hers done. I can't thank Your Royal Highness enough for the business your patronage has sent my way."

"I should set up a salon here and charge them a little extra." Wallis laughed that too-loud laugh of hers, and somewhere outside, one of the terriers barked.

"That isn't a bad idea." Mrs. Bethel removed the cape from around Wallis's neck and handed her a mirror.

"But I won't create competition. I must do everything I can to help the local ladies." Wallis examined Mrs. Bethel's work, gifted at pretending to be magnanimous or concerned about Bahamians when she couldn't give a fig. "Very good, thank you again."

The hairdresser was as talented as Antoine or any French maid in making sure not one strand of Wallis's hair was ever out of place or frizzed in the humidity.

"I look forward to seeing you at your appointment, Mrs. Montague," Mrs. Bethel reminded as she packed up her things.

"I'll be there." Amelia might be in Nassau under interesting circumstances but it didn't mean she had to let herself go.

Mr. Hale came to escort Mrs. Bethel out, through the back door, of course. No amount of polite reasoning with Wallis had changed that.

"I have your letters," Amelia said.

"I don't know why I bother reading them. I should simply call the censor's office and ask what's in them."

"I spoke to Sir Walter again about your situation. He says the Colonial Office won't budge on the matter. Every letter has to go through the censors."

"Treating us like common criminals, how typical." Wallis jerked the robe sash tight and walked into her closet to select her afternoon attire. Amelia heard the familiar turn and click of the carnation-shaped lock on Wallis's safe.

She must be picking out her jewels. What Amelia wouldn't give to see inside there, but the safe-breaking lessons from the thief hired by the Bournemouth spy school hadn't included antique locks.

Amelia sat at the desk and sorted the mail, using it as an excuse to linger. The secret key to Wallis's desk sat heavy in her pocket. It wouldn't take much to slip it in the lock and peek inside. It was dangerous, but if Shangri-La was receiving or sending coded messages about merchant ships that could put them at risk for U-boat attacks, and cost innocent people their lives, then Amelia had to take the chance. Wallis always spent at least fifteen minutes matching her jewelry to her outfit. It'd give Amelia a little time to snoop. While Wallis bustled around her large closet, Amelia unlocked the drawer. She poked inside, careful not to disturb too much. Most of the correspondence was receipts for New York department stores and bills from Wallis's favorite ateliers, but then she discovered a small batch of letters from Herr von Ribbentrop at the bottom. They were written on smaller than usual paper and had more folds than a regular letter. They certainly weren't anything Amelia had seen and none of them had the official censor stamp. These had arrived through some other channel.

Amelia read the letters, keeping an ear out for Wallis or anyone who might enter the room. The first was from Herr von Ribbentrop.

The offer of the Swiss francs is still on the table, especially if the order for more of that lovely Mexican perfume you adore is placed. Charles is sending another batch of it to Axel who'll properly deliver it. It should arrive by the 15th. I assure you this scent will make you feel like a Queen. You already are one in our eyes.

This was about more than Chanel No. 5. Same with the other three from Herr von Ribbentrop about this special Mexican perfume and the payments made to Wallis's Baltimore bank account, one Amelia knew nothing about.

Amelia froze when she heard Wallis's footsteps, then relaxed as Wallis entered her bathroom and turned on the sink taps. She quickly flipped through the rest of the letters to see if any of them mentioned the Shangri-La shortwave but they didn't. There was one from Mrs. Bedaux.

All those American shipments to Britain are delaying the inevitable. America shouldn't help Britain but should look after itself the way my friends will look after you when all this dreadful nonsense is finished. My friends thank you for the lovely pictures you sent of

Axel's estate. He's done so much with it and they plan to visit soon and take advantage of his hospitality.

Amelia quickly copied the letters in shorthand. If Wallis happened to look at the notepad, which she never did, she wouldn't be able to read it. She returned the letters to exactly where she'd found them, slid the drawer closed then locked it. She'd just dropped the key in her pocket and picked up her pencil to feign working when Wallis returned from the bathroom. She wore a blue suit with white pinstripes and pale pink pockets, a matching pale pink blouse, and a Van Cleef & Arpels ruby and diamond feather brooch pinned to the lapel.

"What are you doing?" she demanded, startled to see Amelia.

"Recording your letters."

"You don't usually work at my desk."

"I didn't want to accidentally misplace or miss a letter by carrying them around, especially the invitation from Mr. Wenner-Gren for our dinner on the *Southern Cross*. I can't wait to see it. I've heard so much about it."

She could tell Wallis suspected her of something by the way she studied her but it was clear Wallis couldn't quite put her finger on what it was beyond Amelia sitting where she didn't normally sit. "It is impressive. He bought it from Howard Hughes."

Amelia was about to use one of the many Bournemouth skills she'd learned for deflecting attention from herself when Mademoiselle Moulichon entered carrying Wallis's formal dresses.

"Your evening dresses arrived from the cleaner in New York. Which one would Madame like to wear tonight?" Mademoiselle Moulichon asked.

"Hang them up and I'll choose," Wallis instructed without looking away from Amelia. "You may return to your office."

"Yes, ma'am."

"THE DEFEATIST DUKE, that's what the American papers are calling him." Eugenie handed Amelia a copy of *The New York Times* as the two of them strolled down Bay Street. Laura Young, the Bahamian cook who assisted Chef Pinaudier, had recently given birth and Wallis had asked Amelia to buy a layette for her new baby girl.

They stopped to look in the window of a women's dress store, admiring the newest looks that were ages old by Paris standards. Amelia checked the reflection in the shop glass of the people passing behind her to make sure she wasn't being followed. Certain no one was watching, she slid a sealed envelope out of her pocket, tucked it under the newspaper, and passed it back to Eugenie. After copying Herr von Ribbentrop's and Mrs. Bedaux's letters, Amelia had coded them then burned the notepad paper before calling Eugenie to arrange this meeting.

"I'm not surprised he's earned that moniker. The two of them complain to anyone who'll listen how much they hate it here and want to leave." Until today, it was the only thing of interest Amelia had overheard to report to Lady Williams-Taylor since December.

Eugenie waved to someone down the street. "Here's the woman I wanted you to meet."

A young colored woman no more than eighteen or nineteen and rail thin, with her dark hair pulled up into a neat bun at the crown of her head, hurried up to them. She wore a simple maid's dress and held her white apron draped over one arm.

"Barin Rolle, this is Amelia Montague, the Duchess of Windsor's secretary," Eugenie introduced.

"I've been waiting to meet you," Amelia said. "Eugenie has told me all about you. Is your father a bootlegger too?"

Barin laughed and shook her head. "He's a reporter for the *Nassau Daily Tribune.* Some people think that's just as bad."

"Her Royal Highness has complained about a few stories from that paper. Do you write for it?"

"No, I'm training to be a secretary. I've seen the glamorous life you two lead and I want in on it."

"Careful getting mixed up with us," Amelia said, half jokingly. She didn't want anyone getting hurt because of the shady things she, Lady Williams-Taylor, and Eugenie were embroiled in.

"My father taught me to stand up for what's right whenever and however I can, that's why I'm helping you. I don't want to see our beautiful islands used for awful plans." A ship's horn sounded from the docks. "I'm on my way to catch the ferry. It's a pleasure to meet you. I'm sure we'll see each other again."

"I look forward to it." It was nice to have someone else in on their secret, and another person to help.

With a bright wave, Barin hurried to the ferry filled with

people crossing Nassau Bay to jobs at the resorts and homes on Hog Island.

"If you can get your duchess to volunteer at the Infant Welfare Clinic, you'll see Barin. She does administrative work there when she isn't at Shangri-La."

"I'll see what I can do. At least Wallis is finally taking an interest in her duties." In a shocking show of selflessness, Wallis had purchased a car for the clinic and helped get supplies in from New York. It'd garnered her good press and given Wallis more to do than sit around Government House worrying about her clothes and plotting to bring down Britain. "Unfortunately, it hasn't convinced her to give up whatever scheme she's embroiled in. I've watched her all week and I still can't figure out how she's sending or receiving the secret letters or what the fuel is really for. There isn't enough industry in The Bahamas to need that much oil."

"I still say it's a way to launder Axel's German payments for the munitions."

"Launder." Amelia stopped dead, forcing a man to step around her. "That's it, that's how she's getting the letters. The New York dry cleaning."

"I'll tell Lady Williams-Taylor and she'll pass it on to the bigwigs. Brace yourself for the storm when the command comes down from on high for those shipments to stop."

THE STORM BROKE when the cable from the Colonial Office arrived a week later putting an end to Wallis's dry cleaning packages to and from New York.

"They're doing this to torture us," Wallis screeched to the Duke. "The country is supposedly in peril but they have time to worry about my blouses."

"Don't forget the matter of your title." The Duke tugged at the gold silk cravat above the collar of his orange polo shirt, looking as if he missed his daytime drinks.

"The title doesn't mean anything if they keep torturing us like this. People can bow and scrape to the garbageman but he's still picking up trash. You were a king once. You deserve more and better than this awful place."

The Duke walked to the brass bar cart and poured a finger of whiskey into a cut crystal glass.

"I told you, not before seven o'clock." Wallis knocked the glass out of his hand and he stared mournfully at the wasted whiskey soaking into the green carpet. "You're the Governor-General, not the town drunk. Act like it, show Buckingham Palace what you're made of, how good you are at commanding; make them take notice of you and your talents so we aren't stuck here forever."

"Yes, darling." The Duke knelt down to mop up the mess with one of the linen napkins.

"We have servants to do that. Mr. Hale!"

The butler entered as the Duke rose. "I spilled my whiskey. Please see to the mess."

"Yes, sir."

"I think I'll see what Phillips is up to; we need to work on that bill about the thing." The Duke hurried off to find his equerry and escape Wallis's fury.

Amelia wasn't so lucky.

"I'll give Sir Walter a piece of my mind about His Majesty's orders." Wallis snapped at Amelia to follow her and the two of them went upstairs to her room. "They treat me like I'm Mata Hari, reading my letters and filling the house with spies. The Americans don't treat us this way, even the local rag can be better than that. Look at their glowing story about my work with the clinic." Wallis snatched a copy of the *Nassau Daily Tribune* off her desk and shoved it at Amelia. It was folded to show the story about Wallis securing canned milk, medicine, and other essentials for the poor mothers of the Out Islands. "They appreciate what I do."

Which wouldn't have happened if Amelia hadn't urged her to do more than sit around and complain about living here, but she didn't say so.

"Include that article in the letter to Sir Walter. I want him to see we're more than someone to irritate but people of real significance. Britain needs us for the war effort."

Wallis's sudden interest in impressing the Duke's homeland surprised Amelia. Maybe something had changed or, in typical Wallis fashion, she was hedging her bets. "Do you think Britain will survive?"

"Of course not. Their undefeatable image is all smoke and mirrors, with nothing propping it up. It won't be long before the whole deck of cards collapse, and I say good riddance. Someday they'll regret the way they've treated me. I'll see to it."

A knock ended Wallis's tirade and Amelia's chance to ask her about the remark. Wallis, in a stunning transformation, settled herself enough to calmly open the bedroom door, giving no inkling that she'd been in near hysterics over His Majesty's Government only seconds before.

"This arrived by special courier for you, ma'am. I was told it's important." Mr. Hale held out a letter on a silver salver.

Wallis took it, her eyebrows rising in surprise. "That'll be all, Amelia. I have business to take care of."

"Is it anything I can help you with?" The Duke was the only one who ever received courier messages, not Wallis.

Wallis shook her head. "Prepare the list of medicines and supplies we need for the clinic from New York. I'd like to get it off before Buck House decides I can't send anything to civilization for any reason."

Amelia left as Wallis settled in a wicker chaise to read the letter. Whatever the letter was, Amelia sensed it had nothing to do with her charities. Robert had told her to trust her instincts. The end of communication between Wallis and New York had caused someone to risk sending her a note without doing much to conceal it. If Amelia weren't sailing on the *Southern Cross* tonight with the Windsors, she'd try and sneak into Wallis's room while she was gone and get a look at it. However, being aboard the *Southern Cross* might reveal more than anything hidden in the shadows of Government House.

Chapter Twenty-Five

"This is a lovely ship. Tell me, what's that?" Amelia asked one of the *Southern Cross* sailors coiling rope on the stern deck just beyond where the guests were enjoying cocktails. She pointed to the large antenna on the top of the ship. She knew exactly what it was, a shortwave antenna, but she feigned innocence the same way the sailor pretended not to speak English.

She wandered to the railing along the other side.

Barin approached with a tray of hors d'oeuvres. She and a few women in black dresses with crisp white aprons served food and drinks to the guests and were the only non-Swedish crew members on board. "Don't let them fool you. They speak English. They're eavesdropping. There's no other reason for them to be fiddling with the rope this close to the dinner party."

"I suspected as much. But so are we, so I suppose turnabout is fair play. Heard anything good yet?"

"No, but if I have to listen to either of the Windsors complain one more time about her title or dry cleaning, I might swim back to Hog Island just to get away from it."

"I don't blame you." Amelia noticed one of the sailors eyeing them. "You'd better get back to work."

"You too." She winked then took the tray of food to the guests, who smoked and drank or danced to the music.

Amelia leaned against the railing, enjoying the peace of the ocean. The wake crashing against the side of the boat mingled with the stringed quartet; Wallis's, the Duke's, and the other guests' conversations; and the gentle hum of the yacht's engine. In the distance, she could just make out the green starboard lights of a cargo vessel traveling through the islands on the way to America or Britain. She could see them from her room sometimes at night, and once in a while one moored at Prince George Dock to take on supplies. The dark water spread out around them, the moonless night allowing the stars to shine overhead. Amelia stared up at them, trying to spot a constellation, when another light caught her attention. A blue aura glowed around the top of the antenna, turning on and off at short intervals.

They're sending a message.

She'd been taught to watch for the blue light at Bournemouth, a rare phenomenon that, under the right conditions, could alert her to secret transmissions. She didn't know if this transmission was secret but someone was defiantly radioing something somewhere. She peered out into the darkness at the cargo ship, wondering if the *Southern Cross* had radioed it out of a seagoing courtesy she wasn't familiar with. She tried to see if a similar blue light illuminated the top of the other ship's antenna when, all of a sudden, the vessel erupted in a ball of flame. Pieces of the hull shot into the sky with an explosion that echoed over the water and silenced the musicians and the guests.

Everyone hurried to the railing, surrounding Amelia with gasps of horror.

"What is it?" Wallis said from beside her, the fear that had paralyzed her during the Paris air raid making her voice quaver. The woman could bluster about her title and standing but the minute she encountered a real threat, she crumpled like a paper bag.

"I'd say the poor bastards were torpedoed," the Duke said. "U-boat, most likely."

"Torpedoes?" Wallis nearly hyperventilated at the possibility that they could be the next vessel to go up in flames from the unseen U-boat. The danger hung in the air with the thick smoke and the cries from the sailors flailing in the water.

"We have to help the survivors," Amelia said. "We can't leave them to drown."

"We have to go back to port before we're attacked." Wallis looked ready to walk on water to get there.

"We're perfectly safe," Mr. Wenner-Gren assured her. "They wouldn't dare attack us."

He exchanged a look with Wallis that immediately settled the panic in her blue eyes and made the hair on the back of Amelia's neck rise. Of course they were safe; he'd probably told the Germans they were in the area, along with the coordinates of the cargo ship.

Amelia looked at the antenna. There was no blue glow coming from it.

"We should help them," the Duke said.

"At once, Your Royal Highness." Mr. Wenner-Gren picked

up the ship's phone and gave directions in Swedish to whoever was on the other end of the line.

The engines whirred into life and the wind whipped the guests as the yacht sped up to carry them to the quickly disappearing ship. The flames were doused as the ship stood, stern up out of the water, and slowly slipped beneath the waves, casting the flailing survivors into darkness. As they steamed toward them, the *Southern Cross*'s crew prepared the lifeboats.

"We should get blankets and coffee ready for the survivors," Amelia suggested to Wallis. "Imagine what the newspapers will say when they find out you're involved in saving their lives."

"They'll be positively ecstatic." The plotting tone in her voice was sickening. "Ladies, we have to prepare food and accommodations for those poor souls. Amelia, get some blankets."

"I'll show you where they are," Barin offered. "Follow me."

Barin led Amelia inside, past the dining room, the smoking room, and down the stairs to the lower deck with the staterooms. She then led her to a linen closet, checking to make sure no one was around before she spoke. "This isn't the first time we've picked up survivors from a torpedo attack. Last year, before the Windsors arrived, we rescued three hundred people from the SS *Athenia*."

"How fortunate the *Southern Cross* was so close." They both knew it wasn't a coincidence.

"THAT WAS QUITE an evening you had," Eugenie said, reading the newspaper article about the hundred sailors they'd rescued from the SS *Malta*. *The New York Times* article praised Wallis, writing as if she'd rowed the lifeboats back and forth between the yacht and the survivors for the four hours it had taken to get them all on board.

"She's practically been canonized." Amelia lay on the cabana chaise, trying to relax in the sun but she couldn't. She could still see the wounded and haunted men they'd pulled from the ocean and the many others they couldn't save.

Eugenie tossed the newspaper on the sand beside her bag. "Your suspicions about the *Southern Cross* radioing the U-boats about the *Malta*'s position are probably right. With the Lend-Lease Act signed, convoys will soon be crossing the Atlantic with supplies and if Britain doesn't get them, they won't survive."

"Neither will the sailors on those attacked ships. The *Southern Cross* can't be at every sinking. Even if it is, it won't be long before Mr. Wenner-Gren turns his back on what's left of his humanity and leaves the survivors to drown."

"Lady Williams-Taylor says they need to know how U-boats are operating this far south. They have to be refueling and taking on supplies somewhere. We have to find out where."

They met each other's glance, the answer so obvious they were ashamed they'd both missed it.

"The deepwater harbor," they said in unison.

Eugenie nodded. "We need proof."

"He's throwing a party in Wallis's honor at Shangri-La tomorrow night. I'll see what I can find." Then she'd see Wallis, Mr. Wenner-Gren, and their black hearts go to hell.

"Amelia, there you are," Wallis said when Corporal Sawyer held open the car door at Government House and Amelia stepped out. "There's someone here to see you."

"Who?" She wasn't expecting anyone.

Wallis waved her into the State Drawing Room and there, standing beneath Wallis's portrait, was someone she'd never expected to see.

"Peter."

"Hello, Melly."

"What are you doing here?" He was the same but different, a few pounds heavier, his dark hair a touch thinner. They had the same brown eyes but her jaw was rounder like Mother's and his square one resembled Father's.

He glanced between her and Wallis, who for once readily relinquished attention. "I'll leave you two alone. I'm sure you have a lot to discuss."

Amelia remained rooted to the floor, not sure if she should hug him. There weren't etiquette books for reunions, and after her last one with Theodore, she was cautious. She didn't have to decide. Peter opened his arms and gave her a firm, heartfelt hug.

"I've missed you."

"I've missed you too." She clung to him, and memories of loss combined with a relief she hadn't experienced in years flooded through her. He still loved her. She didn't know if he'd forgiven her but he loved her. She backed out of his embrace. "What are you doing here?"

He glanced uneasily at the portrait of Wallis. "Is there somewhere we can speak privately?"

"I'll show you the garden." She led him outside. They followed the main path beneath the palms and the poinciana trees with their vibrant red flowers and spreading branches where iguanas lounged or tugged at the bright petals. The Bahamian gardeners worked near the house, trimming the bougainvillea while chatting with each other in Bahamian Creole. Amelia understood only a word or two and left them to their conversation as she led Peter to the far end of the garden, where the Caribbean pines and yellow elder trees offered shade and privacy. "What brings you here?"

"I had business with the railroad in Miami and decided to take a plane over to see you. Wallis was kind enough to invite me here when I called to arrange it. I rather wanted to see it and you for myself. Theodore said you were looking well."

"I know he didn't say that."

"Well, not in so many words. He said you were as chic as the high-class whore you worked for."

"That sounds more like him." A bright green anole lizard darted across the path in front of them as Amelia debated asking the next question. "What did Mother say?"

"That if you're going to work for a whore, at least it's one who's finally given you some sense of style."

"Practically a compliment."

"Mother is Mother the way Wallis is Wallis and she isn't going to change any more than Wallis will. We simply have to accept them as they are and work with them as best we can. But you've changed. You're nothing like you used to be."

"Good." She never wanted to be that meek and gullible mouse again.

He glanced around to make sure no one was near them. "Your friend Mr. Morton called on me in Baltimore and told me what you've been up to these last few years."

Amelia touched the *bonne chance* charm, shocked as much by this as seeing Peter in the flesh.

"He said you worked at the Embassy in London during the Blitz. I could hardly believe it. You in the middle of all that, it's really something."

"I just did what everyone else did. The sound of planes still makes me want to dive for cover."

He sat beside her on an iron bench beneath a rubber tree. "I'm serious. It took a lot of guts to do that, and what you're doing here."

She cocked her head at him. "My work for Wallis?"

"No." He tugged his tie and looked around again, as if expecting a gardener to jump out from behind a bush. Then he leaned forward and whispered, "The other stuff."

It wasn't possible. "How do you know?"

"Mr. Morton told me something of it, at least what he could. He said I'd be shot if I told anyone else. I don't think he was kidding. I don't know much about it but I know enough." He took her hand and held it tight. "You've done well for yourself with school and your job and now this. It's what I came here to tell you. I'm proud of you."

She covered his hand with her other one. "You don't know what that means to me."

"I do. I'm sorry I wasn't always there for you after Father died, and all the things with Jackson. If I hadn't been so wrapped up in college and my life, maybe I could've stopped you from getting in trouble, but I was and I regret it. I want to make it right."

"What about Mother?" She'd never expected this. Perhaps there was another miracle waiting for her.

"When the war is over we can tell her about you and she might soften."

She shot him a skeptical look.

"Or not, but it's worth a try. I can't wait to hear your stories when you're free to tell them."

Peter stayed for lunch with Amelia and Wallis, who was in top form as hostess, reminiscing about summers at Cousin Lelia's while laying on a simple but substantial offering of rock lobster and pigeon peas and rice. The Duke dropped in to eat his usual fruit tart before leaving to meet with the Governor's Executive Council.

At the end of the day, Wallis and Amelia stood at the front door to wave Peter off before Corporal Sawyer drove him to the airport. It was hard to see him go but she was glad he'd come.

"I think that went very well," Wallis said with the same pride as when one of her dinner parties was a success.

"Thank you for arranging it. It was good to see him." It gave her hope for a different future, Thanksgivings with family and new and better memories of home.

"I had to make him welcome, on your behalf. That bitch

mother of yours will never come around, but I want you to have someone on your side the way I've had you and Aunt Bessie on mine."

Amelia didn't know what to say. Peter was right: Wallis was Wallis, and she could be caring and a witch at the same time. She'd done something so sweet for Amelia, who was actively working against her.

She held paying my debt over my head in Paris then used me as a pawn. She'd do it again if given the chance. Amelia had to remember that and not be taken in by her kind gesture and the cozy afternoon. If push came to shove, Wallis would look out for no one but herself.

Chapter Twenty-Six

Shangri-La, March 15, 1941

"To Her Royal Highness, the heroine." Mr. Wenner-Gren raised his champagne glass to Wallis.

"To Her Royal Highness," the guests cheered in unison.

Wallis blushed with the required humility but the satisfaction in her eyes gave her away. She basked in their admiration and radiated it back like her tiara did the torchlight around the massive square pool. The water sparkled blue in the center of the green grass of Shangri-La's massive tiered garden. Beyond it, stone terraces led up to a folly of multiple arches overlooking lily ponds. Amelia could hear croaking frogs competing with the waves from the nearby beach. Somewhere down that beach was the deepwater harbor.

The band began to play and with Wallis occupied with Mr. Wenner-Gren, Amelia slowly made her way through the highest of Bahamian society, wandering behind groups of people who strolled up the terraces toward the folly. She reached the arched stone with a view of the ocean. The waves were louder here than the band's melodious bass drums and accompanied the chirping frogs and insects, bringing the night alive. Below, on the white strip of sand between the foliage and the dark water, a cargo truck drove toward the spit of land separating the Shangri-La beach from the deepwater harbor. She couldn't see much in the sliver of the crescent moon except the white foam waves washing across the pale sand. Amelia checked to make sure no one noticed or cared what she was doing, then started down to the beach. She kept close to where the windswept autograph trees and tangles of sea grapes met the sand, her dark silk dress allowing her to blend into the shadows and obscure her from anyone who might be watching. Sand chafed her skin and stockings as her kitten heels sank with each step but she kept going. The hum of a truck engine over the hill was barely audible during the slight pauses between the waves. Something was happening there and she wanted to see what it was.

She followed the beach until it curved toward the jutting point of the spit. She found a path through the foliage that crossed the spit and would save her time. She crept along it, stopping more than once to carefully free her skirt from a bush. She couldn't return to the party looking as if she'd had a roll in one of the dunes and have Wallis questioning where she'd been.

She followed the narrow, rocky path until it stopped near the crest and gasped in horror at the sight below. In a natural cove that protected it from the waves, a long U-boat sat at the surface, the hatches open as sailors unloaded crates and supplies from the truck into the ship. The faint smell of diesel fuel mingled with the ocean air from the large metal tanks on the dock between where the U-boat sat and the other side, where the *Southern Cross* bobbed against its moorings.

I have to tell someone. I have to tell Lady Williams-Taylor. It wasn't her mission to stop anything, simply to observe and report, but she had to say something to someone before the U-boat slipped into the open ocean and sank another ship.

Amelia picked her way back down the path, struggling to keep to the barely marked trail, until she reached the soft sand that tugged at her feet and slowed her steps as she hurried to Shangri-La. Her calves ached from rushing through the sand and she slowed down when the band's music began to mingle with the constant breaking waves. She couldn't rush into the party like a crazed madwoman but had to appear calm and composed. In the shade of the folly, she picked leaves off her dress and removed her stockings, tossing the torn-up things into the bushes, glad her dress was long enough to cover the tops of her shoes. When she was suitably put together, she walked down the terraces and back to the pool, looking around for Barin but she didn't see her among the Bahamian maids and footmen circulating with trays of cocktails and hors d'oeuvres.

"Where have you been?" Wallis hissed when she took her place beside her on the terra-cotta-tiled terrace.

"Exploring the gardens. They're so big I didn't realize how far I'd wandered until I had to turn back." That was enough of a truth to hide the lie.

"I think my hem is coming loose. Please get me a safety pin."

"Yes, ma'am." Amelia was glad to have a reason to go inside the breezy home with wood-beam ceilings, limestone floors, and fine art.

A large bedroom with wainscoting and an attached bathroom was where the numerous female guests came to freshen their lipstick or get help with a torn stocking or a falling coiffure from the female attendant.

"She's dressed like a queen," plump Mrs. Stewart said to Mrs. Mackintosh as they left the restroom.

"She's certainly acting like one but I guess this is as close to a throne as she'll ever get."

Their voices faded as Amelia wandered past the ladies' room and deeper into the house.

I need to find a phone. Barin had given her a rough sketch of the house, and the office was near the back with a view of the ocean. She crept along the hallway, keeping a careful eye out for Mr. Wenner-Gren's Swedish footmen. If they caught her here, she wasn't sure they'd fall for her innocent smiles or lies about getting lost. From what she'd seen on the *Southern Cross*, his employees didn't look like the type of men to be put off by a simpering woman.

She turned another corner, sure she was near the study, when footsteps against the tile sounded up ahead. She ducked into the closest room, her heart pounding in her chest as she pressed against the wall in the darkness behind the door while someone passed.

Once they were gone, Amelia peeked into the hall and

noticed the room across from her, catching the silhouette of a phone at the corner of the large Honduran-mahogany desk in front of the ironwork-covered windows.

Amelia slipped across the hallway and slowly closed the door behind her. She lifted the phone receiver and listened to see if anyone was on the line but there was no one. She dialed Lady Williams-Taylor's number, her home close enough for Amelia not to need the operator. It was risky to call her directly but she had no choice. That submarine had to be stopped.

"Pick up, pick up," Amelia urged as the phone on the other end rang and no one answered.

She hung up, not sure what to do, then tried again, nearly collapsing against the desk when the butler answered, "Williams-Taylor residence."

"Mrs. Montague calling for Miss Heastie."

"One moment, please."

Amelia twisted the phone cord around her finger, listening for footsteps in the hallway while she waited for Eugenie to come on. The line crackled and popped, and the noise of the waves from outside drifted through the windows.

Eugenie came on at last. "Amelia, what's wrong?"

"I'm at Shangri-La. There's a submarine at the deepwater harbor taking on supplies. I saw it. I don't know how long we've got until it sets sail but it's here."

"I'll tell Lady Williams-Taylor. Fingers crossed they can get a plane out of Florida to take care of it before it gets away. Stay safe, Amelia, and hope for fireworks."

"I will." She hung up, careful to return everything to exactly where she'd found it. She cracked open the office door and, not seeing anyone in the hallway, scurried out. She retraced her steps to the main room, making sure to get a safety pin from the bathroom attendant.

"Is Barin working tonight?" she asked the young Bahamian woman attending to the guests.

"She is, but I haven't seen her."

"If you do, tell her Mrs. Montague would like to speak with her." The more people she could get the word out to, the better.

"I will."

Amelia dropped a dollar bill from her clutch purse into the young woman's tip jar then hurried back outside to the party.

"What took you so long?" Wallis snapped when Amelia returned.

"It was busy in there. Too much champagne."

"This is an island of morons and drunks." Wallis took the safety pin, distracted by one of the morons who came to speak to her. Amelia stepped back, standing on the fringes as usual but on the lookout for Barin. She didn't see her, and with Wallis in a terror about Amelia being gone for so long, she had to remain close by.

Amelia checked the Cartier watch Wallis and the Duke had given her for Christmas. Time was ticking, and in between the band's songs she listened for the hum of fighter planes but there was nothing except the chatter of guests. Wallis and the Duke were speaking with members of the General Assembly when Mr. Wenner-Gren joined them. He stood beside Wallis and leaned down to whisper something in her ear.

Amelia felt a bead of sweat roll down her back, afraid he knew about the call and her sneaking around and was telling Wallis.

He didn't stay with Wallis long before wending through his guests for more conversation, and Amelia allowed her tense shoulders to relax.

"My hem is worse than I thought. We have to go inside and see to it before it gets worse," Wallis instructed a few minutes later and led Amelia inside.

"The restroom is this way, ma'am." Amelia pointed as Wallis headed toward the east wing of the house.

"It's too crowded in there and I'll have no privacy. The last thing I need is women whispering about the color of my garters and having it end up in the gossip columns. Axel put one of his rooms at my disposal. We'll go there."

Wallis led Amelia deep into the house and into a bedroom with a four-poster bed and white wainscoting on either side of the large, plantation-style windows with a view of the ocean. Inside, Mr. Wenner-Gren stood waiting for them.

"Mrs. Montague, how nice of you to join us." He strode around her, closed the door, and turned the key in the lock then dropped it in his tuxedo pocket. "I understand you've been making telephone calls from my private office?"

"I don't know what you mean, sir." The clicking phone line. Someone must have been listening.

"Of course you do. Who were you calling and what was it about?"

"I didn't call anyone."

"Don't be difficult, Amelia, tell him what you were up to and why," Wallis insisted. "I want to know too. I expect this from the local footmen and maids but not you."

"I don't know what he's talking about."

"One of my men heard you on the line. He doesn't speak English but he heard you speaking with another woman."

"How does he know it was me? It could've been any of your guests calling for their car or their stockbroker in New York."

"See, it's nothing," Wallis assured, as eager to stay in his good graces as she was to return to the party.

"It isn't nothing. Mrs. Montague is a spy."

"Nonsense." Wallis laughed but it faded as fast as it came.

"That's ridiculous. I'm nobody. No one would be interested in me and what I have to say."

"You're Her Royal Highness's cousin and close to her. I have contacts in very high places, people who owe me for all I've done for them. They wired me this afternoon of your friends in the American Embassy, and that you weren't delayed in London but trained there and were sent to Her Royal Highness to spy on her and report back to the U.S. and British intelligence services."

"No one wants to hear about shopping and golf." Amelia tried to look bored with the conversation, as if it were all too ridiculous to believe.

"You informed the Colonial Office of Her Royal Highness's correspondence and had it stopped; you were also there when we discussed King Carol and his Mexican oil interests, ones that have recently come under heavy scrutiny by the State Department."

Wallis stared in horror at Amelia as if she were a jigsaw puzzle and the pieces were putting themselves together. "You're the one who went through my desk drawer. I knew someone had been in it the moment I opened it. After everything I've done for you, how could you betray me like this? I raised you from a penniless nobody to somebody and this is how you repay me."

"You believe this warmonger who's bought your friendship over your cousin, the person who's stood beside you for the last three years?" She wasn't about to admit anything.

"Who did you call and what did you tell them?" Mr. Wenner-Gren towered over her, bending and menacing with his white hair and piercing eyes. She knew he was capable of underhanded things but until this moment she hadn't thought he was dangerous. She was wrong.

"I didn't call anyone."

"You'll tell me one way or another." He brought his hand down across her face and she saw stars as she stumbled to the floor, her head ringing from the blow.

Wallis bit hard on her knuckles but didn't stop him as he marched up to Amelia again. She tasted salty blood on her tongue and scooted away from him, worried he'd kick her with his pointed and polished dress shoes.

"I said tell me." He grabbed her by the arms and pulled her to her feet, his fingers digging into her skin.

Wallis said nothing but continued to watch, willing to let

her be manhandled by this traitor to maintain his favor, influence, money, and power. That was all Wallis wanted, all she'd ever cared about, and she wouldn't allow anyone, not Ernest, Mary Raffray, Alice Gordon, the Duke, not anyone she'd ever known, to get in the way of it.

Terror ripped through Amelia as much as the pain in her arms. Wallis would let him kill her if she thought it might gain her the crown.

He drew back his hand and Amelia braced for another blow when an explosion and a flash of flames from the harbor tore through the room. He let go of her and she crumpled to the floor, her ears ringing from his strike, but she heard the Spitfire engines as they roared over Shangri-La. The *rat tat tat* of machine-gun fire crackled through the night as the Spitfires strafed the submarine.

"We're under attack," Wallis screeched, as another explosion just over the dunes lit up the night sky. She turned this way and that, not knowing what to do or where to run.

One of Wenner-Gren's men banged on the door and called to him in Swedish.

Axel removed the key from his pocket and unlocked the door. The man said something to him in Swedish and he turned to Wallis. "The house is safe. They're attacking the harbor."

"You don't know that. They could change their minds at any minute and kill us all," Wallis screeched.

"Stay with her. I'll be back and we'll get to the bottom of this."

He followed his man out, leaving Wallis and Amelia alone as another explosion lit up the harbor and the room.

"I won't stay here to be bombed to bits." Wallis hurried past Amelia, who grabbed the silk hem of her dress, nearly tripping her. "Let go of me."

"How dare you run, you traitor."

"Let go!" Wallis pulled at her silk skirt but Amelia held on tight.

"You're selfish, you've always been, but you won't get the crown, do you hear me, you won't get it."

"Let go!" Wallis yanked so hard the dress ripped as it came free of Amelia's tight grip. "Axel can deal with you."

Wallis grabbed the key out of the lock and left, closing and locking the door behind her.

Amelia pulled herself off the floor, clasping the back of a chair to steady herself before she staggered to the window. Three fighter planes crisscrossed the sky above Shangri-La, and the guests scattered in terror across the sunken garden. One plane flew so low past the window, Amelia could see the pilot against the flames, and then smoke rising from the deep-water harbor.

I have to get out of here. Wallis wasn't going to help her, and if Axel and his men came back, she'd end up at the bottom of the ocean or worse. She opened a window but iron grates blocked any chance of escape. She pushed on them but they wouldn't budge. She searched for a latch or something that might open them but she couldn't find anything. Amelia snatched a bronze dolphin statue off the dresser and raised it over her head, about to hit the iron, when the door clicked open behind her. She whirled around, gripping the dolphin tight, determined to fight, when Barin stepped in.

"Quick, before the planes leave and there aren't any more distractions."

Amelia dropped the statue and hurried after Barin out of the room. They crept along the hallway, stopping every now and then when a voice yelling in Swedish sounded too close.

Gunshots thundered in the chaos and Amelia and Barin ducked down out of sight of the windows then crept up to peek through them. Axel's men were firing at the planes. The rest were heading to the harbor to fight the flames, dodging the guests scrambling to reach their cars.

"If we can get in the crowd, we can sneak you past his men." Barin led her through the now empty kitchen and out a side door and around the house. They pressed against the shadow of a palm tree when Axel's men hurried by carrying fire hose coils over their shoulders.

They ran to the parking area, where people were frantically searching for their cars, and drivers were nearly colliding with one another to get down the long drive to the main road.

Barin led Amelia to the Duke's car and pulled open the back door. "Get in."

Amelia locked eyes with Corporal Sawyer. "No. I don't trust him."

"I'm one of you. Get in," he ordered. Wallis was right. There were spies all over Government House.

"He is." Barin pushed Amelia into the plush back seat, and

the bruises on her arms from Axel's hands smarted. "Get on the floor."

Barin tossed a blanket over her then slid onto the seat. Corporal Sawyer drove to the main road in the caravan of white-capped butlers and fancy cars ferrying the terrified guests away from Shangri-La. The car bumped along for what seemed like ages before it stopped.

Barin lifted the blanket off Amelia. "You can get up now."

"Where are we?"

"The edge of Lady Williams-Taylor's property." Amelia peeked out the window to see Eugenie waiting on the dark and deserted road with Lady Williams-Taylor's car. "She'll take you from here. We have to get back. We don't want anyone to suspect anything."

Amelia hugged her tight. "Be careful. Mr. Wenner-Gren is dangerous."

"I can handle myself," Barin assured her. "Goodbye, and thanks for the most interesting cocktail party I've ever served."

"If you ever need anything . . ."

"I'll have Eugenie let you know."

Barin climbed back into the car with Corporal Sawyer and they drove off as Amelia hurried to Eugenie.

"YOU'LL BE IN Miami within the hour," Lady Williams-Taylor said as they sat in the back of her Cadillac on the private runway at Oakes Field waiting for the plane to taxi to the hangar. She handed Amelia a fresh towel of ice from the bar compartment in her car for her swollen mouth. In her ripped dress and borrowed coat and with a broken lip, Amelia looked like a mess but she was safe.

"What about you? If they know about me then they must know about you."

"Eugenie and I leave for Canada tomorrow and we'll stay there until things calm down. There's too much excitement here and I don't want to be bombed to bits by the next German air raid, at least that's the story we'll give to everyone, including the newspapers."

"Did they get the U-boat?"

"They did, thanks to you." The plane pulled to a stop and the mechanic slid wedges under the tires. The pilot didn't cut the engine. They'd leave the moment she was on board, but the stairs lowered and a tall figure stepped out. "Now off you go. There's someone waiting for you."

Amelia threw open the car door and rushed across the tarmac to Robert. He sprinted to close the distance, scooping her up in his arms and twirling her around in excited relief. He set her feet on the ground, ready to kiss her, but her nasty lip stopped him.

"I'll make them pay for what they did to you."

"We both will."

Chapter Twenty-Seven

Miami, Biltmore Hotel, March 1944

"Are you sure you want to do this?" Robert asked.

Amelia checked the tea in the teapot and adjusted the cups and saucers to make sure everything on the table was perfect. Working at the FBI in Washington, D.C., might not be as glamorous as planning dinners for European aristocrats, but even in the midst of war work she hadn't forgotten how to lay a proper table, write a perfect thank-you note, or dress with distinction. She also needed the armor of her Chanel-inspired blue suit to help her face Wallis.

"I'm quite sure."

"Good, because they're here."

The door opened and the suited FBI gentlemen showed Wallis and the Duke into the suite. After a couple of years of good behavior, the Colonial Office had finally granted the Windsors permission to travel to Miami for Wallis to have dental work. If Amelia didn't do this today, she might not get another chance.

Wallis stepped over the threshold and glared at Amelia. "I have no desire to speak to that woman." Wallis clutched her white leather purse that matched her white suit and tried to leave but the FBI agents stepped together in front of the door to block her way.

"How dare you," the Duke thundered at being treated like a commoner.

"If Your Royal Highnesses would be so kind as to join me, we have some very important matters to discuss." Amelia motioned for them to sit.

"I have nothing to say to you," Wallis spat.

"They are issues of national importance concerning Your Royal Highnesses," Robert said, and the Duke perked up at the prospect of being let in on something as important as state secrets. "You'll want to hear what Mrs. Montague has to say."

The Duke looked over the table and at Amelia standing behind it like the perfect hostess.

"I hate to let a good fruit tart go to waste." The Duke escorted a stiff Wallis to the chair Robert held out for her.

She exchanged a wary look with the Duke as she sat down across from him.

"Are you enjoying Miami, Your Royal Highness?" Amelia sat and poured the tea, preparing the Duke's exactly as he liked it before she handed it to him along with his fruit tart.

Wallis waved hers away, sitting sour-faced as if she'd noticed a bad smell. "It's quite nice being in real society, even if the present company is lacking."

"Have you heard from Mrs. Bedaux? I understand she's under the protection of her Nazi friends at Château de Candé." Amelia's composure never changed and neither did Wallis's except for the slight narrowing of her hard eyes.

"I don't know anything about that."

"Perhaps you've heard from Mr. Bedaux? He was in Africa overseeing the construction of oil lines for the Germans, until he was arrested by the U.S. Army and brought to D.C. That's why Mrs. Bedaux is no longer free. After everything she did for them, that's how they treat her."

"I haven't heard from Charles since we left Europe."

"Nor will you. He killed himself with sleeping pills last week. The evidence against him was so damning, he decided to take matters into his own hands."

Wallis's hand went to her neck and the Duke stopped eating his tart.

"I understand Mr. Wenner-Gren is in Mexico City; of course, it's the only place willing to take him since the U.S. government seized his assets, including his account on your behalf at the Bank of Baltimore."

"How dare they. They have no right to touch that money, it's mine!" Wallis screeched.

"You're free to argue your case with the U.S. government. I'm sure they'd love to see any documents connecting you to the account and where the money came from. You have some very interesting financial backers, including Mr. Wenner-Gren, who's been blacklisted by the U.S. government."

Wallis's square jaw clenched tighter in barely concealed anger. "The Bahamas is British territory. U.S. laws don't apply there."

"They didn't until today." Amelia motioned for Robert to come forward. "The Colonial Office asked us to present His Royal Highness with an order to seize Mr. Wenner-Gren's Bahamian assets, including Shangri-La, the cannery, his beach resort, docks, and oil import business."

Robert opened a leather folio and laid the seizure orders from the Colonial Office in front of the Duke. He uncapped a fountain pen and held it out to the Duke.

The Duke read the document, then looked to Wallis for what to do.

"Sign it," she ordered.

The Duke took the fountain pen, letting it hover over the document a moment before he finally pressed the nib against the paper and signed his name.

"Thank you, Your Royal Highness." Robert slipped the paper out from under the pen and tucked it back into the folio.

The Duke laid the pen on the table beside him, shoulders hunched in defeat.

Wallis remained ramrod straight in her chair. "You think you have the upper hand, but I know the ways of the world. You'll be a nothing and nobody soon enough while I'll be so much more. I taught you everything you know."

"You did, and many other lessons, especially how to be grateful for what I have instead of always wanting more."

"You'd have nothing if it wasn't for me."

"A pathetic woman afraid of failure, anonymity, poverty, so desperate to be someone, you'd sell your soul to the Germans, and your life to the Duke, the Nazis, or anyone who'd offer it to you. But you won't get it because there's nothing behind your carefully constructed façade except selfishness and fear."

"I'm not afraid of anything."

"Except everyone seeing the weakness hidden by your clothes, manners, and money. I assure you, they see it, the way Mary Raffray, Mr. Metcalf, Her Majesty, and I do, and they see the grasping woman it's made you, but you'll never get what you want because you've shown your true colors, your lack of loyalty to anyone but yourself and your interests, and you'll pay for it. His Majesty's Government will not grant you another official position once your tenure in The Bahamas is over, and you won't be allowed to return to Britain. You'll be stuck forever in this false and meaningless life you've created."

Wallis said nothing, more truth in those few words than she'd heard in a lifetime.

"And the press, the British people?" the Duke asked, tugging at his tie.

"In deference to Their Majesties and the reputation of the royal family, no one outside this room and the intelligence community will ever know the truth about your attempt to help the Nazis defeat Britain and install you on the throne."

The Duke and Duchess stared at the table, taking in what

Amelia had said and everything it meant for their lives, future, and all their ambitions. They'd been defeated and they knew it.

With nothing more to say, Amelia set down her napkin and stood, forcing the Duke to rise in respect. Wallis grabbed his arm and pulled him into his chair then glared at Amelia.

Amelia gathered up her purse and gloves and settled her hat over her perfectly coiffed hair. Robert offered her his arm and they walked out of the room.

"No one will ever know what happened in there," Robert said as they waited for the elevator.

"Wallis knows and I know. That's all that matters."

Washington, D.C., January 1953

"Dad, here's the newspaper. Mom, the postman brought you a letter." William, Amelia's son, tossed the items on the kitchen table as he raced through the kitchen to the living room, where his sister, Anne, sat coloring.

Amelia tore open the letter. "It's from Eugenie."

"How's she enjoying Hollywood?" Robert poured a glass of orange juice from the bottle in the Frigidaire and sat down to his usual breakfast of toast and eggs. He always ate with Amelia before catching the train to the Office of Naval Intelligence.

"She loves the weather and being at the center of gossip. She says Marlene Dietrich is as interesting in real life as she is on the screen." Marlene's maid had left her around the same time Lady Williams-Taylor had passed away and Amelia had arranged the employment. "She and Barin are tearing up the town. Between them, they know more gossip than Louella Parsons and Hedda Hopper combined."

After the war, Barin had come to America and been one of the first women Amelia had trained and placed through her new agency. Barin had been in Hollywood for years and currently worked for Lauren Bacall. Amelia had placed secretaries all over New York, Hollywood, and Paris. After the war, all the socialites, aristocrats, and celebrities she'd known in France before the war had resumed their old lives as if nothing had happened, and clamored for personal secretaries to manage their revived social calendars.

"Have you seen this?" Robert handed her the newspaper, folded back to reveal a photo of Wallis and the Duke sitting together on a couch wearing paper crowns. According to the caption, Jimmy Donahue had thrown a New Year's Eve party and the Windsors had been the guests of honor. He'd staged a mock coronation, and while the Windsors smiled a good game, Amelia recognized the strain along the edges of Wallis's lips, the lack of fire or joy in her eyes. She despised being made fun of and this ridicule cut to the core.

"She's been crowned at last." Amelia didn't feel sorry for her. She hadn't consciously followed the Windsors since walking away from them at the Biltmore in '44, but there was no avoiding news of the world's most famous socialites.

According to her intelligence sources, the Windsors had returned to France after the war and the Duke's tenure in The

Bahamas. Their precious houses, linens, china, and antiques had miraculously survived. While Amelia had left the FBI to build her secretarial placement agency, helping the many women whose careers had ended with the peace, Wallis and the Duke had spent the postwar years as aimless, wandering aristocrats with no real friends or purpose.

In true Windsor fashion, Wallis and the Duke had run to the worst people they could find, Mrs. Woolworth Donahue and her playboy son, Jimmy. Mrs. Donahue had the money to court the notorious couple, paying their jeweler and clothing bills and foisting her son off on Wallis, who spent too much time with Jimmy, who was half her age. Judging by the picture, all Wallis needed to do in return was sacrifice what remained of her dignity, another in a lifetime of Wallis's poor decisions.

"I never thought I'd be grateful for Wallis but I am." Amelia turned the picture of her cousin facedown on the table. "If it hadn't been for her, I wouldn't have everything I have today, including you."

He took her hand and raised it to his lips and Amelia smiled.

Wallis had said the best revenge was a life well lived. She'd been right.

Acknowledgments

Amelia Montague is a fictional character, but I drew on accounts from various Windsor secretaries to help flesh out her story. Those memoirs and recollections paint an overly rosy picture of what it was like to work for the Windsors. However, flashes of the truth can be found in other sources. Letitia Baldrige, social secretary to the American Ambassador to France and later to Jackie Kennedy, mentioned in her memoirs an encounter with the Duchess of Windsor's personal secretary. Mrs. Baldrige related how the woman cried because she hadn't enjoyed a day off in a year, and the Duchess had canceled her one day off for a trivial reason. Other servants give hints here and there that Wallis was a difficult and exacting boss who also didn't pay well.

Amelia might be fictional, but much of the Windsors' desire to regain the British throne and the events of 1937 through 1944 are taken from reality. You can read more about the Windsors' alleged treasonous activities in many Windsor biographies. The biographies also discuss how free the Windsors were with their admiration of Germany and their belief that England would lose the war. Wallis's dislike of Queen Elizabeth and her lifelong grudge against England were well known, as was her overbearing and insulting manner with the Duke, often in front of others, especially in later years. Most of the FBI documents that Robert shows Amelia are amalgamations of actual FBI documents on the Windsors, and they are available to read on archive.org and various other websites. Some of the letters from German officials that Robert shows her are from the Marburg File, a German Foreign Ministry file found after the war that detailed much of the Windsors' dealings with the Germans. The Marburg File was kept secret for years but was published in the 1950s in *German Documents on Foreign Policy*, where it can still be read. Most of Mr. Metcalf's telegram to Amelia saying that he is through with the Windsors comes from his letter to his wife after the Duke abandoned him in Paris. Eugenie is a fictional character, but Lady Williams-Taylor is real and she did spy on the Windsors in Paris and The Bahamas. Mademoiselle Moulichon is real and she was the person that Wallis sent to occupied Paris to retrieve a number of their things. She had a harrowing three-month journey trying to rejoin them in The Bahamas and was briefly arrested. Sadly, she never wrote a memoir of her experience. Whenever possible in the novel, I used real quotes or turns of phrase from Wallis and the Duke or those who knew them.

I hope you enjoyed reading the novel as much as I did researching and writing it. A special thanks to my editors Lucia Macro and Asanté Simons, and my agent, Kevan Lyon, for their help in bringing this interesting story to life.

DISCOVER MORE BY
GEORGIE BLALOCK

AN INDISCREET PRINCESS

From the acclaimed author of *The Other Windsor Girl* and *The Last Debutantes* comes a brilliant novel about Queen Victoria's most rebellious and artistically talented daughter, Princess Louise, showcasing her rich life in Georgie Blalock's signature flair.

"A royal princess determined to create a hidden love, and a demanding queen who vows to keep her in her place—I couldn't turn the pages fast enough. Rich in period detail, *An Indiscreet Princess* is a beguiling story of duty, power, and a young princess's passion for art and love. A thoroughly engaging read."

— Shelley Noble,
New York Times bestselling of *Summer Island*

THE LAST DEBUTANTES

Fans of *The Kennedy Debutante* and *Last Year in Havana* will love Georgie Blalock's new novel of a world on the cusp of change...set on the eve of World War II in the glittering world of English society and one of the last debutante seasons.

THE OTHER WINDSOR GIRL

If you love *The Crown* and *The Gown*, then this is the book for you!

Diana, Catherine, Meghan…glamorous Princess Margaret outdid them all. Springing into post-World War II society, and quite naughty and haughty, she lived in a whirlwind of fame and notoriety. Georgie Blalock captures the fascinating, fast-living princess and her "set" as seen through the eyes of one of her ladies-in-waiting.

DISCOVER GREAT AUTHORS, EXCLUSIVE OFFERS, AND MORE AT HC.COM